Princess of Hanover

Princess of Hanover

A Novel

Helene Lehr

St. Martin's Press
New York

PRINCESS OF HANOVER. Copyright © 1989 by Helene Lehr. All rights reserved. Printed in the United States of America. No part of this book may be used or reproduced in any manner whatsoever without written permission except in the case of brief quotations embodied in critical articles or reviews. For information, address St. Martin's Press, 175 Fifth Avenue, New York, N.Y. 10010.

Library of Congress Cataloging-in-Publication Data

Lehr, Helene.
Princess of Hanover / Helene Lehr.
p. cm.
ISBN 0-312-02967-5
1. Sophia Dorothea, consort of George I, King of Great Britain, 1666–1726—Fiction. I. Title.
PS3562.E4417P7 1989
813'.54—dc19
89-30100
CIP

First U.S. Edition

10 9 8 7 6 5 4 3 2 1

In appreciation of her unflagging support and encouragement, this book is dedicated to Kay Kidde.

Celle

November 1682

The castle of Celle was ablaze with light, although the rain that pelted the yellow stone walls obscured all but the faintest glow from shining through the tall narrow windows.

A great deal of activity was taking place inside the imposing structure that was situated on a rise overlooking a bend in the Ahler River. Footmen, lackeys, and chambermaids scurried about the 180 rooms that comprised the castle, for guests were expected to arrive the following day. None of them could be expected to know that their efforts were in vain. Anthony Ulric, Duke of Wolfenbüttel, was scheduled to arrive with his son, who was the primary candidate being considered as a husband for Sophie-Dorothea, the young daughter of the house of Celle.

But at this very moment a change in those plans was occurring, a change that would prompt Anthony Ulric to leave in a huff, refusing even to set foot inside the castle.

From the brightly lit, high-ceilinged entrance hall, a carpeted corridor led to a small reception room in the east wing. A young girl stood outside the closed door, her manner attentive, her expression grim.

The door, though heavy and of solid walnut, did nothing to mask the voices of her parents. Dorothea, only child of the Duke and Duchess of Celle, eavesdropped with shameless curiosity and a sinking heart. Not yet sixteen, her slim body was, nevertheless, endowed with the softly rounded hips of womanhood. Small breasts strained against the green satin bodice as her breath quickened with the words she was hearing.

They were discussing her marriage – arguing would be a more apt description. Each word increased the heavy feeling in her chest. There was no doubt, Dorothea thought in dismay as she listened, ear pressed against the cold carved surface. In spite of her mother's protestations, she was to be married to her cousin, George Ludwig, rather than to the handsome son of Anthony Ulric, who was her own personal choice. Married to that taciturn, humorless, colorless individual. It was impossible. It was not to be thought of. For a moment Dorothea wondered whether her father's decision had anything to do with the recent visit of her aunt, Duchess Sofia of Hanover. The imperious duchess had been closeted with her father for more than an hour the day before. In view of the fact that it had been many years since her aunt had set foot in Celle, it seemed a reasonable, if unfathomable, assumption.

Dorothea closed her eyes tightly, as if to blot out the awful vision, the awful certainty. And certainty it was; she could hear it in her father's voice.

Opening her eyes again, Dorothea made her way back to the front hall. She stood there a moment, trying to make sense of what she had just heard. Then, almost in a daze, she climbed the stone steps that led to the second floor. At the top, after hesitating only briefly, she wended her way along the drafty corridor to her own rooms, which were in the southern tower of the castle.

By the time Dorothea entered, she was in tears. Her companion, Lenore Knesebeck, rushed to her side.

'I'm to be married!' Dorothea's plaintive cry held such an expression of agony that Lenore's rosy face grew pale before the meaning of the distraught words registered. Only a few years separated the fifteen-year-old Dorothea and the nineteen-year-old Lenore Knesebeck. In spite of the difference in their station, they were close friends. Aurburn-haired and blue-eyed, Lenore was a quiet, serious young woman, almost the exact opposite of her raven-haired young mistress, who could, at times, be volatile.

Lenore put her arms about Dorothea. 'Of course you

must marry,' she exclaimed, observng the tearstained face. 'Why does the thought upset you?'

'I won't marry him.' Dorothea drew away from the comforting arms, dark eyes flashing, slender body taut.

Used to the sometimes impassioned outbursts of her young mistress, Lenore just sighed. She placed her hands gently but firmly on Dorothea's slim shoulders. 'Has the duke informed you of this, *ma chère*?' she asked softly.

The tearstained face raised itself. 'No. The duke doesn't need to inform me. I … heard.'

Lenore's mouth formed a straight line, adding years to her otherwise youthful countenance. Her blue eyes were speculative as she regarded Dorothea. 'You were eavesdropping again.' It was a statement and required no affirmation.

'And why shouldn't I?' was the quick response. 'It's my life they are discussing. How can they decide my future, my happiness, in such casual tones?'

'You know the duke and the duchess have only your welfare in mind,' Lenore murmured, undeterred by Dorothea's heated observation.

'If they did, I would have been consulted.' Dorothea's chin thrust out defiantly.

Lenore's expression altered subtly. 'Who is it?'

Tears began again, sparkling through thick dark lashes. 'My cousin, George Ludwig of Hanover.'

Lenore raised her brows, dismayed. Dear God, there were few men who were so solemn, so ill used by nature, as that one. With full sympathy now, she put her arms about the weeping girl.

Downstairs the Duke of Celle was speaking softly, intensely, as was his way. While his wife heartily disagreed with his words, she was, nevertheless, captivated by the sound of his voice. It had always been so, from the very first day she had met him.

They were in a small reception room off the main hall, a room Eleanor referred to as the Blue Salon due to the fact that all the furniture was upholstered in pale-blue damask. Even the richly embroidered tapestries on the walls were worked predominantly in that color.

Eleanor sighed as she listened to her husband. With a graceful white hand she absently toyed with the double strand of pearls about her neck. Somewhat lavishly gowned in gold brocade, Eleanor was small and dainty, possessing a patrician beauty that had caught the eye of more than one man.

She turned her head slightly, still listening to Wilhelm. It wasn't that she didn't want this marriage for her daughter. On the contrary, it was an excellent match. It was just that she doubted Dorothea could be happy with George. The girl was so spirited, so alive, and Prince George was so rigid and unbending. Too, there was that business with Catherine Busche, sister of Countess Elizabeth Platen. Eleanor couldn't imagine what her sister-in-law, Duchess Sofia, was thinking about, allowing her oldest son to indulge in such scandalous behaviour, right under her own roof. It was no secret that George was involved in an affair with the woman.

'You see the beauty of it, my dear?' Wilhelm was looking directly at her, commanding her attention. 'If Dorothea marries George, Celle and Hanover will be united. And our goal will be that much closer to fruition.'

Ernst's goal, you mean, Eleanor thought to herself with some resentment. It's always Ernst, always your brother. 'I do see, Wilhelm,' she replied softly, unable to repress a sigh.

She watched as Wilhelm turned to the other man in the room. But Andreas Bernstorff, Minister of Celle, needed no convincing. He was very much in favor of this marriage. As was Ernst, Wilhelm's brother. If Ernst's dream of uniting Celle and Hanover came true, there was a distinct possibility that the emperor would agree to make Hanover the ninth electorate.

Eleanor was well aware that if such a thing came to pass, George Ludwig would eventually be elector – a position equal to a king. It followed then, that the woman George married would become electress. An enviable circumstance for any girl.

Again there was that small sigh. That was another problem. Dorothea wasn't just any girl. I have spoiled her, Eleanor thought, but she wasn't in the least sorry.

'Eleanor!' Wilhelm sounded digruntled. His dark eyes, however, were soft as they rested on his wife. He was a handsome man, in his late forties, trim, erect, and youthful-looking despite the touch of silver at his temples.

Startled, Eleanor looked up at him.

Although he frowned petulantly, Wilhelm couldn't find it in himself to be angry. He could never be angry with Eleanor. He loved her now as much as the day he had first met her. Even as he frowned, he wondered at her beauty. She was forty-three, but the years seemed to have brushed her lightly. Her hair was still glorious, still the rich color of burnished copper. How sad that Dorothea, while she had inherited her mother's beauty, had not had the good fortune to inherit those incredible blue eyes, though he had to admit that his daughter's dark tresses were every bit as lovely as Eleanor's lighter shade of hair.

Wilhelm cleared his throat and turned away from his wife. 'You haven't heard a word I've been saying,' he chided. 'I should think your daughter's future would be of more interest to you.'

Eleanor straightened, her brocade gown rustling with her movements. 'I care deeply, Wilhelm,' she responded in her low voice. 'So much so that I have been unable to think of anything else all day.'

He frowned again. 'What objection could you possibly have?' he demanded. 'The marriage will unite Celle and Hanover, keep our wealth, our property, where it belongs. In the family.'

She nodded, then spoke firmly. 'Very well. I will agree to this union … on one condition.' She stared at her husband steadily. As he tilted his head inquiringly, she continued. 'That creature that your nephew is consorting with must be sent away.'

Wilhelm drew a breath that verged on exasperation. After a quick glance at Bernstorff, he again addressed his wife. 'These things should not concern you, my dear,' he murmured uncomfortably.

'They do not concern me, Wilhelm,' Eleanor pointed out quietly. 'They concern my daughter. I will not have her go into that house as the situation exists. It's one thing for a man to …' She faltered, at a loss for words, briefly annoyed by Bernstorff's presence. It would be so much easier to speak to her husband alone. She wet her lips. 'It's one thing to carry on an affair. But to have the woman in his own house ... It's offensive.'

'Catherine Busche is one of the duchess's ladies,' her husband remarked, as if that explained the reason. He toyed with his neckcloth and avoided her eye.

'I don't care who she is,' Eleanor insisted in a strong voice. 'She must leave the court before Dorothea enters it.'

Almost without being aware of it, Wilhelm smiled in relief. Eleanor had accepted the union. The matter of the boy's mistress was of no real importance. He chewed his lower lip. He supposed that women attached much more importance to such trivia. Eleanor was right, he decided. If it upset her, no doubt it would upset Dorothea as well.

Standing by the stone fireplace, hands clasped behind his back, Andreas Bernstorff watched and listened to the exchange between the Duke of Celle and his wife. He was a stocky man in his early fifties with a paunch that attested to his liking for good food and wine. A small curl of his lip was the only indication of the contempt he felt for the duchess. Bourgeois, he thought, not for the first time, completely ignoring the fact that Eleanor came from the distinguished Poitous family. She was a pretty piece, well enough, but it escaped him why the duke had taken up with her in the first place. She was, after all, common. No woman of nobility would have consented to living with a man as she had done. He listened to her silly demands and made a sincere effort to control his rising impatience.

Bernstorff wondered what Duchess Sofia would say when she heard of this ridiculous demand. The duchess was a lady, a royal lady. Through her veins ran the blood of the Stuarts. Through her, George Ludwig was a prince. And here was this stupid woman insisting that the prince's mistress be sent packing.

Bernstorff thought of Count Platen, Duke Ernst's minister. Turning slightly, he glanced at the gilded clock on the mantel behind him. Platen should have been here by now; no doubt the rain was delaying him. At times, the twenty-mile road between Hanover and Celle deteriorated into little more than oozing mud.

He returned his attention to the duke and duchess. The woman that they were obliquely discussing was none other than the sister of Platen's wife, Elizabeth. He smiled as he thought of Elizabeth, wondering whether Eleanor, with her high-and-mighty attitude, knew that Elizabeth was Ernst's *mâitresse en titre*; had been for years. Platen knew, but wisely kept out of the way. She was a shrewd one, that Elizabeth. It was due to her that Platen had risen from tutor to George Ludwig to Minister of Hanover.

Shrewd or not, he wouldn't want to cross her, Bernstorff thought, shifting his weight to a more comfortable position. She was beautiful, but deadly as a viper. She wouldn't take it kindly to hear that her sister was to be sent away. And she would be. No matter how Duke Ernst felt about Elizabeth, he wanted this marriage to take place. For that matter, they all did. All except this frivolous woman. Bernstorff eyed Eleanor resentfully. What did she want for her bastard? he wondered, irritated. She was damned lucky that Ernst even gave it a thought.

Glancing toward the door just then, Bernstorff saw the servant's discreet signal. That meant that Platen had finally arrived. Unobtrusively, so as not to interrupt Eleanor as she continued with her boring tirade, Bernstorff left the room, making his way to the large and spacious front hall. He was in time to see Count Platen hand his dripping cloak to a footman.

Tall and gaunt, Platen was, nevertheless, a handsome man, if one did not look too closely at his eyes, which were calculating and cold. They were the eyes of a self-centered, self-serving person – a man Bernstorff admired unabashedly.

Platen expulsed his breath sharply. 'The road is almost impassable,' he complained, viewing his colleague. 'I could use a drink.'

Bernstorff nodded and beckoned. 'Come in here. The duke and duchess are still arguing. I'm sure we won't be missed for a few minutes.' He led Franz Platen into a small study, then closed the door. After walking across the carpeted floor, he picked up a silver decanter and poured the amber liquid into two silver cups as Platen sprawled wearily in a comfortable chair.

'They expect me to get back before the night is gone,' the count said, a short laugh following his words. He brushed a few raindrops from his velvet doublet. 'I hope that the duke has his answer ready.' Gratefully, he accepted the brandy and swallowed it quickly before again speaking. 'The right answer, that is,' he added, handing the now-empty cup back to Bernstorff.

'I think so,' was the reply. Bernstorff refilled the cup. 'There is one point, however, which may be a problem.'

'What do you mean?' Platen accepted the brandy. This time he held it, staring at Bernstorff in an almost accusing manner. He didn't like the thought that he had made this journey under execrable conditions, only to have the plans go awry. 'Ernst has already spoken to his brother,' he pointed out. 'He seemed amiable.'

'He still is,' Bernstorff quickly assured. 'There is no problem with Wilhelm.'

Platen gave a sound of disgust as he again drained his glass. 'The duchess?'

Bernstorff nodded, then raised a hand as Platen was about to continue. 'She agrees,' he said, before the other could speak. 'Under certain conditions.'

Platen's dark brows dipped in a frown. 'What conditions could she have?' His irritation mounted. 'The duke shows her great favour by offering his son. After all, the girl's legal status is questionable.'

'Of course, of course,' Bernstorff placated. He drained his own cup. 'There is the slight question of the prince's ... lady friend.'

Platen's face grew blank, on him a ludicrous expression. 'Are you serious?' He didn't know whether to laugh or not. It was too absurd. But then, the Duchess of Celle herself was absurd. How ridiculous, he thought to himself.

Bernstorff, seeing the disbelief, grew serious. 'I'm afraid she means it, Franz,' he murmured quietly. 'If the woman is not sent away, there will be no wedding.'

Leaning back in the chair, Platen's frown deepened. Elizabeth wouldn't like this, he thought irrelevantly, ignoring for one moment his own duke's displeasure. She wouldn't like it one bit. And when Elizabeth was displeased, everyone suffered. 'Is that the only obstacle?' he finally asked.

'As far as I could tell.'

Platen nodded and put his cup on the ornately carved table beside his chair. Whatever else Eleanor was, she had exquisite taste. The thought came grudgingly as he mentally compared the delicately molded furnishings in this room with the heavy, almost overbearing pieces that Sofia seemed to choose. 'Well, let's get this over with,' he said, grunting as he got to his feet. 'I'm expected back before the night is gone.'

The two men walked to the door. Bernstorff opened it, allowing Count Platen to precede him. A few moments later he entered the Blue Salon, announcing the count's arrival.

Relief sharply etched Duke Wilhelm's features as he greeted his brother's minister, but Eleanor regarded the man with a cool eye. In Platen she recognized no friend of hers.

Platen bowed perfunctorily and moved closer, waiting for Wilhelm to speak, all the while comparing him with his own master, the Duke of Hanover. One weak, one strong; one, a man of action; one, a man who acquiesced too often – and to his own wife.

'Count Platen ...' Wilhelm's tone was warm in its greeting. 'I won't even ask how your trip was. I suspect that it was less than comfortable.'

Painful visions of the past three hours prodded Platen's consciousness but he smiled affably. 'Please do not concern yourself, milord. The trip was worth the discomfort.' He regarded Wilhelm with a hopeful expression. 'Your brother is most anxious for your decision regarding the union of his eldest son and your lovely daughter.'

Wilhelm smiled. How like Ernst, he thought. So impatient. And of course, why shouldn't he be? He was the one with the brains, the one with the dream. 'Ah, yes,' he responded. 'But you must be chilled. Can we offer you a brandy? Certainly you will stay for dinner?'

Memories of the delicious French meals with which Eleanor graced her table assailed Platen's senses. Firmly he pushed them aside. Foolish and no account she might be, but she certainly knew how to cover a table with delicacies. 'I could have no greater pleasure, milord, than to sit at your table. Regretfully, I must decline. I have promised the duke that I would return without delay.'

Wilhelm beamed. 'And you must keep your word. But, a drink at least.' He beckoned to the footman by the door, who immediately hastened to obey.

'Duke Ernst instructed me to convey his fervent desire for a favorable reply,' the count prodded gently, using his most respectful tone. 'He has already spoken to George Ludwig, who is overwhelmed by his good fortune.' Platen almost smiled as he said that, thinking of George's uncharitable remark when he had been informed of this marriage.

'Is he so overwhelmed, Count Platen, that he has discarded his mistress?' Eleanor ignored her husband's distressed face. Bernstorff's pained expression went completely unnoticed by her.

'I'm certain that the prince will do the honorable thing, milady,' Platen replied coolly, thankful that Bernstorff had warned him of what to expect.

'My dear,' Wilhelm interrupted in a mild voice. 'Please see to it that some refreshment is served to our guest. We will eat informally, so as not to unduly delay the count.' He turned to Platen. 'In the meantime we can go over the final contract.' He walked to the far end of the room and sat behind a highly polished walnut desk with delicately carved panel inserts.

Kindly but firmly dismissed, Eleanor hesitated only a moment. Then she got to her feet and, without further words, left the room.

After his wife had gone, Wilhelm again addressed Count Platen. 'She's right, you know,' he murmured. 'The woman must leave before the wedding. And,' he emphasized sternly, 'she must not return afterward.'

Platen nodded slowly, disappointed that Wilhelm apparently backed his wife's foolish notions. There would be the very devil to pay, he thought, repressing a sigh. And the problem would not be with the duke or George Ludwig. 'Very well, milord,' he answered quietly. 'And the rest of the marriage contract?'

Wilhelm picked up the papers and glanced through them, although he was thoroughly familiar with the contents. Still, it would be better not to leave anything to chance. Actually the contract had been drawn up by Ernst; but it was ordinary enough. All of Dorothea's holdings, property, money, would be turned over to George Ludwig.

'It seems all in order,' he said at last.

'Excellent!' Platen smiled. 'Now all we need is your signature and that of the duchess. Your daughter must sign as well,' he added unnecessarily.

At that moment the door opened to reveal Eleanor, followed by two footmen in blue-and-silver livery holding large trays covered with steaming bowls.

'Ah, good.' Wilhelm rubbed his hands together and nodded approvingly at his wife. He motioned to the footmen to place the trays on the table. Then, picking up a quill, he hastily affixed his signature to the marriage contract. Extending the quill to Eleanor, he said, 'After you sign, my dear, would you be kind enough to take it up to Dorothea for her signature?'

Platen, who had begun to walk in the direction of the table, drawn by the aroma of food, exchanged a brief glance with Bernstorff at the placating tone Wilhelm used when addressing his wife. Such was the rapport between the two men that no words were necessary. Platen again returned his attention to the food. It was one more thing he grudgingly respected about Eleanor d'Olbreuse. She set a fine table. Of course, all the food was French and he supposed that one would, after a while, tire of such rich fare. He suddenly realised just how hungry he was and turned around almost impatiently, waiting for the duke.

Eleanor had read and signed the contract. Now, for the first time, she smiled cordially at Platen. 'Please sit down and eat,' she invited. 'You've had a long journey, and another ahead of you. Are you certain that you cannot spend the night? I'm afraid the weather is worsening. The rain is turning to sleet.'

Platen bowed. 'Thank you, milady. But it's quite impossible for me to delay any longer than is necessary.'

'I understand.' She looked at Wilhelm. 'I'll take the papers up to Dorothea.'

In the hallway, Eleanor stood at the front of the staircase and thoughtfully viewed the contract in her hand. It had all happened so suddenly, she thought, dismayed. Dorothea was barely sixteen; in fact, would not be sixteen until next week. With the wedding a scant two weeks hence, there would be no time to prepare for anything but the ceremony itself. There would be no gala wedding for Dorothea. There wouldn't even be time to make a proper gown.

She glanced up, her blue eyes following the row of brass wall sconces that led to the second floor and which were now lighted with flickering tapers. But she made no move to ascend the stairs. The union was a good one; she didn't fool herself as to the reason for it. The Duke and Duchess of Hanover wanted Dorothea for no other reason than that she was heir to Celle. And without Celle, there could be no ninth electorate.

With a start, Eleanor realized that she had been standing in the hallway for many minutes. She gathered her skirt in one hand, raised it slightly, and began to climb the stone steps.

Moments later she entered her daughter's bedchamber.

Dorothea was seated at her dressing table while Lenore was artfully pinning up her hair. Seeing her mother's reflection in the looking glass, Dorothea spun around, her expression wary.

With a sigh, Eleanor drew a straight-backed chair closer to the dressing table, then sat down. 'Duke Ernst has proposed marriage on behalf of his son, George Ludwig,' she said quietly.

Dorothea's fair skin paled. 'Mama, you cannot be serious.' She took a breath. 'George is …' She waved a hand in helpless confusion, at a loss as to how to describe her moody cousin.

Eleanor moistened her lips. 'You do George an injustice, Dorothea,' she stated firmly. 'It's true that he is a serious young man – '

'I will not marry him,' Dorothea interrupted, ignoring her mother's frown of disapproval.

Eleanor glanced at Lenore. 'Fetch a quill and the inkpot,' she instructed, then again regarded her daughter's angry face. Even with the unlovely expression, Eleanor had to admit that her daughter was more than pretty. She would one day be a beautiful woman. Right now, though, she was too slender – and given to fiery outbursts of temper. Eleanor reached out to clasp Dorothea's hand. 'It is all settled. It would do you well to count your blessings. You will be a princess. And, if all goes well, one day you may very well be electress.'

Dorothea shrugged at her mother's words. The prospect didn't excite her.

Eleanor was about to make a sharp retort but just then Lenore returned with the writing materials. The young woman placed them atop the dressing table, then stood there uncertainly.

Unmindful of her mother's expression, Dorothea continued. 'Besides, George has a mistress. He has boasted of it. Surely you can't expect me to marry a man who carries on like that!'

Eleanor flushed. She had hoped that her daughter was unaware of that particular situation. 'It has been taken care of, Dorothea. And you're right. I wouldn't send you into that sort of environment. Neither, for that matter, would your father. He was very insistent on that point,' she lied. Her tone softened. 'You must remember, my darling, that men are different. You cannot judge a man harshly simply because he has a mistress. And certainly not before he is married.' She stood up. 'Your father is waiting, Dorothea.' There was now a curtness to her tone. 'If I don't return the document to him soon, he is certain to come up here.'

With little grace, her slender body tautly conveying her thoughts on the matter, Dorothea affixed her signature just below that of her mother's. What did it matter? she thought with irascibility. Sooner or later she would have to marry someone. At least George was her own age and lived close enough to Celle so that she would still be able to visit her home. Her thoughts brightened somewhat. Perhaps it wouldn't be so bad after all. The wedding was most likely a year or more away. An eternity.

Her newfound optimism was, however, dashed with her mother's next words.

'We will be going to Hanover a week from Sunday. The wedding will be performed there.' Eleanor felt a tug of sympathy as she regarded her daughter's stricken face. 'I'm truly sorry that there will not be time for a proper gown. But your pale-yellow satin will do nicely. The duke has promised you a whole new wardrobe, so plan on taking only those things that you want.' She kissed Dorothea's smooth cheek and hurried from the room.

Speechless, Dorothea sat there for a moment. Then, in an angry gesture, she swept her arm across the dressing table, sending paint pots, brushes, combs, ribbons flying. The inkpot, too, joined the clutter, leaving a dark-purple stain on the muted green, hand-woven rug. Staring at the mess, she burst into tears.

Immediately Lenore knelt down and gathered her in her arms. 'Why are you so unhappy, *ma chère*?' she crooned. 'You will be a princess. And who has more right?' She rocked the girl in her arms and continued to murmur until the sobs lessened.

'What if that woman is still there?' Dorothea cried out.

After taking a silk handkerchief from her pocket, Lenore dried the tears on Dorothea's face. 'The duchess does not lie,' she admonished. 'If she says the woman will be sent away, you must believe it.' She smiled. 'And think of your new wardrobe. No doubt you will have your own residence, your own servants. You will be a real princess.'

Dorothea clutched at her friend. 'You will come with me, won't you? You must! You will be my lady.'

Lenore flushed with pleasure, then got to her feet. 'You do me honor, your Highness.' She dipped in an exaggerated curtsy.

Clapping her hands, Dorothea laughed through her tears. 'As long as you are with me, Lenore, it will not be too bad.' Her impish expression returned, heralded by deepening dimples. 'Perhaps we shall teach those staid Hanoverians a thing or two.' Her face grew somber. 'When my mother first came to this country, she and my father lived at Leine for a time. Do you know that Duchess Sofia made my mother sit at a separate, lower table than the rest of the court?' She nodded at Lenore's suitably shocked expression. 'It's true.' Her chin lifted defiantly.

'But that will not happen to me. The daughter of Eleanor d'Olbreuse will return to Hanover and will be given a proper seat, according to her rank.'

Downstairs, Eleanor again entered the Blue Salon. A quick glance at the table told her that the men had finished eating and were now enjoying a glass of wine. Wilhelm stepped toward her, his face reflecting mild annoyance.

'I was about to come after you, my dear,' he chided. 'We have detained Count Platen long enough.'

'I'm sorry,' Eleanor quickly apologized. She handed him the document and smiled. 'You'll forgive a mother's sentimentality at a time like this?'

'I will forgive you anything, my dear.' He planted a fond kiss on her cheek, then handed the document to Platen. 'Please tell my brother that we look forward to seeing him in two weeks' time.'

'I'll accompany you to the door, Franz,' Berstorff offered in an amiable voice, falling in step with his colleague.

When the door closed, Wilhelm faced his wife. 'Was there any problem?' But of course there was, he was thinking, well aware of his daughter's high-spirited independence.

Eleanor tilted her head. 'Not really,' she replied. 'She was a bit upset with the swiftness of it all. But then – ' she laughed sadly – 'so am I.'

Wilhelm frowned. 'I see no reason to delay,' he stated firmly. 'Dorothea is of age. Ernst is right. Once we have reached an agreement, things ought to move ahead swiftly and smoothly.'

Ernst, Ernst! Eleanor repressed a surge of irritation. She had never doubted Wilhelm's love for her in all these years. But she suddenly wondered what would happen if Wilhelm had to make a choice. Who would it be? His brother, or his wife? She turned her mind away from that, uncomfortable with the thought. Of course Wilhelm would choose her. How foolish of her to think otherwise. She had told Dorothea to count her blessings. It might be a good idea if she did the same, Eleanor thought ruefully. She had married for love, a rarity in itself, and her husband had never cast his attention elsewhere.

She smiled again, this time warmly. 'The hour is late,

Wilhelm,' she whispered. 'And it has been a long day. Perhaps you will look in on me before you retire?' She placed a soft hand on his cheek and he immediately clasped it, kissing her open palm. 'I'll wait for you, my love,' she said softly. She held his gaze a moment longer, then, in rustle of brocade, left the room.

Smiling, Wilhelm poured himself another glass of wine, then glanced at the clock. Fifteen minutes, he knew from years of experience. That's how long it would take her to undress and perfume herself with her favorite fragrance. God, how he loved her. He reached for the decanter again, hesitated, then put his empty cup on the table. He wanted a clear mind for the night ahead.

Hanover

November 1682

The carriage left the muddied road and bounced along the cobbled street, jarring its passenger. Platen woke with a start and peered outside, noting with relief that he was almost at his destination.

He reached inside his cloak and patted the pocket of his jacket, checking to see that the marriage contract was still there. Satisfied, he leaned back, blinking his eyes in an effort to clear his sleep-drugged mind. It was still raining, although not so heavy as it had been. Perhaps it would clear before morning. He yawned, stretching his booted feet out at an angle to relieve his cramped muscles.

No doubt they would all be awake at Leine, he thought. Certainly the duke would be, in spite of the late hour. He wished he could go to Monplaisir first, to see Elizabeth. But then, perhaps she was at Leine too.

In any event, he had little choice. Duke Ernst was nothing at all like his easygoing brother. To cross him was to place one's head in jeopardy.

The carriage bumped sharply and Platen knew that they had entered Leine's courtyard. Through the curtain of rain he could now see the huge gray-stoned castle, its turrets rising into the damp blackness of night. Tall narrow windows on all three floors beamed with yellow light, attesting to the wakeful state of the inhabitants. At last the carriage stopped. With a final pat on his pocket, Platen got out and hurried up the front step.

Without speaking, he removed his cloak, handing it to the waiting servant. Then, with brisk, purposeful steps, he walked in the direction of the study. He had hoped to find the duke alone but now saw that Duchess Sofia and George Ludwig were in the room, although the prince was sprawled out on the divan, sound asleep.

'Your Highness,' Platen murmured in a quiet greeting to the man seated behind the desk. He withdrew the marriage contract from his pocket and laid it on the desk, remaining silent as Ernst studied it.

The duke was two years younger than his brother, Wilhelm, but his face appeared older, harder. It was a face unused to being disobeyed, or even disagreed with. The dark eyes were steady, unwavering, commanding; except, perhaps, where Elizabeth Platen was concerned. Franz turned his mind away from that. And, in truth, it was not a situation that overly concerned him. He wouldn't be where he was today if it were not for his wife's ... persuasive powers. Elizabeth had her life – and he was free to live his. It was a not-unpleasant arrangement after all.

Ernst completed his perusal and glanced up at his minister. 'All is settled, then?' he inquired, appearing pleased, satisfied.

'Yes.' Platen's response was a bit hesitant. He glanced at the duchess and the still-sleeping George Ludwig. The boy really was a dolt, he thought, eyeing the slumbering figure; and he should know, he had tutored him for many years. The young prince was slow thinking, slow speaking, and even slow to anger. That was not to say that George didn't have a temper. He had a fierce one, even more terrible because it was unpredictable.

'Well, speak up, Frank,' Ernst snapped irritably. All pleasantness vanished in an instant, as if it had never been. 'I can see that something is amiss. What is it?'

Platen cleared his throat, conscious of the piercing stare of the duchess, who was regarding him in silence. 'Nothing of any great importance,' he answered quickly and softly, suddenly glad that George was asleep.

The duke was now regarding him with narrowed eyes and Platen hastened to explain. 'Somehow, it has come to the attention of the Duchess of Celle that ... the prince is overly fond of Madame Busche.' He stopped and took a breath, not noticing the flush that stained the face of Duchess Sofia. Had he noticed, he might have considered it embarrassment.

In truth, it was anger. Just the name of Eleanor d'Olbreuse was enough to provoke anger within the Duchess of Hanover, but to have her disapprove! How dare she, Sofia thought, her black eyes glinting as she looked at Platen. The little upstart, she fumed silently. She compressed her lips tightly, knowing that it was beneath her to even indicate that she had heard such an utterance.

Turning her head slightly, Sofia stared fixedly at her husband. The years seemed to melt away, as if they had never been, and instead of Ernst, she was looking at Wilhelm.

Wilhelm. Even the name tore at her heart. She had met him long before she had met Ernst. He had proposed, and she had accepted. But then something happened. It wasn't her, that much she knew. It was just that Wilhelm wasn't ready to settle down, to meet his obligations. He had been so handsome, so gentle, the first time that they had met. Was it really twenty-four years ago? They had had one brief meeting alone in the gardens. In that hour, Wilhelm had won her heart. For always.

Sofia lifted a hand and patted her graying hair. It hadn't always been gray. That summer it had been golden; the whole world had been golden. She was Princess Sofia, granddaughter of James I, and her Stuart blood had set her apart from her contemporaries.

Wilhelm, for reasons of his own, had approached her father and asked for her hand in marriage. The consent had been given. Her heart, too, had been given.

But instead of Wilhelm, it was Ernst who stood by her side when her marriage vows were spoken. Still, when they had returned to Hanover after their wedding journey, Sofia had found at least a measure of happiness. Wilhelm lived with them and his smile and occasional fond kiss on her cheek had been enough. For five years it had been enough.

Then Wilhelm had taken a trip to Brede. That was where he had met her: Eleanor d'Olbreuse. Wilhelm had brought her home, here to Hanover, and the look of love upon his face had chilled Sofia's heart.

Oh, she had been pleasant enough, she could do little else; but deep inside her, Sofia had thought it was just another casual affair. Time, however, had proved her wrong. It had not been casual.

It shouldn't have been that way, Sofia's mind raged, while her face remained passive. *She* should have been the one; not Eleanor d'Olbreuse, not that – commoner. Until recently, Eleanor and Wilhelm had not even been wed because Wilhelm had, many years ago, agreed to never marry. It was all there, in the Act of Renunciation he had signed. Eleanor was little better than a kept woman, despite the dry, official contract that had taken the place of a wedding ceremony.

Things remained that way until Dorothea became of marriageable age, her legal status in question.

Now, because Ernst had finally relented, finally agreed to allow Wilhelm and Eleanor to wed, morganatically, with benefit of clergy, Sofia was forced to give her eldest son in marriage to Dorothea.

And this was the woman who dared take exception to George's innocent liaison. Sofia's breath came rapidly just thinking of the insolence of it. Calming herself, she brought her attention back to Ernst, who had this while been pondering the statement of his minister.

'I fail to see that my son's attachments are of any concern to the Duchess of Celle,' he stated tersely, regarding Platen with a devastating expression that made the minister pale.

'Indeed, I was of the same mind,' Platen quickly agreed. 'But I'm afraid that the Duke of Celle has made it a condition. Not only must the association cease, Madame Busche must leave the court.'

'Must?' Ernst repeated, eyes bright.

Platen wondered briefly if he should soften his tone but then realized that if he did, the negotiations could crumble. That, he knew, would upset the duke even more than his brother's inane condition.

'I'm afraid, Highness, that he was quite adamant. She goes, or there will be no marriage.'

Ernst was silent a moment. It wasn't his son's feelings that concerned him. He just wasn't used to Wilhelm demanding anything. Ernst reflected dourly that he had done Wilhelm a favour that should last a lifetime – he had married his betrothed. Not that Sofia was such a bad bargain. She was tiresome, but she *was* a lady. A royal lady. At all times she conducted herself properly. His own liaison with Elizabeth Platen had never once been mentioned by his wife. That sort of thing was beneath her notice. A real lady.

No, it was Wilhelm's insistence that Ernst found annoying, although no doubt it was at Eleanor's instigation. Ernst allowed himself a deep sigh. His brother was besotted where that woman was concerned. As Ernst considered this, he tapped his blunt fingertips on the desk, producing a curious rhythmic sound. For a time it was the only sound in the room, if one ignored George's guttural snoring.

'Very well,' he said at last. 'The woman will be sent away.' He regarded Sofia, who nodded her acquiescence.

Following his duke's glance, Platen observed the duchess's calm demeanor. Not for the first time, he marveled at her poise. Dressed in pale-green satin, her graying hair cleverly interwoven with pearls, she appeared quite unperturbed. Nothing bothers that woman, Platen thought. Nothing ruffles her except, perhaps, a lack of protocol. It was the only thing he had ever seen make Sofia angry; even then, it had been a contained, icy anger she displayed. Platen doubted that the duchess had a thought in her head except who preceded whom into the dining hall.

'I'm certain that you must be tired, Franz.' Ernst waved a ringed hand in dismissal. 'You may retire.'

Platen bowed slightly. 'Thank you, Highness,' he murmured. With a further bow in the direction of the duchess, who graciously inclined her head, he withdrew.

For a moment, Ernst studied his wife's placid face, then he spoke. 'You will take care of this annoying condition, Sofia,' he instructed, without smiling.

'Of course,' Sofia replied calmly. 'If you really feel it necessary,' she murmured.

Ernst gave her a sharp look. 'What do you mean?' he demanded. 'Of course it's necessary. Wilhelm has agreed to all our terms. All. He has made one request. And a not-unreasonable one,' he conceded, rubbing his chin.

Sofia shrugged her plump shoulders delicately. 'I would agree with you, Ernst,' she said, 'if I thought that it was Wilhelm's request. You and I both know it was Eleanor's condition.' Her voice hardened and she rapped her lace fan sharply on the arm of her chair. 'What right has that woman to demand anything! Especially in view of the fact that we are allowing George to marry a girl of doubtful heritage.'

Ernst frowned. 'Let's not get into that again,' he growled in annoyance as he got to his feet. 'Wilhelm and Eleanor are now married.'

'Through your good graces, milord,' Sofia interjected smoothly, inclining her head.

The frown deepened, creasing Ernst's broad forehead with sharp lines. 'Be that as it may,' he noted quietly. 'They *are* married.' He began to walk toward the door. 'Frankly, madame, the subject tires me. The only thing of importance is the girl's dowry. Celle.' He paused, his hand on the knob, and glanced at his still-sleeping son. 'Make certain the woman leaves by the end of the week. She must not be here when my brother arrives.'

'I will take care of it, Ernst,' Sofia responded in a pleasant tone.

With the departure of her husband, Sofia turned a speculative eye upon her slumbering son. A deep sigh escaped her lips as she rose. After walking to the divan, she bent over, tapping the young man on the shoulder with her fan.

George Ludwig grunted irritably, then opened his eyes, viewing his mother.

'Get up, George.' Sofia walked across the room to the desk. While her son roused himself, she studied the marriage contract. Casually, she noted the signatures: Wilhelm's – careful, methodically penned; Eleanor's flourishing, bold script; and Dorothea's juvenile scrawl. She turned and observed George, who now, sitting up, was running his hands through his tousled hair.

'Has Platen returned?' he mumbled, stifling a yawn.

'He has,' his mother affirmed.

George looked up. 'It's settled then?' he inquired dully. A flash of annoyance crossed his heavy features. 'I cannot understand how you could have let this happen,' he complained.

Sofia raised a brow. 'I had little choice,' she answered brusquely. 'You know the reason for this marriage. It's certainly to your advantage. The emperor would never consider an electorate for Hanover unless Celle is a part of it.'

George threw her an annoyed look. 'A dream,' he muttered. 'That's all it is, you know. A dream.'

'Not necessarily, my son,' replied Sofia. 'At any rate, even to petition the emperor, Hanover and Celle must be united. You are the heir of Hanover. Your cousin is the heir of Celle. When you marry her, it will all be yours.'

'My cousin. You yourself have often told me of Eleanor d'Olbreuse. She is a slut, so you have said, time and again. Now you insist that I wed her daughter!' And no one, he thought grumpily, had even asked him for his opinion.

Sofia's mouth tightened. 'I will not lie to you, George. I would have it otherwise. However, we must lay aside our personal feelings in the light of practicality.'

'All right, all right. Since Father began this whole thing, I've known the outcome. It isn't exactly a surprise.' He stood up and stretched again. 'With your permission, Mother.'

'One moment, George.'

He turned, regarding her with a scowl.

'The Duke of Celle has accepted all our terms. All of the girl's property and allowances will be yours when you marry her.'

'So?'

The duchess regarded him steadily. 'He has made one condition.'

George made a face, annoyed with his mother's digressions. He did not, however, speak. He was tired and wanted nothing more than to go to his room and sleep.

'Catherine Busche must leave Leine,' Sofia said to him.

George stared blankly, not certain that he had heard correctly. His mother had never acknowledged his affair with Catherine. She neither approved nor disapproved, merely accepted.

'I myself will tell her,' Sofia went on, when her son made no comment. 'You needn't concern yourself with this matter.'

For a fleeting moment, George was tempted to protest. The urge left him as quickly as it had come upon him, for it was based more on annoyance than any real conviction. Besides, he had begun to tire of Catherine weeks ago. He had been uncertain as to how to end the tedious affair; now, here was his mother with the perfect solution. He walked toward the door. 'If the weather clears, Friedrich and I are going hunting tomorrow,' he remarked casually. 'It might be a good idea for you to tell her then.'

When Platen had left the Duke and Duchess of Hanover, he went to the suite of rooms occupied by Elizabeth when she was in residence at Leine. Ernst had given her a separate residence of her own, Monplaisir, which was situated midway between Leine and Herrenhausen. Technically, Monplaisir was his too, but Platen seldom went there. It was always filled with officers and courtiers, all of whom passed the time drinking and gambling. Not that he blamed them, Platen had to admit to himself. The Duchess of Hanover ran a very staid – and boring – court.

The door to the outer salon was open as Platen entered. It was empty, save for a sleepy footman who leapt to his feet at the sight of the count.

'Has the countess retired?' Platen inquired of the man.

'I do not believe so, sir,' came the reply. 'May I – '

'Never mind,' Platen interrupted. He strode across the black-and-white tiled floor and entered Elizabeth's bedchamber without knocking. The interior was furnished lavishly, if with little taste. Carved and gilded wood and plaster were very much in evidence. In the corner of the large room was a cast-iron tub, which he knew from experience was normally concealed by a screen. Now the screen was folded and carelessly propped against a wall.

At the sight of his wife, Franz grinned. 'Still taking your milk baths, my dear?' He leaned over and kissed her black hair, piled atop her head, noting the few wispy tendrils that floated charmingly about her face as she moved. 'I'm surprised to see you up at this hour, much less bathing,' he commented as he sat down in a velvet upholstered chair; God, she was lovely, he thought.

No wonder she had held Ernst's interest all these years. She was in her late thirties, but her body was as firm as that of a young girl.

Her red lips curved in a condescending smile. 'You knew I would wait up for you, Franz. How did it go? Is everything settled?' She motioned to the maid and the young woman immediately fetched one of the two pails of water close by. Elizabeth stood up. Her body glistened whitely, like a statue. She stood still while the maid poured the water over her, then repeated the process, reserving a bit of it. Resting a hand on the woman's shoulder, Elizabeth stepped out of the tub, then permitted the maid to rinse her lower legs.

The countess glanced at her husband, a trace of impatience in her manner. 'Well, Franz? I'm waiting. Or do you plan to sit there, staring?'

Franz grinned again. 'You'll forgive me, my dear Elizabeth,' he remarked, unperturbed. 'A husband does have a few prerogatives.'

She slipped her arms into the outheld negligee, then tied the belt carelessly. The material was so flimsy that it revealed more than it concealed. She sat down at her dressing table as the maid unpinned her hair and began to brush it with long strokes.

'The contract has been signed,' Platen said, enjoying the view.

She turned towards him, the parted lace negligee revealing one firm, high breast. Her expression, however, was neither coy nor inviting. 'What is it, Franz?' she murmured in a low voice. 'I know you too well. There is more.'

He shifted in the chair, uncomfortably stirred by the sight of her. Damn, if only his news was to her liking, she might let him stay the night. She did that occasionally, when Ernst was away – provided she wasn't involved with her lover of the moment. Currently, so he'd heard, she was enamored of an officer, Count Philip Königsmark.

'Franz!'

He got up and began to pace slowly. 'They accepted all conditions,' he responded, then halted, facing her again. 'And made one of their own. The duke accepted it,' he added quickly.

Elizabeth frowned but said nothing. Franz would tell her in his own good time. And from the look of him, she was now certain that it would be something she didn't want to hear. 'Enough, enough,' she said curtly to the maid, dismissing her.

'Catherine must leave the court,' Platen stated in a quiet voice.

She laughed. 'That's absurd!'

He shook his head slightly. 'I'm afraid it's true. The Duchess of Celle feels that her daughter should not enter into a marriage while the prospective groom is ... otherwise occupied.'

Elizabeth's face hardened; strangely, it didn't detract from her somewhat exotic features. 'The duchess.' She spat. 'So, she thinks that her daughter is too good for us, does she?' She drummed her fingernails on the table in a rapid, furious tempo. 'She dares insist that my sister be sent away?' She glared at her husband. 'Why didn't Ernst object? He can wrap Wilhelm around his little finger.'

Platen cleared his throat. 'Not this time. If Catherine does not leave, there will be no marriage.'

'The little chit isn't even here and already she's disrupting the household.' Elizabeth picked up the brush and flung it across the room. 'Do you know how long I worked to get Catherine in the prince's good graces?' she demanded, eyes blazing.

Elizabeth, he could see, was working herself into one of her rages; never a pretty sight, Franz thought. It was time for him to leave. Besides, the night was almost gone and he suddenly realized how weary he was. 'I'm certain it will all turn out for the best, my dear,' he murmured. With a brief kiss, which she seemed not even to notice, he took his leave.

Elizabeth sat there, staring about her angrily. At the thought of Eleanor d'Olbreuse's daughter, she almost laughed aloud. That such a one would dare presume to dictate moral standards! Then her face grew grim. Very well, it appeared that Catherine would have to be sent away; but the girl would pay for her effrontery, Elizabeth decided. Before the marriage, her whims would be granted. But afterward ... Elizabeth smiled coldy. If she knew George Ludwig, nothing would so overwhelm him with distaste as a high-spirited, temperamental wife. Placidity and docility were George's fare.

Again the fingers tapped, this time contemplatively. She knew just the one. Really, it was perfect. Eleanor's daughter would have to be taught a lesson.

Turning, Elizabeth called to her maid, who immediately appeared in the doorway. 'Ilse, do you know where Mademoiselle von Schulenberg lives?'

'Yes, madame.'

'Good. Then tomorrow, I want you to take a message to her. Tell her I would very much like to receive her at Monplaisir Thursday afternoon at two-thirty.'

'Yes, madame.'

'We'll be returning to Monplaisir in the morning,' Elizabeth stated as she walked toward the canopied bed. After allowing the negligee to drop about her feet, she crawled between the satin sheets. Tomorrow, she mused, she would be at Monplaisir – and with Philip. He had to leave for Hamburg before the week was gone, but they would have a few nights together before he had to go. During that time, Ernst would be occupied with the wedding. By then, Philip would be gone, and she would be able to return her full attention to the Duke of Hanover.

Dorothea and Lenore rode in the carriage following the one that held Wilhelm and Eleanor. The third carriage held the staff who would be joining Dorothea at her new court; among them, young Christopher Chappuzeau, who would be her gentleman-in-waiting. Lenore, of course, would be her first lady.

Dorothea plunged her hands deeper into the fur muff on her lap. Sighing, desultory, she gazed outside. The view was changing in a dramatic way. They were almost in Hanover. Gone were the quaint little houses with colorful window planters that dotted Celle, and gone was the gleaming countryside that was so richly massed with pines and lindens. Even now, in winter, the land retained its sparkle.

Here the land was flatter, being closer to the sea, a condition that also inspired an uncomfortable dampness. Too, the houses were constructed of a brick material that was a dark, dull gray. Trees were sparse and grew in small clumps. Even the horizon was dark, for one could see the outline of the Harz Mountains, which hosted gloomy, almost impenetrable forests.

Lenore smiled faintly as she observed Dorothea, although her blue eyes were sympathetic. 'You don't look like a girl on her way to be married,' she noted after a while.

Dorothea turned her gaze from the bleak view and regarded her companion. 'Neither will I look like a bride,' she observed tartly. 'I have neither gown nor veil, nor will I even be wed in a church. The ceremony is to be held in the castle chapel.'

'Still, it's the days and years to come after the ceremony that matter.'

'I fear they will be as dreary as my wedding day.' Dorothea sighed.

'When was the last time you saw the prince?' Lenore inquired, looking at her.

Dorothea shrugged beneath her fur cloak. 'During last winter's carnival. It has been almost a year.'

'Well,' Lenore pointed out logically, 'people do change in a year.'

The girl didn't bother to answer this.

'I understand that Prince George, when he was not yet sixteen, fought with the Imperial Army at Treves,' said the determined Lenore. 'A young man who volunteers for such an assignment must have a great deal of courage.'

'George is a soldier at heart,' Dorothea agreed, although her tone conveyed distinct disinterest. She glanced outside again. They were just passing Herrenhausen, a summer residence of the Duke and Duchess of Hanover. To the rear, as the carriage rolled by, she could see part of the orangery, its glass walls reflecting gray sky. She knew from experience, however, that inside it was lush and green and warm, even now, in November. It provided oranges and pineapples for most of the year.

Dorothea leaned back, dozing, and when next she became aware, they were in the town itself. The castle of Leine was situated on the banks of the river by that name. It was much larger than the castle of Celle although, in Dorothea's opinion, not nearly as beautiful.

At last the carriage rolled to a stop. She sat quietly until a footman opened the door and aided her in alighting. Then she walked slowly to where her mother and father were standing. Wilhelm nodded once, then led the way up the wide steps. No one spoke. They felt, rather than saw, that their approach was being observed. Then they were conducted to the reception room where the whole family was waiting.

Dorothea curtsied to Duchess Sofia, a princess in her own right. She repeated the gesture for her uncle, Duke Ernst. Then she glanced at her cousins. George Ludwig bowed, then straightened. He was not smiling. His heavy features and slightly protruding blue eyes gave him the look of being older than twenty-two.

By his side was Friedrich, who was eighteen, and who greatly resembled his older brother.

Next was Maximilian, who was her own age, sixteen, and who grinned at her as be bowed. Of all the boys, Maximilian mostly resembled his father. He was good-looking, with inquiring, challenging eyes.

Then came Charles, a year younger, who appeared to Dorothea the most friendly. He was smiling at her in a welcoming manner.

The two youngest boys, Christian and Ernest Augustus, smiled shyly and quickly looked away.

The only girl in the family was the thirteen-year-old Charlotte. She stood by her mother's side, regarding Dorothea in a haughty, disdainful manner.

There were others in the room, but Dorothea recognized only Count Platen and his wife, Elizabeth, who was Sofia's lady.

Ernst and Wilhelm were greeting each other with an affection that was not spurious, but with an unusual amount of joviality, which was. Neither man had to be told that their wives loathed one another and so they made a sincere effort to disguise this fact.

Sofia stood stiffly while Eleanor curtsied, merely nodding her head in acknowledgment of the obeisance. Then, catching the duke's signal, Sofia led the way to the chapel, which was situated in the rear of the castle.

The ceremony began immediately after they entered.

As she walked down the aisle at her father's side, Dorothea hardly noticed the lovely diffused light that poured in through the stained-glass windows. It was just past one o'clock in the afternoon and the gray clouds had parted briefly, allowing a pale sun to break through.

Carefully she knelt on the scarlet velvet-covered stool beside George and listened apathetically to the murmuring voice of the clergyman. Behind her, the chapel was so silent that Dorothea had the impression she was alone in the room.

At last it was over. George offered a perfunctory kiss, then, taking her hand, led her from the chapel.

Awhile later in the large dining hall, Dorothea observed the heavy meal with a protesting lurch of her stomach. Venison she could abide. But the inordinate amount of red cabbage and sauerkraut, with its tangy, vinegary smell, nauseated her. She glanced down the table to where her mother was seated, but Eleanor was conversing with the courtier who sat by her table. Miserable, Dorothea toyed with her food. George made several, halting attempts at conversation. Then he too fell silent.

Finally the interminable meal was at an end. Dorothea brightened when she saw the musicians. She loved to dance. However, to her dismay, she saw that they were going to give a recital.

An hour later it was time for her parents to leave. Fighting back her tears, Dorothea watched her mother and father enter the carriage that would take them back to Celle, back to home.

She was still standing by the tall narrow window even after the carriage was gone from view when her new mother-in-law approached her.

'It has been a long day,' the duchess observed. 'Perhaps you would like to retire to your chambers.'

Dorothea managed a smile. 'Thank you, your Highness,' she murmured.

'Come along, then,' Sofia said, leading the way. To Dorothea, in her present state of mind, everything looked gloomy and dark. Even the sun had once more retreated. 'I hope you'll be comfortable,' Sofia said conversationally as they climbed the stairs to the second floor. 'I've had some fine pieces put in your suite.' She halted midway down the hall, then opened a door.

With relief, Dorothea noted that Lenore was already in the room. They had entered the salon, which in turn led to a sitting room. All of the walls were hung with tapestries of muted color and design. The walnut furniture was heavy and massive. As they entered the bedchamber, Dorothea's eye lit upon the wardrobe, the front of which bore the appearance of a two-story façade, complete with columns, pilasters, and portals. In a corner was a lovely writing table made of ebony, with delicate floral marquetry of wood and ivory. But even the charming piece couldn't lighten her mood.

After receiving a brief, cold kiss planted on her forehead, Dorothea bade her mother-in-law good night. When the door closed, she fell into Lenore's arms in tears. 'How am I to live here?' She wept.

'Everything seems strange to you right now,' Lenore comforted her. 'Why, carnival is about to begin. I've heard that there will be a grand ball in only a few days.'

Dorothea lifted her head. 'Is that true?'

'Yes, indeed. And tomorrow the dressmaker will be here. Countess Platen plans a masque at Monplaisir this weekend. There's plenty of time for you to have your costume made.'

In spite of herself, Dorothea had to laugh. 'How on earth did you discover all this?'

Lenore began to unfasten buttons and ribbons as she helped her mistress disrobe. 'While you've been getting married and moping about, I have been making inquiries and listening carefully.'

'You're right,' Dorothea agreed, ashamed. 'I'm being silly. All that will stop right now.' She hugged Lenore again, grateful for her presence.

Awhile later, Dorothea was dressed in her nightclothes and sitting in the huge four-postered bed. The damask curtains were left parted on one side.

'I'll leave the candle lit,' Lenore said quietly. 'I'll be in the next room if you need anything.' She smiled sweetly and then left.

Dorothea pulled the eiderdown coverings closer about her body and waited. George's rooms adjoined hers – as did Lenore's on the opposite side – and she sat there, staring at the door as if it were a living thing about to attack her if she looked away.

At last it opened. George, in a light-brown dressing robe, entered. He had removed his wig and his dark hair was tousled and uncombed. He stood there uncertainly for a moment, then said, 'If it's inconvenient, I can return later …'

He looked so uncomfortable that Dorothea began to relax. She started to laugh, then fell silent at the affronted look upon his face. 'Please come in,' she said at last, wondering why no one in this house seemed to laugh.

Her husband approached the bed, removed his dressing robe, then climbed in beside her.

'The light …' Dorothea murmured, suddenly frightened once more.

Turning to look at her, George stared blankly for the moment. 'Oh, yes. Forgive me.' He extended a hand. A moment later the room was plunged into darkness, relieved only slightly by the pale moonlight that crept in between parted draperies.

George reached for her, wishing he dared ask her to remove her nightclothes. Catherine always did that. But, he supposed, a trifle annoyed, that was not the proper attitude toward one's wife.

Dorothea lay beneath him, rigid and unresponsive. She bore the penetration and the pain that followed in a stoic manner. Eleanor had, only that morning, told her what to expect. The first time will be painful, her mother had said. But after that it will be much easier, perhaps even enjoyable. Somehow, Dorothea doubted that.

George had neither spoken nor kissed her during the entire ritual, which had lasted only a few minutes.

Afterward, he got up and, fumbling about in the dark, located his dressing robe. Then, with a murmured good night, he returned to his own room.

Hanover

March 1683

The following weeks were pleasant enough. As Lenore had foretold, carnival season began in earnest. The dressmakers came and went. New, lovely gowns crowded Princess Dorothea's wardrobe. George visited her most evenings but never spent the night in her bed, which did not unduly concern her. He was off hunting for days at a time. Both Prince Charles and Prince Maximilian were attentive and friendly. Occasionally even Duke Ernst danced and laughed with her.

The others, however, treated Dorothea with a reserve that bordered, at times, upon rudeness.

One part of her day truly annoyed Dorothea, and that was the daily walk the duchess insisted upon after the midday meal. Rain or shine, snow or cold, Sofia was adamant. Naturally all the ladies of the court, including Dorothea, had to be in attendance. The only excuse was illness. However, this was difficult to feign unless Dorothea wanted to absent herself from the evening's activities as well.

The walk wouldn't be so bad, Dorothea reflected on this blustery March day as she trudged along, if the duchess didn't walk so fast. Briskly, she called it, although it left everyone in her wake breathless. Then, too, there was her constant harping about her heritage. Sofia's mother had been Queen of Bohemia, her grandfather, James I. Dorothea knew it by heart, though why her mother-in-law would want to lay claim to the English succession escaped Dorothea, who was perfectly content to stay in her own country. Other countries were fine enough, but only to visit.

Now Dorothea walked, trying to take big steps so as to keep up. She listened with only half an ear to her mother-in-law. The sausages she had eaten a short time ago lay heavily and uncomfortably in her stomach. Dorothea was certain she would never get used to the execrable food. Why, she wondered resentfully, couldn't she have wine instead of beer; beef bourguinon instead of sausages and fried cabbage?

Suddenly, in spite of the freezing temperatures, Dorothea felt hot and dizzy. The path before her wavered and blurred and seemed to rise up at her. Uttering a cry, Dorothea put a hand out and pitched forward into the snow before any of the startled ladies could reach her.

Then there was nothing.

When she awoke she was in her own bed. The first thing Dorothea saw was a ring of faces about her: Lenore's frantic and concerned; the physician's, grave and unsmiling; George's – as usual, his face revealed little; the duke's, who for some reason looked pleased; and Sophia's, whose expression, for once, reflected concern and chagrin.

It was the duchess who stepped forward and spoke.

'My dear,' she said softly. 'Forgive me, but you should have let us know.' Sofia's manner and attitude conveyed a slight accusation, despite her concerned look.

'Know what?' Dorothea retorted, gritting her teeth against a rising wave of nausea.

Sofia raised a brow at this obstinacy. 'You are to have a child,' she stated, quickly, blinking her eyes. 'You should have told me. Certainly I would not have allowed you to walk in the cold had I been aware of your condition.' Regarding the surprise on Dorothea's face, Sofia suddenly realized that the girl hadn't known. But of course she hadn't, the duchess further speculated with annoyance. Eleanor didn't even know how to raise a daughter properly. Bending over, Sofia patted Dorothea's hand. 'You may rest as long as you wish. You will not, of course, be allowed to walk with us during your confinement.'

Nausea disappeared in a wave of relief. Gratefully, Dorothea closed her eyes, aware that everyone was now leaving the room. When next she opened them, only

Lenore was there. They grinned at each other as they each thought the same thing: no more of those horrendous walks, at least for the coming months.

By far the person made most happy by the coming event was Duke Ernst. He sent for George Ludwig that night after the evening meal.

George, entering, was surprised to see that his father was alone in the study. While his mother was rarely in attendance on those occasions when the duke sent for him, Count Platen most invariably was. Tonight, however, the duke was alone.

'George!' Ernst motioned his son forward. 'Again, my congratulations.'

'Thank you, sir,' George automatically responded as he sank down in the chair indicated by his father.

'I want you to know that I'm proud of you.' Ernst emanated an air of satisfaction. 'From the time you conducted yourself so admirably at Treves, I've watched you grow from a boy into a man. Now you're married and will soon have a child. I hope it will be a son.'

'I too, sir.' George flushed with pleasure at this unusual outpouring of compliments.

'How much do you know of the history of our family?' Ernst inquired quietly. He leaned back in his chair and clasped his hands on his stomach.

The question was so unexpected that George merely stared at his father.

'I daresay you're more familiar with your mother's family than my own,' Ernst noted dryly with a slight smile. 'But it's time you learned,' he went on, 'because I have great plans for you.' He regarded his eldest son with new seriousness. 'More than thirty years ago, the house of Brunswick was divided. Half of it went to the Wolfenbüttels, which is headed now by my cousin, Anthony Ulric. The other half was given to our family, the Luneburgs.'

George nodded, puzzled by this recitation of facts he already knew, but he didn't interrupt his father.

'There were four of us originally,' Ernst continued. 'Wilhelm is the oldest. He became the Duke of Hanover when he was only seventeen. My brother Christian and my brother John were both dead, as you know. I'm certain that you've heard the story from your mother as to why Wilhelm began, at seventeen, as the Duke of Hanover and yet now I hold that title.' He gave a short, humorless laugh. 'However, your mother may have colored the facts somewhat, so I shall try to explain it to you.'

Ernst took a breath, then continued. 'Wilhelm, in his younger years, loved life and women with an equal passion.' He smiled fondly. 'So much so that when the time came for him to settle down and raise a family, he simply couldn't do it. He was away more than he was home at that time. Needless to say, affairs here suffered as a consequence.'

'He certainly stays home now,' George observed sarcastically.

Ernst frowned at this levity but chose to ignore it. 'At that time, his life suited him. Consequently, he asked me to fulfill his obligations as head of Hanover. Frederick was alive at that time and he was governing Celle.' Ernst got to his feet, went across the room, and poured himself a brandy. 'Help yourself,' he said to his son as he returned to his seat.

George got himself a drink while his father continued.

'Your mother and I were married and settled down in Hanover, while Wilhelm lived his exciting life.' Though Ernst was uncertain as to whether his son knew that Sofia was originally betrothed to Wilhelm, he made no mention of it.

George smiled as he again sat down. '*Was* it exciting?' he asked, beginning to enjoy himself.

Ernst's answering smile was indulgent. 'I would certainly imagine so. He was quite the gallant.' Then the duke grew serious again. 'Wilhelm signed a contract renouncing all rights to Hanover – and he swore that he would never marry.' He twirled his glass, absently noting the amber colors in the liquid. 'He didn't count on falling in love, I suppose,' he mused, almost to himself. 'Yet he did. He brought Eleanor d'Olbreuse home here to Hanover. Naturally, neither your mother nor I would release Wilhelm from his promise. After all, to have done so would have been to place you and your brother, not to mention ourselves, in great jeopardy of losing Hanover.

Well, we had thought that Wilhelm would get over it. He had had many love affairs – your mother and I felt that this was just one more.' Ernst glanced briefly at George, then looked away.

'There was no real problem,' he went on, 'until our brother Frederick died. Wilhelm then became Duke of Celle.'

Ernst fell quiet for a minute and George got up to get another drink. All very interesting, he was thinking, although he already knew most of it. But why was his father telling him all this? He returned and sat down again, waiting in respectful silence.

Then Ernst turned to him. 'The land that has been in our family for generations has been split asunder by all these events. It shouldn't have been that way. The Duke of Saxony was able to keep his holdings intact and under one rule. As a consequence, the emperor granted him an electoral status. As you know, there are eight electorates.'

Ernst paused and stared intently at his son. 'I plan for Hanover to be the ninth. I, and then you, in turn, will sit in council with the emperor. This is why you had to marry Wilhelm's daughter. Celle and Hanover will be united, as they should be. As they once were.'

'Yes, Father,' George murmured. The brandy began to make him feel drowsy and he leaned his head back, eyes closed.

'Our land must never again be divided,' his father was saying. 'And there is only one way for me to do that. That is why I have sent for you tonight. For generations it has been the custom to divide our lands between our sons. I shall discontinue that trend.'

George opened his eyes and stared at his father.

'I plan to leave you, intact, everything I possess.'

Dumbfounded, George now sat up, straightening his wig, which had gone slightly askew. 'But what about Friedrich, and Christian, and …'

'Exactly,' his father interrupted. He fixed George with a hard stare. 'There would be nothing left, nothing of any size, that is. Oh, don't worry. The money will be there for the others. And I charge you, George, to see to it that your brothers and their families will always be taken care of.'

Still amazed, George leaned back again. 'The others,' he said slowly, unable to take it all in. 'Do they know? Do they agree?'

Ernst frowned. 'There is nothing for them to agree upon,' he stated harshly. 'The decision is mine to make, and I have made it. As for them knowing, they will know soon enough.'

'Mother?'

'She, too, will be informed in due time.' He stood up and George stumbled to his feet. 'Franz will see to the necessary papers.' He clapped George on the shoulder. 'It's a heavy responsibility I place upon you, my son. If I didn't deem you worthy, I would not hesitate to choose someone else.'

George couldn't suppress a tremor of apprehension at those words. 'I'll do my best, sir,' he said fervently.

They walked toward the door and Ernst said, 'By the way, my boy, I understand that you have installed Mademoiselle von Schulenburg in the suite that adjoins yours.' He laughed heartily at George's sudden pallor. 'Now, now, I'm not the one to bandy the news about. But I suggest that you keep your wife blissfully uninformed. Especially now. We don't want to upset her.'

'Yes, sir,' George mumbled as he hastily withdrew.

Leine castle had two dining halls. The small one in the west tower was used for family meals, and the large one in the east tower, facing the river, was used for more formal occasions and state banquets.

The midday meal, the heaviest one of the day, was served promptly at two o'clock. Seating and protocol were rigid and Duchess Sofia frowned on any but the most correct behaviour during the daily ceremony.

There was one exception, which she bore with fortitude, as a member of her rank should. These occasions were when Countess Platen was in residence in Leine, as she would be for the next month or so. Painful though they might be, Sofia discreetly ignored these incidents as much as possible. Strictly speaking, the countess should enter the room and be seated with the other ladies of the entourage – at a separate table. As it was, Elizabeth Platen entered directly behind the duke and duchess and was seated to the duke's left. A distressing situation, but one that must be tolerated. It would never do for Sofia to even acknowledge such a deviation in protocol.

As the court entered the dining hall on this April afternoon, it was with some consternation that Sofia saw Princess Dorothea come into the room, her hand placed lightly upon the arm of her husband. The princess had been confined to her apartments in these last weeks on the advice of the physician until her condition was stable enough so as to cause no threat to the child she carried.

Apparently the girl was feeling better and had taken it upon herself to join them for the midday meal. With a stab of uneasiness Sofia realized that Dorothea would have no way of knowing that the countess would be seated to Ernst's left, which was Dorothea's privilege as second lady of the court.

From her position at the other end of the table, the duchess watched in dismay as both women headed for the same chair.

Elizabeth, older and wiser, stepped in front of Dorothea. As the footman pulled out the chair, Elizabeth sat down gracefully, flashing a warm smile at Ernst. Sofia tore her gaze away from the intimate look that passed between her husband and her first lady, and saw that Dorothea was, for the moment, standing there in bewilderment. Gently George tried to take her arm and direct her to a vacant chair. Dorothea shook her head until her curls bounced in angry protest. Memories of her mother's treatment in this court now came to her and she remembered her own resolve never to condone such a situation.

'Madame!' Dorothea said in a clear strong voice that rang through the room with painful clarity. 'I believe that you are sitting in my chair.'

The countess arched a black brow and regarded Dorothea coolly, a slight smile on her red lips.

Ernst frowned, Sofia paled, and George, together with the rest of the assemblage, looked decidedly uncomfortable.

'Dorothea,' he whispered, tugging at her arm again.

Astounded, Dorothea realized that the woman had no

intention of moving. Worse, neither the duke nor the duchess, much less her own husband, was about to reprimand her for her forward and presumptuous behaviour. Angrily shrugging off George's hand, Dorothea glared at them all, spun around, and with quick, furious steps, left the dining hall, her head held high.

With a brief, apologetic glance at his father's dark expression. George followed.

'How dare she!' Dorothea screamed when in her own apartments.

'Please don't excite yourself,' George exclaimed, thoroughly alarmed at the sight of his wife's reddening face. He knew that she had a temper, it had fallen on him on more than one occasion, but he had never seen her so enraged. 'Your condition ...' he began. Oh, God, he thought, his father would be even more upset if anything happened to the child.

'Damn my condition!' Dorothea retorted in a loud voice. 'I am not sick. I am pregnant.' She glared at him, dark eyes flashing. 'How dare you let such a situation occur?' Her voice rang with indignation and, in fact, she had never before been so humiliated.

Helplessly, George waved a hand. 'It wasn't my doing. I have no say in such a matter. The countess always sits there when she's in residence. You haven't noticed because she has been in Monplaisir these past months.'

'It will have to change,' Dorothea stated firmly. What was the matter with him? she wondered crossly. Such a thing would never occur at the court of Celle. Her father would never permit such an insult to her mother.

Exasperation at her attitude grasped George. 'I don't see why you consider yourself insulted,' he argued testily. 'If my mother can conduct herself graciously under the circumstances, I fail to see why you cannot do so.'

'Your mother!' Dorothea shot back in scathing tones. 'I do believe that she lectures me by the hour as to the proper protocol. She, who sets great store by such things, ignores that ... that creature with her painted face and overbearing manner.' The words tumbled forth in breathless fashion.

George was about to retort when the door opened to

frame Duchess Sofia. She glanced briefly at her son. 'If you would be kind enough to leave us,' she suggested midly, 'I would like to speak with the princess.'

Grateful for this interruption, George nodded once. Without further words he left the room, closing the door behind him.

For a long moment Sofia stared at her daughter-in-law, resisting the impulse to grasp the girl and shake her by the shoulders. Such behaviour was inexcusable, she thought, irritated. The girl really was not brought up properly. Good heavens, one would have thought that she came from a family of burghers. Sofia sighed deeply. She supposed that allowances would have to be made for Dorothea's condition.

'You conducted yourself badly, Dorothea,' Sofia said at last, not unkindly. As the girl opened her mouth to speak, the duchess raised a hand. 'Come, let us sit down over here by the window so that we may talk.'

With an audible sigh of exasperation, Dorothea followed her mother-in-law. When they were seated, the duchess observed the wife of her eldest son. She folded her hands primly in her lap. 'You are correct when you say that Countess Platen was not seated properly at the table,' she remarked almost conversationally. 'It's unfortunate, perhaps, that you have been here these months without this situation occurring.'

'Unfortunate!' Dorothea sputtered, eyes wide.

But the duchess continued as if uninterrupted. 'Countess Platen is in a unique position,' she explained, averting her eyes. 'The duke thinks highly of her, and is comfortable and relaxed in her company.'

Astonished, Dorothea just stared at her mother-in-law. How could she speak so? she wondered, truly amazed. How could she ignore the fact that her husband's mistress brazenly seated herself at table in view of the whole court, flaunting her position? And with her *own* husband seated nearby. In spite of her own emotions, Dorothea fell into wonder at the calm, almost unconcerned face before her. 'I am not the one who should be reprimanded, Highness,' she remarked at last in a softer tone.

For the first time, the duchess smiled. 'I'm afraid, my

dear, that you are exactly the one,' she murmured. 'The countess did not disrupt the meal. You did. What if we had had guests?' she pointed out, inclining her head. 'Surely such a scene would be unforgivable. Now,' she went on briskly, her back straightening. 'I suggest that you observe and study the behaviour of my daughter, Charlotte.'

Dorothea made a face. She and her young sister-in-law were barely on speaking terms. The young Charlotte was an insufferable bore. Since it had been announced that she was to wed the Elector of Brandenburg, the girl had become intolerable.

'Charlotte is well versed in deportment,' continued Sofia. 'She has been well brought up and is perfectly suited to the marriage arranged for her. If you are in doubt at any time as to how to conduct yourself, I suggest that you look to my daughter and follow her lead. One more thing, Dorothea,' the duchess said before Dorothea could comment. 'Later this week, the Dowager Duchess of Friesland will be joining us for a visit. You are, of course, above her in rank. Yet, while she is here, she will be accorded special treatment.'

'Am I then to move further down the table?' Dorothea retorted acidly. 'Perhaps I should dine with the maids in the kitchen.'

Sofia cast her a pained look. Lord, the girl was incorrigible, she thought unhappily. 'The duke hopes to secure Friesland as an ally, Dorothea,' she explained with exaggerated patience. 'There are times when special considerations must be extended for political reasons.' She peered intently. 'You do understand? Please assure me that you will not treat our guest in a rude manner.' She placed a hand on her ample bosom as if to still the disquieting thought.

Dorothea flushed. 'I am not accustomed, Highness, to treating guests rudely.'

'Your behavior toward Countess Platen can be termed no less,' Sofia remarked softly.

'I hardly call her a guest!'

'Nevertheless,' Sofia persisted firmly. 'I must insist that you never repeat today's performance while you are in my house.' She stood up. 'Perhaps we can now join the others,' she suggested.

Dorothea's eyes widened. 'Surely you don't mean for me to go down there again?' She was appalled at the idea.

'I do indeed,' Sofia stated firmly with a level look.

'I won't do it! I will not be humiliated twice in one day.'

'You have little choice, Dorothea.' Sofia's manner was unsympathetic. 'The countess will be in residence until the court moves to Herrenhausen, eight weeks from now. Do you plan on not eating for that length of time? If you wait until tomorrow, it will only be harder on you.'

Dorothea turned away. 'I will eat in my room.'

Sofia raised a brow, her only concession to anger. 'Very well. But if you do, you needn't present yourself at the evening's festivities – tonight, or for any night you choose to disregard your obligations.'

Dorothea chewed her lip, sorely tempted, but the thought of weeks on end alone in her rooms save for Lenore's company provided a bleak picture.

'If you choose to absent yourself,' Sofia noted in a quieter voice, 'then the countess has won.'

Dorothea glanced up, startled. She stared at her mother-in-law for a long moment. Then, resigned she got to her feet.

Smiling now, Sofia led the way from the room. Together they entered the dining hall once more. There was an immediate scraping of chairs as the men got to their feet.

Taking her place on the other side of George, Dorothea sat down, conscious that her face was flaming. But she held her head high. Deftly, the duchess began a conversation with Field Marshal Podewils, who sat to her right. Heinrich Podewils, many years at court, was a gracious and kindly man in his early fifties. Immediately he responded to Sofia. In only moments the buzz of conversation was at a normal level.

For a time Dorothea ate in silence, aware that George was speaking to Countess Platen, seated on his other side.

'You certainly showed her,' came the whispered murmur. Surprised, Dorothea turned to look at Prince Charles, who sat next to her. The young man was grinning in absolute delight.

She flushed, not altogether displeased, and resumed eating.

'Not everyone could have stood up to the countess,' Charles continued in low tones. 'I admire your spirit.'

Dorothea turned to look at him. 'You're the only one,' she observed tartly, relaxing. She glanced across the table and saw Prince Maximilian openly staring. He flashed her a wide smile and, disconcerted, Dorothea averted her eyes.

Chuckling, Charles said, 'That's it, Dorothea. It's easy when you know how to play the game.'

'Thank you, Charles,' she said to her younger brother-in-law. 'If I must sit next to someone, I'd rather it be you than anyone else.'

The following morning as Dorothea was penning a letter to her mother, George entered her sitting room. She looked up, surprised to see her husband at this hour. 'Why are you dressed like that?' she asked, noting the military uniform he was wearing.

He stared steadily. 'With the duke's permission, I have joined the Imperial Army,' he announced, sounding somewhat pontifical.

Dorothea was amused. 'The uniform looks well on you,' she remarked, not realizing the impact of his statement. George, she thought, was always playing soldier.

'I'm leaving this morning,' he said quietly. 'I came to say good-bye.'

Dorothea blinked. 'Leaving? Where are you going?'

'Right now, to Hungary,' he replied. 'The emperor needs all the help he can get to stem the advance of the Turks.'

'But,' she said in a small voice, 'what of me?'

George stared at her, amazed that she could be so selfish at a time like this. 'You will be well attended,' he pointed out, annoyed.

She stood up and went to him. 'Will you be back before the child is born?'

George flushed. 'I'm ... not certain,' he responded vaguely. He seemed uncomfortable. Dorothea had the impression that he was performing a distasteful chore, one he wished would end swiftly.

'But you cannot leave me now!' she cried out, close to tears.

George was regarding her with distaste. His mother was right, he thought to himself. More and more, he was ashamed of his wife and her outbursts. They had been married little more than six months and already it seemed a lifetime.

Dorothea looked at him sharply, recognizing his expression of revulsion. 'Go, then,' she said coldly, in command of herself once more. 'Go and be damned!'

He bowed stiffly. 'Good day, madame,' he murmured, backing away. Out in the corridor, George took a deep breath, relieved to have it over. Then, with a quick glance at Dorothea's closed door, he hurried to the far end of the corridor. Without knocking, he entered. Regarding the woman seated on a brocade-covered divan, placidly embroidering, George smiled softly.

Melusine von Schulenberg looked up from her handwork. Her lips curved sweetly. 'George,' she said quietly. She laid the embroidery on a table and held out her white arms. Quickly he crossed the room and sat down beside her. Their kiss was long and deep as they clung to each other. At last, breathless, she pulled away.

In appearance Melusine was the opposite of Dorothea. She had such fair hair that it shone whitely in the sun. Her eyes, while reflecting little spirit, were a vivid shade of blue. She was plump and pink and utterly feminine. George loved her with all the feeling he had to give to such an emotion. He had met her at Monplaisir during one of Countess Platen's glittering masques and had fallen completely under her spell. He was still amazed that such a glorious creature could care for him.

Even now, after all these months, he marveled at how easily Melusine had consented to be with him. He was not a great admirer of Countess Platen, for that woman was too bold, too flamboyant to suit his tastes, but George would be forever in her debt for introducing him to Melusine. Naturally the countess could not have known how devastating the meeting would be; it had just been a happy coincidence.

'I'm so proud of you.' Melusine's voice was tender as

she stroked his cheek. Then she clasped him close. 'You will be careful? I couldn't bear it if anything happened to you. You are my life!' Nor was Melusine speaking an untruth. As Elizabeth had foreseen, these two were ideally suited to one another.

George put a fingertip to her rosy lips. 'Nothing will happen to me,' he promised. 'Not when I have you to return to.'

'Will it be all right if I stay here while you're gone?' she asked, worried. 'Perhaps I should return to Monplaisir.'

'No, no. I want you here.' George frowned. 'There are too many temptations at Monplaisir.'

She rested her head on his chest. 'There is no other man for me, my darling,' she assured him.

'I've made arrangements for you to join my mother's suite. You will be given the post of lady.'

'She knows about me? About us?' Melusine's wide blue eyes regarded him doubtfully. She was quite in awe of Duchess Sofia.

George hesitated. 'I would venture to say that she suspects,' he replied slowly. Then he brightened. 'But my mother is a lady. She will never cause you any discomfort.' He pulled her close again. 'There is so little time,' he murmured, his breath quickening with her nearness.

'Enough, my dearest,' she assured him, gasping as his hand encircled her ample breast.

With her husband's departure, Dorothea's life settled into a routine. She spent her mornings writing letters, mostly to her mother, and consulting with her dressmaker or hairdresser. After the midday meal, no longer able to join the duchess on those horrendous walks, she napped. Occasionally she received visitors. But, disgruntled, Dorothea discovered that Countess Platen managed to receive the most interesting people available. As a result, on some days only Prince Charles joined her. Charlotte, too, showed up periodically, to gloat and to boast of her coming marriage.

In October, because her condition would no longer permit it, Dorothea retired from court merely to languish in her apartments, awaiting the birth of her child. She missed the dances, card parties, and, most of all, dressing up in her jewels and magnificent costumes.

Toward the end of the month, Dorothea was surprised to see Charlotte enter her sitting room. The girl was dressed lavishly, for the evening offered a ball. Jewels sparkled at her throat, in her hair, at her wrists, and on her fingers. She wasn't pretty, but she had a certain haughty flair that was attractive. Resentfully, Dorothea noted the slim waist and couldn't help but compare it with her own burgeoning stomach. God, but she was tired of being pregnant, tired of being cooped up, tired of being bored, and tired of being tired!

'What is it, Charlotte?' she questioned in an irritated manner.

'I see that you are in your usual petulant mood,' Charlotte observed with a lift of her brows. She smiled disarmingly at Lenore, who was bent over an embroidery frame. Not receiving an answering smile, she continued. 'The duchess instructed me to see if there is anything you need. She is quite busy now, seeing that all is in order for the evening. William of Orange arrived this morning. The ball will be in his honour. My, but he is a handsome man,' she concluded breathlessly.

With a heavy sigh, Dorothea got up and walked about the room in an aimless fashion. 'There is nothing I need,' she retorted. 'Go and enjoy yourself. Soon you will marry,' she added spitefully. 'Your times of careless enjoyment may be few.'

But Charlotte merely laughed, refusing to be goaded. She was anxious to be married, anxious to be Electress of Brandenburg. With a light step, she spun around, billowing the full skirt of her blue taffeta dress. It was cut daringly low and hugged her small waist tightly. Around her slim white neck a diamond collar glinted and sparkled with her movements. 'How do you like my new gown? I had it made especially for tonight.'

Grudgingly, Dorothea had to admit that it was beautiful. Charlotte began to walk to the door, then halted on the threshold. 'Oh, I do have some news, Dorothea,' she said brightly. 'We have received word from George. He'll be returning in time for my wedding next month.'

Dorothea paused, glaring angrily. Her husband would be in time for his sister's wedding – but not for the birth of his child.

'I must hurry,' Charlotte went on, ignoring the look. 'I don't want to miss any of the dancing.'

As the door closed, Lenore looked up from her needlework, mouth grim. 'That one has an acid tongue,' she noted quietly. 'I do hope that you don't let her upset you.' She regarded the small tapestry again. 'She will soon be married and gone.'

There was no answer. After a brief moment, Lenore looked up again. With a cry, she stood up, heedless of the fallen embroidery, then rushed to Dorothea's side. 'What is it?' she cried, alarmed.

Dorothea, her hands gripping the back of a chair, could not, for the moment, speak. The pain thrust its way upward, as if rending her in two, and she could only groan.

Running into the hall, Lenore screamed at a passing servant, who hastened for the duchess. It seemed a long time, but it was only moments before the duchess arrived with the midwife in tow and calmly began issuing orders.

Downstairs, the ball was in full swing. Only a few of the almost three hundred persons in attendance knew of what was happening upstairs.

Elizabeth knew. But then, she knew everything, she thought with satisfaction. Thanks to her many informants, little, if anything, happened to Hanover without her knowledge. It heightened her enjoyment for the evening to know that the little chit was upstairs, probably screaming in agony. Serves her right, she thought, smiling brilliantly at her partner, a tedious envoy from Brandenburg.

Turning, she caught her breath as she saw Philip Königsmark enter the room. At twenty-four, Philip had reached his final height of six feet. His tall lean body was hard and muscular under the satin and velvet outfit he wore. Philip knew how to dress, and did so with flair. When he was on leave, he disdained the military uniform, dressing as the courtier he was. His face was ruggedly handsome with the fair coloring of his Swedish ancestors. Elizabeth saw his eyes scan the room. When they found her, his gaze was like a caress.

At last the dance ended and Elizabeth was able to rid herself of the wearisome envoy. As she knew he would, Philip approached and requested the next dance.

'Why didn't you let me know you were coming?' she demanded as he guided her around the floor.

'Careful, my dear,' he murmured with a half smile. 'The duke is watching you. But then, I suspect every man in the room has his eyes upon you.'

'Philip,' she whispered, almost overcome by his nearness. If ever she had loved a man, this was he.

He watched her in amusement, conscious that her hand trembled upon his shoulder. 'You look beautiful,' he noted. 'You should always wear red.'

'How long can you stay?' she asked, keeping the noncommittal smile in place.

'Only tonight. Podewils was most insistent that I return to my regiment in the morning,' he advised, speaking of his commanding officer.

'Where will you be going?'

'Vienna,' he replied. As she drew a sharp breath, he added: 'There is no danger. The city is secured and the Turks have been driven back. We'll be there just to make certain that they don't return again.'

'Can you come to Monplaisir this evening?' she whispered in hurried tones, for the dance was almost at an end. Her mind working quickly, Elizabeth reasoned that the duke, as well as the whole household, would be engrossed with the events now taking place upstairs.

Philip raised a brow. 'Wouldn't it seem odd if you left Leine tonight?'

'I don't believe so,' she replied, then laughed in earnest. 'Our little princess is about to bring forth an heir.'

'George's wife?' Philip enquired, remembering the little Dorothea of Celle. He hadn't seen her since she came to Hanover. 'I met her once when she was just a child.'

'I daresay she hasn't changed much,' Elizabeth remarked dryly. 'She is still a child, and a very irritating one, at that.'

The dance ended. Reluctantly, Elizabeth accepted a new partner. Now she wished for the evening to end so that she could join Philip at Monplaisir.

Königsmark walked aimlessly to the far end of the hall to avail himself of refreshments.

'Philip!'

He turned, then smiled broadly, showing white, even teeth. Enthusiastically, he grasped the outstretched hand. 'Charles! How good to see you. I was hoping that we would have some time together before I have to leave again.'

Prince Charles, adorned in a dark-green doublet, clapped his friend on the shoulder. 'I hope you can stay awhile.'

'Regretfully, no,' Philip answered. 'I must leave in the morning for Vienna.'

Charles's eyes brightened. 'George is there! We've had word that he'll be home in time for Charlotte's wedding.'

Puzzled, Philip regarded his young friend. 'I was under the impression that George will imminently be presented with an heir. Wasn't he able to get leave?'

Charles shrugged and helped himself to a canapé. 'I don't know.' Then he laughed. 'But the baby will be here when he returns.'

Philip laughed too. He liked Charles. Of all the sons of Duke Ernst, he felt closest to the engaging young man before him. He disliked George, who was a pompous bore. And he didn't like Maximilian a whit. That young man was too much like his father.

Charles gripped his arm firmly. 'Philip, if you have no other plans, I would like to have a talk with you.'

Königsmark hesitated and glanced in the direction of Elizabeth, who was still dancing, her eyes bright, her red skirt billowing about her slender figure.

'It's important,' Charles went on earnestly, seeing the hesitation.

Philip shrugged and put down his glass. Elizabeth could wait. She was always available. It wasn't as if he loved her, or felt anything like it. 'Very well,' he agreed. 'Let's go where we can talk.'

Awhile later Charles closed the door to his private

bedchamber on the third floor. At this distance, not even the faintest strain of music penetrated. They had met no one. Everyone was either in the ballroom or attending the princess.

'I hope all goes well with her,' Charles murmured as Philip settled himself comfortably in one of two large wing chairs. The young man opened a cabinet and brought forth a silver decanter and two pewter cups.

'Who?' Philip asked, stretching out his long legs.

'The Princess Dorothea. She is at this moment giving birth. You've never met her, have you? The last time you were in Hanover, I believe we all were at Herrenhausen.'

Philip nodded. He reached for the decanter placed on the low table between them and poured himself a brandy. 'It does seem that each time I arrive, the mysterious princess is unavailable.'

'I'll make a point of presenting you the next time you're here.' He grinned as he sat down. 'This evening would not be the appropriate time.'

Laughing, Philip had to agree. 'Hardly. Actually, I did meet her many years ago when I was at Celle for a short time. But she was barely nine at the time, and we had little to discuss. I was almost seventeen,' he added, as if that explained everything.

'You'd like her, I think.' Charles helped himself to a drink. 'She's gay and loves to laugh. And when she does, it's difficult not to join in. She has a bit of a temper, though. That plunges George and my mother into a sea of disapproval.'

Philip smiled as he sipped from the cup, beginning to understand Elizabeth's attitude. 'I cannot imagine the little girl I knew having temper tantrums,' he mused idly.

'Oh, it isn't her fault. At least I don't think so. But she's quite fearless about it,' Charles went on in evident admiration. 'She even took on Countess Platen one day.' He shook his head. 'I'm afraid Mother called her to task on that one.'

Interested, Philip asked what had happened, then chuckled in delight as Charles related the events that had occurred in the dining hall.

'I say, you're not in love with her, are you?' Philip asked

at the conclusion of the story. He watched, amused, as Charles flushed a bright pink.

'Of course not!' the young man protested. 'She's my sister-in-law.'

Philip leaned back and put his feet up on the low table, carefully avoiding the silver decanter. 'Very well, Charles,' he said firmly. 'What was so important that you had to drag me away from the festivities?'

Charles lowered his head and his face grew somber. He was slightly drunk, his relaxed features appearing even more youthful than was ordinarily the case. 'My father has informed us that George will be his sole heir.'

'What does that mean?' Philip asked, not understanding.

'It means that George gets everything. Hanover, Celle, all his wife's property, all the money. Everything.'

Philip frowned in perplexity. 'But what of you and your brothers?'

Charles gestured. 'George is to provide an allowance for us as he sees fit.'

'That's disgraceful!' Putting his feet on the floor again, Philip sat up. 'What have you done that prompted this?' He was mystified. Certainly George would become Duke of Hanover. But what of Celle and Herrenhausen and Osnabrück? he wondered.

'We've done nothing. It's not that at all,' Charles hastened to explain. 'My father hopes to make Hanover the ninth electorate. The emperor will not even consider the petition unless Hanover and Celle are united. Obviously, there can be only one elector.' He sighed. 'And that will be George,' he murmured dispiritedly.

Philip pursed his lips. 'I'm sorry, Charles. Truly I am.' He spread his hands in a helpless gesture. 'But what can I do about it? If the duke has said it must be this way, why, I suppose that's the way it will be. No one has the authority to question him.'

Charles shook his head and the room seemed to spin before his eyes. He took a breath. 'I don't question my father's decision. And you're right, it has to be as he says.' His face grew morose. 'That's just it, Philip. My brother Friedrich refuses to accept it. He has gone behind Father's back and has secretly written to Anthony Ulric for assistance. He wants to petition the emperor in behalf of what he calls his rightful inheritance. Friedrich has done this in all our names, even though I want no part of it. Christian agrees with me. As for Maximilian, well, he won't lift a finger to either help or hinder. Don't you see what this will mean?' The young brow creased in anxiety.

Frowing, Philip nodded slowly. 'If the emperor grants Friedrich's request, he will have to automatically turn down the duke's petition for an electorate. Split up between the five of you, there won't be enough left of any size to qualify.' He looked at Charles, suddenly fearful for the young man. The duke had a most violent temper and there was nothing in the world he wanted more than the electorate.

'What shall I do, Philip?' Charles pleaded. Leaning forward, he rested his arms on his thighs, hands clasped between his knees, his attitude one of profound dejection. 'I cannot betray my brothers. And I cannot betray my father.'

'Who else knows of this, besides Ulric?'

'Only Count Platen.'

'Platen!' Suddenly agitated, Philip got to his feet.

Bewildered, Charles looked up at him. 'Why, yes. He has been most helpful. Someone had to word it correctly. I know he's Father's minister, but he is sympathetic to us. He thinks it's wrong.'

'Oh, my God.' Philip ran a hand through his wavy hair. Like babes in the woods, they had all walked into a trap. He'd bet money on it. Platen had sympathy only for himself. Philip turned and faced Charles, who by now was looking decidedly ill. Glancing at the clock, he saw that it was close to one-thirty in the morning. If the ball was not already over, it was close to being so. 'Go to bed, Charles,' he said gently. 'I'll see what I can do.'

He would have to hurry, Philip thought, making his way downstairs. He had to be back in camp by six. On the second landing he heard a high-pitched scream and paused momentarily. Then, remembering the princess and her travail, he hurried onward. That was no concern of his.

The ballroom, he saw, was indeed vacated, except for the servants, who were cleaning up, and the musicians, who were availing themselves of leftover food. Moving out into the chilly night, Philip summoned his carriage.

Moments later he was speeding toward Monplaisir, some three miles distant. The October night was clear and cold and moonless, the sky a tapestry of brilliant stars. With a little luck, Philip told himself, Franz would remain in Leine tonight and Elizabeth would be alone.

She was. Dressed in a thin negligee and little else, she greeted him warmly. 'Where have you been?' she scolded, leading him toward the bed. 'I left early and have been waiting for you.' Her black eyes narrowed. 'You weren't with anyone else, were you?'

Philip forced himself to smile, then kissed her, holding her close against him. In spite of his distracted state, Philip felt himself responding to the sensuous movement of her voluptuous body.

'It's been so long,' she murmured breathlessly. 'I've missed you.' Her hands wandered over his body, demanding, insisting. After a moment, he picked her up in his arms and carried her to the canopied bed. Unceremoniously, he deposited her there. Without even taking time to remove his clothing, Philip took her roughly and without a hint of tenderness.

Elizabeth, however, was used to his gruff, almost brutal manner, especially at first. He spent long months with his regiment and was not predisposed to the niceties when he had only a few hours to spend with her.

Finally he sat up and looked down at her. Her negligee was torn and tattered. 'I'm sorry about your robe,' he said with a half grin that belied his words.

'You are welcome to tear them all, one by one,' she answered, smiling up at him.

'Still, it's unfortunate that I was so careless,' Philip persisted, toying with a strand of her black hair. 'Especially now, when I have a favor to ask.'

She raised herself up on one elbow. 'A favor?'

He nodded slowly. 'I assume that you're aware that the duke plans to leave his entire estate to Prince George?'

She laughed, throwing her head back to reveal a white,

slim neck. 'That's old news, my dear Philip. In fact, I suggested it to Ernst. It's the only way that he can secure an electorate for Hanover. Ernst will make a good elector,' she mused, swinging her well-shaped legs over the side of the bed. Standing there, she carelessly undid the belt of her torn negligee and let it fall to the floor, pirouetting invitingly.

'It's late, you vixen,' Philip said to her. 'Put some clothes on.' Watching her, he suddenly wondered if he were making a mistake. Perhaps Elizabeth didn't know of Friedrich's plans. To put such a weapon in her hands would not be wise. 'Do you think the duke's sons will accept his conditions gracefully?' he asked, choosing his words with care.

Elizabeth laughed again. She walked to her wardrobe and drew forth another negligee. 'Gracefully is hardly the word,' she commented as she slipped it on.

Philip checked a frown. Damn her, he thought, noting the time. It was after five o'clock. He still didn't know if she knew. It was one of her favorite tricks, pretending that she did know something, thereby getting the other person to reveal what they knew. 'What do you mean?' he said at last, trying to act casual.

Her eyes narrowed. 'Come now, Philip. What I mean isn't important. What is it that you want?'

He hesitated, then wet his lips. 'I know of Friedrich's plans,' he said simply.

This time, she laughed with genuine mirth. 'My goodness, you *have* been busy. You've only been here for a matter of hours and already you're a fountain of information.' She grew serious. 'Yes, it's true. Friedrich has foolishly involved himself and his brothers in what could be termed an act of treason.'

'I told you I wanted a favor, Elizabeth,' Philip repeated, staring at her.

Elizabeth walked over to where he was still seated on the bed. Standing close to him, she drew his head to her breast. 'And I'm prepared to grant you whatever you want,' she whispered in a low voice.

Absently he ran his lips over the white and scented flesh. Then he stood up and put his arms about her, cupping her buttocks in his hands. 'Neither Charles nor Christian were involved in this,' he said to her. 'And I doubt seriously that Maximilian had any active part. The duke will be angry enough when he learns of it. There is no need to involve the others, is there?' There was no immediate answer as Elizabeth nuzzled his neck. His put his hands on her shoulders and firmly held her at a distance. 'Does the duke already know?' he asked, suddenly concerned. He was aware that his fingers sunk deeply into her soft flesh, but she didn't wince. Instead, she smiled lazily.

'No, my dear Philip,' she answered. 'Not yet. I was going to bring it to his attention this evening. But the little princess has upset my plans. Ernst is in no mood for problems on this gala evening.'

'Then I want you to stress that Friedrich acted alone,' he said quickly.

She pursed her lips in thought. 'Very well. Franz has secured copies of Friedrich's letters to Ulric and to the emperor. I don't believe that he mentioned the others, except in a general sense. Friedrich is a very self-centred young man, you know. As the next eldest, he has the most to lose.' She put her arms about his neck. 'Now that I have granted your favor, my darling, I have one of my own.'

He glanced at the clock. 'My God, it's five-thirty,' he exclaimed, breaking away. 'I must go, Elizabeth.' He blew a kiss at her pouting face. 'When I return, you'd better clear your calendar for a week. I don't plan on sharing you, even with the duke!'

When Dorothea awoke, the late-morning sun flooded her room. Only the duchess, Charlotte, and Lenore remained of the sea of faces that she had seen all night long.

Amazingly, the duchess smiled down upon her warmly, almost affectionately. Charlotte looked pale and chastened. There was no hint of hauteur left upon her young face. She appeared shaken by what she had seen. Her mother thought it was in her best interest to witness the birth, in view of her own impending marriage. Charlotte now regarded Dorothea with a new respect.

'You have a son,' Sofia said to her, still smiling.

Astonished, Dorothea felt the dry lips brush her brow. 'He is a fine son, and healthy. As soon as you're rested, we shall bring him to you.'

Dorothea took a deep breath, immeasurably relieved that it brought forth no pain. She was thankful that it had been a boy. Not for herself; she really didn't care, one way or the other. But everyone else seemed to attach great importance to it. She smiled weakly, acknowledging the congratulations.

Patting her hand, Sofia continued. 'We will leave you to rest now, my dear.'

As her mother left, Charlotte turned and took hold of Dorothea's hand. 'I'm so sorry,' she whispered. 'I've been wretched to you. I hope you'll forgive me. You were very brave,' she added solemnly.

Dorothea pressed the warm hand. 'Thank you, Charlotte. How unfortunate that it took so long for us to become friends. I'll miss you.'

'I will visit,' the girl offered quickly. 'And when I have my own court, you'll always be welcome. Now, you must hurry and get well. There are all kinds of festivities planned. Father is having a masque that will be the best ever! You and I will plan our costumes together. There will even be a torch dance. Have you ever seen one?'

Dorothea smiled sadly. 'Once,' she murmured. The dance was a traditional German ceremony, performed mostly at weddings. It was quite spectacular when executed by experienced dancers. She thought of her own wedding, a scant year ago. There had been no torch dance, no masque, no festivities at all.

'I'm tiring you.' Charlotte was contrite. 'I'll be back in the morning. We can talk then.'

The following day George returned, bringing with him, of all things, two Turkish prisoners. Only they weren't really prisoners. They had started out that way, but George had inexplicably offered them positions as his servants and they had gratefully accepted. Mustapha and Muhammed were their names, but Dorothea was never able to tell them apart.

Some days after that, Friedrich stood by the window in his

father's study, contemplating the happy scene outside. At nineteen, Friedrich possessed the same slightly protruding blue eyes and somewhat heavy features as did his older brother George. He was, however, more intelligent, more quick to temper; in that, he resembled his father. He moved closer to the window. From this vantage point, he could see the cobbled streets of the city, now made festive with hundreds of gaily painted lanterns. Visitors had been arriving all week and the burghers, dressed in their traditional costumes, greeted each newly arrived carriage with high enthusiasm. They came from near and far because Hanover's carnival season was a notable event; that, combined with Charlotte's wedding and the birth of George's son, promised to make the coming weeks memorable.

Friedrich was thinking about his older brother; he had caused quite a stir with his two Turks. They had been his prisoners but somehow George had gained their loyalty. Now they served him as attendants. Everyone had been intrigued and amazed at the sight of the strange individuals who could barely speak an intelligible word.

But then, George seemed to get everything he wanted, Friedrich reflected with no little bitterness. George had a rich wife, a healthy son, a beautiful mistress – a secret, so far, successfully kept from his wife. He had proved himself courageous in battle. And now it appeared that he would have his brothers' inheritances as well.

Behind Friedrich, his father was continuing with his angry tirade. Ernst had been at it for more than an hour now, with no sign of tiring. Friedrich wondered if it had been Ulric who had betrayed him. It didn't seem likely, he mused, only half listening to his father, who was now beginning to repeat himself. It was in Ulric's interest that primogeniture not be established in Hanover.

My interest too, Friedrich thought desultorily. What could he or the others expect as a handout from the tight-fisted George? Nothing, that's what. Only enough to keep them in a bare existence. It was intolerable. Even his mother had seen the disadvantages. She had pleaded ardently on behalf of her younger sons, all to no avail. The electorate meant more to Ernst than did his own family.

How fortunate Charlotte was, he thought grimly. At least she would marry and be out of it.

For a moment Friedrich's thought shifted to his younger brothers; fortunately for them, his father seemed to hold him solely accountable. Young Ernest was, of course, still too immature to understand fully what all this meant. Even Christian and Charles seemed not to grasp the import; however, Friedrich had hoped that Maximilian would stand by his side. But Max, the chameleon, had hastily withdrawn his support when he discovered that the plan had come to light.

'Friedrich! Are you listening?' the duke demanded, regarding his son's back. He had never liked Friedrich, he realized suddenly. He had all of George's weaknesses but none of his strength. And, Ernst now reflected, he didn't much care for Maximilian either; but at least he knew his place. As for the younger ones, it was too early to tell. Not for the first time, Ernst was grateful that fate had seen fit to bestow upon him a son of George's worth.

'Yes, I am listening, sir,' Friedrich responded, but didn't turn around. Her had little desire to view his father's face, a mask of rage and contempt.

'Who are you to question my decisions?' Ernst was shouting now.

'I am your son,' Friedrich pointed out, mentally wincing at the sound of his father's snort of derision.

'Son,' Ernst muttered. 'You call yourself a son? You are no son of mine.'

Now Friedrich turned and faced his father. 'That much you have made apparent, sir,' he stated coldly.

'I might have forgiven you for what you've done,' Ernst went on, glaring at him, cheeks flushed with his anger. 'But I can never forgive you for dragging Ulric in on this. Don't you understand that the Elector of Hanover would be in a position to challenge Ulric? He has for too long had things his own way. You fool!' Ernst spat contemptuously. 'He wasn't trying to help you, he was trying to block me!'

'He was the only one, aside from Mother, who would listen,' Friedrich argued doggedly. 'It is unfair! George is not your only son. You must think of the rest of us.'

Amazement momentarily displaced anger. 'Must? Must?

How dare you speak in such terms?'

Friedrich turned away again. It was useless.

'Your brother George has returned from battle,' Ernst now continued in a more normal voice. 'He has acted with valor and with courage. It has made a man of him. I have sent word to the emperor it can make a man of you too.'

Slowly, Friedrich turned to his father. He had expected a severe reprimand, perhaps even a thrashing. He hadn't expected to be sent away. Yet maybe it wouldn't be all that bad. The life of an officer was not difficult and had many compensations. 'What will be my commission?' he asked at last, only to be somewhat startled by his father's answering laugh.

'Commission? You will be a soldier, Friedrich,' he replied softly. 'A common soldier.' He stood there, hands clasped behind his back, thoroughly enjoying the look of dismay he was seeing.

Friedrich paled. Surely his father couldn't mean it. 'You intend to send me unaccompanied, without a regiment, without equipment?' he asked, stunned, still not believing it. George had left with a small army trailing in his wake, a commission as a colonel, even a personal chef!

The reply was blunt. 'That is exactly what I mean,' Ernst confirmed. 'You will leave here with the clothes on your back and any personal possessions you can carry. One horse, one saddle, one musket. You will join the army in Vienna. Report to the emperor. He will assign you wherever he feels the need.'

'When?' Friedrich managed to ask through dry lips. He'd be damned, he thought, if he'd ask for anything. If his father wished to send him out as a beggar, then so be it.

'In the morning.' Ernst turned away. 'You may go now. We have nothing further to discuss.'

Herrenhausen

January 1684

With the departure of his obstreperous son and carnival in full swing, Ernst held a masquerade. From the meanest burgher to the highest nobleman, everyone was arrayed in costume and dominoes. Music spilled out of the castle into the streets, where rich and poor alike danced. The revelers flowed from Leine to Herrenhausen, six miles away, and back again. Ballets, concerts, plays, and card parties were held simultaneously, and the guests rushed from one event to the other, dancing in the streets as they went.

Charlotte, her seamstress having artfully captured the Turks' apparel, was decked out supposedly as Mustapha.

Dorothea was likewise attired as Muhammed. Both girls were in high spirits, and Dorothea was happy that she had recovered in time to join the festivities. Even George, dressed as Scaramouche, appeared rakish and in a cheerful mood

But it was Charles and Maximilian who stayed close by her side, acting as escorts and dancing partners. Eleanor and Wilhelm were in the crowd of revelers and Dorothea had received their warm congratulations upon the birth of her son, George Augustus.

It was late in the evening at Herrenhausen when the young people finally paused long enough to eat. Trestle tables were covered with snowy linens, with bowls and plates of delicacies. There were pâtés, saddle of venison, pickled pork, steaming platters of sauerbraten, smoked pork ribs, and mountains of potato dumplings. One table was devoted entirely to pastries, with colorful tortes and hot strudels dominating the aromatic repast. The orangery was opened at one end of the reception hall, and everyone found it a novelty to dance among blossom-laden orange trees in January.

Charles, dressed as a smuggler, had fetched a blanket and spread it on the warm earth of the orangery. Now the four of them – Dorothea, Charlotte, Maximilian, and Charles – wearily sat down to eat. The music filtered in and several dancers glided in and out among the trees.

'Father's outdone himself this time,' Charles noted happily. He reached toward his plate, plucked out a piece of sausage, and popped the steaming morsel into his mouth.

'Father loves to exceed himself,' Maximilian noted dryly as he chewed on a piece of pheasant.

A couple danced close by. Dressed as a gypsy, the girl had black hair that swung loose, her face, as was everyone else's, partially covered with a mask. Her partner was lavishly costumed as a harlequin.

Dorothea leaned over to Charlotte, who was busily scraping her plate free of the remaining crumbs of a cherry torte. 'Who is that?' she whispered. 'I have not seen her before.'

Charlotte glanced at the couple, then exchanged an oblique look with Maximilian. The young man smiled sardonically at his sister but made no comment. 'That is Countess Platen's daughter,' Charlotte responded slowly. 'She has only recently returned from Paris, where she has been attending school. Her name is the same as mine: Charlotte.'

Something in Charlotte's tone precluded Dorothea from asking any further questions. But she already suspected the reason for the suddenly closed looks. Elizabeth Platen was even more brazen than she had thought, Dorothea mused, still watching the couple. Or more firmly entrenched. There was a distinct possibility that the girl was Ernst's daughter, Charlotte's half sister.

'May I have the pleasure of this dance, milady?'

Dorothea looked up, surprised. It was the harlequin she had seen only moments ago. Beneath the mask, his mouth was curved in an engaging smile. From behind the black satin domino, his blue eyes smiled, just as engaging. She extended her hand and he assisted her to her feet. A moment later they were wending their way through the fragrant-smelling, artificially contrived orchard.

At first he hadn't known who she was, but the dimpled smile was not to be hidden by a mask. He had been watching her, surreptitiously, for the past thirty minutes while he danced with Elizabeth's daughter. Thankfully, someone else had claimed her. The girl had only a fraction of her mother's beauty and none of her charm or mystery. He found her incredibly tedious and vacuous and was glad to be rid of her.

Happily, Ernst had claimed Elizabeth's attention for the evening. Elizabeth had begun to bore Philip; her demanding possessiveness was beginning to suffocate him. Besides, Philip thought, Elizabeth was nearing forty. Even her practiced art with cosmetics couldn't hold back years.

'I've not seen you before,' Dorothea commented, dimpling.

'Nor have I ever seen you,' he lied.

'I am – '

'No, no,' he said hastily, laughing. 'That's the reason for the masks. I know only that I hold a beautiful woman in my arms.' His brow rose in amusement. 'What else is there for me to know?'

Dorothea's laugh mesmerized him with its silvery sound. She was weightless in his arms as her dark eyes viewed him with mischief.

'Perhaps your gypsy will be looking for you,' she noted archly. 'If you don't return to her, maybe she will cast a spell on you.'

Philip tilted his head. She couldn't even see the color of his hair, covered up as it was under the cap he wore. 'Someone *has* cast a spell on me, milady,' he remarked quietly. 'But I find it delightful.'

She flushed, hoping her mask hid that. 'I think I should return to … to my friends.'

The music had momentarily ceased and they now stood to the rear of the orangery, effectively concealed by thick green foliage.

'Look!' Philip pointed at the glass wall. 'Here we stand,

among scented blossoms, and there, only inches away, is snow.' He raised his eyes to look at the black sky. 'There are millions of stars. They look close enough to touch.'

Dorothea watched him, captivated by the sound of his voice. He still stood with his arm about her waist, but she made no move to pull away. Who was he? she wondered. Was he a visitor, a burgher, a king? He could be any of those. No, he spoke too well to be a burgher. The arm about her waist was hard and muscular, but that could simply be because he was young and well built.

'Do you really want to return to your friends?' he whispered. He leaned close to her, so close that she could feel his warm breath on her cheek. The heavy scent of blossoms, the wine she had drunk, and the lateness of the hour combined to make her feel dizzy, and Dorothea swayed slightly.

His arm tightened and he held her closer. 'Are you all right?' His voice was still a whisper, but now touched with concern.

'Yes,' she replied weakly. 'It's just so close in here.'

He grasped her hand. 'Come on, you need some air,' he pronounced firmly. Over her murmured protests, Philip led her out of the orangery.

Only minutes later, cloaked and with a fur robe across her legs, Dorothea found herself in an open sleigh. Beside her, the strange young man held the reins confidently in his gloved hand. They didn't speak for a moment, and as Dorothea breathed the clean cold air, she began to feel better.

He led the horse over a little-used roadway behind Herrenhausen, until, at last, on a rise, he halted the sleigh. Then he turned to her. 'Are you all right now?' he inquired solicitously.

'Yes, I am. But I think we should return.' Dorothea wondered if her voice sounded as unconvincing to him as it did to her.

He put an arm around her shoulder and, with his free hand, pointed. 'We can see everything from here,' he remarked.

It was true, she realized, gazing down at the breathtaking sight. Lights and brightly arrayed revelers shimmered below, framed in the snow-covered land beneath a black starlit sky.

'You must have been here before,' she said, almost accusing, not knowing why the thought should upset her.

'I?' he responded with a small laugh. 'No. It was the horse who led us here. He is a smart fellow.'

Dorothea looked up at him. 'What am I to call you?' she murmured, wishing he would remove his mask. 'I don't even know your first name.'

He shrugged, as if it were of little importance. 'I don't know yours either. But I shall call you my angel.' He leaned toward her and Dorothea drew back instinctively.

'Did I frighten you?' The eyes were again concerned. He lifted her hand to his lips and kissed it. Then he held it tightly in his own.

Dorothea was at a loss to explain her feelings, for the simple reason that she had never before felt this way. She felt a strange affinity for the man beside her, as if she had known him for a long time. His touch made her feel weak and giddy, yet she knew nothing about him. Not even his name.

Again he leaned forward. Dorothea made no resistance as he placed his lips on hers. He still held her hand, but made no move to embrace her.

It seemed to Dorothea that time stood still. There was nothing in the world but this gentle kiss.

At last he drew away. For a moment he stared at her. She couldn't see his face, he wasn't smiling. His eyes, behind the mask, held an odd, contemplative look.

Abruptly he turned, releasing her hand, and picked up the reins. A sharp snap prodded the horse, who had this while been contentedly munching on a pine bough. The animal moved forward briskly.

The young man didn't speak again until they were back at Herrenhausen; this greatly confused Dorothea. Perhaps she had angered him, she thought. And hoped that it was not so.

In the courtyard he halted the horse, then leapt lightly to the ground. With long strides he came to her side and assisted her as she got out.

Dorothea regarded him uncertainly as he took her hand

again, kissing it lightly. 'My angel,' he murmured huskily.

Before she could speak, he was back in the sleigh. A moment later he disappeared into the night. Bemused, Dorothea stood there until she could no longer hear the sound of bells on the trappings.

During the following days of carnival and festivities, Dorothea searched for him; a difficult task, since she had never seen his face. She would recognize him, though. She was certain of it.

But he was nowhere. He had driven into the night and vanished. Once or twice she spied Countess Platen's daughter again, but she was never with the man who had been dressed as a harlequin.

All too soon the gala weeks were over. Charlotte left for Brandenburg. George returned to his regiment, and the duke, accompanied by both Count Platen and Elizabeth, left for Venice.

The months dragged by in utter, unrelenting boredom. The duchess had insisted that Dorothea and Lenore again join the afternoon walks. 'The exercise and fresh air will be good for you,' Sofia asserted when Dorothea had demurred.

In the spring they went to Wiesbaden to take the waters; in the summer they moved to Herrenhausen, where Dorothea was briefly able to visit with her parents; and in the fall they returned to Leine. The winter carnival was bleak in comparison with the exciting year before. Dorothea was not unhappy to see it end. She had never again seen the young man. As the months slipped by, even the memory began to fade.

She hadn't seen George in over a year, although he wrote with some degree of regularity – stilted, formal words inquiring after the health of his son and commenting perfunctorily on her own well-being.

At last, in January of 1686, the duchess informed Dorothea that Duke Ernst had sent for them to join him in Venice. 'George is there now,' Sofia explained. 'And we will stay until carnival.'

'How marvelous!' Dorothea exclaimed, delighted for a change in routine.

Sofia smiled thinly at the enthusiasm. The girl would

never learn to control herself, she thought in despair.

'How long will we be staying?' Dorothea inquired, mentally reviewing her wardrobe.

'Several months at least,' Sofia answered. 'When carnival is over, we shall all be returning.'

Hanover

September 1686

Although summer was at an end, the weather seemed unable to comply with the seasonal change. The days remained mild and warm. Only at night did the dipping temperatures give warning of approaching fall.

Dorothea sat in the open carriage, her parasol shielding her fair skin against the afternoon sun. Beside her, Lenore chattered gaily, reminiscing on their trip to Venice. And it had been wonderful, except for George, who had become even more moody and withdrawn. They had quarreled frequently, to the distress of both the duke and the duchess; the latter urged patience and restraint.

Patience! Dorothea thought disdainfully, only half listening to Lenore. Her husband had brought Melusine with him to Venice. When she had discovered that, Dorothea flew into a rage. George had been unmoved, but under the insistent urgings of his father had sent Melusine back home and spent the rest of the holiday with his wife.

Well, their mission had been accomplished, Dorothea now fumed resentfully. She was pregnant again. The only thing good about being pregnant, she reflected ruefully, was that she was able to ride in a carriage instead of walking with the duchess. She had wanted to drive to Celle, but the duchess had firmly forbidden this. And so, with Lenore in attendance, Dorothea consoled herself with an afternoon drive about Hanover.

As they drove through the cobbled streets, Dorothea smiled, at times waving and nodding to those burghers she recognized. Occasionally one of them would call out a 'good day to you, princess,' for she was well liked. But the smile on her face wasn't genuine. Dorothea was miserable, angry, frustrated. When they had returned to Hanover some weeks before, George had immediately taken up with Melusine again. He rode with her almost every day and danced with her every evening. Now there was no more trying to hide it from her, or from anyone else. And since Dorothea had discovered she was pregnant, neither the duke nor the duchess made any effort to interfere. Dorothea had complained to her uncle, who had merely looked pained; and to Sofia, who merely shrugged, as if it were of little importance.

At the end of town the driver dutifully turned the horse about and once again headed back to Leine. As they neared their destination Dorothea leaned forward, studying the large house whose property bordered on the gardens of the castle itself.

'I thought that house was vacant,' she remarked to Lenore, noting that gardeners were busily at work restoring the grounds.

Lenore, too, looked. 'I believe you're right,' she mused, watching the activity. 'Someone must have purchased it. It's been vacant for months now.'

Dorothea leaned back again, suddenly losing interest. Her own problems were too overwhelming for her to dwell upon anything else for any length of time. 'I have half a mind to leave him,' she speculated moodily, her thought returning to her wayward husband.

Lenore regarded her mistress and friend, shocked at such an announcement. 'You mustn't think of such a thing,' she said in a low voice, casting an anxious glance at the driver. She patted Dorothea's hand. 'Come on,' she comforted her, 'You're distraught with all that's happened recently and the pregnancy is making you edgy.'

Dorothea didn't bother to answer. Besides, this time she felt fine.

The carriage rolled to a stop and a footman hurried forward to assist them in descending.

The large house that adjoined Leine had indeed been

purchased – by Count Philip Königsmark, who was now standing by a front window. Behind him, his sister Aurora was busily informing carpenters and workmen as to her wishes. Under her guiding hand and eye the large old house was taking on a semblance of elegance. They had been in Hanover for over three weeks now. Philip had not yet left the house, preferring for the moment to keep his presence secret. Especially from Elizabeth. Unfortunately, his arrival had coincided with the return of the court from Venice. His regiment had been disbanded and Philip was currently without commission, although not without money. He had plenty of that. But soldiering was his life. He had no desire to do anything else. He could have gone almost anywhere; yet, he had come back here.

Incredible that he had not been able to get her out of his mind. It had been almost two years and still her face haunted him. He had seen her during that time, but was always careful not to let himself be seen.

To what purpose? Philip wondered morosely. She was a princess, she was married – very much so, for since his arrival he had learned that she was to have another child.

Worse, for the three weeks that he had been here, Philip had stood by the window each day at this time just to glimpse her carriage as it came and went. When he saw her laughing, his heart constricted. Even though he couldn't hear the sound, his ears rang with the memory of it.

Today, however, she had not been laughing. She looked peaked, ill, and it was all Philip could do to restrain himself, to keep from rushing out into the cobbled streets, calling her name.

A sad smile drifted across his lips. She wouldn't even recognize him, probably wouldn't even remember him. Why couldn't he get her out of his mind? The question was one on which Philip dwelt only briefly, now and then. Suffice it to say that he could not. Suffice it to say that he loved her, and would never cease loving her.

Why was he here? What did he hope to accomplish by purchasing a house so close that he could see her window from his side garden?

The smile disappeared and his mouth tightened. He

knew what he hoped to accomplish: a degree of proximity that would allow him to exist.

'For heaven's sake, don't drop that!' Aurora exclaimed to a servant in a sharp voice. 'It's porcelain. Put it down carefully. That's it. No, move it to the side just a bit.'

Philip turned and regarded his sister. At twenty-eight, Aurora was at the peak of her beauty, unmarried because she chose to be. His younger sister Amelia was married to Count Lewenhaupt. Aurora was, Philip reflected with some pride, probably the loveliest woman in all of Europe. His friend Prince Augustus of Saxony certainly thought so. On more than one occasion the prince had tried to win her affections. But Aurora was like a swiftly moving mountain stream. She shimmered and glistened but refused to stay in one place.

She turned now, her silver-blond hair catching the light, her tapered finger tapping her lips. 'Philip, do you prefer the tapestry from Holland or the Flemish one?' She looked at him inquiringly and he gave a short laugh.

'You don't expect my taste to compete with yours, do you?' he answered with a sigh. 'Whatever you decide is fine with me. I've given you carte blanche. Do as you will.'

Aurora frowned and came closer. 'Philip, you must stop acting this way. You are like a man possessed.' She gestured in annoyance. 'Each day you stand by that window as if a saint were passing by.'

'I can't help myself,' he said simply. 'You don't understand how I feel.'

'Obviously,' she remarked archly. 'Nor do I care to learn. If what you're feeling is love, then I want no part of it.'

There was no answer and she was immediately contrite for her flippancy. Philip had a marvelous humor and a keen sense of the ridiculous. But on this particular subject, he was positively morbid. He had taken to hiding in the shadows of buildings just to catch a glimpse of that girl. During last year's carnival he had been so disguised that even she hadn't recognized him, padded as he was to resemble a fat old merchant. At that time, Philip had simply followed the princess, keeping at a distance, never speaking to her. And all because he had once spent a few hours in her company.

Aurora put a hand on her brother's arm. 'Forgive me, Philip,' she murmured. Then she brightened. 'Has it ever occurred to you that she might feel the same way?' If only he would engage the girl in an affair, she thought desperately. Then he might get it out of his system. Certainly it had happened to her often enough.

'She doesn't feel the same way,' Philip responded sharply, moving back toward the window. 'She's pregnant! That means she's been with her husband.'

Amazed, Aurora could only stare at him. 'My God, Philip, be reasonable .... What choice has she?'

'I don't want to discuss it,' he raged. He glared briefly, then stormed from the room.

She stood there, feeling helpless. Aurora knew where Philip was going and what he was going to do. He had chosen for his own a room that faced Leine. Here he would sit and stare at her window, hoping to catch sight of her, even for a moment.

Again Aurora gestured irritably. Well, she couldn't stand around all day, she thought. Nothing would get done.

Hanover

November 1686

The late afternoon offered snow. Flakes fell gently but with purpose, covering streets and trees and houses with a soft white mantle.

Dorothea was more out of sorts than usual. Carnival was only weeks away, but this year she would be unable to participate. She had slept badly the night before. Her dreams had been filled with the sound of a woman screaming. Once she even woke up, but Lenore had been there and had soothed her back to sleep again.

Dorothea had done nothing all day but write a few letters and visit her son in his own apartments. He was plump and healthy and amply cared for, by a nurse and a governess who were in constant attendance.

Now the maid entered and Dorothea allowed herself to be dressed for the evening meal. She refused to think about the inevitable, boring musicale that would follow supper, concentrating instead on the card games to be held later. That, at least, was something to look forward to.

Dorothea viewed her reflection with critical eyes as Lenore assisted the maid in pinning up her abundant hair. It had a natural wave and, under Lenore's skilled hands, curled prettily about her head. She had chosen a taffeta gown of dark burgundy, with elbow-length sleeves that flared revealing inserts of white lace.

'Lenore,' Dorothea said suddenly. 'You look pale. Are you ill?' Her brow creased in concern. She often took Lenore's services and companionship for granted, but Dorothea now realized how bereft she would be without the one person she could call a friend.

Quickly, Lenore smiled as she regarded her mistress in the mirror. 'Of course I'm not ill, *ma chère*. I'm just a bit tired.' Lenore prayed silently there would be no more questions. Apparently Dorothea didn't remember the sound that had caused her to awaken in the middle of the night. All day Lenore had waited in apprehension, fearing the princess would inquire as to the cause of the disturbance. Lenore knew what had happened. Presumably, everyone else in the castle knew too – everyone except Dorothea.

'I'm sorry, Lenore.' Dorothea reached up and patted her lady's hand. 'I promise you, we will retire early this evening. And I command you to sleep, no matter how many nightmares I have.' Despite her imperious tone, the concern shone in her eyes.

Lenore bent over and kissed Dorothea on the top of her curls. 'You know I'll be there whenever you need me,' she murmured softly.

A few moments later Dorothea and Lenore left the bedchamber and proceeded down the wide staircase to the dining hall.

George was waiting by the entrance. Formally, he offered his arm and escorted her to the table. Dorothea noted sourly that Elizabeth Platen would be joining them. At least Melusine was nowhere in sight. Of course, Melusine wouldn't dare sit anywhere except with the other ladies at their own table. Not even the duke himself would get Dorothea to accept otherwise.

George was silent, even for him, and Dorothea spent the entire meal exchanging witticisms with Charles and with Maximilian, whose dry wit could be, at times, stunning.

Afterward, led by the duchess, they retired to the drawing room. Halfway through the tedious musicale, Dorothea noticed that George had absented himself. For that matter, Elizabeth Platen was nowhere about, either. Why was it, Dorothea thought, irritated, that everyone was able to avoid these things except her? She fidgeted in her chair, opening and closing her fan. But then, under the reproving eye of her mother-in-law, Dorothea settled down with a sigh, resigning herself to another thirty minutes of boredom.

At last it was over. Dorothea got stiffly to her feet. She now didn't feel like playing cards, or anything else for that matter. Abruptly she motioned to Lenore. 'I'm going to retire,' she said. She began to walk from the room and, when Lenore followed, Dorothea paused. 'You needn't come. You've been cooped up with me all day long. Stay and enjoy yourself.'

'No, no,' Lenore protested, falling in step. 'I too am tired.'

With slow steps, Dorothea ascended the stairs, Lenore matching her pace. At the landing Dorothea looked up, startled to see Elizabeth Platen, gowned, as usual, in an elaborate manner. 'Countess,' she murmured tartly, as she reached the top step. 'Was the musicale not to your liking?'

Elizabeth smiled coldly. She was dressed in pale-blue silk that effectively set off her vivid coloring and dark, almost black, hair. 'There are more interesting things, Princess,' she replied enigmatically. 'Perhaps there are things that would even interest you, if you knew where to look.' The smile lightened to amusement.

Nervously Lenore tugged at Dorothea's sleeve. 'Let's go,' she whispered urgently. But Dorothea shook free of the hand. Even the sight of Elizabeth was enough to make her angry, but this haughty, knowing air enraged her.

'You enjoy speaking in riddles, Countess,' she stated, annoyed. 'If you have something to say – although I doubt that – then say it, and be done.' She raised her chin and glared at the older woman.

By her side, Lenore was trembling and gazing on Elizabeth Platen with absolute hatred. She wouldn't dare! Lenore was thinking. She just wouldn't dare. Had Lenore thought otherwise, she would have forcibly moved Dorothea away. As it was, she thought Countess Platen merely up to her usual trick of baiting Dorothea. The woman never lost an opportunity to do that.

'Do you see that room at the end of the hall?' Elizabeth asked sweetly and, before Lenore could protest, continued. 'I suggest, my little princess, that you see what lies behind it. Then perhaps you will learn your proper place.' With that, Elizabeth swept past them in a swirl of silk and heavy perfume, descending the stairs without a backward glance.

'Let us go!' Lenore said frantically, again grasping hold of Dorothea.

'Stop pulling on me,' Dorothea said sharply, quite astounded at the untoward behavior. She stood there only a moment, then determinedly headed for the door. Helpless in the face of this obstinacy, Lenore followed, her lips working in a feverish prayer.

Pausing outside the door, Dorothea listened, but all was silent.

'There is nothing in there,' Lenore declared in a hushed voice. 'She was merely being nasty, as always,' she said of Elizabeth.

Dorothea viewed her friend suspiciously. 'Then why are you whispering?' she asked quietly. Before Lenore could answer, Dorothea opened the door with a swift motion of her hand.

It was difficult to take in the scene all at once, even though her eyes saw everything with one look. There was a bed and in it, her yellow hair plaited in two thick braids, was Melusine. Her nightgown was pulled down off one plump shoulder, baring a full white breast. In her arms she held an infant, who was contentedly suckling. Sitting on the bed, watching the procedure with tender interest, was George.

For a long, shocked moment, everyone stared. Only the baby seemed unconcerned.

Her face white with anger, Dorothea stepped into the room. No wonder she hadn't seen Melusine lately, no wonder George kept disappearing. And the screams she had heard last night had not been in her dreams at all. It had been Melusine giving birth to her bastard. George's bastard!

'My God, how dare you?' Dorothea screamed, lunging toward the bed. 'I'll have you thrashed within an inch of your life!' she shouted at Melusine, whose face blanched in terror at the sight of the enraged princess.

George had jumped up and now placed his hands on Dorothea's shoulders, effectively halting her progress. His fingers pressed painfully into her skin as he tried to restrain her. Control gone, Dorothea bit her husband's wrist and he howled in pain, releasing her. In a quick motion, Dorothea lunged at the bed again, this time getting close enough to grab one of Melusine's braids, at which she gave a vicious tug.

Clasping her around the waisit – no easy thing to do, in view of its swollen size – George lifted Dorothea off her feet and took a few steps across the room. Then he set her down. Immediately he returned to Melusine, who had fallen back on the pillow in a faint. The child, unsupported, had rolled off its mother's breast onto the bed, and was now crying in lusty anger over its interrupted meal.

The sight of the unconscious Melusine and the crying child quickly dampened Dorothea's temper. She stood there breathing heavily with the unaccustomed exertion.

The sight, however, had the opposite effect on George. With an angry cry, he spun around and reached for his wife, putting his hands around her throat. He shook her until Dorothea lost her balance and fell to her knees. Adjusting his position, George kept his hands in place, bending over to do so.

Gasping for air, Dorothea put her hands around George's wrists, trying to loosen his hold. The contact seemed to enrage him further. She heard him screaming at her, cursing her, and she heard Lenore's high shriek as she called for help.

Then Dorothea heard nothing.

The duchess viewed her son with stern eyes. They were in her private salon, drapes closed tightly against the worsening weather. In the tiled hearth, a fire burned brightly, casting a glow on one side of Sofia's pale face.

George, despite how much the duke admired him, was not Sofia's favorite son. Despite the fact that George was her firstborn, it was Charles who was her favorite, with the gay, irrepressible Maximilian a close second. Regardless of her feelings, however, George was her son and heir. In fact, with her own claim to the throne of England, distant as it might be, there was the outside possibility that George might even one day be the King of England. That thought, she already knew, was displeasing to him. Imagine the thought of being king displeasing to anyone. George was a brave soldier, a good son – within limits – and an able administrator. He was an abominable husband and father.

Sofia had dismissed the servants and her ladies. This was not a matter for outsiders. Not that the distressing events could be kept from them, she thought with resignation.

For once, Ernst had refused to interfere. With an unaccustomed shirking of his responsibility, he had retired to Monplaisir. Sofia momentarily wondered what would have happened if she had acted like Dorothea had when Elizabeth gave birth not once but twice, over the past years. Of course, Elizabeth was married and it was easy to pretend that her two children belonged to Franz. Indeed, they just might. Sofia had never troubled to find out. But what would have happened? she mused. Ernst had a violent temper, but it was cold rather than heated. In that, George was like him – most of the time. Because of this, Sofia sincerely doubted that he'd meant to murder his wife deliberately.

Nevertheless, he almost had.

Dorothea had lain unconscious for hours. Even now the physician was uncertain as to whether or not the child would survive. There had been some bleeding but, fortunately, that had stopped. The physician, however, had given strict orders that Dorothea remain in bed until the child was born.

Now, viewing her son, Sofia said, 'Whatever possessed you?' Her tone was almost sad. Thoughts of Charlotte suddenly crossed her mind. The letters from her daughter had not been encouraging; the girl was unhappy. But then, what woman had the right to be married and happy? She knew of very few. A woman made her own happiness. Perhaps only Eleanor, Sofia thought bitterly, then turned her mind away from that old wound.

George was glaring at his mother in defiance, irked that she still had the capacity to make him feel like a child. 'She attacked Melusine,' he pronounced, as if that explained it all.

Sofia raised a thin brow. 'She pulled Melusine's hair. And for that you nearly killed her,' she stated flatly.

George prowled the room, hands behind his back. 'She would have harmed her further had I not been there.' His jaw jutted out in a further display of defiance.

Sofia ignored the juvenile display. She shifted her weight on the brocade upholstered chair and rearranged the folds of her skirt. 'When a man attacks a woman,' she noted placidly, 'he merely accents his own weakness.'

'I will not have it,' George shouted. 'I will not have her near Melusine.'

Sofia sighed, dissatisfied with George's stupidity. 'Then I suggest that you get Melusine her own residence,' she offered shortly. 'It should have been done in the first place. It is unseemly to keep your mistress,' she accented the word harshly, 'in the same house as your wife.'

George paused and stared at his mother, then his features relaxed. He had thought she would condemn him for keeping Melusine; that had put him on the defensive. But her suggestion was the perfect solution. He cursed himself for not having thought of it sooner. It would have saved Melusine from so much anguish. He regarded his mother with new respect.

Sofia saw, and disdained him. 'You are not the first man to form a liaison,' she pointed out with heavy sarcasm. 'However, you must remember that society recognizes your wife and your family. Not your mistress, nor any spawn she may produce. You owe it to your wife and to your family to treat them with the utmost respect.'

George's mouth tightened sullenly. 'Respect?' he muttered in a low voice. 'You talk to me of respect – for Eleanor d'Olbreuse's daughter?' A ripple of shock, colored by disbelief, coursed through him.

'She is your wife!' Sofia's voice rose. With one part of her mind she deplored her shrill voice, and ... yet if ever there was an occasion that warranted it, it was now. 'Do you understand the meaning of the word, George?' she demanded sharply, leaning forward. 'Love has nothing to do with it. Background has nothing to do with it. She is no longer Eleanor d'Olbreuse's daughter. She is your wife.' She took a breath, calming herself once more. 'A man does not attack his wife when she discovers his mistress,' she continued in a calmer voice. 'Do you realize what a shock it must have been for her? She is pregnant. With your child! The daughter born to Melusine can never, never be yours, insofar as society is concerned. Dorothea has given you a son.' She regarded George in some bewilderment, bemused by his indifferent expression. He appeared to be only half listening to her. Sofia blinked. 'Have you no feeling for her at all?'

George turned away and studied the flames in the grate. 'I cannot abide her,' he confessed at last, his low voice conveying more conviction than had he shouted.

Sofia's mouth tightened until it was a thin line. 'Hear me, George,' she said quietly. 'And know that I speak with your father's approval.' She peered closely, almost hating him. 'Your father's approval, George,' she repeated for emphasis. 'Do you doubt your father's respect for me?' she demanded, straightening in her chair. Her eyes were bright as she watched her son.

Guiltily, he met her eye. 'Of course not. He ... loves you.'

She gave a short laugh. 'You are not that stupid,' she stated flatly. 'Look at me,' she commanded when he again turned away. 'Your father loves Elizabeth Platen.' She raised her chin. 'But *I* am his wife. I am the mother of his sons. I am the one he respects!' Her look challenged him to say otherwise.

George slumped in a nearby chair. His mother didn't understand, he thought, dejected. She didn't realize how much he cared for Melusine. It wasn't the same. It just wasn't the same.

'Have you been to see Dorothea?' Sofia asked, staring at him attentively.

'No,' he responded, viewing the pattern in the carpet as if he had just discovered it.

'She has regained consciousness,' Sofia went on. 'Although the bruises on her throat are fearsome. There has been some bleeding, but that has ceased. The physician is as yet uncertain as to whether she will lose the child. The next week will tell.' She regarded her son intently, fiercely, but he seemed unmoved by this announcement.

George's thoughts were on Melusine. All this fuss and

bother over Dorothea, he was thinking resentfully. No one had asked about Melusine's welfare. Only Countess Platen, who had seemed genuinely concerned for her friend, had made inquiry. Melusine had been terribly upset. So much so that Countess Platen had had to make arrangements for a wet nurse. Melusine's milk had dried up due to the shock she had sustained. Even now she was pale and trembling. And that, after the ordeal of birth, George thought, growing more agitated.

'I want you to stay with Dorothea for the coming days,' Sofia was saying. George stared at her, dumbfounded. 'You must reassure her, calm her, until the child is safely born.' Sofia observed him with a dark restlessness, suddenly feeling empty and bereft. This was her child, even though he was a grown man, but their minds would never touch, never communicate, except superficially.

Was she mad? George wondered. His face reflected his disbelief. Stay with Dorothea! The woman who had caused Melusine such distress. 'I ... cannot do that,' he protested strongly. 'I never want to see her again.'

'Your wishes do not concern me,' Sofia interrupted coldly. 'Your obligations do.' She leaned back in the chair. 'You will spend a part of each and every day with your wife. You will assure her that you care, that you are sorry for these unfortunate events. This you will do,' she repeated slowly, eyes level and compelling, 'or your father may consider it expedient to choose another heir.'

The blood drained from his face. He thought of Friedrich, in the army, fighting as a nonentity. He was not even an officer. George viewed the carpet again, his thoughts whirling. It was only for a short while, he reasoned, making an effort to conceal his concern over his mother's harsh ultimatum. Soon Dorothea would have the child. Then he could return to Melusine, to warmth, to peace, to contentment. And one day he would be his own man. Imperceptibly, his face hardened. Once his father died, not even his mother could dictate to him.

Thus fortified, George stood up. 'Very well, Mother,' he said evenly. 'If you think it necessary, I will go to her.'

With that, he walked from the room. For a long time Sofia sat there, staring into space. After a while she got to her feet and made her way to her writing table. It would not be long before Eleanor heard of the events that had taken place. Sofia would have to write and set her mind at ease. It would not do if Eleanor thought that her daughter's life was in danger.

It would not do at all.

Dorothea opened her eyes, again conscious of pain. It seemed of late that each time she awoke, it happened. She could barely speak for the ache in her throat. Her voice sounded thick and unintelligible, even to her own ears. The sharp throbbing in her side had, however, subsided. That at least was something to be thankful for. Turning her head on the pillow, Dorothea glanced at Lenore, disturbed to see the pale-purple smudges under the young woman's eyes. Poor dear, Dorothea thought, but could not voice it. It was agony to speak.

And what did it all mean? she wondered, closing her eyes again. Did she really care about Melusine? Did she really care about George?

No, not really. That's why it was all such a waste. The whole thing had no meaning. Her whole life had no meaning.

If only she could go home. Dorothea moved restlessly in her bed. Home to Eleanor, good food, quiet, peace. If only …

'Dorothea?'

She opened her eyes again, surprised to see that the tapers had been lit. It was already evening. She glanced at George, seated on a straight-backed chair placed close by her bed.

'Dorothea?' he said again, not certain that she was fully awake. For the past hour now she had opened her eyes intermittently, only to close them in sleep again.

Dorothea made a sound that was quite unintelligible, then gave it up. She swallowed, sighed, and was still. But her eyes remained open.

'Dorothea,' George began again in a determined voice. 'You have my profound apologies. My actions were inexcusable. We were both … upset.'

She moved her head on the pillow, turning her face away from him.

Damn her, George thought. His face flushed with his rising anger. He had apologized when, by rights, it was *she* who should have done so; and she was still acting incorrigibly. He noted the stubborn set of the chin, the firmly clamped mouth, and was repulsed. Briefly he viewed the dark bruises on her throat, then averted his gaze. He too was not without bruises. He had teethmarks on his arm, scratches on his wrists. God, he had fought the Turks with less wounds than he had received from this temper-ridden woman he had the misfortune to call wife.

With an audible sigh, George made the effort to relax. He would stay until she fell asleep again. Then he would leave. Perhaps tomorrow she would be more receptive.

George spent a goodly portion of the following day making arrangements for the purchase of a modest but well-furnished house in town for Melusine and her baby daughter. That evening he returned to his wife's bedside. Dorothea still could not, or would not, speak.

The next day he assisted Melusine to her new residence, making certain that the papers were safely tucked away. He spent the afternoon with her to see that she was comfortably settled, the house adequately staffed.

That evening he visited Dorothea again. This time she spoke, albeit in a whisper, and seemed in a more amiable mood. She was even sitting up in bed. A good sign, George thought, relieved. His mother had insisted that he visit Dorothea only until the danger was past.

When he left his wife, George cornered the physician, listening in further relief as the man assured him that all was well. Having done his duty to his own satisfaction, George made haste to rejoin his regiment on the outskirts of Vienna.

This time Dorothea was glad to see him go. Melusine was out of the castle and out of sight. Dorothea spent the following weeks resting and, on the physician's orders, doing nothing more strenuous than writing letters.

Only an occasional visit from the steadfast Charles livened her days and when, in early March, her pains began right on schedule, Dorothea was grateful.

The new child was a girl. She was named Sophie-Dorothea.

Hanover

August 1687

'Philip!' Prince Charles grasped Königsmark's hand firmly, shaking it with undisguised enthusiasm. 'My God, when I got your note, I was astounded.' The young man entered the newly refurbished house, blinking in surprise. It was as elegant as Leine itself. And, he noted, it appeared as fully staffed, with footmen, pages, and servants scurrying busily about, all dressed in bright green livery. 'You've been in town, practically next door, for months,' he complained, 'and have not let me know. I shall not forgive you for that.'

Philip laughed. 'The house has just been finished this past week, Charles. You are our first guest. We wouldn't have it otherwise. Besides,' he said, sitting on an oversized settee, 'Aurora has had me running about, gathering pieces she insists are an absolute necessity. I've just returned from Brede the day before yesterday.'

'Our?' Charles viewed Philip with interest. 'Are you married now?'

'No, no. I speak of Aurora, my sister. She'll be joining us in a moment.' Philip glanced toward the door. 'Ah, here she is.' He got to his feet, amused to see Charles's face light up. Aurora always had that effect on men when she entered a room. Her silver-blond hair was piled into shimmering curls in the latest style, her fair coloring set off to perfection by the pale-lilac satin gown she was wearing.

Philip stepped forward. 'My dear, may I present Prince Charles.' He looked at his friend. 'My sister, Countess Aurora Königsmark.'

Charles bowed and kissed the extended hand, holding it

a moment longer than necessary. 'Countess, my life is complete,' he said gallantly. 'I can now say that I have met the most beautiful woman in the world.'

Aurora laughed, delighted. The young man could be no more than eighteen, she judged, amused. 'I certainly hope your life is far from complete, Prince Charles,' she murmured, sitting down.

Philip sat down at her side. Charles positioned himself comfortably on the opposite settee as a footman placed refreshments on a low, intricately carved table displaying marquetry of a delicate blue tortoiseshell.

'Does this mean you'll be staying in Hanover?' Charles asked Philip when they were settled.

'It does,' Philip affirmed. 'Although Aurora doesn't stay in one place too long,' he added with a laugh.

'Then we must be entertaining enough to change her mind,' Charles declared, his eyes returning to Philip's sister. 'This weekend there is to be a grand party at Herrenhausen. I insist that you both come. My mother has even had gondolas shipped in from Venice. It will be great fun.'

'It sounds as if it will be,' Aurora concurred, smiling. 'Is it a special occasion? Or does Hanover amuse itself like this often?' She tilted her head, observing the young prince. She thought him most attractive.

'Often enough.' Charles flushed slightly at her direct look. 'But you're right. The occasion is somewhat special. My sister-in-law, the Princess Dorothea, has recently given birth to a daughter. My mother has planned the festivities in her honor and, of course, to celebrate the birth of her new granddaughter.'

Philip smiled stiffly, but it was Aurora who responded. 'I'm happy to hear that she has been safely delivered,' she said with an engaging smile. 'I've heard that the princess has been ill these past months.'

A frown drifted across his face as Charles replied. 'The physician had advised her to rest,' he admitted, hoping they hadn't heard that George had actually tried to throttle Dorothea. 'However, she's in fine health now. I see her most every day.' He brightened. 'Perhaps you would like to join me. And you too, Philip. It seems that each time you've visited us, the princess has been indisposed. It's time you met her.' He regarded them both eagerly.

Aurora glanced at her brother, but his expression was unreadable. 'We would be honored, your Highness,' she replied graciously. 'You need only name the day, and Philip and I will be at your disposal.'

'Please, call me Charles.' He looked from one to the other. 'Would tomorrow at three be convenient? Wednesday is normally the day the princess receives visitors.'

Aurora frowned prettily. 'Tomorrow is Tuesday, Charles,' she pointed out.

The young man grinned. 'I know. But I would like her to meet you both in private. That way we can chat comfortably, without others interfering.'

Aurora nodded, then stood up. The young prince immediately got to his feet. 'It was a pleasure to meet you, Charles. I'll leave you two alone now. I'm certain you have a lot to discuss.' She held out her hand. 'Until tomorrow then.'

Charles watched as she gracefully made her exit, then sat down again. 'She's lovely, Philip,' he exclaimed enthusiastically. 'I'm surprised you've waited this long to present her.' He glanced at his friend with mock severity. 'That's two things I will not easily forgive you.'

Philip shrugged his broad shoulders. 'Aurora travels a great deal,' he murmured vaguely.

For the first time Charles noticed how pale Philip was. He had lost weight too. 'I say, you haven't been ill, have you?' he asked, genuinely concerned.

'No,' Philip replied, then smiled. 'Most likely my condition can be ascribed to boredom. You see, my regiment has been disbanded. I've been without a commission these past months. I'm unused to so much leisure.'

'Why didn't you come to me immediately!' Charles admonished. 'I'll speak to the duke today. Before the week is gone you shall have a commission with the Hanoverian Army.' He stood up and Philip followed suit.

'You're certain it's no imposition?'

Charles's face grew serious as they walked to the front door. 'Don't even think such a thing, Philip. After what you've done for me, I'm only too happy to be of service.' He halted at the door, which a footman respectfully opened. 'You know what's happened to Friedrich?'

'I've heard that he was sent to join the Imperial Army.'

Charles nodded solemnly. 'That he was. But he has no commission, he's only a common soldier. Father has not provided him with funds. We've heard nothing from him since he left. He hasn't even written to Mother. I suspect that that would have been the fate of us all had you not intervened.' He regarded Philip quizzically. 'You never did tell me how you accomplished it.'

Philip grinned. 'Nor am I about to.' He clapped the young prince on the shoulder. 'It's good to see you again, Charles,' he said quietly. 'I hope you have success in my behalf.'

'I will,' Charles assured him. 'Don't forget tomorrow. I'll meet you in the reception hall just short of three.'

'I'll be there,' Philip promised and, turning, made his way back inside again. He sat down, quite unnerved. Tomorrow he was to meet her, face to face. Would she remember him? Did she have any idea of the impact she had had on his life?

He shook his head slightly. No, that was foolishness. Since he'd met her she had grown two years older, had had another child, and had suffered at the hands of the beast she was married to. Oh, he knew what had happened. The thought had crazed him when he had learned of it. The monster had almost killed her! Philip clenched his hands into fists. Just the thought of George sent him into a rage.

He got up and prowled the room aimlessly. Tomorrow, he thought. Tomorrow, tomorrow; it was an eternity away.

Dorothea finished penning the letter to her mother. Folding it, she glanced at the small silver clock that sat atop her writing table. It was almost three. No doubt Charles would be there any moment. He had told her last night that he was bringing some friends along that he wanted her to meet. Dorothea's brow furrowed as she searched her mind for the names. Oh, yes, Count Philip Königsmark and his sister, Aurora. Dorothea had tried to talk Charles into bringing them by tomorrow, which was her normal day to hold court, but the young prince had been most insistent. She smiled fondly. Charles, insistent, was quite irresistible.

As she stood up, Dorothea gave momentary thought to changing her gown; she was dressed informally in the pale-yellow silk dress she had worn all morning. But then she decided against it. Besides, it was already three o'clock. Lenore, appearing in the doorway, announced their arrival. Nodding, Dorothea followed her into the salon.

'Dorothea.' Charles stepped forward. 'May I present Count Philip Königsmark and his beautiful sister, Countess Aurora Königsmark.'

Dorothea smiled as the count bowed and murmured, 'Your Highness.' At least he was good-looking, she thought, acknowledging their greeting. Mostly her salon was filled with aging diplomats and envoys, whose boring looks were exceeded only by their tedious conversation. Most of the young men, officers and courtiers spent their time at Monplaisir, where Elizabeth held card parties for high stakes. There was plenty of drinking and there were bawdy plays, which, she supposed, were far more entertaining than her own levées.

'Please sit down,' she said now. 'You may call me Dorothea.' The dimples appeared and deepened. 'Charles has spoken so highly of you I feel I already know you both.'

As they settled themselves, Charles said, 'Philip has been given a commission as colonel in our army. He will soon join his regiment.'

Dorothea tilted her head. 'Oh, I do hope you will be here for the festivities at Herrenhausen this weekend.'

The count smiled and nodded. 'We wouldn't miss it ... Dorothea,' he said quietly. 'I hear it will be a gala event.'

'It should prove to be,' Dorothea acknowledged. 'Have you ever been to Herrenhausen?'

Philip's expression did not change as he replied, but his

heart constricted painfully. 'I have had the pleasure, Highness,' he replied formally.

'But I have not,' Aurora put in. 'And I must say I'm looking forward to it. Even in Hamburg we have heard of the orangery. Is it true that the walls are of glass and the fruit grows in winter?'

Dorothea observed the count's sister. Aurora was the loveliest woman she had ever seen, but her beauty was pleasant and outgoing; it was not threatening and intimidating, as was Elizabeth's. The resemblance between brother and sister was quite startling, she saw, although the count's hair was a darker shade of blond. He was clean shaven and did not wear a wig. 'The walls are indeed of glass,' she responded at last. 'And I myself have seen the fruit in winter.'

'How delightful,' exclaimed Aurora. 'And I understand that you are to be congratulated on the birth of a daughter.'

Dorothea dimpled again. 'She's beautiful. Perhaps you can visit me some morning. I shall be happy to introduce you to both my son, who is now two, and my daughter.'

Aurora, who could think of nothing more boring, beamed and smiled, 'I'd love to.'

Dorothea again regarded the count, a bit disconcerted to find him staring at her intently. He certainly was good-looking, she thought to herself, flushing under the penetrating scrutiny. But what was the matter with him? she wondered. Didn't he realize how rude it was to stare? 'I understand that you've purchased the property that adjoins Leine,' she said conversationally.

He nodded. 'That's true,' he admitted. 'My sister and I will be staying in Hanover for a while.'

'For a short while, unfortunately,' Charles put in. 'Philip leaves for the front next week.'

'So soon?' Dorothea murmured. 'I hope there will be no danger. Are you married, Count Königsmark?'

Philip shook his head. God, she was even more lovely than he remembered. He couldn't keep his eyes off of her. 'I've never been married,' he replied. 'I was engaged some years ago, but she became ill and died.'

'How awful,' Dorothea said with genuine feeling. Then she turned to Aurora. 'And you, Countess?'

Aurora's laugh was like a trilling mountain stream. 'I've never been married or engaged. Only our sister, Amelia, conforms to the proprieties.'

Dorothea nodded and again became aware of the count's intent stare. She regarded him in some perplexity, flushing.

'Forgive me, Princess,' he said hastily, noting her expression. 'Aside from the fact that it's a delight to gaze on someone so lovely, I was merely comparing you with the last time we met.'

Her smooth brow furrowed. 'The last time?' she murmured. 'Have we met before, Count Königsmark?'

'Ah-ha! I can see that you've forgotten,' Philip remarked with a false gaiety that apparently went unnoticed. 'We met at Celle more than a few years ago. Although I confess that I'm crushed at having made so little impression upon you.'

Dorothea's confusion deepened. 'I'm afraid you have me at a disadvantage.'

Charles laughed delightedly and slapped Philip on the knee. 'There! You're not all so irresistible to the ladies as you would have us believe. That ought to take you down a peg or two.'

Dorothea regarded them both. 'I do wish that you would let me in on the joke.' Despite her words, she was beginning to enjoy herself. She was drawn to both Philip and his sister. They were quite the most interesting people she had met in a long time.

'Well – ' Philip leaned forward with a grin that was positively boyish. 'You do deserve an explanation. At one time, you had a pony cart,' he went on. 'If I remember correctly, it was painted red and white.'

She regarded him in genuine astonishment. 'But my father gave that to me when I was eight years old!'

He nodded and continued. 'It was the year after that, when my mother and I visited Celle. Your charming mother and mine were dear friends. They still correspond, I believe.'

Dorothea clapped her hands, eyes sparkling. 'You! You were that wretched boy who laughed so long and so loud when the cart tipped over and I fell into the mud.'

Philip leaned back, pulling on his earlobe. 'I'm afraid so,' he admitted ruefully. 'Although, had I known that you would grow up to be a princess, and a lovely one, I daresay that I would have been more careful of my manners.'

Dorothea was laughing helplessly at the remembered incident. As usual, the sound was infectious. Even Lenore, sitting quietly in a chair across the room, her embroidery in her lap, chuckled, pleased to see Dorothea in such good spirits again. It had been too long since she had laughed, too long that she had lacked the animation she was now displaying.

'I feel as though I've been reunited with two old friends.' Dorothea reached out, clasped Aurora's hand and then Philip's. The pressure with which he grasped her hand seemed apropos to the moment, and she thought nothing of it. 'Will you both join us this evening?' Dorothea released their hands and stood up, indicating that the social visit was at an end. This was not because she wished to see them go as much as because she had to dress for the evening activities. Suddenly it became important as to what dress she would wear. 'The duchess's musicales are positively mind numbing,' she informed them with an impish grin. 'But there will be card parties afterward. Do you play?' As she glanced at Philip, Charles burst out laughing.

'Does he play!' the young prince exclaimed. 'There is no greater gambler this side of Versailles.'

'Marvelous! I'll see you both then.'

After the door had closed, Dorothea turned happily to Lenore. 'Come along. I want you to do my hair especially well this evening.' She walked from the salon, through her sitting room to her bedchamber. 'And I'll wear the green brocade,' she said, a trifle breathless. 'The new one.'

Monplaisir

August 1687

Elizabeth Platen paced her bedchamber with furious steps, hands clenched, nostrils flaring, everything about her indicating rage. Her new chambermaid, Marie, watched her with fearful eyes. She had been with the countess only a week, but she doubted her fear would dissipate even after a year. Her predecessor, Ilse, a personal friend, had been thrown into prison on the countess's orders. That had been a few months back. The girl had finally been released, but she had had to leave Hanover.

The countess claimed that Ilse had stolen a bracelet, but Marie knew that was not so. Ilse, before she had left, had tearfully told her the true story. She had, she said, been returning from town, where the countess had sent her on an errand, when she met Duke Ernst in the courtyard. 'He was most pleasant,' said Ilse, a young girl of fifteen, 'and spoke to me most friendly like.' They had even laughed, she said, and the duke had pinched her cheek and complimented her on her comeliness.

Unfortunately, the harmless exchange had been witnessed by the countess, who had flown into a rage. She had slapped Ilse and screamed for minutes on end. That night the guards had unceremoniously carried her away. She had spent more than two weeks in the rat-infested dungeon of the fortress just outside of Hanover that served as a prison. What had gone on in those two weeks Ilse could not speak of, for each time she thought of it, she wept hysterically. She had at last been released, but the countess had warned her to never set foot in Hanover again.

Now she, Marie, was here. She wasn't happy about it. She watched with cautious eyes as the countess prowled the room, muttering to herself in a crazed fashion. Marie wondered what could have so upset her.

Elizabeth paid no mind to the young maid; in fact, she was hardly aware of Marie's presence.

At last Elizabeth paused before a table. In a quick motion she picked up a glazed Chinese vase and flung it across the room. It smashed against the wall, its delicate structure shattering. Porcelain, water, and flowers went flying, but Elizabeth didn't even look at the mess as she continued her pacing.

How dare he! she was thinking. Her mind and her body were heated with a fury that rose and ebbed in endless waves. With each breath she took, she cursed him, and loved him.

She hadn't even known that Philip was back, had apparently been back for months.

Tonight, when she had gone to Leine for the first time in weeks, she had seen him. She had been so astonished that she had just stood there when first she caught sight of him. He was standing with Charles and Dorothea. The sight of the beautiful blond woman by his side had caused Elizabeth's black eyes to smolder dangerously. But then, after a few discreet questions, she had discovered that the woman was his sister. With that knowledge, Elizabeth had relaxed.

Finally she caught his eye. After only a small hesitation, Philip came toward her.

Even now, in her fury and anger, Elizabeth could see him: handsome, his plum-colored jacket molding broad shoulders, the dark blond hair shining, the blue eyes regarding her speculatively. And that mouth.

Elizabeth passed by her dressing table. Reaching for the jeweled brush, she threw it across the room in a furious gesture. It barely missed Marie's head. Slowly the girl stooped to pick it up, wondering if she should return it to its proper place. But the countess began moving again, so she stood still, hardly daring to breathe.

She had questioned him, Elizabeth was thinking, and Philip had answered, vaguely, as if his attention were elsewhere. But where? Who? The only other woman in the room worth a second glance, besides herself, was his own sister!

Elizabeth paused in the middle of her bedchamber, closing her eyes, reliving her humiliation, much as one worries a sore tooth with an inquisitive tongue.

They had barely begun to speak when Dorothea appeared in a swirl of green brocade and glittering diamonds. Elizabeth had stared at her in astonishment. The princess's face was alive, animated, her cheeks pink and glowing, her eyes sparkling. Dorothea had put her hand on Philip's arm and said, 'Come, Philip. I want you to be my partner. Charles is paired with Aurora, and I'm certain that we can beat them.'

Astoundingly, Philip turned, smiled, and with no more than a backward glance had walked off with the chit. It was insufferable! her mind screamed. Her nails dug into her palms and she was almost grateful for the sharp, biting pain as they tore her flesh.

But there was more, and her mind must go over it, must torment her with the odious vision.

They had seated themselves at one of the tables and, amid much laughter, Charles, that simpleton, had dealt the cards. Casually, Elizabeth had approached the table. Just as casually, she placed a hand on Philip's shoulder.

He had glanced up at her. Only now, in retrospect, did Elizabeth recognize his expression as annoyance. She had said, 'When you're through here, Philip, perhaps you'll join us at Monplaisir? There are many of your friends who would be delighted to see you again.' She had even flashed a warm smile at Aurora, who had regarded her with cool eyes. She would speak to Philip about that, Elizabeth had thought, while awaiting his answer.

Philip had not bothered with the courtesy of standing; he had remained seated as he spoke to her. 'I'm sorry, Countess,' he replied indolently. 'I must convey my regrets. As you can see, I am otherwise occupied.' He had smiled at Dorothea, who was grinning in her stupid fashion; then he picked up his cards, which seemed to have captured his entire attention.

Elizabeth had been left standing there, looking foolish.

She had immediately left Leine and, since her return, had been pacing, reliving the evening, which, each time, seemed more unbearable, more humiliating than the last.

Now Elizabeth opened her eyes, a film of perspiration dampening her brow. 'But he will not get away so easily,' she murmured aloud.

'Mother?'

The voice made her turn quickly and Elizabeth regarded her daughter, who stood in the doorway. The eighteen-year-old girl was gowned in yellow lace, a color that made her appear sallow.

'I came to say good night,' Charlotte said uncertainly, viewing her mother with questioning eyes. That she was angry was easy enough to see; but there was an underlying tenseness that suggested she was feeling a certain desperation. 'Are you all right?'

Elizabeth managed a smile and made a conscious effort to relax. 'Of course I am, Charlotte. Please come in.'

The girl regarded her with doubtful eyes. 'I knew you came home early. I thought perhaps that you were ill.' She glanced about the room, noting the shards of porcelain, and frowned.

Elizabeth laughed lightly. 'Do I look ill, darling? I retired early only because the duchess, as usual, was having one of those insipid evenings for which she is so famous.' She followed Charlotte's gaze to the broken vase, then she glared at Marie. 'Clean it up, you fool! Don't just stand there.' She turned to Charlotte again. 'It's trying, breaking in a new maid. Sit down, darling. I'm glad you've stopped by.' She studied her daughter with critical eyes. Pretty enough, although somewhat docile and placid. She lacked fire, intensity. But then, Elizabeth mused, thinking of George Ludwig, some men thrived on placidity. The fools thought of it in terms of peace and serenity. Perhaps Philip had reached that stage. Certainly it was time for him to marry. If he married Charlotte, she thought suddenly, he could live here, in Monplaisir. There was more than enough room.

'My dear, Philip is back in Hanover.' Elizabeth smiled at her daughter, making a mental note to advise her against ever wearing yellow again.

Charlotte flushed pinkly. She liked Philip well enough, she supposed, although he was so … intense. Too, she had the uncomfortable feeling that she bored him, and suspected that he was kind to her only because of her mother. Charlotte regarded Elizabeth with envious eyes. How she wished she could be like her mother. Elizabeth was always so assured, so very beautiful …

'Do you like him?' Elizabeth inquired, almost too casually.

Charlotte swallowed visibly and wet her lips, not certain how to answer. She knew of her mother's relationship with Philip Königsmark. If she said yes, would her mother be displeased, thinking that she had designs on him? If she said no, would Elizabeth take that as a criticism?

'I find him gracious and kind,' Charlotte said at last, watching her mother hopefully.

Elizabeth nodded and smiled, and Charlotte relaxed. 'Excellent,' she murmured. Leaning over, she patted her daughter's hand. 'Run along now, Charlotte. I have things to do.'

Herrenhausen

September 1687

The evening was mild under a clear sky with little, if any, breeze. Herrenhausen sparkled with the light of hundreds of lanterns and candles.

Where the lawn sloped down to meet the river, poles had been placed at intervals from the house to the water's edge. These were united with rope that had been cleverly entwined with foliage sporting gaily painted lanterns. On the river itself, black except where the lights made golden slashes, numerous gondolas drifted along, each one poled by an expert gondolier.

In the courtyard rows of open carriages, each manned by a liveried driver, awaited the pleasure of guests who wished to ride about the grounds. The orangery was opened, softly lighted, and scented. In the reception halls the tables sagged under the repast. Musicians played enthusiastically, sending strains of music through open windows, into the gardens, the orangery, and across the river. In various rooms plays and ballets competed for one's attention. Soon after dusk the whole estate was dotted with guests and revelers.

Dorothea, her arm linked through Philip's, looked back at Aurora and Charles, who followed. 'Shall we eat, or dance?' she called out to them.

Aurora, looking especially fetching in white satin, smiled and replied, 'We shall dance. The food will wait.' She placed her hand lightly on Charles's arm. 'However, you must take me for a gondola ride before the night is gone.'

As they entered the extravagantly decorated ballroom, Philip took hold of Dorothea and they merged with the already dancing guests.

She gasped slightly, feeling a tremor course through her.

'Is anything wrong?' he asked quickly.

'No ...' She smiled then, shaking off the strange feeling that had suddenly gripped her when he had put his arm about her waist. 'These past days have been marvelous,' she said breathlessly. 'I do wish you didn't have to leave so soon.'

His arm tightened about her. 'Let's not think about that,' he said lightly. 'I haven't had occasion to compliment you,' he went on. 'But it has only been because I'm overwhelmed by the sight of you.'

Dorothea flushed and dimpled prettily. 'I do believe that I have never been complimented as much as I have been in these past days,' she remarked. And it was true. She felt beautiful when Philip looked at her. Whether she was or not, she didn't know. But she *felt* that way when he was around.

The music ended and Philip halted. 'Are you hungry?' he asked. At the sight of her face, he said, 'No, neither am I.' He took hold of her hand. 'There are the gondolas.' He laughed. 'We mustn't forget them. Come along.'

Almost running, they left the ballroom and went outside. The grass felt cool and damp on Dorothea's slippered feet. At the water's edge he raised a hand and immediately a gondolier expertly positioned his long narrow boat against the small wooden dock.

With Philip's assistance Dorothea entered and sat down on the cushioned seat, moving over to make room for him. A moment later they were on the river.

Leaning back, Dorothea viewed the sight. The boat rocked gently, causing the black water to lap in a rhythmic pattern against the side. The moon was just rising and added its pale-white slash to the golden glow of the lanterns.

'It's beautiful,' she said in a quiet voice, absorbed in the glorious scene. The trees were black, standing like sentries against the shore. The night was so still that the music was clearly audible. She felt like crying but didn't know why. Certainly she wasn't sad. In fact, she had never been more content than she was tonight. She turned her head slightly and was almost startled to meet Philip's lips.

He did not embrace her, but their lips met gently, firmly, and for a moment neither one moved. A moment in which Dorothea's mind flew backward, weeks, months, years, to a snow-covered hillock not far from where she was right now. A moment that encompassed years, a lifetime, a second.

At last Dorothea drew back, her dark eyes searching his face. His dear face, his forever-remembered face, his never-before-seen face.

'You ...' She breathed the word in wonder. She was at once astonished and angry with herself, as if deep down she had always known but had not recognized. 'It's you!' she said again.

'Did you think I would ever leave you?' he said simply. 'Once having found you, did you think I would ever let you go?'

'I looked for you,' she said, unable to prevent the accusatory tone that crept into her voice. 'I looked for you for weeks. For months. And during carnival I searched everywhere!'

Philip lifted her hand and kissed the inside of her wrist. 'I was there,' he whispered softly. 'I have never been far from you. Nor shall I ever be.'

Her eyes filled with tears. 'Oh, Philip.' She flung her arms about his neck and he clasped her close to him.

'My angel,' he murmured, breathing the fragrance of her hair. 'My dearest angel.'

Years later, Dorothea would try to recall their words of love, but all she would be able to remember was the feeling. The night melted into a bittersweet symphony of emotion and discovery. It was a lifetime, captured in a few blissful hours.

They didn't leave the gondola until the sky was brightening. They talked endlessly, relating to each other how they felt, trying to explain the inexplicable. They kissed, and each kiss was almost a farewell, as if there would be no other.

The evening dissolved into memories that were later to be remembered, each one in exquisite detail.

But at the time, it was not an ending, it was a beginning.

On Monday, two days before he was scheduled to join his regiment, Philip was at Leine for the evening. He and Dorothea had not been able to speak privately but he had written to her. The glow in her eyes told him all he needed to know. Philip felt as if he had been reborn at the recognition in her eyes when he had kissed her. He felt a great relief. It was no longer necessary for him to dissemble, except around others, and they didn't matter at all. Nothing mattered, no one mattered. Only Dorothea. He loved her so desperately that he was occasionally amazed at himself. Then he was grateful to fate. How many men lived, he wondered, and had not been fortunate enough to know and to experience the pure love that he felt?

Philip was playing cards, but actually he was looking at Dorothea, at her dimpled smile, her flawless skin, her shining hair, her eyes that seemed to be reservoirs of emotion, when Elizabeth Platen approached the table.

Elizabeth spoke. Philip looked up at her as if he were viewing a stranger. He didn't notice her hard eyes, the white, almost pinched look about her nostrils, the stiff, almost unnatural way she held her body – she was no more than an intrusion. Slight, but irritating, for she took his eyes from the one human being he wished to gaze on for the rest of his life.

'Philip,' Elizabeth said in a lilting, brittle voice. 'I understand that you must leave us soon.'

'I am leaving Wednesday, Countess,' Philip answered, trying to repress his mounting annoyance with the interruption.

Elizabeth issued a light laugh. 'Not before you visit Monplaisir,' she advised, tapping him with her fan. Although her tone remained light, there was the undercurrent of a command in her words.

Across the table, Dorothea watched the small scene with inquiring, bewildered eyes. In the face of that look, Philip cringed, and Elizabeth smiled coldly.

'I insist that you visit me this evening,' Elizabeth went on, the smile planted firmly on her face. When there was no immediate answer, she said, 'Philip!' in such a loud voice that those at the adjoining tables glanced at them curiously, half interested and half annoyed at having their play interrupted.

'I will be there, madame,' Philip replied stiffly, ignoring Dorothea's look of hurt outrage.

The rest of the evening was a nightmare for Philip. There was no opportunity to speak with Dorothea, who viewed him with eyes alternately accusing and hurt. Aurora kept up her usual bright chatter. Charles seemed unaware of the emotions flowing about him.

When Philip arrived at Monplaisir, it was almost dawn. Elizabeth greeted him in a negligee, parading insolently about her bedchamber as she viewed her recalcitrant lover.

'Philip, you amaze me,' she said to him in a softly admonishing tone. 'You have neglected me, but I forgive you for that. However, your obvious attention to the princess shocks me. I would imagine that her husband would frown on the untoward attention you seem to be showering upon her.' She paused and viewed a fingernail critically. 'I doubt, too, that the duke would smile upon such a ... liaison.'

Philip's face remained noncommittal as he watched her. 'There is no liaison,' he advised smoothly, without a hint of the emotion he was feeling. 'The princess is charming enough,' he went on casually. 'However, it was Charles's company that I sought. I'm sure you know that he was responsible for obtaining a commission for me in the duke's army.'

Elizabeth raised a brow. She hadn't known. With the knowledge, she relaxed a bit. Then she smiled. Of course. How could I have been so stupid? she thought, eyeing him fondly. Philip could never care for Dorothea, for that washed-out little creature who always seemed on the verge of tears or temper. The thought was positively ridiculous when looked at logically. Her jealousy had clouded her reasoning, Elizabeth decided, almost contrite. 'I'm sorry, Philip,' she murmured. 'It was inexcusable of me to jump to conclusions.' She walked toward him, smiling tenderly, and was unaware of his slight withdrawal.

'Now that Charles has secured a commission for you,' she whispered softly, 'we will be able to see each other regularly. There will be no more of these painful separations.' She put her arms about his neck, and her eyes narrowed as he drew back.

'Because of that,' Philip said firmly, removing her clutching arms, 'we must end our association. The duke would certainly frown on our … liaison. I've no intention of insulting him.' His blue eyes regarded her sternly, without a hint of desire, of love, or even fondness.

Seeing that, Elizabeth moved away again, her motions as graceful and lethal as a cat's. So, her first instinct had been correct, she thought, pursing her red lips. He no longer wanted her. But damn it, she wanted him! Nor would she let him go. Certainly not to the insipid Dorothea. Composing herself, Elizabeth faced him, smiling sweetly. 'You are right, my dear Philip,' she noted calmly. 'I'm afraid that you misunderstood me. Actually I wanted to talk to you about a very important matter.'

He eyed her warily, but made no comment.

'My daughter is of an age where she should be wed.' She regarded him candidly. 'I'm afraid that she is hopelessly in love with you, Philip. I would be most pleased, and most grateful, if you would consider her as your wife.' Her laugh was artless. 'Certainly it's time for you to think of marrying.'

Philip stared, dumbfounded. Of all things, he had never expected this. He peered closely to see if Elizabeth was jesting, although lightheartedness was not one of her characteristics. But no, he saw, regarding her expression; she was serious. Dead serious. 'I must decline your gracious offer, Countess Platen,' he replied at last. Two spots of crimson appeared on her cheeks, but relentlessly he continued. 'Please don't think that my refusal reflects in any way on your lovely daughter. The life of a soldier is, at best, uncertain, and I would not want to inflict it on any woman. I have no plans now, or in the future, of marrying.'

With that, Philip bowed formally, then made his way to the door, leaving the speechless Elizabeth standing in her bedchamber, in her new negligee, furious.

Hanover

September 1687

Although it was not Dorothea's normal receiving day, Philip presented himself in her salon. For the first time, he was wearing the dark-blue uniform of the Hanoverian Army. Lenore was gone for such a length of time that he had a moment's panic, thinking he would be refused permission to see the princess. But then Dorothea entered the room, stunningly arrayed in a velvet morning gown the color of sapphires. As always, her hair was piled high in soft curls.

She was pale and distant, but greeted him courteously enough.

Looking at her, Philip's heart ached. She is so lovely, he thought. How is it that one woman could embody so much appeal? 'Forgive me,' he murmured, coming as close to her as he dared. 'I realized that I may be acting in a forward manner, but I felt that I had to see you before I left.'

'Please sit down,' Dorothea invited, biting her lower lip. Why did she feel this way? she wondered. She had no claim on this man. He was free to come and go – and to visit Monplaisir if he so chose. Most young men did. There they could gamble, drink, carouse; wasn't that what all young soldiers wanted? She sat down, folded her hands in her lap, and tried not to cry.

'I wanted to explain …' Philip began, hesitant.

'Explain?' Dorothea raised her chin. 'Surely you owe me no explanation, Count Königsmark. But I am pleased that you came to say good-bye.'

Philip took a breath. 'The reason I left last night – '

'I understand the reason,' she interrupted quickly, raising a white hand. 'Most of the young men in our court prefer the atmosphere at Monplaisir. It offers attractions that we cannot possibly match.'

He ran a hand through his hair before he responded. 'I must contradict you, your Highness. You have no idea of why I went to Monplaisir.'

'To see Countess Platen, was it not?' Dorothea observed coolly, trying to keep her composure.

'Yes.' He nodded. 'I told her that I would no longer be visiting Monplaisir. I find I need only your company to be content,' he finished softly, noticing the flush that stained her fair skin. He clenched his fists tightly in an effort to keep from reaching for her. And if Lenore had not been so obviously present, Philip realized that he might have done just that.

Dorothea was regarding him doubtfully, as if she couldn't quite believe him. She longed to ask him if he had ever made love to the countess, but she feared knowing the answer.

'The countess was of the opinion,' Philip tried to explain, 'that I might favorably consider a union with her daughter.'

Dorothea's eyes widened in surprise. 'You mean she wants you to wed Charlotte?' She caught her breath, almost afraid to hear his answer.

He nodded again. 'I advised her that I have no intention of marrying.' He glanced about the room until his eyes spied the clock, then he turned to Dorothea again. 'It's time for me to leave,' he said quietly.

'How long will you be away?' Dorothea asked in a small voice. She viewed her folded hands and realized that she didn't want him to go.

Philip shrugged his broad shoulders. 'Several months, I suspect.'

'Months?' she murmured, looking up at him.

Philip leaned forward, lowering his voice. 'May I have permission to write to you?' he asked impulsively.

Dorothea blinked as if the question had taken her unaware, as indeed it had. She wavered and hesitated.

'Please,' he whispered, seeing her uncertainty.

She regarded him for a long moment. 'Very well,' she said at last. 'But address the envelope to Mademoiselle Knesebeck. Lenore picks up the post. She will deliver it to me directly.'

After getting to his feet, Philip bowed, then walked from the room without further words. He hadn't said good-bye, Dorothea thought inanely, staring at the closed door. She turned then and looked at Lenore, who had been sitting quietly in her usual chair, her attention apparently centered squarely on her needlework.

Almost a month passed before Dorothea received the first letter. It was polite and friendly and brief. Time and again she picked up a quill, then laid it down again. It would, she knew very well, be improper to write. Yet, what harm?

Harm enough, she thought. Countess Platen had been decidedly unfriendly since Philip had left. Her biting wit and caustic tongue seemed forever aimed at Dorothea when they happened to be in each other's company.

Dorothea still hadn't answered the letter when, eight months later, George came home on leave.

That evening the talk at table was sobering and afterward, in the large, high-ceilinged drawing room, it continued. The duchess had cancelled the evening's musicale; instead they all listened attentively to George and Marshal Podewils, who had also taken a brief leave.

The Palatinate, that magnificent castle wherein the Count Palatine, one of the secular electors of the empire, resided, had been captured and occupied by the French.

'They couldn't hold it,' George related bitterly. He stood with his back to the fireplace, facing them all. His face was haggard and livid and he looked incredibly weary. 'We were advancing daily. But they must have known that it was only a matter of time. When we finally entered Mannheim, it had been reduced to rubble. We had long seen the smoke,' he explained, 'but we hadn't believed that the French Army would destroy it all.'

'What of the people?' Sofia asked, stricken.

'Madame,' Heinrich Podewils responded, 'they are homeless. With winter only months away, I fear that they will have a bad time of it. The French confiscated most of their supplies and food, and what they couldn't carry they laid to waste.'

'Horrible,' the duchess murmured, putting a hand to her trembling lips.

'During the following weeks, as we entered Oppenheim and Spires, it was the same,' George went on.

Sofia's eyes widened. 'And what of Heidelberg?'

'I'm sorry, Mother,' George retorted, knowing that she had lived for many years as a child in that city. 'It fared no better.'

'They must not be allowed to get away with this,' Duke Ernst declared in outrage.

'Father.' Charles spoke up. 'It's time that I be allowed to join the fighting.'

'No, Charles,' Sofia murmured quickly, alarmed. Wasn't it enough, she thought to herself, that two of her sons were risking their lives?

But Ernst nodded, pleased. 'You will be nineteen in a few week's time. Soon after I'll secure a commission for you.' He glanced at Maximilian, but he didn't offer his services.

Nor was he about to, Maximilian was thinking as he observed his father with cool eyes. He had no intention of dying at the hands of a Frenchman. Besides, with Friedrich out of the way and George in the thick of it, there might yet be a chance for him to inherit. Even though his brother Friedrich had blundered badly, he himself had every intention of laying his own plans with care.

Unobtrusively, Maximilian glanced at the man seated beside him on the divan. Count Otto Moltke, Master of the Hunt, was his only confidant. But it will have to be soon, Maximilian was thinking, listening in amusement as Charles tried to convince his father that there was no need for him to wait until his birthday. The duke, however, was adamant.

Right now, Maximilian thought, the emperor and the eight electors are too busy stemming the French tide to give much thought to my father's petition for an electorate. But as soon as things calmed down again, the threat would be a very real one. In the meantime, let George fight, let Charles risk his life. I, Maximilian, have my own concerns.

*

Later that evening George visited Dorothea. He presented her with a small, narrow box. In some surprise, she opened the gift.

'I hope it isn't damaged,' he ventured apologetically. 'I purchased it some months ago in Venice and have been carrying it about since then.'

Dorothea opened the box and gasped in genuine delight. It was a pair of gloves. Of pale-rose satin, they were embroidered with the most exquisite stitchery she had ever seen. The gold thread was artfully woven into an intricate floral pattern. 'They're beautiful,' she exclaimed.

George smiled slightly. 'I'm glad you're pleased,' he murmured. He began to walk toward the door.

'Where are you going?' Dorothea called out. 'You're not leaving already, are you?'

George paused, his face flushed. Damn it, the woman was always making a scene. 'It's late,' he offered, trying to speak calmly. 'And I'm leaving early in the morning. I thought to get a good night's rest.'

Dorothea's eyes narrowed. So, she was thinking, the gift was not a gift at all, merely a placebo. He couldn't wait to get out, to go to Melusine. A good night's rest, indeed! Angrily Dorothea flung the box at him. It opened, spilling the gloves to the floor.

George stared at them for a moment, then at her. He really was weary, he thought. Weary of Dorothea and her continuous tantrums. 'Good evening, madame,' he said quietly. Before she could speak, he was gone.

Dorothea opened her mouth to call to him, then closed it again. She would not so humiliate herself as to beg for her husband's company. Her eye lit on the gloves. They were lovely. Quite the loveliest that she had ever seen. Stooping, she picked them up, admiring them once more. Just because she was angry with her husband was no reason to discard them.

Only a week after George had left, Dorothea came down the stairs, intending to go into the dining room for the midday meal. In the front hall, she came on the duchess, weeping in such a distraught manner that her ladies had to support her.

It was only moments before Dorothea discovered the reason: Friedrich had been killed in battle.

Moving forward, Dorothea assisted the ladies as they helped the duchess to her room, wondering why the duke was so conspicuously absent. A few discreet questions revealed the answer to this too. On hearing the news, Ernst had departed for Monplaisir, unable to deal with his wife's collapse.

The weeks turned into months. Even carnival was muted, more perfunctory than gay. As for the duchess, she attended none of the festivities. Dorothea spent most of her time in her own apartments. Whether this was because George and Charles were both gone, or because Philip had been unable to get leave, she didn't ask herself.

Toward summer, Dorothea asked for, and was granted, permission to visit Celle and her parents. When she returned, three weeks later, there was another letter from Philip. Like the first, it was friendly, noncommittal, but a bit longer in length. As Dorothea was reading it for the third time, Lenore asked, 'What are you going to do, *ma chère*?'

'Do?' Dorothea looked up from her perusal, startled.

'About the letter,' Lenore enlarged patiently. 'You have been reading it, over and over.' She smiled, but her heart felt heavy and saddened. Did Dorothea know, Lenore wondered, that she was falling in love? Somehow, Lenore doubted it. Married, the mother of two children, Dorothea was still an innocent, her heart untouched. And why should it be otherwise? Lenore reflected morosely. Dorothea's husband didn't love her, had never loved her, had never even made the pretense of loving her.

But *this*, Lenore thought to herself, still waiting for an answer, was not the solution. Oh, she had seen the look in Königsmark's eyes when he gazed at the princess. It was there for anyone to see. And that was what so troubled Lenore. If Philip had been a dashing courtier with nothing more on his mind than a brief fling, Lenore would encourage her mistress. But whatever Philip had on his mind, it was not a brief fling.

'Well, *ma chère*?' Lenore persisted in the face of continuing silence.

'I ... don't think I shall answer,' said Dorothea, and never saw the relieved look in the eyes of her lady.

Hanover

November 1688

The Imperial Army and the French Army were at a standoff, strung out along both sides of the Rhine. With the comparative quiet, both George and Philip returned for carnival and a well-deserved rest.

Almost every day, in the company of Prince Charles, Philip called on Dorothea. Occasionally Aurora joined them. Then, during the evening, they all gave themselves up to carnival. George claimed little of Dorothea's attention, preferring Melusine's company. But now Dorothea didn't care; in fact, she was relieved to be rid of his ponderous, taciturn, disapproving presence. After the long months of boredom and quiet it was good to dance, to laugh, to be happy.

Philip's attention brought such a glow to her cheeks and sparkle to her eyes, it was not long before they were the subject of many speculative looks.

Charles, perhaps not surprisingly, was the first to notice the change in Philip. Gone was the rakish grin and easy-going banter that had formed an intricate part of his personality. He laughed only when in the company of Dorothea. When she left, even for a brief dance with someone else, his eyes followed her progress about the room.

Newly observant, Charles watched, noticed, and, dismayed, came to the conclusion that Philip was in love with the princess.

There was to be a splendid ball at Monplaisir on this cold November evening. Dorothea had let it be known that she was spending the day readying herself for the event. In consequence, Philip and Charles took the occasion to take the hounds and go hunting in the dark forests that surrounded Hanover.

The day was cold but calm enough. A brittle sun tried and mostly failed to penetrate the deep stand of trees.

For an hour they hunted, enjoying their companionship. Charles shot a deer, a fine buck, which was now being hauled by attendants back to Leine.

As the horses ambled along, returning to town at an easy pace, Charles glanced at Philip, who had been silent for many moments now. Charles wanted to speak of what was on his mind, knew he had to speak, and prayed that his words wouldn't jeopardize their friendship.

But how to begin? How to tell Philip that he must not love Dorothea, must not gaze on her as if she were the only woman in the world? Dorothea, Charles tried to console himself, was only being kind. She was merely enjoying the attention; she was high-spirited and fun-loving. It was what made him like his sister-in-law. Of course she was beautiful, she seemed to grow more so each year. Even Maximilian, not usually given to fanciful prose, admitted that he was most fond of Dorothea.

Charles cleared his throat. 'Philip,' he said, hoping that his tone was casual, 'perhaps you should escort Charlotte Platen to the ball this evening. Or,' he laughed, wondering if it sounded as hollow as he knew it to be, 'Mademoiselle Vault. She has been looking at you with cow eyes since carnival began.'

Turning his head, Philip regarded Charles as though he, Philip, had just woken from a dream-filled sleep. 'Escort Charlotte,' he repeated inanely.

'Why, yes,' Charles continued affably. 'We've been monopolizing too much of your time. I'll see to it that Dorothea is not left unattended. And as for Aurora, we both know that she has more admirers than any other woman at court.'

Philip carefully led his horse around a broken tree stump. 'No,' he answered slowly. 'I've no desire to escort anyone else.'

Charles frowned. 'George will be there,' he observed, hoping that Philip would take the hint.

He did not. 'George has eyes only for Melusine von Schulenburg,' he noted acidly. 'He's oblivious to everything and everyone else.'

As you are, my friend, Charles thought sadly. 'I'm afraid,' he went on, feeling uncomfortable, 'that your persistent attention to the princess is being noticed.' When there was no immediate response, Charles injected a note of sternness. 'Surely, Philip, you cannot wish to damage her reputation?'

Philip halted his horse, startled. Charles did the same. Bright color flooded Philip's cheeks, but Charles wasn't certain if it was anger or embarrassment that caused it.

'Has Dorothea told you to speak to me?' Philip demanded at last.

'No, no. She has said nothing,' Charles assured him with a wave of his gloved hand.

Philip leaned forward in his saddle. 'Then who has?'

'No one, Philip.' Charles tried to calm him. He shook his head. 'Perhaps I'm the only one who has noticed. But it's so obvious.'

Philip eyed his friend with a wary look. 'What is obvious?' he persisted in a low voice, eyes narrowed.

'That you're in love with her,' the young prince replied, averting his face. He took a determined breath as he regarded Philip once more. 'If I thought otherwise, I'd call you out. But, sincere or not, it must stop now, before Dorothea is hurt.'

'I've no intention of hurting her,' Philip protested. He prodded his horse forward again, ignoring the feeling of despair that settled on him. Was it really so obvious? he wondered. He had tried to be careful, circumspect. After a while he spoke to Charles in a low voice. 'You're right, I do love her.' He almost smiled at the silly little word. It was so inconsequential for what he felt. I love my sister, I love the feeling I get just before a battle, I love to hunt. How could he apply such a word to his feelings for Dorothea? He didn't merely love her, he worshipped her, idolized her, adored her. She was his life.

Charles heard this admission in dismay. 'You can do nothing about it, you know,' he said, feeling helpless. Philip didn't answer. The feeling of dismay grew. Surely he wasn't thinking of doing anything foolish? Charles thought, alarmed. If Dorothea were compromised, there would be hell to pay. His mother would never stand for such a scandal.

'Don't worry, Charles,' Philip said, brusquely now. 'The princess doesn't know how I feel. I promise I will do nothing to harm her.' He forced himself to speak with confidence.

With these reassuring words, Charles relaxed somewhat. No doubt he really was making too much of it all. In only a few weeks Philip would be returning to join his regiment along the Rhine. By then this whole thing would have blown over. Charles grinned and changed the subject. 'I've spent these last months getting no farther than the outskirts of town. But when you leave, I'll be going with you,' he confided happily. 'We'll teach the French a thing or two.'

Relieved, Philip had to smile at the young man's enthusiasm. He made a mental vow to be more careful in the future. 'I'm proud, Charles,' he said, then gave a mock salute. 'We shall be comrades-in-arms.'

With a howl of youthful glee the young prince spurred his horse to a gallop. When they arrived back in Hanover he was breathless with exhilaration, convinced that his suppositions with regard to Philip and Dorothea had been all in his mind.

Monplaisir

November 1688

'Hurry, Lenore. You must find them,' Dorothea urged. 'The carriages are in front and everyone is waiting.'

'I've already found them,' Lenore soothed, handing her the exquisitely embroidered gloves.

Dorothea slipped them on quickly, then viewed herself in the mirror. She wore a pale-pink gown sewn at the bodice with small white pearls. The narrow sleeves were off the shoulder and the decolletage revealed a pert, high bosom. Over the rose-colored gloves she now slipped on a diamond bracelet, which Lenore fastened for her. A matching diamond coronet rested in the dark curls.

'How do I look?' she asked, still viewing her reflection.

Lenore laughed gently. 'If you looked any lovelier, you would sprout wings.' She picked up a fur cloak and draped it about the princess. 'Come along now. You're the one who's dilly-dallying.'

The carriages were waiting in the forecourt. Philip, Charles and Aurora turned to look at her as Dorothea descended the steps.

Philip immediately stepped forward and took her hand, assisting her into the first carriage. With a frown, Charles, with no alternative, helped Aurora into the next one. The horses danced, excited, breathing out puffs of warm mist that hung on the cold air like little wisps of smoke. Then they were on their way to Monplaisir, three miles distant.

Dorothea viewed Philip with a shy smile. It was the first time they had been alone in better than a year.

'Everyone has gone on ahead,' he said, turning to look at her. He would never tire of looking at her, he thought with no small amazement.

'I'm glad you waited,' she murmured, thankful that the dimness hid her flushed cheeks.

Philip took her small hand and held it tightly. 'I'll always wait for you,' he whispered fervently.

She removed her hand, conscious of how warm it felt from his touch. 'Perhaps I should have ridden with Aurora,' she said with a light laugh. 'I'm certain that it's improper for us to be alone like this.'

Philip's mouth tightened. 'I'll stop the carriage now, if you like.' He leaned forward and raised a hand to tap on the window separating them from the driver.

Dorothea put a hand on his arm hastily. 'No ...' She waited until he settled back again. 'I ... would much rather ride with you.'

There was a small silence. Philip viewed her intently in the shadowy light. 'Why didn't you answer my letters?' Although his voice remained quiet, there was an edge of urgency to it.

Dorothea bit her lip. 'I ... was going to,' she responded, not looking at him. 'But ...'

'But what?' he persisted, leaning closer. Her fragrance washed over him. He clenched his hands, trying to stem the rush of longing that engulfed him. 'I waited. Each day that I didn't hear from you I counted as a lost day. I couldn't sleep for thinking of it.'

'Just when I had made up my mind to answer,' she tried to explain, 'George came home.'

In an abrupt movement, Philip turned away, staring moodily outside. 'George,' he muttered.

Dorothea was uncertain as to how to respond to that, so she said nothing. For a time they rode in silence.

'Do you know how much I love you?' Philip's voice was barely audible. He kept staring outside, afraid to look at her, afraid of what he would see. Surprise? Shock? God forbid, amusement? All he heard was the sharp, indrawn breath that told him that she had heard and understood. Slowly he turned to her, his eyes anguished. 'Do you care for me at all?' he implored.

For a long moment Dorothea studied his handsome face. Then she nodded, toying with the small purse in her lap. The moonlight filtered in through her side of the rocking carriage. It played about the diamonds in her hair, sending tiny prisms of light that ventured fearlessly into the dark shadows. 'I have cared for a long time,' she mused, almost dreamily. 'Perhaps since that first night when I didn't even know who you were.' She laughed softly. 'I had even supposed that you might be a burgher, or a king.'

'I wish we both were burghers,' Philip said simply. His heart soared with her words.

With a start, Philip noted that they had reached their destination. Never was he so unhappy to see Monplaisir. He was oddly torn between exultation and despair, happy because she did care, morose because there was nothing he could do about it. Charles had been right, he was forced to admit as he helped Dorothea alight. Nothing must harm her.

Monplaisir was ablaze with light. Music and laughter reached them before they reached the front door.

Elizabeth, as hostess, greeted them with a frozen smile. She, too, was wearing a pink gown, although it was a shade darker than Dorothea's.

They deposited cloaks and hats with the ever-attentive servants, then wandered into the vast ballroom. Both the huge crystal chandeliers were adorned with hundreds of candles. The yellow light glittered and wavered as it played over the swirling dancers below.

Philip held out his arms and Dorothea entered them as if she belonged there. Round and round they went, their eyes never leaving one another. People watched, not entirely because of their absorbed attention with each other, but because both Philip and Dorothea were superb dancers. And when the music ended, more than one person came to tell them so.

Laughing, flushed, and happy, Dorothea accepted all the acclaim with a feeling of immense excitment. I feel alive, she thought. It was an almost unbearable sensation. Feeling warm, both from the dance and the excitement, Dorothea went into the wide front hall. After removing the long gloves, she laid them carefully on a table.

'Dorothea ...'

She turned and broke into a delighted smile. 'Mama!' She embraced Eleanor affectionately. 'I'm sorry I didn't get to ride with you. I'm afraid my toilette took longer than I anticipated.'

'It was worth it, my darling,' Eleanor said quickly, viewing her daughter. 'You look lovely.' She herself was splendidly arrayed in pale-blue satin, her coppery hair swept high on her head.

They walked into the ballroom again, but as Dorothea began to head toward Philip, her mother's arm detained her. 'Dorothea, we must talk.'

The princess viewed her mother in dismay. Talk! Tonight of all nights. 'Mama, can it wait until morning?' she entreated. But Eleanor shook her head firmly and drew her back into the hall once more. Dorothea saw Philip looking at her. Then Aurora approached him. A moment later he led his sister onto the dance floor.

Turning, Dorothea regarded Eleanor with some impatience. She had been in Hanover for weeks now and and they had spent a part of every day in each other's company. Yet now her mother wanted to talk. It was maddening.

'You are heading for trouble,' Eleanor was saying. 'And I feel I must warn you.' She glanced about, but no one was in their immediate vicinity.

Dorothea's annoyance increased. 'Must you speak in riddles, Mama? What are you talking about?'

Eleanor studied her daughter, vastly relieved by the reaction she was seeing. It was quite obvious that nothing had happened. Yet. Probably never would; but that was a chance, as a mother, she couldn't take. Ever since Eleanor had arrived in Hanover she had seen what was going on. She suspected everyone did, except George, who was either too engrossed in his own affairs or simply didn't care.

'You're spending entirely too much time in the company of Count Königsmark.' At the sight of Dorothea's flushed face, Eleanor's dismay returned, stronger now. The terrible thing was, Eleanor thought frantically, that it didn't appear to be a flirtation, a mild infatuation, even a physical attraction that, once satisfied, would dissipate. Although *that* would be bad enough, No, it was more, she thought, still studying her daughter. She had seen the expression on Philip's face when he looked at Dorothea; he always seemed to be looking at her. Now she was seeing the same look on Dorothea's face. It confirmed her worst fears.

'I spend just as much time in Charles's company,' Dorothea pointed out, in control of herself once more. 'It's not that I spurn my husband's company,' she remarked tartly. 'But as you may have noticed, George all but ignores me.' She lifted her chin in that defiant manner. 'But of course you've noticed that, haven't you, Mama? You seem to be noticing a lot these days.' Although she tried, she couldn't quite control her aggravation with what she took to be her mother's interference.

Eleanor winced at the accusation. 'I do not pry,' she said earnestly. 'You are a grown woman, a married woman, the mother of two children. I will not presume to dictate how you live.' She took her daughter's hand and squeezed it tightly. 'You must act with discretion. You cannot go around flushing each time his name is mentioned.' She increased the pressure of her hand. 'And you must tell him – insist – that he stop gazing at you as if you were a saint he reveres!'

In spite of herself, Dorothea grinned at the allegory. Her dimples deepened charmingly. At the sight, Eleanor just shook her head and embraced her daughter. 'I love you very much, my darling,' she whispered. 'Please promise me that you will take care.' She held Dorothea at arm's length and searched the lovely face with worried eyes.

Dorothea hesitated a moment. 'I will, Mama,' she replied at last. 'I promise.'

Standing by the front door, having just greeted some late arriving guests, Elizabeth watched Dorothea and Eleanor, a slight smirk on her face. She'd give anything to know what they were talking about. Although, knowing the two women, the conversation could be no more than insipid. And Philip. Elizabeth's expression hardened. Damn him. His attention never strayed from Dorothea. He didn't even have the courtesy to dance with his hostess.

Just how far, Elizabeth wondered, had their little love affair progressed? Her eye lit on Dorothea's gloves, still lying atop the hall table. Casually she walked toward it. She picked up one of the gloves and balled it in her hand. Turning, she called to a footman. 'Come with me,' she commanded.

Once in her study at the end of the hall, she scribbled a note. Folding it tightly, she handed it to the footman. 'Deliver this to Count Königsmark,' she instructed, 'as soon as this dance is over.' She stood up and eyed the man sternly. 'Do it discreetly, do you understand?'

'Yes, Countess,' he replied, bowing in his most deferential manner. He was definitely a bit put off by her intense expression. She isn't a person to cross at the best of times, he thought, backing from the room. But when she looks like that, she chills a man's soul.

Elizabeth returned to the hallway. The dance had just ended and she watched as the footman approached Philip with a tray laden with champagne glasses. Smiling, Philip accepted the refreshment. Elizabeth could see his startled look when he received a small, folded paper with his glass. It took Philip only a moment to recover. His glance at the note was brief. Then he casually deposited it in his pocket, nodding affably at a friend across the room.

Well done, Philip, Elizabeth mentally applauded. I can always count on your discretion.

With a quick look at Dorothea and Eleanor, who were still in deep conversation and regarding each other with misty eyes, Elizabeth slipped out the front door.

Holding her skirts high, she made her way through the garden to the balcony that adjoined the ballroom. With a bit of difficulty, due to her voluminous skirt, Elizabeth managed nevertheless to climb over the two-foot wall that surrounded the balcony.

Then she waited in the shadows, shivering with the cold. But Philip wouldn't keep her waiting long; that much she knew.

The words burned in his mind. 'Meet me on the balcony as soon as you can.' It was signed 'Dorothea'. Darling little fool, Philip thought, slowly making his way toward the

French doors. She shouldn't have used her own name. He would speak to her about it. Her safety was paramount.

Philip was by the doors now. Catching his breath, he saw the flash of a pink skirt. She was in the shadows; at least she had that much sense, he thought tenderly. Suddenly he spied George, with the blond Melusine, heading in his direction. Philip froze, not daring to move, cursing his luck.

But George paid him no mind. Repositioning a straight-backed chair, he smiled at Melusine. She sat down and George bent his head, listening to her words.

Philip watched them for a moment. He was a bare ten feet away. When he was certain that George, who had his back to him, was sufficiently engrossed in his conversation, Philip quickly opened one of the French doors and stepped outside. The cold air hit him with force after the warm interior of the ballroom, causing him to take a sharp breath.

'Dorothea?' he called softly.

'Over here.'

Philip walked into the shadows, and stopped short. 'Elizabeth! What the devil ...'

She began to scream, her voice loud and shrill, while Philip stared stupidly.

The balcony doors were flung open. George and a few of the guests, Charles included, stepped out. As soon as the doors had opened, Elizabeth had departed. With an alacrity that utterly astounded Philip, Elizabeth scaled the low wall and disappeared into the darkness.

Coming forward, George peered, seeing only a flash of pink. 'What is going on?' he demanded, frowning at the commotion.

Philip turned, still bewildered by the foolishness of it all. 'I just stepped out for a breath of air,' he tried to explain.

'We heard a scream,' Charles said, looking about.

Philip grinned with a trace of his old charm. 'So did I. But I don't know where it came from. As you can see,' he spread his arms, 'I'm alone out here.'

George stared at him, suspicious, and, still frowning, looked past him.

'Is anything wrong?' Elizabeth stepped out onto the

balcony. Her voice held only concern. Viewing her, Philip marveled at her duplicity.

'No,' George answered, turning to look at her. 'It's nothing. Let's go back. It's cold out here.'

Before anyone could move, Elizabeth's delicate laugh rang out like silver charms. 'Philip,' she said, still laughing, 'it appears that you have lost your glove.' She pointed a tapered finger at the ground.

George took a few steps forward. Stooping, he picked up the rose-colored glove. In silence he contemplated the exquisite embroidery, then viewed Philip somberly. 'It's not his, Countess,' he replied evenly, his thoughtful gaze still on Philip, who appeared a trifle confused. 'I'll return it to its rightful owner.' With that, George again entered the ballroom.

Charles, shaking his head unhappily, followed his brother. Elizabeth, with only a slight hesitation, joined them, without so much as a glance in Philip's direction.

Too late, Philip realized that he'd been duped. But the agonizing thing was that Elizabeth knew of his feelings for Dorothea. First Charles, then Elizabeth. My God, George? Quickly he entered the room again, in time to see George heading toward his wife, who was standing by one of the food-laden tables. He saw her turn and smile at her husband. A moment later her brow wrinkled in perplexity as George handed her the glove.

But George, for all his failings, was not a fool. He noted Dorothea's puzzlement. Then, casually, he touched her arm. It was warm, almost damp with perspiration, for she had just finished a dance with Maximilian, who was, if not a good dancer, an enthusiastic one.

As he returned to Melusine's side, Elizabeth intercepted him. 'I must apologize, your Highness,' she said sweetly. 'I'm most annoyed that this incident spoiled my evening's entertainment.' She pouted prettily.

George inclined his head, noting with grim amusement that Elizabeth was wearing a pink gown. 'Rest assured, Countess, your evening's entertainment was in no way spoiled. At least not for me.'

Elizabeth flashed a warm smile and tilted her head in what she thought to be a beguiling gesture. 'Thank you, your Highness. You are so like your gracious father.'

But, George thought to himself as he returned to Melusine, there is no smoke without fire. There was a reason why Elizabeth had done what she had done; he was almost certain now that it had been her he had seen on the balcony. Whatever else Dorothea was, she was not a liar. Certainly not an accomplished one. On the contrary, she had the distressing habit of openly speaking her mind, regardless of how it affected others.

And if Dorothea was attracted to Königsmark, so be it, George thought. Just as long as she did it discreetly. He smiled down at Melusine, grateful to be back in her quiet company.

Standing there, watching it all, Philip seethed with fury, the emotion almost overwhelming him. If he could, he would have walked over to Elizabeth Platen and struck her. Her had never in his life hit a woman, but now the urge was almost irresistible.

'Philip?'

He turned and gave a start as he saw Dorothea approach. Didn't she know? he wondered frantically. 'You shouldn't be here,' he said lamely. The hurt look on her face was like a blow to his heart. 'Dance with me,' he said then. Before she could even respond, he drew her out onto the dance floor. Quickly, in a halting voice, he told her what had happened.

'How dare that woman do such a thing,' she said, outraged.

He held her tighter. 'Please, Dorothea,' he begged. 'Don't cross Elizabeth Platen. She's a viper.' He looked at her with concerned eyes. 'What did your husband say to you?'

She shrugged slightly. 'Not much. He said "I think this is yours," ' she related. 'Then I asked where he had gotten it. I had left it on the hall table. He told me he found it on the balcony.' Her brow furrowed. 'I had no idea what he was talking about. Then he touched my arm, smiled, and walked away.'

'He didn't seem angry or upset?' Philip persisted.

Dorothea shook her head. 'Not at all.'

Things are moving too swiftly, Philip was thinking. And

in the wrong direction. 'I'm leaving tomorrow morning,' he said, with a firmness that surprised Dorothea.

Her face paled and she stumbled slightly. 'You're not due back for two weeks!' she protested, striving to keep her voice low.

'I know,' he said in the same tone. 'But your safety is all that matters to me.'

Dorothea raised her chin in the way he was beginning to recognize. Strange how such a simple gesture melted his heart. He so longed to clasp her to him, to kiss her, that he was gripped with an almost physical pain.

'Is it my safety or yours that you're so concerned with?' she asked pertly, perversely ignoring his anguished look.

'Dorothea ... I love you so very much.' His voice faltered. He wanted to ask her to come away with him. Anywhere. 'Will you write?' he asked instead. When she made no immediate answer, he added, 'If you don't, I shall die. I swear, I'll step in front of the first Frenchman I see.'

Dorothea regarded him, alarmed.

'I will,' he insisted fervently, tightening his hold on her. 'I can no longer bear my feelings.'

'I will write,' she said quickly, suddenly believing him. He meant it and the thought made her cold. 'You will remember to address your envelopes to Lenore?' she reminded him.

He nodded. The dance ended. Philip escorted Dorothea back to Charles, who would not look in his direction, and Aurora, who regarded him with a profound sympathy that he chose to ignore. Charles had told Aurora of what had taken place on the balcony. Aurora was more than a little worried about her brother. She remembered the day when a servant had reported that George had attacked the princess, coming close to killing her, in fact. Philip had behaved like a madman, pacing the floor, pounding the walls with his fists until Aurora feared he would do himself bodily harm.

Dorothea seated herself next to Charles. When next she looked, Philip was gone. There was no need to question herself as to why she felt so desolate. Carnival had two weeks to go. But for Dorothea it was over.

*

The letters came. Slowly at first, then one, even two a day. Dorothea spent all of her mornings writing to Philip and all of her afternoons and evenings thinking about him. She knew she was thinking about him far too much, but she couldn't help herself. She was irresistibly drawn to him. And it wasn't just his strong good looks that so attracted her. She wondered if what she was feeling was love; if so, it was nothing like what she had thought it would be. And did Philip really love her? That was a question that had tormented Dorothea on more than one sleepless night: yes, no, maybe, perhaps.

Lenore watched and worried and was saddened. No good could come of it, she decided. If Philip was obsessed, Dorothea was becoming more so. It was difficult now even to gain Dorothea's attention. She lived from post to post, occasionally reading his words aloud. She carried the most recent letter in her bodice, refusing to part with it until the next one came.

More than once Lenore had tried to talk to Dorothea, but it was no use. All she could do was try to protect her mistress, as she had always done.

And then something happened that even captured Dorothea's attention. Word came that young Prince Charles had fallen in battle. For a time it was hoped that he was alive. But then the report came: Charles had been killed.

The duchess collapsed. Even Dorothea wept profusely. 'He was so young,' she lamented, recalling his irrepressible ways and keen wit. For once she commiserated with her mother-in-law. She didn't have to be told that Charles had been his mother's favorite. Charles had been everyone's favorite. Except, perhaps, for the duke, who could see no one of his children save George.

Dorothea accompanied Sofia to Karlsbad where the physician had sent her to take the waters, but was unable to notify Philip of the trip. Without his letters, she fretted and grew distraught. Fortunately her nervous state was attributed to Charles's death.

In a way, the assumption was correct. Dorothea suddenly realized, with a painful clarity, the frailty of one's hold on life. She suffered moments and hours of agony as she worried over Philip's safety.

She no longer fooled herself. She loved him. And when they at last returned to Leine, she wrote and told him so. The realization didn't surprise her. It was as if she had been born to love Philip. All else receded. There were varying degrees of annoying intrusions: letters from George, from her mother, lectures from the duchess, who continually told her how fortunate she was to be married to George. 'You may one day be Queen of England,' Sofia said on more than one occasion, then tediously reported on her lineage to the English throne yet one more time.

But as near as Dorothea could see, there were a dozen or more claimants to the coveted crown. Besides, it didn't matter. She didn't want to be electress, she didn't want to be Queen of England. She wanted Philip. Desperately, unreasonably, with all her heart, she wanted Philip.

Hanover

June 1689

Conrad Hildebrandt was worried. The longer he studied the neat row of numbers he had set down on the paper before him, the more concerned he became.

He was a short, rotund man who liked nothing better than to eat and to apply himself to the myriad of secretarial details that comprised the handling of Count Königsmark's estate. He had held this post now for three years, ever since the court had purchased the large house that adjoined Leine. He was diligent and meticulous, and he knew that his figures were correct.

The vast wealth of the Königsmarks was dwindling, fast. The man lived on what could only be termed a lavish scale. Hildebrandt consulted another list, noting the surprising number of footmen, pages, butlers, maids, and servants. Leine itself had not much more.

And then there were the gambling debts. Whether he played cards at court or in his off-duty hours with his fellow officers, Königsmark seemed to lose – on a grand scale.

He picked up a letter delivered only that morning, the letter than had prompted his own detailed inventory. He studied it with care, even though he knew it by heart. If Königsmark didn't act, didn't return home to Sweden, he was in danger of losing his family estates, which were in the process of being confiscated by the crown.

Hildebrandt shook his head. Königsmark's pay as a colonel in the Hanoverian Army was minuscule. He had received offers from Denmark, from Bavaria, from Saxony, all offering him a commission as general. Philip had firmly declined them all. He would not, he said, leave Hanover. Although what could prompt such madness Hildebrandt didn't understand.

He sighed and leaned back in the chair. He was hungry. He discounted the fact that it was midmorning. When he grappled with problems, he always wanted to eat. Leaning forward, he rang the little silver bell on his desk and moments later a maid entered.

'Are there any scones left over from breakfast?' Hildebrandt inquired, eyeing the buxom figure with appreciation.

'I believe so, sir,' came the reply.

Hildebrandt rubbed his plump hands together. Lascivious thoughts retreated. He could have the maid anytime he wanted. Scones were baked only once a week. 'Well then, bring me a few,' he ordered. 'Perhaps a small plate of honey and jam. And some coffee. And don't forget the cream!'

As the maid turned, Hildebrandt called out: 'The Countess Aurora, is she awake?'

'Yes, sir,' the girl confirmed. 'She's having breakfast in her room. The count was up, but he was feeling poorly and went back to bed.'

Hildebrandt nodded and waved a hand, sending her about her business.

There was, he reflected glumly, no purpose served in speaking to Königsmark. He had done that before. The man was simply not interested in his own financial situation. The money had always been there; as far as the count was concerned, it would always be there. Since the countess ran the houes in her brother's absence, and for that matter even when he was in residence, it was time that the facts be brought to her attention. Perhaps she could cut down on the staff, not to mention her endless purchases of *objets d'art*. At the very least she might be able to persuade her brother to go back for a while and set his affairs in order.

The doors opened. Hildebrandt looked up, viewing the laden tray with a smile. With a quick motion, he brushed aside the papers and gave his wholehearted attention to his midmorning snack. Königsmark's financial affairs had waited this long, he thought, happily spreading jam upon a hot scone; they could wait a few more minutes.

As he ate, Hildebrandt wondered what was ailing the count. Königsmark was not a man to lie in bed for no reason.

At last he leaned back, contentedly belched, and patted his ample stomach. It would be almost two hours before lunch was served. He hoped there would be some cold pheasant left over from last night's supper. There should be, he thought, getting to his feet and gathering his papers together, if the staff had not already devoured it. And that was another thing, he mused grumpily. All those people ate like pigs!

In the hallway he glanced up the wide, curving staircase that led to the second floor. With a sigh, he resignedly began to ascend the steps.

He was puffing when he reached the landing. With a hand on the bannister, he stood there until his breath came easier. Then he adjusted his small morning wig, clutched his papers tightly, and headed for the door that led to the countess's apartments.

Aurora, in a pale-green morning gown, was seated at her writing table. Looking up, she greeted Hildebrandt cordially. With not much regret, she laid aside the uncompleted letter to her sister. Amelia was a voracious letter writer. Aurora had to discipline herself to answer any correspondence. She found letter-writing a chore. It always amazed her to learn the amount of time that her contemporaries delegated to this task.

'Sit down, Monsieur Hildebrandt.' She smiled in amusement at the sight of the little man. He was so busily efficient each time she saw him. He was also incredibly tedious. Aurora permitted herself a small sigh as she watched him neatly arrange a pile of papers before her. When this had been accomplished to his satisfaction, he sat down and regarded her with a stern expression that rested uneasily on his round face.

'Have I exceeded my allowance?' she inquired amiably. 'I fear from your grim expression that you're about to scold me again.' She pouted prettily.

Hildebrandt reddened, not certain how to take her

words. In fact, the countess managed quite easily to unsettle him each time he had occasion to speak with her. He was never quite sure how to take her light, sometimes flippant, manner.

'Milady, I would never presume ...' he began awkwardly, then paused at the sound of her trilling laughter. 'What I have to speak to you about is most serious,' he commented earnestly, and with just a touch of reproof.

'Very well, Monsieur Hildebrandt.' Aurora glanced down at the papers in a sincere effort to make sense of the row on row of figures that greeted her eye.

Somewhat mollified, Hildebrandt reached forward and tapped one of the sheets. 'These figures represent the upkeep of this house for one month.'

She looked at the total. Twenty-five thousand talers! It is imposible, she thought, suddenly sobered. Where did the money go? she wondered, bemused. But it was all there: food, wages, maintenance, even the feed for the horses was itemized. Still, it wasn't all that bad, Aurora reflected.

'I don't see where we can cut down.' She flashed a bright smile at the secretary, who merely frowned at her.

'Perhaps, milady, the household could be run just as efficiently with twenty footmen instead of twenty-two,' he suggested.

Again she laughed. 'That would hardly make a dent, Monsieur,' she pointed out. She returned her gaze to the figures. 'I don't really see any cause for concern,' she pronounced, growing bored.

'Permit me, milady.' Hildebrandt placed another sheet before her.

Aurora's eyes widened. Eighty-seven thousand talers for one ball? For one evening's entertainment? 'Quite remarkable,' she murmured, more surprised than upset.

Seeing her lack of concern, or understanding, Hildebrandt repressed his exasperation. Without speaking, he put another sheet before her, detailing to some extent Count Königsmark's gambling debts. The list was probably incomplete, he thought to himself, because the count paid some of his debts immediately with money he had on his person. There were only the notes presented to Hildebrandt, as secretary, to honor.

Aurora turned to him, frowning. 'It is a sizable amount, I agree. But I can hardly cut down *these* expenses. After all, it is my brother's money to do with as he pleases.' She was growing a bit annoyed. Next, Hildebrandt would show her the expenses for her own monthly allowance. Certainly he didn't expect her to reduce that!

But he didn't. Prudently Hildebrandt reasoned that the countess already knew that amount. Instead, he placed before her the letter he had received that morning from the Swedish minister.

She read it quickly. 'But this is absurd,' she declared, outraged. 'Those estates have been in my family for generations. They cannot confiscate them.' She glared at the secretary as if he were at fault.

Hildebrandt looked unhappy. 'I'm afraid they can, milady. They have been vacant for years. And the count is apparently residing in a foreign country. Nor have the taxes been paid. The crown is within its right if it chooses to claim the land, and the estates on it. This is the main reason I wanted to speak with you – '

'Well, pay the taxes,' she interrupted him. 'That is your job.'

Hildebrandt straightened. 'I would be happy to pay them, milady,' he replied, somewhat affronted, 'if there was money available.'

Aurora stared at him blankly.

'Your expenses are exceeding your income,' he explained patiently at her lack of understanding. 'Within a year, two at the outside, the principal will be exhausted. If I were to send the money for the taxes ...' He shrugged. 'Then you would have only six months.'

Aurora put a white hand to her breast. 'What do you suggest?' she inquired in a faint voice.

'Well, milady,' he responded. 'I would suggest that, first, you convince the count to drastically curtail his expenses. Second, persuade him to return to Sweden and meet with the minister. Probably something can be worked out, especially if he were to occupy his residence there.'

Aurora sat quietly for a long moment, viewing the secretary in dismay. At last she stood up. Hildebrandt automatically did the same, gathering his infernal papers into a neat pile.

'I'll speak to my brother,' she said, acknowledging his slight bow with a nod of her head.

In the hall again, Hildebrandt plucked a linen handkerchief from his pocket and mopped his brow, wondering if it was time for lunch to be served.

With the secretary's departure, Aurora went to the window, letting her eye gaze on the restful scene that the gardens offered.

Incredible, she was thinking. She had never thought about money; one does not, when it's always available. They were wealthy, or had been. Now they were almost impoverished! Of course it wouldn't affect her personally too much. There was always Amelia. I can go and live with my sister in Hamburg, Aurora thought, if worst came to worst.

The door opened and Aurora turned, half expecting to see Hildebrandt return with yet another forgotten expenditure. But it was Philip's personal servant, Hans, who haltingly reported that his master was gravely ill. 'I wanted to summon the physician, milady,' he said earnestly, blinking watery blue eyes. 'But the count will not hear of it.'

'I'll come immediately,' said Aurora, already walking toward the door. There seemed no end of trouble this day, she thought irritably.

When she entered Philip's room, it needed only one look to see that he had the fever again. She relaxed somewhat, because these attacks were nothing new. He intermittently fell victim to bouts of fever and delirium. Aurora knew from experience that it would rage for up to eight hours and then would subside, leaving him shivering and cold. Occasionally he would be well only a day, then, unaccountably, the fever would return.

'There's no need for the physician,' Aurora stated calmly. 'I will care for him.'

'But he should be bled, milady,' Hans protested in a wavering voice, wringing his hands in consternation.

'Nonsense! It does more harm than good,' she answered curtly. 'I've seen him this way before. Bring some water,' she instructed, 'and get more sheets.'

Briskly she approached the bed. Philip thrashed about, his skin hot and dry. No doubt earlier he had been shivering with cold, she thought as she tried to remove his shirt. He had apparently dressed and then lain down again.

Hans returned with two servants in tow, each carrying a pail of water. He himself held an armful of linen sheets.

'Help me remove his clothes,' Aurora said, ignoring the man's shocked look. However, he promptly did as he was told.

'Now the sheets,' Aurora instructed calmly. 'Dampen them and wring them out.' Philip had begun to murmur incoherently, his voice occasionally rising shrilly. He waved his arms about and Aurora took care to avoid them.

The sheets ready, she said, 'Now wrap them carefully around his body. Keep his arms at his sides if you can.'

With doubtful eyes, Hans and the two servants followed her instructions. If the count doesn't die from this, Hans thought to himself, tucking the wet sheet firmly under his master's bed, it will only be due to God's intervention.

Aurora sat down. 'Now we wait,' she announced firmly.

Thirty minutes later she had the servants change the sheets. At intervals throughout the afternoon and evening, the procedure was repeated. At times Philip became violent. During those times, Aurora instructed the servants to hold him down, lest he injure himself.

By nine o'clock in the evening the fever began to abate and Philip finally calmed down.

'Remove the sheets,' she commanded. 'But keep them here. Replace the bedding and get more blankets.'

Philip smiled at her weakly. 'How long?' he asked, wetting his parched lips. Aurora brought him water and he drank thirstily.

'Since morning,' she responded, placing her hand on his brow. 'You should have called me immediately,' she admonished.

Philip didn't answer. He rolled to one side of the bed while the servants replaced the damp bedding, then to the other side while they completed this chore.

Aurora covered him with a blanket, then sat down with a sigh. 'Send for some food,' she said to Hans. 'But only a bit of broth for the count.'

Aurora knew from experience that there would be at least one more bout of the fever, probably within a few hours' time. She drew her chair closer to the bed. Philip was huddled beneath the blankets and the whole bed shook with his violent, convulsive movements.

'So cold,' he murmured. Aurora took another blanket from the pile on the floor and covered him.

The food came and Aurora and the servants ate at a common table, while Philip dozed fitfully. Afterward, Aurora returned to her vigil. Philip was quiet now, then he murmured, 'Dorothea.'

Aurora frowned. His voice mumbled on, interspersed with the single name. She looked at Hans. 'Remove the blankets and ready the sheets,' she said shortly.

Toward dawn the fever again broke. When Philip finally awoke to clarity, he smiled at the sleeping Aurora. She was curled up on the divan. By the side of the bed Hans dozed in what looked like a very uncomfortable position on a straight-backed chair. The other two servants were on the floor, asleep. Philip stretched and yawned and was conscious of hunger.

'Milord?' Hans was immediately on his feet.

'Bring me something to eat, you old devil,' Philip grinned.

Aurora sat up and winced, placing a hand on the small of her back. 'I don't think much of your sleeping arrangements,' she grumbled. Then she smiled. 'You're looking better.'

'A bit of food and I'll be as good as new,' Philip declared cheerfully.

'You'd best stay in bed for a day or two,' Aurora advised strongly. 'You remember what happened last time when you tried to rush it. I've no desire to spend another night listening to your rantings and ravings.'

'Did I carry on much?' Philip's rueful grin suggested that he wasn't overly concerned. Thank God, he thought, that I only have these attacks every two or three years. His whole body ached as if he had been beaten.

Aurora was about to reply when Hans returned with a tray, which he carefully deposited on Philip's lap. 'Milady?' he inquired, looking at her.

Aurora shook her head. 'Just coffee for me. I plan on going back to bed.' She took the proffered cup, then said: 'Please leave us. See to your own breakfast.' When they were alone, she faced her brother, her expression grave. 'You did nothing but call her name.' She took a sip of her coffee. 'Philip, this madness must stop. You cannot go on this way. It was one thing when only you and she knew about it. But now – ' she gestured in exasperation – 'the whole damn court knows of your infatuation.'

Philip looked uncomfortable, took a few bites of his food, then said simply, 'I will never leave her. There's no use in even discussing it.'

Slowly, as if she were speaking to a child, Aurora explained the situation as Hildebrandt had told it to her. When she finished, however, Philip repeated himself. 'I'll never leave her,' he said in a toneless voice that conveyed more conviction than a firm one might have.

Aurora made a sound of disgust at the declaration. He is bewitched, she thought, dismayed and angry at the same time. 'If you love her so much, then have you no care for what happens to her? People are already whispering,' she went on, willing him to understand the gravity of the situation. 'This sort of thing is always more difficult for the woman. People view a man's affairs with a tolerant eye. They show no such tolerance for a woman. Especially one who is married.'

'Her marriage is a farce.' Philip scraped the last of the eggs off his plate.

Aurora took a breath. 'It doesn't matter a damn whether it is or not!'

Philip pushed the tray aside. He didn't look at her. 'I want you to bring Dorothea here,' he said, wiping his mouth on the linen. 'I want to see her.'

'Are you mad?' She stared at him in genuine astonishment. But he now regarded her in an almost excited manner, as if he had just solved a problem that had been plaguing him.

'Don't you see?' Philip said quickly. 'I agree with you. I must no longer show her any attention in public. In fact, it would be best if we were to completely ignore each other. I shall not even dance with her.'

That, at least, makes sense, Aurora thought glumly. She drained her cup and put it down on the table. It was the first sensible thing Philip had said with regard to Dorothea since he had met her. 'I'm glad you feel that way,' she commented carefully. 'But bringing her here is, of course, out of the question.'

'But Dorothea and I must speak,' he insisted, sitting up straighter. 'We must plan. She will be coming to see you, at your invitation,' he pointed out.

'No one will believe that,' she retorted flatly.

'Nevertheless!' Philip flung the covers aside in an angry gesture and swung his legs over the side of the bed; his mouth was tight and grim as he viewed his sister. 'If you don't bring her here, I shall go to her.'

Quickly Aurora stood up and put her hands on his shoulders, gently pushing him back against the pillows. 'It might work once,' she allowed, alarmed by his attitude. Perhaps he still has a touch of fever, she thought frantically. 'But only once, Philip,' she stressed, searching his face. 'I must have your word.'

'Yes, yes,' he quickly agreed. They needed only an hour or so alone, he was thinking. That's all. It would be time enough to decide their future together. And as he lay back, Philip was determined that, regardless of the cost, they would have a future together. He would move heaven and earth and sell his soul to the devil, but they *would* have a future together.

Aurora watched her brother with worried eyes. Now, she could see, was not the time to continue with her discussion regarding their financial state, desperate as it might be. Tomorrow perhaps, when he felt better. Surely Philip couldn't have meant what he said. That attitude would soon leave him penniless.

Philip's determination was matched only by Dorothea's, which was no less resolute. George's persistent neglect had begun to rankle. Enough! she thought. There is only this one life, there is only here and now. She weighed her life as Princess of Hanover and as a woman loved by Philip Königsmark. She didn't need to ask herself which one she preferred. Philip's love beckoned, George's antipathy repulsed her.

And what business did Eleanor or Sofia have to interfere? They were old, they didn't even know the meaning of the word love. Few people apparently knew, Dorothea mused, gazing out of her window. They placed precedent on many other things: duty, religion, obligation, society. None of them mattered, she told herself firmly. Not really. There was only Philip and his love for her – and hers for him.

When the courier arrived with the message from Aurora Königsmark, Dorothea stared at it for a moment. It was properly worded, a short note requesting her presence for refreshments and conversation. The only odd thing about it was the date. It was for today; in fact, in less than an hour's time. She glanced at the courier whom she recognized as one of Philip's footmen. He was standing respectfully, awaiting an answer that he could bring back to his mistress.

'Thank Countess Königsmark,' Dorothea said, grateful for the steadiness in her voice. 'Inform her that I shall be pleased to join her for tea.'

Less than an hour, she thought in rising excitement as the servant withdrew. Less than an hour and she would see Philip. There was no doubt in her mind that he would be there. In an urgent voice, she called to Lenore to assist her in dressing. Lenore, who would have to accompany her, would have to go as she was. There would be no time for her to change.

'*Ma chère*,' Lenore murmured as she deftly pinned up Dorothea's hair. 'It may not be prudent to make this call.'

'I must go,' Dorothea insisted. 'You know as well as I that since Philip's return two weeks ago, we've not been able to speak privately. Not once.' She bit her lip in agitation. 'And every time he attends my court, the duchess appears.' She made a face. 'She has never before attended any of my levées, yet now she appears faithfully. And then engages Philip in constant conversation!'

Lenore finished, then regarded her mistress with thoughtful eyes. 'And you know why that is,' she observed quietly. 'That's why I'm against this visit. I don't believe you should go.'

Dorothea stood up impatiently. 'We are visiting Countess Königsmark.' She viewed her lady's crestfallen face, then impulsively threw her arms around her. 'You won't fail me, Lenore?' she pleaded earnestly. 'You will help me?'

'I will always help you, *ma chère*.' Lenore fought to repress her own misgivings. 'If this is a course you feel you must take, then I shall offer no obstacle.'

'I knew I could count on you,' Dorothea murmured softly, smiling.

Lenore sighed deeply as she followed Dorothea downstairs to the waiting carriage. Although they could see their destination from where they stood, walking was out of the question.

As she settled herself in the carriage, Lenore was aware of a cold feeling of apprehension that engulfed her despite the warm summer day. She didn't think that Dorothea was capable of a simple love affair. If it were no more than that, there would be no problem at all. The trouble was, in spite of being headstrong and willful, Dorothea was entirely without deceit. If she made the decision to commit herself to this man, then it would be totally. In her mind, her husband and everyone else would be relegated to second place in her thoughts; only Philip would command her loyalty. Nor would Dorothea be content with a brief fling. And that road led nowhere. It would be endless, with no turning back, once she took that first step.

And from the look on Dorothea's face, Lenore mused unhappily, she had already taken that step, at least in her mind.

So be it, Lenore thought in resignation, seeing that they had arrived at their destination. Her fate was irrevocably bound up with Dorothea's, and where the princess led, Lenore would follow.

Aurora Königsmark, properly dressed as always, came outside to greet them. For the benefit of any observing eye, she was highly visible as she welcomed them effusively, leading them inside to the modest reception room just off the main hall.

As Dorothea knew he would be, Philip was in the room. He looked pale. When he saw her, he got to his feet slowly and stood there, wavering.

'Please sit down,' Aurora said to her brother in a sharp voice. 'I'm certain that her Highness will understand if you remain seated.' She looked at Dorothea. 'My brother has been very ill,' she explained. 'He should not be up and about as yet.'

'Of course,' Dorothea said quickly. Taking a few steps forward, she put a hand to her lips. 'You do look ghastly,' she exclaimed, alarmed. 'What has happened?'

Philip sat down on the divan again, then gave his sister a meaningful look.

With only a slight tightening of her mouth, Aurora turned to Lenore. 'Perhaps you would care to join me in my own salon for refreshments?' she inquired pleasantly, relieved when Mademoiselle Knesebeck immediately agreed as though it were quite the accepted procedure to leave her mistress alone in a room with a man.

'Philip, I've been so worried,' Dorothea said to him when the door closed. She walked across the room and sat down beside him. 'I've not seen you for several days. If I'd know that you were ill ...'

He took her hand and raised it to his lips, kissing her palm and the inside of her wrist as he always did. Her arm tingled and the skin felt hot where his lips touched her. 'It's nothing serious,' he assured her. His arms went around her and they kissed, clinging to each other with rising emotion.

When their lips parted, Dorothea settled herself contentedly, her head on Philip's chest, thoroughly enjoying the feel of him, the security his arms afforded.

'My angel, we must talk,' Philip said at last, resting his chin on her soft and fragrant hair.

Dorothea sighed. She didn't want to talk, she didn't want to do anything but just sit there while Philip held her. But of course he was right, she reflected. They had far less than an hour left. After that she would have to leave. A call of this sort lasted from two to three in the afternoon; no more, no less.

'I can't tell you how I felt when I received your letter,' he said softly. 'I requested leave as soon as I read it.' He tilted her chin with his hand. 'Tell me,' he whispered. 'I want to hear you say it.'

'I love you, Philip,' she said simply. 'Now and for always, I love you.'

He gazed at her for a long moment, as if she were the most precious thing in the world. As indeed she was. 'We can no longer speak to each other in public, except in the most formal and casual manner.' He drew her closer. 'You do understand?' She nodded but made no comment. 'Nor must we dance together.' His brow creased in a severe frown. 'Although each time I see you with another man's arms about you, I shall suffer the most agonizing torments.'

'I shall not dance at all,' she declared with such fervor that he smiled. Then her eyes clouded. 'I suppose this also means that you won't be coming to my levées?'

'I dare not,' he affirmed. His arms tightened about her again. 'But I must see you,' he said in a fierce whisper. 'Tell me how. Can you come here?'

'No, no. That would be too dangerous.' Her brow furrowed in thought. 'I don't know,' she said at last. 'Let me speak to Lenore. Together we'll find a way.'

'Promise me,' he urged in the same tone, only partially convinced by her reassuring answer.

'When do you have to go back?' Her eyes searched his and Dorothea wondered frantically how she could live without him, even for a short time.

'In four days,' he replied, his thoughts paralleling her own.

'I'll find a way before then, I promise.'

A discreet tap on the door informed them that their brief time was at an end. Quickly they kissed and Dorothea got to her feet, smoothing her hair. 'Stay there, my dearest,' she whispered. Touching her lips lightly with her fingertips, she blew a kiss. Then, reluctantly, she joined Lenore and Aurora who were waiting in the hall.

'Thank you, Aurora,' Dorothea murmured. She kissed the older woman's cheek.

Aurora smiled sadly at Dorothea's flushed and happy face. She looked as if she had just gained the world instead of being on the brink of losing it all. 'You'd best go, Highness,' she said quietly. 'It's almost three o'clock.'

Dorothea nodded and together with Lenore walked out into the sun-filled day.

As Dorothea had known she would, Lenore found a way. At the far end of the corridor that led to her rooms was a small door that opened onto a narrow, little-used staircase. Only servants availed themselves of the ill-lit passage, which led outside to a small garden area that was enclosed with a high wall. The only access was a solid wooden gate that bolted from the inside. It would be a simple matter for Philip to walk across the garden area from his house to the gate. Lenore would wait for him, unbolt the gate, and lead him to Dorothea's apartments. It would of course have to be late at night when everyone was asleep. There were no guards in the corridors, so the procedure should be relatively safe.

Their plans made, Lenore wrote a letter to Aurora, who delivered it to Philip. On the night before he was to return to his regiment, he came to Dorothea.

'My angel,' he breathed. He reached for her and put his arms around her, unaware that Lenore had discreetly closed the door and returned to the adjoining room, where she would keep watch.

Dorothea swayed in his embrace, dizzy with the unexpected feeling of passion he aroused in her. Philip picked her up and carried her to the bed. There was a single candle burning on the bedside table. Dorothea leaned over, intending to snuff it out, but Philip put a hand on hers.

'No,' he whispered. 'I want to see you, to fill my eyes with your loveliness. There is nothing we must hide from each other.' Gently he removed her nightgown.

For a long time he gazed on the white perfection, letting his hands trace the pure curve of her breast to the narrow waist and swelling thighs. As his lips followed the same path, he felt her tremble. He murmured soft endearments against her warm flesh.

Time became meaningless. There was no time, there was only sensation. This was how it was meant to be, Dorothea realized ecstatically. She gave herself to Philip, gave herself completely, without reservation. All else was false. It was the other part of her life that was a sham, not her feeling for Philip. They spoke only in endearments, the language of lovers, so meaningless to everyone else; and, time and again, they reached for each other.

Too soon, Lenore tapped lightly on the door. Opening it just a crack, she whispered, '*Ma chère*, it will soon be light, perhaps in thirty minutes.' She closed the door again.

The candle was almost gutted. In the uncertain flickering light, Dorothea regarded Philip in dismay as he got up and hurriedly began to dress. Today was the day he would have to return to his regiment. Watching him, Dorothea felt as if this night had been her wedding night.

'Will there be fighting?' she asked him in a quavering voice. I will die, she thought, if anything happened to him.

'There is always fighting,' he replied quietly. Sitting on the bed, he picked up his soft leather boots, then put them on, fastening the buckle at the top.

Dorothea bit her lip. 'You will be careful?'

He turned and drew her to him again. The material of his jacket felt rough on her bare flesh, but she pressed tightly against him.

'Don't worry,' he murmured, stroking her hair. 'Now that I have your love, I am invincible. But even as I leave, my heart remains here, with you.'

Dorothea's eyes brimmed with love and sadness. 'That is a gift I shall never return.'

Philip kissed her, tender now, then stood up as Lenore's light tap on the door reminded him of approaching dawn. 'Write to me,' he whispered as he left. 'Please write to me each day.'

'I will. I promise,' she assured him, striving for a smile. But she couldn't prevent the tears that coursed down her satin cheeks when the door closed and he was gone.

Herrenhausen

February 1690

It was the last ball of carnival and Elizabeth, dressed in a Grecian-style gown that accented her full breasts and slim hips, danced gaily. But it was a forced emotion, she didn't feel any emotion save desire. It tortured her body in the most agonizing manner. As she gazed up at Philip, with whom she was dancing, her breath felt rapid and pulsing in her throat. She was all too aware of his muscular body, the nearness of it, the heat of it. It made her quite giddy.

Philip hadn't wanted to dance with her, she knew that. But she had insisted. Where Philip was concerned, she seemed to have no pride, no willpower. Just the sight of him made her legs weak and her breasts ache.

At least he seemed to have gotten over his foolish infatuation for the princess, Elizabeth told herself with satisfaction. Dorothea was here this evening but Philip hadn't danced with her, not once, and had only briefly spoken to her. But of course Dorothea couldn't hold a man like this, Elizabeth mused, filling her eyes with the splendor of him.

The music ended. As Philip bowed, she grasped his arm. 'No, let us walk in the orangery,' she urged, annoyed that her voice sounded so unsteady.

Seeing his hesitation, her nostrils grew white and pinched. 'I insist.' Her eyes glittered malevolently. 'Or do you wish to cause a scene?'

'And you are very good at making scenes, aren't you?' Philip noted quietly as they began to walk from the ballroom. He pressed his lips together in a straight hard line. He had no doubt but that Dorothea was observing his exit. He prayed that she would understand.

Toward the rear of the orangery, Elizabeth halted. Turning abruptly, she flung her arms about Philip's neck, pressing her body so tightly against his that he almost lost his balance. She murmured incoherently as she kissed his face, his neck, his lips. She thrust her hips against him in an insistent, demanding fashion. In spite of himself, Philip could feel his body respond to her animal-like abandon. Elizabeth realized it and clutched him even closer.

Then, in a quick motion, Philip grasped hold of her upper arms, tightening his grip in a painful manner. He pushed her away from him. Holding her at arm's length, Philip regarded the countess with cold eyes, amused by her obvious torment.

'You requested a dance, Countess Platen,' he said cruelly. 'And you have gotten your wish. I've nothing more to give you.'

Elizabeth stood there, breathing heavily, her eyes slightly wild. 'Please, Philip,' she muttered in agony. 'You're still angry with me for what I did that night on the balcony.' He made no answer. She went on in an almost eager voice, ignoring the contemptuous look in his eyes. 'I apologize for that. I swear I never meant you any harm. It was just a joke, a silly prank. No one was harmed by it.'

'Only because Prince George is not the fool you make him out to be,' Philip observed, still holding her in the painful grip.

'Please, Philip. Forgive me,' she cried out. 'It's only because I love you so much.' Her eyes searched his face, pleading, imploring his understanding. 'You loved me once.' She tried to move closer to him, but his grip remained firm and unrelenting as he held her at a distance.

'I have never loved you,' he stated flatly. 'And you're a fool to think otherwise.' With one part of his mind Philip knew that he was speaking in a dangerous manner. But he also knew that he wanted no part of Countess Platen.

At last he released her. Again freed to move Elizabeth again flung herself at him. Really annoyed now, Philip put his hands back on her arms, intending to push her away. Then a movement caught his eye and he turned.

'Dorothea,' he whispered. He took a sharp indrawn breath as he saw her standing there. She looked at him for only a moment, eyes wide, then spun about and ran out of the orangery.

Elizabeth reacted to the spoken name as if doused with a pail of ice water. The tone of Philip's voice was unmistakable, as was the look in his eyes. Now Elizabeth drew back of her own accord. Gone was the look of desire, of adoration, of love; in its place her black eyes glittered with an emotion too strong to term anger. She stood stiffly, her body rigid and taut. Then her hand suddenly flashed out and she struck Philip in the face. She opened her mouth as if to speak, but her rage was so great that she could manage no more than a strangled cry.

With a look only slightly less angry than her own, Philip turned and walked quickly back to the ballroom.

Hesitating briefly in the doorway, he headed for Dorothea, who was standing next to the duchess. George, as usual, was elsewhere with Melusine.

Determined, he walked toward them. 'Good evening, your Highness,' he said to the duchess, bowing.

'Ah, Colonel Königsmark,' Sofia responded graciously. 'I'm glad you were able to get leave in time to join us tonight.'

Right now Philip was disinclined to agree with that, but he replied amiably enough.

Listening to her mother-in-law exchanging pleasantries with Philip, Dorothea turned away, conscious that her face was flaming. She wished fervently that she was able to simply walk away, away from his nearness, away from the searching gaze and inquiring eyes that seemed to beg for understanding.

Oh, I understand, all right, Dorothea thought, furious. She understood that Philip's relationship with Elizabeth was just as she had first suspected. They had been lovers, they were still lovers. And he dared proclaim his love for her!

With a start she realized that Philip was addressing her, requesting a dance. Dorothea opened her mouth to refuse, but Philip had already extended his arm and was smiling, taking his leave of the duchess.

'How dare you speak to me?' she murmured in a low, furious tone as they joined the crowd of dancers.

He was silent for a moment, then said, 'What do you think you saw?'

'Think?' she replied in a scathing voice. 'I know exactly what I saw.'

'Tell me,' he said pleasantly.

Dorothea stared at him in astonishment. 'I'm in no mood for games,' she replied coldly, averting her face.

He watched her for a moment, then smiled. 'I did not seek out the countess. Nor do I wish her company.'

Dorothea turned to him again, eyes blazing. 'If she carried you off by force, I was not aware of it.' Her tone was caustic and she was startled by his laugh. 'I see nothing amusing,' she retorted, angry again.

'My angel,' he murmured, almost pleased by her display of jealousy. 'No, don't look away from me,' he said firmly. When she again met his eyes, he continued. 'If I had refused to accompany her, she promised to cause a scene.'

Dorothea was not mollified. 'You were holding her in your arms,' she said, accusing, glaring at him.

He raised a brow. 'Was I?' He seemed to consider that statement.

Dorothea regarded him, doubtful for the first time. Then, glancing over Philip's shoulder, she saw Elizabeth standing in the doorway. Her face, beneath the artificially contrived Grecian coiffure, was a mask of icy anger as she stared at them. Suddenly Dorothea felt a chill of apprehension so strong that she trembled with the force of it.

Philip, always sensitive to her every nuance, tightened his arm in a protective manner, his face reflecting immediate concern. 'What is it?' he said quietly, not turning. She didn't speak and as he danced, Philip turned Dorothea so that he could see what she had been looking at. Without expression he briefly observed Elizabeth, then looked away again. He cursed himself for a fool. He shouldn't have approached Dorothea, much less danced with her. Never, never, must he make the same mistake again, regardless of the provocation.

'Do you believe me now?' he murmured. With a short,

ashamed glance, Dorothea nodded. 'Never doubt my love for you,' he said urgently, aware that the dance was almost over. He regarded her intently. 'May I come to you tonight?'

'Yes,' she whispered, amazed at the turbulent feeling within her.

Hanover

September 1690

Duchess Sofia eyed her daughter-in-law with a slight frown. What was the matter with the girl? she wondered irritably. For weeks now Dorothea had been walking about as if she were in a trance. She barely ever went out, receiving visitors only when she couldn't avoid doing so. And one had to address her directly to get even so much as a word out of her. Only Aurora Königsmark seemed to spark any interest, any animation in Dorothea of late.

Sofia nodded and offered a polite response to the envoy seated to her right, meanwhile continuing with her own thoughts.

That was another thing she wasn't too happy about, Sofia reflected. Dorothea seemed to spend an inordinate amount of time in the company of Countess Königsmark. Actually it wasn't the countess per se as much as her brother that Sofia found so objectionable. Thank heavens that situation had apparently dissolved. It took but a glance to see that Königsmark had been quite infatuated with the princess there for a while. But he obviously had come to his senses and, of late, had begun to act in a proper manner.

Again Sofia observed Dorothea. Perhaps the girl was ill, she mused, watching the princess toy with her food. She certainly did look peaked. Annoyed, Sofia saw the Dowager Duchess of Friesland try to engage Dorothea in conversation. The princess merely smiled wanly and made no effort to respond.

At last the evening meal ended. Sofia rose.

In the hallway, Dorothea approached her. 'Madame,'

she said. 'may I be excused this evening? I have a terrible headache.'

Sofia's thin brows drew together. 'This is the third time this week,' she observed sternly. 'Perhaps we should summon the physician.'

'Oh, no,' Dorothea protested quickly. 'I assure you, an evening's rest is all that I require.'

Sofia hesitated, but then said, 'Very well, run along. I'll look in on you later this evening.'

Gravely Dorothea nodded and, with Lenore by her side, returned to her rooms. Once there she immediately sat down at her writing table. From her bodice she drew forth Philip's latest letter, received only that morning, and, though she knew it by heart, read it again.

'He says,' she remarked to Lenore, 'that his sister has been urging him to return to Sweden.'

Sitting herself down in a comfortable chair, Lenore looked surprised. 'Whatever for?' she asked.

Dorothea shrugged slightly. 'It has something to do with his estates there. He doesn't make it entirely clear.' She flashed Lenore a bright smile. 'But he refuses! He will, he says, go nowhere except Hanover.' Dorothea read in silence for a while. Then she picked up the quill. After dipping it into the inkpot, she began to write her daily letter.

She was still writing an hour later when the door opened and Sofia entered.

With remarkable calmness Dorothea covered the written pages with a blank sheet of paper, then faced her mother-in-law.

'Dorothea! I had expected to see you in bed.' Sofia's face was full of disapproval as she took in the scene.

'I'm about to retire right now,' Dorothea replied serenely. 'I thought I would answer George's letter before I did.' And this, strictly speaking, was the truth.

Sofia's expression softened a bit. 'Of course.' She nodded. 'I've been speaking with the duke,' she went on. 'We are both concerned for your welfare. I think that a visit to your parents would be beneficial. A change is always good, now and then. The Duchess of Friesland will be leaving for Celle tomorrow. Arrangements will be made for you to accompany her.'

Dorothea paled, but the duchess's expression left no room for argument. She offered a weak smile and didn't have to pretend that she felt ill. She did.

'Now you get your rest,' the duchess said briskly as she left.

'What am I to do?' Dorothea looked at Lenore, upset. 'His letters will come here. And I will be at Celle!'

Lenore nodded at the unfinished letter. 'Tell him that you will be at Celle for a few weeks. With luck, he'll receive word in two days. Only two letters will come here. Since they're addressed to me it should cause no undue comment.'

Dorothea sighed and again picked up the quill.

The following day, in the gently rocking carriage, Dorothea only half listened to the dowager duchess's irritating prattle, leaving it to Lenore to make conversation.

She was home for a bare two weeks when Count Philip Königsmark presented himself at the Court of Celle.

Celle

October 1690

'Well, you must do *something,*' Wilhelm declared as he paced up and down the bedchamber. He paused before the brightly burning fire in the grate. The room was chilly. Even the heavy hangings that obscured the windows and most of the stone walls did little to prevent the cold October night air from creeping inside.

Seated at her dressing table with a flannel robe over her nightgown, Eleanor brushed her hair. She regarded her husband's reflection in the mirror with thoughtful eyes. 'I'd be grateful for any suggestions,' she commented tartly. 'I can hardly refuse hospitality to Count Königsmark and thereby precipitate the very scandal that we're both trying to avoid.'

'He has his nerve,' Wilhelm complained in a terse voice. He turned, standing with his back to the fire. 'Has he no sense of proprieties? Does he not realize how his actions reflect on our daughter?' His jaw thrust out as he viewed his wife, a sign of rising anger.

'I don't believe that Dorothea knew he was coming,' Eleanor said quickly, laying down the brush. 'In fact, I'm certain that she knew nothing. I saw the look on her face when he arrived.'

'So did everyone else,' her husband remarked dryly. Then his face flushed a dull crimson. 'I will not have it. Do you hear me, Eleanor? I will not have it!' He began to pace again. 'She must learn how to conduct herself properly. She is a disgrace to the House of Celle. What will Ernst think of all this?' he lamented.

Eleanor sighed, frankly unconcerned with Ernst or his

feelings. Dorothea was the only one who mattered. Nothing had happened yet, Eleanor was certain of it, if for no other reason than the foolish way Königsmark was acting.

'I'll speak to her,' she said at last, seeing her husband's angry glare. 'And I'll make arrangements for her return to Hanover tomorrow morning.'

'Yes, yes,' Wilhelm agreed, greatly relieved that his wife was going to act. 'I myself would speak to her – ' he gestured vaguely – 'but I don't think that would be appropriate.' He looked at Eleanor again, concern returning. 'When will you do it?'

Eleanor got to her feet in a graceful movement. 'Right now,' she replied, walking from the room.

A few minutes later she faced Dorothea, suddenly uncertain. The subject was, to say the least, a delicate one. But then she took a breath, resolve strengthening. Delicate or not, this situation simply could not continue. As it was, tongues were busily wagging. Even the dowager duchess had voiced a few thinly veiled innuendos as to the sudden appearance of Count Königsmark at just the time that Dorothea was visiting.

'I came to say good night,' Eleanor began. 'And to have a few words with you.' She smiled tentatively at Dorothea, who was already in bed, an open book on her lap.

'Come in, Mama.' Dorothea put the book on the bedside table.

After crossing the room, Eleanor sat down on the bed. She reached out a hand and smoothed Dorothea's silky hair. 'You know what I want to speak about, don't you?' she inquired, sadly noting her daughter's suddenly wary expression. Dorothea was twenty-four, she realized with a bit of surprise. No longer a girl. Why, Eleanor wondered, did she persist in thinking of Dorothea in those terms? 'Once before we have discussed Philip Königsmark,' Eleanor persisted in the face of her daughter's silence. 'But I can see that you didn't heed my advice.'

'I had no idea that he was coming,' Dorothea said truthfully.

Eleanor nodded. 'I believe you. Nevertheless, he is here. And I can hardly ask him to leave, can I?' She didn't wait for a response. 'But you are another matter. You must return to Hanover in the morning. I will accompany you.'

Dorothea sighed. Why was it that everyone sought to run her life? Only she knew what was best for herself. And it was the one thing she couldn't have. A clandestine affair with Philip was not what she truly wanted. And from this standpoint Dorothea sympathized with her mother's obvious distress. Yet living without Philip was unthinkable.

'You must ask him,' Eleanor was saying. 'No, you must *tell* him that he must no longer bother you. He must no longer even speak to you,' she concluded strongly.

'That would be difficult, Mama,' Dorothea pointed out quickly. 'He is a member of the court.'

Eleanor's face hardened. 'If he's not careful,' she warned sharply, 'he will be welcome at neither Hanover nor Celle. Do you understand me, Dorothea? He will be sent away. Then you will *never* see him again.' She noted Dorothea's pale face, but pursued relentlessly. 'You have it within your power to stop this now, before things get out of hand.' Her voice grew gentler. 'You love him, don't you.' Eleanor didn't feel it necessary to even phrase that as a question.

Dorothea viewed her folded hands. 'Yes.' The reply was no more than the merest whisper.

'I thought so.' Eleanor patted Dorothea's hand in a consoling manner. 'Believe me, it will pass. It's no more than a passing fancy.' Her voice grew quiet. 'And listen to me, Dorothea,' she went on with urgency. 'If you fall into an affair with this man, love or no, you will live with the constant fear of becoming pregnant. Have you any idea what would happen in such an event?' Even she shuddered at the prospect. Wilhelm would never, never forgive his daughter for such a disgrace. And Eleanor was perfectly aware, for Dorothea had told her, that George had been absent from her bed since their daughter was born. 'You would be ostracized,' Eleanor continued, answering her own question. 'Your father would never forgive you.'

'Would you, Mama?' Dorothea questioned in a small voice.

Eleanor threw her arms around her daughter and held her tight. 'I'll always love you, my darling. There's nothing I wouldn't forgive you.' Tears welled up and spilled down her cheeks. 'But even I couldn't help you if such a thing happened. That's why you must stop it now, while there is still time.'

Dorothea bowed her head and her own tears fell on the satin coverlet. *While there is still time,* she thought wryly. 'Very well, Mama,' she said at last. 'I'll try.'

'Good,' Eleanor breathed in relief. 'You must speak to him in the morning before we return to Hanover.'

After her mother left, Dorothea lay on her bed wide awake. She had agreed to send Philip away. But when the time came, could she do that? About one thing her mother had been absolutely right. The danger of pregnancy was a recurring nightmare. Not that she would mind all that much. The worst George could do would be to divorce her, then she would be free to marry Philip.

But her children, Dorothea reflected somberly. She'd have to give them up. *That* was not a step to be taken lightly. She loved them both: her son, and her little adorable daughter.

No, Dorothea decided. She couldn't give them up. But Philip ... Oh, God. Dorothea turned and buried her head in the pillow, weeping.

The next morning, pale but composed, Dorothea informed Philip that she had no wish to see him again.

He stared at her, white-faced. 'You can't mean that,' he said, and she winced at the anguish in his voice.

'It has to be this way,' she said doggedly. 'Too many people are aware of our feelings. We can no longer hide them.' Her hands were trembling and she clasped them together tightly. What was she saying? her mind cried out. Never see Philip again ...

'I don't want to hide my feelings,' Philip objected in a ragged whisper. He took a step closer. 'Can you send me away?' He glared at her with fierce eyes. But even in his agitated state he was aware of her loveliness, of the vision she presented dressed in yellow silk with diamonds threaded through her hair. 'Can you say that you no longer love me?' he demanded in a broken voice.

'I'll always love you, Philip,' she said, sighing deeply. She tried not to look at him. 'But yes, I'm sending you away. If I learn at any time that you are in court, I will stay in my apartments.'

He took a step back, his eyes distant and bleak. 'Very well,' he said stiffly. 'When I return to camp I'll request a transfer to Morea.'

Dorothea's eyes widened and her color blanched. The most intense fighting, the heaviest casualties, occurred in Morea.

Philip picked up his hat and walked toward the door, where he turned and faced her with a cynical look that barely concealed his hurt. 'Perhaps when I am dead, you might remember me in the years to come.' His jaw tightened. 'Unless the memory of me fades completely with time,' he added bitterly.

The sarcasm in his voice cut right through her and it took a moment before she could speak. 'Philip! You're not actually going to do this thing?' She was fearful, utterly dismayed.

'I've every intention,' he stated with cold finality.

'Wait!' she called out. He turned at the door. In a moment she was in his arms. 'How can you torture me so?' She wept, clinging to him.

Philip put his hands on her shoulders. 'I will give up everything for you,' he said in quiet measured tones. 'Even my life. But I will never give you up.'

Later that morning, Eleanor sat facing Dorothea and Lenore in the carriage as they made their way back to Hanover. Her own two ladies were riding in her personal carriage, which trailed some distance behind. She would make the return trip with them in the morning. Things have gone much better than I'd hoped, Eleanor thought, with no little relief. She had half expected that wretched man to follow them. Thankfully, Philip had left first, announcing that it was his intention to return to his regiment.

Dorothea looked pale and lines of weariness etched her fine features. But that was normal enough, Eleanor reflected, with no little sympathy. She, of all people, knew what it was to love a man so desperately as to give up everything for him, even damage her own name and threaten her child's future. But neither she nor Wilhelm had been married at the time of their affair. That, Eleanor reasoned, made all the difference in the world.

Besides, Eleanor mused, half dozing with the rocking of the carriage, she wanted better for Dorothea than she had had. There was the distinct possibility that Dorothea would one day be electress. The emperor had at last reviewed the petition, and with favorable eyes. A few of the others, notably Anthony Ulric, were posing problems, dissenting, as it were, to the swelling of their ranks. But the problems were not insurmountable.

She had done the right thing, Eleanor finally concluded. Thank God she had been in time to nip it in the bud. However, just to be on the safe side, it would be wise if she were to have a frank discussion with her sister-in-law, Eleanor decided. Sofia would be the one who would be close enough to keep an eye on things when Königsmark returned to court.

Eleanor's complacency lasted until they neared Hanover. There, to her dismay, she saw the bulk of the army camped – as they always were when not actually out in the field – on the outskirts of town. Was that wretched man's regiment among them? she wondered uneasily.

The carriage at last rolled across the drawbridge and halted before Leine. Cramped and weary, all three women got out. When they entered, Dorothea tersely announced her intention of going to her rooms to rest.

Sofia, who had come into the hallway, regarded Eleanor inquiringly. As far as she could see, Dorothea looked no better than when she had left. But then, breeding will tell, Sofia thought with resignation. With a mother like Eleanor, little more could be expected from Dorothea. Poor George, she thought, with an unaccustomed surge of maternalism for her eldest son. He really does have a cross to bear.

'Would you like to rest before dinner?' Sofia offered graciously, looking at Eleanor. But Eleanor shook her head.

'I'd like to speak with you in private,' she replied in a strained voice.

'Of course. We can use the study. Ernst is presently out.' She led the way. 'Would you like some wine?' she asked, noticing Eleanor's unusually agitated state. Normally the Duchess of Celle was serene, composed. Sometimes irritatingly so. Today even her lips were trembling. Sofia noticed that she repeatedly compressed them in an effort to maintain her composure.

'I would indeed.'

Sofia walked to the table by the tall narrow window. 'Well, then, we must serve ourselves if you wish privacy.' She filled two glasses with red port. Returning to where Eleanor had sat down, Sofia handed her a glass. She put her own glass on the low table and sat down opposite the Duchess of Celle. 'You seem upset,' Sofia commented. 'I hope the trip went without mishap. I remember once, some years ago, we were on our way to Wiesbaden. Right in the middle of the journey, we lost a wheel. I must say, I was bruised for weeks afterward.'

Eleanor finished her wine in a long swallow. 'The trip was uneventful, thank you,' she responded. 'We did not lose a wheel.'

'I'm glad to hear that,' Sofia murmured, still bemused by her sister-in-law's manner. Even the wine didn't seem to calm her down.

Now that she was here, Eleanor was uncertain as to how to proceed. How did one tell the mother-in-law of one's married daughter to keep watch so that that daughter would not take a lover? It was quite impossible really, when one thought of it.

'Did you wish to speak of Dorothea?' the duchess prompted. 'I've been aware that she's been upset of late. It was the reason I sent her home to Celle. I thought perhaps that you might be able to help.'

'Dorothea is fine,' Eleanor said quickly. 'Actually the problem is not with Dorothea at all.' She regarded the duchess with level, determined eyes.

Sofia raised her brows. 'Then what *is* the problem?' she inquired.

Eleanor frowned. 'The problem, madame, is Count Philip Königsmark. He's making quite a nuisance of himself. Were you aware that he presented himself at Celle a few days ago?'

Sofia wasn't. In spite of herself, she paled. That really was too much. Then she remembered the dowager duchess. Good heavens, the tale would be on every tongue throughout the empire! Philip Königsmark was well known; so was his reputation. 'This is dreadful,' she murmured. Extending a hand, she reached for her untouched wine. Pretence fell away as the two women faced each other with a mutual problem. 'Have you any suggestions as to how we should handle this?' she asked at last.

With those words, Eleanor relaxed, aware that in one sentence her sister-in-law had admitted to a problem and had also admitted that she knew what the problem was.

'I've had a long talk with Dorothea,' Eleanor advised. 'And she has spoken to Count Königsmark. She told him in no uncertain terms that she no longer cared for his attentions.'

Sofia looked pleased, but inwardly she admitted to some reservations. 'Has he agreed?' she asked tentatively, leaning forward.

Eleanor looked angry. 'I certainly hope so,' she declared. 'He left soon after to rejoin his regiment.' She remembered the troops camped just outside of town. 'Have you any idea where they are?' she asked, then listened in dismay as Sofia confirmed her worst fears. Königsmark's regiment *was* stationed right outside of town. That meant he would join the court each evening. 'Perhaps,' Eleanor said carefuly, 'it would be wise if you were to ...' She faltered, but Sofia nodded briskly.

'Have no fear,' she said. 'I'll see to it that Count Königsmark stays away from my son's wife. Rest assured, it will be to the benefit of all concerned that he keep his distance.' She observed Eleanor with satisfaction. For once she had acted promptly and with just the right degree of concern. There was, of course, no real danger of anything scandalous occurring, but rumors could be just as damaging and must be halted immediately.

'I want you to know that nothing has happened,' Eleanor stated firmly. 'It's important that you realize this.'

Sofia appeared genuinely shocked. 'I never thought

otherwise,' she said truthfully. Getting to her feet, she smiled, almost friendly. 'Would you like to see our grandchildren? Sophie-Dorothea has grown in these past months.' She laughed fondly. 'That little girl will be a true beauty when she is grown.'

Eleanor, too, smiled. In expectation. She dearly loved the children. 'I would like nothing better, Sofia. Let us visit them together.'

Hanover

November 1690

The night was still and calm and cold. Snow crunched beneath his boots as Philip walked with determined steps in the direction of the barracks that housed Field Marshal Podewils. As he had hoped, his superior was alone, seated at his desk, poring intently over the maps spread out before him. A lamp close by his elbow shone on the small bald spot on the top of his head. Of medium height, Podewils had the thick compact body of a soldier. He looked up briefly as Philip entered.

'Ah, come in, Colonel.' His gaze returned to the maps and he tapped one of them. 'Namur,' he said in a tone of conviction. 'If we can liberate Namur, we'll give the Sun King a run for his money. Louis has had his way for too long now.' Leaning back in his chair he regarded Philip curiously. 'What brings you here at this hour, Colonel?'

'I came to request leave to enter town, sir,' Philip replied, watching the older man with hopeful eyes. He had to see her. That was all there was to it.

Podewils frowned, thinking of the letter of complaint he had received just hours ago from the Duke of Hanover. It seemed Königsmark was smitten with the princess, had actually followed her to Celle. 'You have only returned this morning,' he pointed out mildly.

'I realize that,' Königsmark said quickly. 'But we're not doing anything now. Just waiting.' Actually Philip's request was neither unusual nor out of line. Officers always had leave each night when they were camped outside of Hanover.

Podewils cleared his throat. Personally, he liked

Königsmark. He was a brave man, a more than capable officer, a leader of men. Podewils felt he could do with more like him. Time and again Philip had proven his valor in the field. 'Where did you want to go?' he asked at last in a cautious voice.

Philip stared at him. So, he knew too. Philip went cold. It seemed as if everyone knew how he felt. Philip strove for control. He grinned in his best imitation of his old rakish smile. 'I had planned to go to Monplaisir,' he answered easily, then winked. 'I don't need to tell you the appeal of Monplaisir. I feel lucky.' He patted his jacket pocket. 'And, just having been paid, I think I can double my wages. As to the other attractions,' he continued lightly, with a wave of his hand, 'I don't think I need relate them to you.'

Podewils relaxed visibly. The duke had said that he would not be at all happy if Königsmark went to Leine. He had said nothing about Monplaisir, where most of the officers went anyway. 'Very well, Colonel,' he said, smiling. 'But be back in time for roll call.'

As Philip left, Podewils returned his attention to his maps, which were, after all, much more important than all this foolishness.

Masking his relief, Philip had his horse saddled. A short time later he was in his own residence. Aurora was dressed and ready to go to Leine. There was a new play, she explained, eager to be off.

'Aurora, wait!' Philip grasped hold of her arm. 'You must get word to the princess.'

She frowned. 'Philip.'

He tightened his hold, not caring if he was hurting her. 'You must do it. Tell her to have Lenore unbolt the gate tonight. Two o'clock.'

Aurora hesitated, and his grip tightened until she cried out. 'All right!' she said heatedly. When he released her, she rubbed her arm. 'If you insist on making a fool of yourself, there is nothing I can do about it.'

'Please, Aurora.' His tone became conciliatory. 'You, of all people, know how I feel. They want to separate us, but I will not allow it. I *cannot* allow it.'

'Prince George is home,' Aurora observed, watching

him closely. 'What if he decides to visit his wife for the evening?'

Philip's face flushed a dull red. 'I want no man to touch her,' he declared in a strong voice. 'Dorothea is mine!'

God, he *is* going mad, Aurora thought in amazement. He didn't even want her own husband to sleep with her. Aurora shook her head, but agreed. If she refused, Philip might do something foolish.

A few moments later Aurora went outside to the waiting carriage, never noticing the man who hid in the shadows of the building.

The man watched her go, but didn't follow. Elizabeth Platen's instructions had been firm. It was the whereabouts of Count Königsmark that interested her.

With a slight yawn, the man watched as Aurora drove away, then he settled down to await the count's next move.

When Aurora arrived at Leine the play had already begun, and it was necessary for her to sit through it until the card games followed. It probably is a very good comedy, she thought wryly, watching the actors cavort and mime through their performance. However, she was in no mood to laugh. Occasionally she glanced over to where the princess was seated, the duchess on one side of her and George on the other. Apparently Dorothea, too, found nothing amusing in the performance. Not once did those charming dimples appear.

Aurora had a moment's panic when, after the play, it appeared that Dorothea would retire. But a few words, spoken in a whisper by the duchess, seemed to change her mind.

In the large reception hall, which served a dual purpose, for dancing and card parties, Melusine von Schulenburg was very much in evidence. Aurora had heard that she had given birth to another daughter. Even so, she was looking particularly radiant this evening in emerald-green satin, which greatly complemented her golden hair. Aurora noticed with some amusement that George immediately joined Melusine's table. From the looks they exchanged, one would have thought they were strangers who only just met this evening.

And what a web we weave, Aurora thought cynically as she made her way to where Dorothea was standing. Unfortunately, the duchess was by her side. Aurora waited long minutes, cursing her brother for ruining her evening. At last Dorothea walked to the long table, contemplating the many varied dishes it held. Casually Aurora approached her.

'Philip wants to see you,' she said in a whisper. She motioned for a servant to place a piece of hot apple strudel on her plate. The aroma wafted about and she sniffed appreciatively. It was done to perfection, the crust flaky brown and crisp.

'When?' Dorothea murmured, not looking at her.

Aurora felt a start of surprise at the ready acceptance. The princess was every bit a fool, as was her brother, Aurora decided in exasperation. 'At two. He said to instruct Lenore to open the gate.'

Dorothea nodded once and was gone. Aurora didn't look in the direction of the departing princess. Now perhaps she could enjoy herself for what was left of the evening.

Monplaisir

May 1691

Elizabeth Platen was not fooled. True, she had almost believed it in the beginning. And most likely everyone believed it, or pretended to believe it. However Philip had not been as cautious as he had thought himself to be. At first, Elizabeth had been mystified as to how the assignations came about; now she knew that too. It had taken her quite a few months to piece it all together, but the wait had been worth it.

Oh, they were clever enough, she mused on this May evening. All through carnival they had hardly spoken to each other except in the presence of others, and then only in the most formal manner. Not once, to her knowledge, had they danced together.

Elizabeth had offered Philip another chance to resume their relationship, which he had haughtily rejected, and to reconsider marrying Charlotte, an offer he had politely declined.

The rejections stung, causing her anger to smolder constantly beneath a bright and brittle smile. Oh, he would pay; they would both pay. But for now it amused her to watch their little game of love, knowing that she was the only one who knew.

Informing Ernst at this time would have little effect, Elizabeth reasoned. Philip might or might not be sent away, and the little chit would probably get off scot-free. No, what she needed was proof, visible proof, or to actually catch them *in flagrante delicto*.

That would be difficult, for the simple reason that they met so infrequently. Philip was gone for weeks at a time.

And when he was in Hanover, they didn't meet every night. Indeed, when Prince George was home, not at all. Elizabeth doubted that the lovers had met more than twice in the past six months.

The key to the whole thing was Aurora. Elizabeth smiled in a most mirthless fashion as she thought of the beautiful Aurora Königsmark. There was more than one reason why she would like to rid the court of Philip's sister. Not only was that lovely face annoying to have around, but with her departure the lovers might become less cautious.

Now Elizabeth glanced at the little clock on the ebony desk in her sitting room. Ernst was late; for him, unusual. The physical side of their liaison had, with the years, become intermittent, a situation that didn't unduly trouble Elizabeth because he still sought her company and her advice. Perhaps he wouldn't come tonight, in which case she might as well retire.

Elizabeth was still standing there, undecided, when the duke entered, his expression at once angry and distraught.

'Ernst, what's wrong?' Elizabeth asked quickly, alarmed by the look of him.

'Maximilian,' he sputtered furiously. 'That fool has been plotting for months! Right in my own house, my own son seeks to undo everything I've tried to accomplish.'

'Sit down,' Elizabeth said quietly. With efficient movements she poured him a large brandy. He did as he was told, seating himself in a large deep-cushioned chair that faced the stone fireplace. The flames had died down and bright-red embers glowed among the white powdery ash. He stared moodily, muttering to himself, and received the proffered glass almost absentmindedly. 'Now, tell me what has happened,' Elizabeth said, seating herself in a nearby chair.

'They must have been at it for months,' he muttered in a bitter voice.

'They?' she prompted, leaning forward.

He glared at her. 'Maximilian has been in communication with two of the electors themselves, or at least their ministers. And Ulric, of course.' The bitterness increased. He downed his drink in a long swallow and put the glass on the table beside his chair.

Elizabeth's mind worked rapidly. Baron Bernst was Ulric's minister. That involvement didn't surprise her. Ulric had been against the electorate from the start. 'Who else?'

'The minister of Brandenburg.'

Count Dankelmann, Elizabeth mused, leaning back again. That *was* a surprise. Charlotte was, of course, electress of that small realm.

As if reading the direction of her thought, Ernst nodded. 'It was thanks to Charlotte that I learned of all this. My daughter assures me that her husband was unaware of his minister's involvement,' he explained. 'If it hadn't been for her timely letter ...' He gestured, then his expression turned angry again. 'And here ...' He slapped the arm of the chair with the flat of his palm. 'Here, I breed traitors as well. Count Moltke, my own Master of the Hunt, has openly sided with Maximilian.'

Elizabeth pursed her lips in a thoughtful manner. 'This time, Ernst,' she advised, 'you must act. And in a very definite way. The emperor must see that you are strong. He must know that you are worthy of the electorate. What has happened here is a simple case of treason, something no ruler can ignore.'

'I agree,' Ernst said in a quieter tone. He sighed deeply. 'But I can hardly place my own son on trial. The penalty, if guilty, is death.'

Elizabeth contemplated that a moment. 'So far as the ministers of Wolfenbüttel and Brandenburg are concerned, they are, of course, beyond your jurisdiction. But I suggest a strong letter of reprimand be sent. As for Maximilian, he should be placed under arrest. At least until such time as he agrees, in writing, to honor your wishes.' She shook her head. 'I do not agree that Maximilian cannot stand trial. As for Moltke ...' She smiled coldly. 'I daresay that he is not beyond reach. As an example, his fate might be the best lesson to all of them. Provided, of course, that his fate is execution.'

Ernst fell silent for a time, mulling her words. And then at last he nodded his agreement.

'Franz is at this very time in Vienna,' Elizabeth continued briskly. 'Things must be going well, or we would have heard by now. I suggest you also write to your son-in-law and enlist his active support for the ninth electorate. If Charlotte is correct, then a letter from the Elector of Brandenburg to the emperor may be the final argument in your favor.'

Ernst felt himself relaxing again. He always felt better when he discussed his problems with Elizabeth. Smiling, he reached out a hand, and she immediately rose and came to sit on the floor by his feet. She took hold of the outstretched hand and rested her head on his knee. They sat in apparent quiet contentment, as though they had been married for many years.

'I believe there is one other matter you must take care of, Ernst,' she murmured after a while.

He looked down at her. The firelight played about her hair, bronzing her skin. He thought she looked quite lovely. 'And what might that be, my dear?'

Elizabeth sighed, almost sadly. 'I hesitate to add to your problems. And yet now, of all times, there must be no hint of scandal.'

Alarmed by her tone, Ernst released her hand and sat up straighter. 'What are you talking about?' he demanded. 'If there is something amiss, then you must tell me.'

She nodded solemnly. 'Of course, you're right.' She still sat on the floor and now looked up at him with a serious, concerned expression. 'Do you recall some months ago when there were some rumors involving Count Königsmark and the princess?' She watched him carefully.

Ernst scowled. My God, *that* isn't going to start again, is it? he thought, irritated.

'We both know that it was a tempest in a teapot,' she said quickly, patting his hand. 'Still, this sort of thing cannot be allowed to surface again, especially now. It's not the princess I'm thinking of. And certainly not Königsmark. It's Prince George. There can be no cloud of suspicion where his heirs are concerned.'

Ernst looked aghast, paling at even the suggestion. 'That's absurd,' he said in a faint voice.

Hastily she agreed with him. 'But you know how

tongues wag,' she pointed out. 'It's only proper that you keep abreast of things.'

'Well, what *is* going on?' he demanded sharply, annoyed with her digression.

Elizabeth moistened her lips. 'It's rumored that Königsmark plans to build a larger house on the outskirts of town. *He* says it's for his sister Aurora to live in.' She gestured and shrugged delicately. 'The gossipmongers say that the house is for the purpose of clandestine meetings between the count and his ... paramour.'

'And who is this paramour?' Ernst's voice was cold. There was a dangerous look to his expression.

Elizabeth shrugged again. 'That's the reason why I felt I must bring it to your attention. Supposedly, it is the princess. You and I know that this is pure rubbish,' she added quickly. 'But I believe that we should put a stop to the rumors right away.'

The scowl deepened. 'Damn Königsmark,' Ernst muttered. Naturally it was all rumor, nothing more, he was thinking. 'Yet I hesitate to dismiss him,' he said slowly, rubbing his chin. 'His conduct has been exemplary these past months. And as a soldier ...' He shook his head. 'Podewils sings his praises, insisting that he is the best. But if this sort of thing is being bandied about ...'

'There is no need to dismiss Königsmark.' Elizabeth got to her feet, still watching the duke. 'Aurora Königsmark has the dubious distinction of being named as the go-between for her brother and his lady of the moment. If she were requested to return to Hamburg, I'm certain the whole mess would blow over. Königsmark would have no reason for another house, and Aurora would be removed from any proximity to the princess.' Elizabeth checked a smile. Ernst could not possibly realize that she had presented him with more fact than rumor. Only the tale of the new house was fabricated and pure rumor – which she herself had begun.

Ernst sighed deeply and slapped his knee before he got to his feet. My children are more problems than blessings, he thought irascibly. But one thing Elizabeth was right about. There could be no more rumors that involved George, however indirectly. And any that involved his wife involved him. There was no immediate danger. George was in Venice; Königsmark, somewhere along the Rhine.

The frown returned, and anger with it. 'It's time and more that I set my house to rights,' he muttered. He gave Elizabeth a glance as he headed toward the door. 'As you know, I'm leaving in the morning for Venice. George is there. He'll be returning with me. When I get back, not only will Countess Königsmark be requested to leave,' he stated firmly, 'but I shall see to it that George has a talk with his wife. This will be laid to rest, once and for all!'

'Excellent,' Elizabeth agreed as the duke left. Then, with a sigh of deep satisfaction, she poured herself a glass of wine.

Hanover

December 1691

With all the troubles of the past weeks, Sofia's step was heavy as she went up the stairs to visit her confined son. She had pleaded desperately for this privilege before Ernst had at last, reluctantly, granted it. 'But only once a week,' he had instructed. 'And for no more than one hour!'

She could hear faint strains of music, for carnival was still in progress; although, she mused, people no doubt were more interested in discussing the arrest of Prince Maximilian and Otto Moltke than they were in the festivities. The thought of Moltke filled her with bitterness. Sofia was glad that he was reposing in the fortress prison. If he had not been so actively supportive of Max, perhaps none of this would have happened.

She sighed deeply and paused on the landing, eyeing the two armed guards who stood before Max's door. They stood at attention, eyes forward, but she knew that they were aware of her presence. Wryly, she wondered if they would actually point their weapons at her should she try to gain entrance at any other than her allotted time. She wouldn't put it past Ernst to have so instructed them.

Slowly she approached. Her eyes felt gritty and hot from the tears she had shed this past week. Two of her sons, Friedrich and Charles, were dead. Dead before they had even had a chance to live. And now Max was arrested, with the threat of being convicted of treason hanging over his head.

'Madame!'

Sofia turned, surprised to see Dorothea hurrying along the hall, her silken gown billowing out with her swift approach. 'Please, I must speak to you,' she said, breathless.

'I cannot speak with you now,' Sofia declared sternly, again deploring her daughter-in-law's undisciplined behavior.

Ignoring the frown of disapproval, Dorothea continued in a pleading voice. 'It will take but a minute. I've just learned that Countess Königsmark has been asked to leave Hanover. Is that true?'

'Why should that concern you?' Sofia demanded, her annoyance plain.

Dorothea blinked. 'Aurora is a friend.'

'The countess made her own decision to return to the house of her sister.' Sofia turned to go, but Dorothea put a hand on her arm.

'Then why was I told that she will not be permitted to return?' Dorothea went on, insistently.

'The duke feels that Aurora Königsmark is not a suitable friend for you.' Sofia took a step forward and Dorothea's hand fell to her side.

'Does the duke now think to choose my friends?' she said heatedly. Her mouth tightened until a white thin line appeared. She was so angry that her pulse beat visibly at the base of her throat.

'Dorothea! I suggest to you that the time is inappropriate for this discussion. I have nothing further to say on this matter. There are things of more concern going on here than the countess's change of residence.' Sofia turned quickly and beckoned irritably to the guards, who hastened to unlock Maximilian's door. She entered, leaving Dorothea standing in the hall. Really, the girl is insufferable, she thought.

Maximilian was seated in a chair by the window, a closed look on his handsome face. Of all her sons, Maximilian was the handsomest. He looked like a young Ernst – or Wilhelm. The dark, brooding, almost petulant look in his eyes managed, somehow, to enhance his looks.

'Max?' she called softly.

He didn't turn around. 'Come in, Mother,' he said, apparently still absorbed in the scenery. From there he could see the narrow cobbled street that fronted Leine.

Across the way was the bell tower of the church, the dull bronze of the bell itself glinting faintly in the late morning sun. 'I'm surprised you've been allowed access to my prison.' The comment was bitter. It had been only a week since he had been confined, but he'd never known a week could be so long. All members of his personal staff had been dismissed. The only people he'd seen in these last days were the servants who brought his meals. And to think that it had been Charlotte who had betrayed him. His own sister!

He had almost had it put together too, he thought, feeling a sharp stab of regret. Of the eight electors, the three Catholic ones of Bavaria, Bohemia, and the Palatinate were dead set against Protestant Hanover joining the ranks of Saxony and Brandenburg. As for Ulric, the mere thought of an electoral bonnet being bestowed on his kinsman was enough to make him join any plot to defeat that end.

And it should be defeated, Maximilian reflected angrily. George would have it all; the rest of them, nothing. A fine state of affairs, he brooded sullenly.

'This can hardly be termed a prison, Max.' Sofia sat down and studied her son with care.

'How long does he plan to keep this up?' Max turned to her. There was no contrition on his face, only anger and resentment.

'Until the trial is over,' she answered quietly, hoping that her own face did not reflect the fear that gripped her.

'I suppose the charge will be high treason?' He glanced at her for confirmation and, seeing it, laughed harshly. 'Perhaps in a few month's time he can give a grand banquet to celebrate the execution of his son.'

'Max, please …' Sofia was distressed. 'If you recanted, signed an Oath of Allegiance in favor of your brother …'

'Never!' He got up and began pacing around the room. 'You want me to sign away my birthright? It's unthinkable!' His voice rose alarmingly as his face flushed with his heated emotions. He stopped before her. 'What happens if the emperor will not grant the damned electorate? What happens if Father suddenly dies? Then I will have signed away everything. For what?'

Sofia leaned forward, regarding her son intently. 'Listen to me, Max,' she pleaded. 'Please listen. Count Platen is still in Vienna. He reports that it will be only a matter of weeks before the electorate is granted. There is no question but that it will happen. God forbid, even if your father did die, George is recognized as his heir. And think of this,' she went on quickly before he could respond. 'William of Orange is now King of England. My own claim to that succession is now that much closer. Should William die without issue, I could become Queen of England.' She sighed deeply, hating to part with that long held dream. 'But the years have a way of encroaching upon us all,' she admitted sadly. 'I doubt that I will outlive William and Queen Anne, but George is my successor.

'If things go well, he could become King of England. Then he would have to leave Hanover. Who better to govern in his absence than his own brother?' She stared steadily, trying to will his understanding.

But Maximilian appeared unconvinced. His mother, for as long as he could remember, constantly prattled on about the English throne. It was a dream. Too many ifs, ands, buts – and far too many successors in line. His face revealed a stubborn look. 'I will fight for what is mine,' he stated flatly. 'And I will not be intimidated by the threat of a trial or what may happen afterward. Who knows?' he said with a shrug and, for the first time, smiled. 'The court may find in my favor.'

Sofia wanted to remind him that the court would be appointed by the duke himself. But just then the door opened and the guard respectfully informed her that she must leave.

In the hall again, the duchess descended the stairs with the same slow, weary step that she had used to climb them. It was almost time for the midday meal. Sofia, however, was neither hungry nor even looking forward to her afternoon stroll. George was expected home before the day was gone; despite the fact that she hadn't seen him in more than five months, Sofia wasn't even looking forward to that.

Pausing, Sofia became aware of raised voices. They penetrated her thoughts gradually. She was annoyed by the intrusion. The sounds were coming from the duke's study. At the foot of the stairs Sofia stood and listened. She could hear the voice of her husband, raised in exasperation, and a female voice, shrill with anger.

Oh, my God, Sofia thought with mounting panic, a hand at her breast. The voice belonged to Dorothea! And from the sound of it she had, this time, completely lost her temper. After a moment's hesitation, Sofia headed, determined, for the door, knowing that for once her husband would favor her interruption.

'I will not have you live my life for me!' Dorothea was screaming when Sofia opened the door.

Neither one turned. So enraged were they that they had not even noticed her entrance.

'It's time and more that the prince and I be given our own residence,' Dorothea continued in the same loud voice. 'If you insist on treating me like a child, I will return home to Celle.' Twin spots of crimson colored the pale ivory cheeks as she glared at her father-in-law.

'Dorothea.' Sofia's cool and calm voice caught them both by surprise. The face of the princess was flushed with defiant anger. Ernst's face was a mask of grim exasperation, the mouth clamped as though he were clenching his teeth.

'It's true!' Dorothea exclaimed, staring at her mother-in-law with blazing eyes. 'This must be the only court in Europe that does not have a separate residence for the crown prince and his wife. I'm tired of being treated like a child.'

'Then I suggest that you cease acting like one,' Sofia commented mildly, coming farther into the room.

Faced with the impregnable placidity of the duchess, Dorothea's anger faltered and she stood there uncertainly. 'I don't believe that my request for a residence of my own, with my own household, is an unreasonable one,' she persisted on a quieter tone.

'I agree,' Sofia conceded, still appearing unruffled. 'If you will be kind enough to leave us, the duke and I will discuss your request.' She smiled sweetly but fixed her daughter-in-law with a hard, level look that carried more of a warning than intimidation in it.

Dorothea hesitated. Then her shoulders slumped and with a look at once sullen and stubborn, she stormed from the room without further words.

'I will not have it!' Ernst shouted when the door closed. He glared at his wife as though she had been at fault. 'I will not be involved in these trivial scenes of domesticity. That is your department, madame. I suggest that you pay more attention to what is going on around here.'

Sofia bit her lip. 'Perhaps they should have their own residence, Ernst,' she suggested quietly, ignoring her husband's thundering oration. 'It may alleviate their problems.'

'Their problems do not concern me, madame,' Ernst retorted in a cold voice. 'Except to the extent that they damage the reputation of this house. I need not remind you of certain rumors that have persistently surfaced with regard to our daughter-in-law. Can you just imagine how they would swell if she were in her own residence, with her own household, unchaperoned?'

Unhappily, Sofia had to agree.

'Not only that,' Ernst went on, still glaring, 'but I have an idea that the first thing she would do is defy me. I wouldn't put it past her to invite Countess Königsmark as her first guest.'

'Oh, she wouldn't do that, Ernst,' Sofia protested, genuinely upset by the thought. Aurora Königsmark had been branded *persona non grata* throughout all Hanover. Even the count himself couldn't invite his sister to his home. He would be banned from court.

But the duke had long ago decided that his fiery-tempered daughter-in-law would do anything she damned well pleased if she took a mind to. 'I don't want to discuss this any further,' he said at last. 'And you may inform the princess that she is not to intrude on me in such a manner again. She is to bring her imaginary problems to you.' As Sofia walked toward the door, her husband had one final word. 'You may tell your son when next you see him that the court will convene at the beginning of next week.'

Sofia closed the door without replying. *Your son,* Ernst had said. But of course Ernst had always felt that way, she thought, tired, massaging her aching temples. He had only one son, and that was George Ludwig.

But you have taken two of my sons, Ernst, and you shall not take another, she vowed fiercely.

'May I come in?' George stood in the doorway of their adjoining room as Dorothea viewed him in some wonder. It was most unusual for him to visit her the first night that he returned from his regiment. That sacrosanct time was normally reserved for Melusine.

'Of course you may,' she replied lightly. He looks older, she thought, watching his ponderous entrance. But why should that take her unaware? She had only seen him once or twice in the past year, and not at all for the past five months. This was her husband, she mused, noting that he sat himself down on a chair, rather than on the bed. Yet he was a stranger to her. They had never talked, never exchanged endearments; not once in all the years since they had married had George ever proclaimed love, or even affection.

'I'm surprised to see you,' Dorothea commented, motioning to Lenore to leave them alone. 'Especially tonight.' She smiled acidly. 'I presume that Melusine is waiting for you in breathless anticipation.'

George flushed and averted his face. 'Please, let's not quarrel.' Dorothea had learned little in his absence, he noted sourly. Of course he preferred being with Melusine. Who wouldn't? But he doubted he'd ever seen his father so upset as he had been when they'd had their talk after dinner. And this business with Max wasn't helping, either. Dorothea, he supposed, was just an extra added burden. Unfortunately, she was *his* burden. His father had made that painfully clear.

'My father told me of your ... discussion with him earlier today,' George began, turning to look at her.

'Did he?' Dorothea's voice shimmered with false brightness. 'And naturally you took the side of your wife, didn't you?' she inquired maliciously.

George looked uncomfortable. Damn her. Each time he saw his wife, he disliked her more than the time before. With distance, he forgot her sharp tongue, her abrasive manner. 'My father was perfectly right, Dorothea,' he stated, striving to keep his voice normal. 'In the future we will have our own residence, but for now – '

'Future!' Dorothea took a step toward him. It came again, the surge of resentment, the sharp stab of anger, the outpouring of antipathy she could not repress, had no desire to suppress. 'What *is* the future to you, George? A year, five, ten? How long am I to be cooped up here? Never having a say in my own affairs, my own friends! I cannot even visit Celle without your father's approval.' She glared at him, her breath coming in short gasps.

'It's not appropriate at this time,' he retorted stiffly. He rubbed his moist palms together. Her temper quite unsettled him. It was so ... plebeian.

Dorothea uttered a foul imprecation and his face blanched. 'But you certainly saw to it,' she spat at him, 'that Melusine von Schulenburg had her own residence, didn't you?' Hands on her hips, her tone was scathing. 'For that little slut you will defy your father. But not for me. Never for me.'

George was slow to anger. Usually. But he felt it coming now, like a deep, undulating wave. It engulfed his mind. He thought how pleasant it would be to put his hands about that slim white throat, as he had once before. Perhaps this time no one would reach him before ... He took a deep breath, then another in an effort to calm his wild thoughts.

He got to his feet. 'There will be no separate residence,' he stated coldly. At his sides, his hands were clenched into fists. 'There have been too many rumors about you and Count Königsmark,' he continued spitefully. He himself didn't beleve them, but he knew that Dorothea was aware of the recurring innuendos. 'It would get out of hand if you had your own residence and were unchaperoned.'

Dorothea's face was impassive as she regarded her husband. 'What sort of rumors, George?' she asked quietly.

'They say he's in love with you, that he wants to make you his mistress.'

Dorothea raised a brow and tilted her head. 'What

makes you think they're rumors?' she inquired in a soft voice, eyes deceptively wide and innocent. 'Is it so impossible to believe that a man could love me?'

Again George flushed. 'Of course not,' he protested. 'I merely meant that it's not proper – '

'He *does* love me,' she interrupted in the same soft voice that held a hint of malice.

George Ludwig viewed her in alarm, anger momentarily forgotten. 'Has he spoken improperly to you?' he demanded, confused by her sudden, trilling laughter.

'Are words of love improper to you, George?' she asked in apparent merriment.

George's features settled into heavy disapproval. 'I believe this discussion has gone far enough,' he announced pontifically, heading for the door. He was now convinced that she had been baiting him. If Königsmark were interested in Dorothea, it certainly wasn't because he was in love with her. He'd wager a month's pay on that!

'George.' Dorothea's voice, suddenly calm and expressionless, halted him. 'I wish to return home to Celle.'

He turned. 'That's impossible,' he replied flatly, knowing full well that she didn't mean just for a visit. 'The duke will never allow it.'

'The duke?' Her voice rose again. 'You fool! What does your father have to do with us?'

His mouth compressed. 'Quite a bit, madame,' he noted in that irritatingly stiff and polite tone that set Dorothea's teeth on edge. 'You know as well as I that you may not leave without his permission. Nor, I would venture to say, would Duke Wilhelm receive you with open arms if you arrived without it.' He closed the door then, quickly, not wishing to hear any more of her nonsensical words.

But perhaps a vist with her parents *was* in order, he reflected – after his father spoke with Wilhelm. Dorothea had to learn that she belonged at Hanover. She must also be made aware that she would not be welcome if she obstinately chose to return to the house of her father without consent.

As for Königsmark George almost smiled. Her ruse had been so transparent. Thoughtfully rubbing his chin, George went downstairs to see his father.

Some days later, Dorothea was pleased, if a bit mystified, to see her father arrive at Leine. The reason for the unexpected visit, however, became painfully clear that same day, when Wilhelm spoke to her in private.

They were in her salon. The fire in the grate had been stoked high, a cheery admission of the cold and snowy day outside.

'I'm ashamed of you,' Wilhelm said petulantly, facing his recalcitrant daughter. 'You are a grown woman, a wife, a mother!'

Dorothea flashed her father a defiant look. 'Then why am I not allowed a voice in my own life?' she demanded. She was too restless to sit still and walked about the room in aimless fashion, pausing now and again to look at Wilhelm, who was standing by the fireplace.

'Because you are acting irresponsibly.' The retort was harsh. 'You cannot run home each time you quarrel with your husband.' Wilhelm was truly astonished. He had thought that with Dorothea married, all their problems would be solved. Such was not the case. She was a stubborn young colt, refusing the bit.

'Each time!' Dorothea's eyes widened expressively. 'I've been here for nine years, and this is the *first* time.' She couldn't believe that her own father was speaking in this manner. She had never before doubted his love; it was always there, always considerate, always available. Now he seemed to have deserted her.

Wilhelm sighed deeply. 'Listen to me, Dorothea.' He spoke with a forced patience that grated on her nerves. 'I understand how it is. I understsand that George is involved with another woman …'

'Her name is Melusine von Schulenburg,' Dorothea retorted icily. She regarded her father in wintry silence a moment before continuing. 'And nine years does not constitute an involvement. I am married, but I never see my husband.' Nor, she thought grimly, am I unhappy about that.

'You have two children,' Wilhelm pointed out. 'You have no cause to complain of neglect.' He clasped his hands behind his back and viewed her with placating earnestness.

'And two children constitute the beginning and end of his responsibility as a husband?' she demanded.

Wilhelm shook his head, almost in despair. He was more than ever convinced that Ernst's assessment had been correct. Dorothea was miffed because her husband had temporarily taken a mistress. She refused to accept it as a dutiful wife should. Wilhelm was quite annoyed with his daughter; somehow he had thought that Eleanor had better prepared her for life's realities. He made himself speak firmly, fixing her with stony eyes. 'You are not even to consider returning home unless you have the express permission of the duke to do so.' Without further words Wilhelm made for the door.

Dorothea stared at his receding figure in astonishment. Her own father had refused her refuge. She turned, stumbled, and Lenore was there as always to offer comfort.

But there was no comfort. Dorothea felt as if she were suffocating under the weight of her unhappiness. I cannot go on like this much longer, she thought wildly.

Philip. Philip was her only salvation, her only hope. But Philip was with his troops along the Rhine. Straightening, Dorothea moved away from Lenore and headed for her writing table.

Hanover

March 1693

From her window Dorothea watched the preparations for the departure of the duke, the duchess, George, and both Count and Countess Platen. They were on their way to Vienna. Even from here, she could see the flushed, joyful excitement on Duke Ernst's face.

And why not? His dream had come true. The emperor had named Hanover-Celle the ninth electorate. Now Ernst was on his way to receive, officially, the bonnet that would designate him elector. As heir apparent George, too, would receive official recognition.

As for herself, Dorothea had not been invited. Whether this was punishment for her unruly behavior or simply because they didn't want her company, she didn't know.

Nor did she care. She had already written to Philip, imploring him to come to her.

She turned away from the window, not wishing to view the final departure. She could think of nothing but Philip, and freedom.

Four days later Philip arrived in Hanover. That night he let himself in through the gate, which Lenore had wisely left unbolted for two nights in succession.

'Oh, my darling,' Dorothea cried out at the sight of him. She flew to the safety of his embrace. Their kiss, almost without passion, was a mingling of tenderness and relief at once again being together.

'It has been so long,' he murmured, holding her tightly against him.

At last Dorothea drew away from him and, for the first time, actually looked at him. 'Why are you dressed like that?' she asked in amazement, noting his ragged clothes and several days' growth of beard on his normally clean-shaven face. Even his boots were worn and of the poorest quality.

'It was the only outfit I could think of that wouldn't draw attention to myself.' Philip sat down wearily. Seeing how tired he was, Dorothea was stricken with guilt.

'How long has it been since you've eaten?' she inquired. Aghast at his answer, she immediately sent Lenore for food. Then she came and sat beside him, cradling his head against her breast. 'I don't see why you had to take such drastic precautions,' she ventured. 'I told you that they have all gone to Vienna.'

Philip gave a small, rueful laugh. 'When I received your letter,' he explained in a tired voice, 'I knew there was no hope of a leave.' He looked up at her, his eyes soft with the love he felt. 'But, leave or no, I knew that I had to come to you when you needed me.'

She paled. 'You mean you are here without permission?' she asked in a faint voice. 'That you ... deserted?'

He gripped her in a tight embrace. 'No, my angel. I haven't deserted. And when I return, I shall gladly suffer any punishment Podewils sees fit to bestow on me.' He put his lips against her throat and his warm breath sent shudders of delight coursing through her. 'Whatever it may be, it will be worth it,' he whispered fervently. 'I would suffer the torments of hell for one hour with you.'

Dorothea felt like weeping, her adoration mingled with fear for him. And deep inside her was a core of joy that she knew would always be with her, one that would sustain her all her life. Knowing Philip's bravery, his conscientiousness as a soldier, Dorothea now knew the measure of his love. She felt humbled by the scope of it.

But it was no less than she felt for him.

They were still clinging to each other when Lenore returned with the food. She dared not have a servant bring it, so she had prepared a tray herself, then laboriously climbed the stairs, carrying the repast.

'I'm afraid it's cold,' Lenore said apologetically, offering Philip a small smile.

Philip regarded it appreciatively. 'It looks like a banquet

to me, Mademoiselle Knesebeck,' he said with a grin. He began to eat with undisguised enthusiasm.

Lenore watched him for a moment. Then she returned to the next room to stand guard.

While Philip ate, Dorothea talked. It was an overwhelming relief to speak to someone who listened, who cared. When she had vented herself in a sometimes angry tirade, she concluded, 'We must go away. Go to a place where no one will ever again separate us, a place where we can be together for always.' She looked at him with an expression of profound sadness. 'Do you realize that in the past three years we have been together only a handful of times?'

'Seven,' Philip said, wiping his mouth. Then he took her hand. 'Nor have I forgotten one of them.'

'Can we go away, Philip?' she asked plaintively, close to tears.

'I would take you away now, tonight, if I could,' Philip vowed in a fierce voice. Then his shoulders slumped. 'I have no money, Dorothea,' he said simply. 'There's not enough left to support you. I couldn't bear to have you live the life of an officer's wife. You are used to much more, and deserve much more.'

She shook her head slightly. 'I don't understand,' she murmured.

'My estates in Sweden have been taken over by the crown,' he explained in a low voice. 'I couldn't leave you, and I would have had to, for a long time. And – ' he sighed ruefully – 'I've been less than prudent with my inheritance,' he confessed. 'Even the house here in Hanover is mortgaged.'

Dorothea couldn't quite take it in. Money was to spend, not to worry about. Her face brightened. 'I have plenty for us both,' she exclaimed. 'There are the estates that my father purchased for me. And my own personal allowance.' She laughed. 'And I'm certain there's a lot more, although I can't tell you where.' She shrugged, a delicate movement beneath her blue silken gown. 'I just don't know how much I have, but it's a lot, that much I do know. And – ' her mouth set in a determined manner – 'if I divorce George, there is even Celle. Celle is mine.'

Philip was regarding her with doubt. 'It will all take time,' he cautioned. 'And what of your children?'

Dorothea's face sobered. 'I have no doubt but that my children would have to remain in Hanover,' she said slowly. 'But that is what is best for them. I would never deny them their birthright. But I'm certain I'll be able to see them whenever I wish.' Her face softened. 'And there will be more children. Our children.'

Overcome with love for this woman who had such a hold on his heart, Philip reached for her.

For the following week they rejoiced in other's company, in each other's bodies, in each other's love, knowing that this would probably be the last time they would be together until the day when they were both free.

And, Dorothea prayed, let that day be not too far distant in the future.

They were returning from Vienna, the new elector and electress. Hanover dressed in its finest and the April day dawned softly. The sound of bells began at first light, continuing until the royal party came into view. Then the burghers and court members rushed into the streets, cheering wildly. Even Marshal Podewils came back for the occasion.

While the town and court were otherwise engaged, Philip presented himself before his commanding officer.

As he viewed his insubordinate colonel, Heinrich Podewils looked more sad than angry. He was well aware, as who wasn't, of Königsmark's insane infatuation. 'I never believed, Colonel, that you deserted,' he murmured when Philip was through speaking. 'If I did, I would not hestitate to place you under arrest and have you summarily shot.'

Philip stood stiffly at attention, listening to his commander. But he made no comment. He had already had his say. He could add nothing, nor could he subtract from his grave misconduct.

The marshal fell into silence. Even here, on the outskirts of town, they could hear the bells and music as Hanover celebrated its great victory.

At last Podewils reached for paper and quill and busily

wrote for a few minutes. Then, his face grave, he handed the paper to Philip, who read it with a profound sense of relief. It was a pass. And it was predated to the day that he had left. It ended today.

'This is the first time, and the last time, Colonel,' Podewils said sternly. 'Return to your regiment. You are dismissed.'

Saluting smartly, Philip desperately wanted to convey his thanks, but he suspected that Marshal Podewils already knew.

A week went by before Dorothea could find an opportunity to speak with George alone. She had to humble herself with a request that he visit her in her apartments. As calmly as she could, she told him she wanted a divorce.

Sitting there, George frowned at her words, mildly annoyed by this latest foolishness. He was returning in the morning to his regiment and had planned to spend these last precious hours with Melusine, who was again pregnant. And now here was Dorothea acting, as always, capriciously and inconsiderately.

He stood up. 'Look here,' he said at last. 'I thought you had something serious you wanted to discuss. If you've asked me here just to begin another quarrel ...'

Dorothea viewed him in silence a moment. 'Have you heard what I've said?' she demanded, trying to control the exasperation that George always seemed to provoke. 'I want a divorce.'

George gave a short laugh and began to head for the door, shaking his head with each step. He didn't bother to answer. The idea was so ludicrous that it would not even bear discussion.

Hanover

July 1693

Sofia was frantic. Never before in her life had she been so gripped with a feeling that bordered on terror. The court's verdict, after seven long months, had finally been reached: Maximilian was found guilty.

Her son had been conviced of high treason, as had Otto Moltke, who had been sentenced to death by beheading. Formal sentence had not as yet been pronounced for Max, but Sofia knew that if he would only sign the oath he would at least live. Maximilian refused.

For the only time in their marriage, the duchess, now electress, faced her husband in defiance.

'You must release him,' she cried out, her cool reserve for once deserting her.

'Release him?' Ernst regarded his wife as if she had suddenly gone mad. 'Release him ... so that he can plot behind my back? That's all I would need at a time like this.'

'He is your son,' she pleaded. 'Surely you don't intend for him to ... to be executed!' Her throat constricted. Sofia could hardly speak the odious word. Moltke was scheduled to die in only a few days' time. Sofia had recurring nightmares of the two of them, Max and Moltke, side by side as the executioner's axe descended. 'The electorate is at last yours,' she persisted desperately. 'Maximilian can do nothing now.'

'Nothing?' he thundered. 'You know as well as I that despite the emperor's proclamation both Ulric and the Elector of Saxony refuse to recognise our status. Now would be the worst time for Maximilian to dissent openly. How would it look if my own son sided with our enemies?' He glared at her and put his hands, palm down, on his desk. 'One week after the emperor proclaimed me elector they threatened to send their armies to our borders. The emperor himself had to caution them.'

'I don't care,' said Sofia, her eyes bright with anger and unshed tears. Then her face crumpled, as she wept. 'You will not have him executed?' she begged.

Ernst turned away, annoyed by this unusual display of hysteria on the part of his normally placid wife.

Sofia caught her breath at the hesitation. Her lips compressed and her expression grew as fierce as his. 'If you do, Ernst,' she said through clenched teeth, 'I swear I shall bare my neck beside his! How would that look to the emperor?'

Appalled, the duke stared. The silence grew and lengthened. Actually, Ernst had no wish to condemn Maximilian fatally, not because of their relationship but because it wouldn't look well for the newly crowned elector to condemn his own son.

'Very well,' he said at last. 'But Maximilian will stay under guard until he signs the oath.' Ernst slammed his fist down on the desk. 'And I don't give a damn if he spends the rest of his life in his room. On that I will hear no argument.'

'And when he does sign?' Sofia's voice wavered with relief.

'He will join the army. It's time he proved himself a man instead of a sneaking, cowardly conniver.'

She looked at him through her tears. 'Just as Friedrich?' she whispered.

He smiled thinly. 'Just as Friedrich, madame.'

The following Monday the whole court, including the duchess and Princess Dorothea, together with most of the citizens of Hanover, were required to witness the execution of Otto Moltke. Dorothea, in a small act of defiance, closed her eyes, refusing to watch. But if her rebellion was noticed, no one commented on it.

The only one who did not attend was Maximilian, who still refused to sign the oath despite his mother's frantic pleas.

Everyone agreed that the December snows were the worst ever; no one could remember such a spell of bad weather.

With only intermittent breaks, it had snowed every day for the past month. As a result, the roads were almost impassable. Even the post was delayed for days at a time.

George, however, managed to return from Flanders for the holidays.

It was more than aggravating, Dorothea reflected as she again read Philip's letter, that all these months had passed yet nothing was resolved. But she could hardly have convinced George to grant her a divorce when he was not there to ask. However, he was home now. Dorothea was determined that, this time, he would listen.

She looked at Philip's letter again. He wrote that one of her letters had reached him with the seal broken. No doubt it was only a mishap en route, but he urged caution in the future.

Dorothea was, however, through with caution. The time for that had passed. The time for action had come. They couldn't go on like this, wasting their lives, month by month, communicating only through letters, relying upon circumstances that never seemed to materialize. Money was, she had to admit, a very definite problem. But she was wealthy enough in her own right. George would have to allow her to visit the children periodically. That could be done while he was away. There need be no uncomfortable meetings between them.

That night, soon after the evening meal and before George had time to seek the company of his beloved Melusine, Dorothea again asked him to grant her a divorce. She took great care to control her temper and tongue, trying to speak calmly, to appeal to his reason. She even pointed out that he would be free to marry Melusine. And, she couldn't help adding sarcastically, adopt that woman's two 'nieces.'

This time, George didn't laugh. He simply left the room without speaking. And this time, seeing how serious she was, he told his father.

'Out of the question!' Ernst managed to reply, too dumbfounded for anger.

George looked pensive. 'I don't know as I am entirely averse to the idea,' he said slowly, the tantalizing prospect of marrying Melusine floating before his eyes.

'The situation between us is intolerable. Dorothea can be … difficult,' he concluded.

Difficult, Ernst thought, irritated, was hardly the word. Still, divorce was an unacceptable solution.

'Listen to me, George,' Ernst said to his favorite son. 'There are more things to consider here than a mere divorce. Celle is yours under the marriage contract. Probably it would remain so under a divorce agreement. I say *probably*, but there is a chance that she could contest it. Now, what would happen if she remarries and has other children? Celle, by rights, should go to her heirs. Think of your son, George. Would you want his inheritance muddied?' Ernst leaned back in his chair. 'All you have to do is think about your own brothers to see how easily it could happen.'

Momentarily diverted, George looked at his father. 'Maximilian?' he inquired with a lift of his brows.

Ernst's face hardened and he nodded. 'The fool has at last agreed to sign. But you see what mischief he has caused because of his obstinacy. Would you care for your own son to be embroiled in such plotting?' He shook his head firmly. 'No. There will be no divorce. The marriage contract has been signed in good faith. And so it will stand.'

'But if she keeps insisting, what then?'

'Look here, George.' Ernst put his elbows on the desk and viewed his son intently. 'You must understand how it is with women. You've been gone for long months at a stretch. Your wife is young. And most likely she's bored. I agree,' he said quickly, raising a hand as George opened his mouth to speak. 'Dorothea has a vile temper. But you must assert yourself as her husband. You will be home for several weeks. I suggest that you spend more time with her. Return to your conjugal bed,' he advised, then laughed heartily. 'When she is pregnant again, she will stop thinking about divorce.'

George looked uncomfortable with the suggestion. 'I'll not give up Melusine,' he said doggedly.

Ernst raised his brows. 'Did I say you must? A man has his duty and his pleasure. I do not suggest that you relinquish your pleasure. I suggest only that you do your duty.'

George's nod was a trifle reluctant. With the departure of

the crown prince, Ernst heaved a sigh of relief. While he sympathized with George wholeheartedly, a man must first govern his wife before he could even think of governing his people.

Outside in the hall George looked with contemplative eyes at the wide, curving staircase, and hesitated. Then he shrugged. Dorothea could wait, he decided, sending a servant for his cloak. What he needed now was the soothing comfort of Melusine. After that – and a few steins of beer – he would be ready to face his shrew of a wife.

'What is taking him so long?' Dorothea raged to Lenore. She knew that her husband was closeted with the Elector. She had had Lenore follow George when he had left her apartments.

'*Ma chère*,' her lady advised tactfully, 'why don't you go downstairs for a while? Relax, play some cards …'

'I have no desire to play cards,' Dorothea retorted swiftly. 'And I shall not relax until this business is over and done with.' She paced about the room for a while, eyeing the clock every minute or so, and at last turned to Lenore. 'Go downstairs again. Please find out what is happening. It has been two hours. See?' She gestured. 'It's past eleven o'clock.'

With a small sigh, Lenore nodded. Hurriedly she descended the stairs. She could hear music and laughter from the reception hall as the court relaxed in its usual nighttime activities of cards games, dancing and gossiping. Going to the doorway, she quickly scanned the room. Both the elector and electress were present, each at different tables. Even the Platens milled about. But of George there was no sign.

She moved away and stood there uncertainly for a moment. Perhaps the prince was in his own rooms. No, she discarded that. Her eye lit on the footman who stood by the door. Lenore smiled in her most seductive manner as she caught his eye. Immediately he smiled in return, flushing with pleasure as the attractive lady-in-waiting noticed him.

Casually, Lenore walked over to him. 'Has it stopped snowing yet?' she asked, still smiling.

'No, milady,' he responded, his admiration evident.

She shook her head and sighed. 'I cannot remember such a terrible winter,' she remarked idly. 'I'll wager that a carriage can't get through the streets, even though the servants are diligent enough with their shovels.'

He laughed. 'There's no carriage can get through that.' He gestured in the direction of the forecourt. 'Even the prince had to walk, although I offered to get the sleigh for him.'

Lenore smiled prettily. 'I daresay even the prince will not walk far.'

'He doesn't have to,' the footman agreed. 'His destination is less than a mile away.' He laughed again, as if sharing a joke. 'I don't expect the cold will bother him much.'

Lenore joined his laughter and, as casually as she had approached, walked away, the laughter and smile turning into a sombre expression as she mounted the steps.

'He has gone to see Melusine,' she reported tonelessly as she entered the room again.

Dorothea's face suffused with rage. 'I will speak to the elector myself,' she announced, heading for the door.

Lenore refused to move, blocking the way. 'You cannot do that,' she protested, putting her hands on Dorothea's shoulders. 'He is at the card table.'

'I don't care where he is. He will listen to me once and for all.'

'No, no. You may jeopardize everything.' Lenore tried to reason with her. 'Perhaps it's all settled. You must speak to the prince before you make any further move. Doubtless his pride is wounded and he's merely acting with spite in making you wait.'

Dorothea faltered. It would be just like George to do something like that. And Lenore was right. If it *had* been settled, she could upset everything by angering her father-in-law. Ernst was cool enough toward her as it was. Her mouth tightened. 'Very well. Let George play his little games. I've waited this long, I can wait until morning. But if he doesn't return by then,' she vowed, 'I, too, will visit Melusine von Schulenburg.'

With overwhelming relief, Lenore helped her mistress

undress and saw her safely in bed. Then, with a deep sigh, she went to her own room and did the same.

The noise was a faint one. Dorothea moved restlessly in sleep, coming to awareness for only a brief moment, then sinking into oblivion almost immediately.

But the resulting sag in the mattress as someone sat down on her bed woke her instantly. She sat up, blinking, staring in disbelief as her husband calmly lifted his nightshirt over his head and flung it carelessly to the floor.

'My dear,' he mumbled, his speech slurring, 'your petition for a divorce has not been granted.' He yawned, sniffed, and turned to her as he got into the bed. 'But rest assured I shall make every endeavor to keep you from being bored. From now on I shall share your bed each night.' There. That was just the way he had rehearsed it. George almost grinned as he reached for her.

Speechless, Dorothea felt his closeness and turned her head away from the beer-drenched breath. She put her hands on his naked chest and pushed with all her strength. But against the leaden weight of more than two hundred pounds her efforts were futile; indeed, George didn't even seem to notice. He easily forced her down and lay atop of her, fumbling with clumsy hands at the impediment of her nightgown.

'Get off me!' Dorothea gasped, trying to make sense of his almost incoherent words: conjugal bed ... duty ... boredom ... Maximilian? What the devil was he rambling on about? she wondered, gritting her teeth with the effort of trying to remove the crushing weight from her breast. His hand was between her thighs now. Cursing, he began to rip at the flimsy material of her gown. He raised himself up on one elbow so as to better complete this destruction. With the momentary freedom, Dorothea brought her knee up and crushed it into the soft flesh beneath his chin.

George howled and rolled over, falling out of bed. With a leap, Dorothea, too, was up. Lenore had opened the door a crack; however, seeing that it was the prince who was causing such a commotion, she hastily closed it again. But she sat there on the floor with her ear pressed against the door, ready to aid Dorothea should she need it.

The princess stood in her tattered nightgown, hands on her hips, viewing her husband with furious eyes. Under other circumstances, George would have been a ludicrous sight, lying there sprawled out, naked, one bearlike hand cupped beneath his chin, staring at her accusingly.

'Get out,' she said through clenched teeth. 'Get out of my room.'

George swore, wincing in pain, almost sober now. He got to his feet, wavering. 'You are my wife,' he choked.

Dorothea regarded him disdainfully for a moment. 'That is a situation I am trying to change,' was the crushing reply.

George looked affronted. He'd be damned if he would force himself on any woman, he thought angrily. Even his own wife. And duty be damned too. 'Are you saying that you will not allow me to share your bed?' he demanded, still a little disbelieving.

Dorothea raised her chin. 'You will never share my bed again. And if you dare approach me in such manner as you have tonight, I will kill you!' In a quick motion she picked up a porcelain figurine from her dressing table and flung it at him, but he easily sidestepped the missile. His face was a dull red, reflecting an anger so furious that his temples pounded in protest.

'Then you will sleep alone for the rest of your life,' he declared thickly. 'There will be no divorce, now or in the future.' He lumbered to the door of his adjoining room, still unclothed. After opening it, he turned to her once more. 'No divorce. But I've had enough of your devilish temper. I will write to your father and inform him that we are formally separated and request that he take you back – if he wants you.'

The door slammed. Dorothea stood there, shaking in furious anger, only slightly aware that Lenore came in to help her out of the torn nightgown. Dorothea stared at it ruefully. As torn and as tattered as her marriage. And her life. Clothed again, she fell into Lenore's arms and wept.

Some days later Ernst, Sofia, and George watched in moody contemplation as the sleigh left for Celle.

When it was out of sight, Ernst regarded his son for the

first time with doubtful eyes. Oh, George had explained rationally enough what had happened. Frankly, Ernst couldn't conceive Sofia denying him her bed. It was unthinkable. Certainly he had a mistress; most men did, with, perhaps, the exception of Wilhelm. But one had nothing to do with the other. Women were supposed to understand these things. Most women did. Curse Wilhelm for having raised such a stupid daughter. Ernst recalled the girl's christening. Good Lord, it was as if she had been, well, legitimate, a princess! That is what comes of spoiling them, he thought, disgruntled.

Divorce. That, too, was unthinkable. With Celle at stake, the price was too high even to enter the game.

'I've written to Wilhelm,' Ernst said at last, not looking at any of them. 'I'm certain he will agree with me that this separation must be temporary.' Seeing George's deep frown, he went on quickly, before the prince could speak. 'That is not to say that I am unsympathetic with your problems. And, I agree, a separation at this time could benefit both of you. Let her stay at Celle; for several months, if need be. After a while, she'll learn what it's like to be without her husband and her family. She'll learn what it's like to be a woman alone, with no real place in society.'

'I don't see why she cannot stay there,' George complained stubbornly. Absently, he rubbed his chin. The soreness had lasted a whole day after she had so foully kicked him. God almighty, he couldn't hold her down every minute that he was in her company.

'She cannot stay there because she is your wife.' Ernst's reply was terse. 'And a wife belongs with her husband.'

'I'm certain that the duchess will speak to Dorothea,' Sofia offered in a placating voice, looking first at her husband, then at her son.

Ernst returned his gaze to the window. 'She'd better speak plainly,' he commented in a disgusted tone.

Celle

January 1694

During the ride to Celle Dorothea stared moodily at the passing scenery as the horse-drawn sleigh slipped easily over the white expanse.

It had finally stopped snowing although the gray sky gave promise of more to come. Huddled beneath woolen robes, the hoods on their fur cloaks pulled low, the two young women were reasonably protected from the damp cold air. The sleigh would actually be able to cover the twenty miles in less time than the cumbersome carriage. Dorothea used the time to think.

No divorce, George had said. She lifted her chin. If she had to fight them all, she would do so. A formal separation was only the first step. Soon everyone would know that she had been sent home to her parents. It was as good as a public announcement of the break in their relationship.

A sardonic look crossed her face as Dorothea thought of George. He planned to visit his sister Charlotte for a length of time. Melusine would of course accompany him.

Money. That would have to be the first thing on her agenda. Dorothea had no claim to Celle while her father lived, but there were her other properties. These she owned outright. And her allowance. Dorothea frowned in contemplation. She hadn't received an allowance for years, simply because she had never before had any need for money. When she wanted something, she merely ordered it. The bill was always paid. By Ernst? By George? Dorothea realized that she didn't know.

She had written to Philip, now stationed along the Elbe, and informed him that she was returning home. She had told him of the incident with George, but stressed that she had been faithful to Philip. Nothing enraged Philip as much as the thought that she might be sharing a bed with George.

If the truth be told, Dorothea had to admit that it seemed more an act of infidelity to sleep with George than with the man she loved. Dorothea felt certain that in the sight of God she and Philip were meant to be together. There was no other explanation for their feeling toward one another. It even transcended the mere physical act of love, pleasurable as that was.

No, she belonged to Philip and to no other man, certainly not a husband chosen for her, one whom she had despised even before she had married him. If she had known Philip then, she mused, there simply would never have been a wedding, regardless of the coercion of her parents. What right did they have to so choose the course of her life? What right did her aunt and uncle have? What right had anyone? She had only this one life to live, despite the high platitudes of the chaplain, and Dorothea intended to live it with Philip, regardless of the cost.

Lenore touched Dorothea's arm, shaking her out of her reverie. 'We're almost there.' She pointed to the increasing evidence of civilization. 'Are you all right?' she asked, raising her voice slightly over the hiss of the iron runners and the steady clopping of horses' hooves.

Dorothea nodded briefly. 'I'm glad to be home.'

Glad? Lenore thought, leaning back. She herself was trapped in a feeling of desolation. Life at Celle could in no way compare with the gaiety and splendor of Hanover.

The horses labored along. Ahead, Dorothea, could see the yellow stone walls of the castle in which she had been born. The drawbridge was down; her arrival was anticipated.

Shivering slightly, Dorothea pulled the fur cloak tighter. There was no snow on the drawbridge and the runners of the sleigh made a horrendous clatter as they crossed over and into the forecourt.

Entering the front hall a short time later, Dorothea was greeted by her parents. Eleanor, dressed in a gray woolen gown with a high neck and long sleeves, was almost in tears. Wilhelm was distantly cool. He made no attempt to embrace his daughter. Dorothea didn't care. After a few stilted words, Dorothea gratefully followed her mother to her old rooms.

'You must be tired.' Eleanor's smile was sad as they climbed the steps. 'Rest. I'll have food sent to you and we'll talk in the morning.'

Dorothea murmured a polite reply. But she didn't want to rest. She didn't want to eat. She didn't want to talk. What she wanted was to see Andreas Bernstorff, and as quickly as possible.

Patience, she cautioned herself, acknowledging her mother's tender ministrations as she bustled about the room seeing that all was in order. Patience. She waited until her mother left the room. Removing her cloak, she lay down on the bed, fully dressed. Lenore busied herself with the chore of unpacking.

When Dorothea knew that her mother and father were at their evening meal, she sought out the minister, intending to speak to him in private. Questions needed to be answered and Bernstorff was the only one who could enlighten her.

But almost two weeks went by before an occasion presented itself for Dorothea to speak with her father's minister. Two weeks, during which both her parents were coolly civil, speaking in generalities, addressing her with a politeness that might have better served a guest than a member of the family. The topic of her marriage was studiously avoided.

On this Tuesday morning, having just finished a letter to Philip, Dorothea sealed it with care and handed it to Lenore to deliver to the post rider when he came by.

'Philip answered my last letter,' Dorothea commented, frowning. 'But he made no mention of the one before it.' She viewed Lenore with a worried expression. They both took great care to avoid having their letters fall into the wrong hands. They had even devised a code of sorts.

Lenore tucked the envelope in a pocket of her gown. 'Most likely he read them out of sequence,' she soothed Dorothea. 'You know how often you have received three and even four letters at a time.'

'I suppose,' Dorothea agreed, chewing her lower lip thoughtfully. How glad she would be when all this subterfuge was over, when she and Philip could be together openly. Every night she prayed for that day to arrive.

When Lenore returned some time later, she reported that the duke had gone hunting for the day. Dorothea was already aware that her mother had gone into town to pay a social call. Minister Bernstorff, Lenore further related, was alone in his study, involved with his paperwork.

Dorothea brightened. 'Excellent.' Quickly she kissed Lenore on the cheek. A few minutes later she was standing in the doorway to the small study on the second floor that adjoined Bernstorff's apartment. She viewed the portly man with a dimpled smile.

'Monsieur? May I speak with you?'

Surprised, Bernstorff got to his feet and hastily donned his jacket, which had been resting on the back of his chair. 'Your Highness,' he murmured, blinking. 'Of course. Come in.' He offered an uncertain smile. 'May I say how pleased I am to see you looking so well and rested.'

Dorothea sat down in the chair that faced the teakwood desk. Folding her hands in her lap, she regarded the minister candidly. 'I need your help and your advice.'

As she spoke, Bernstorff's surprise deepened. Never before in their association had the princess approached him directly. 'If there is anything I can do, you need only ask,' he assured her, spreading out his hands.

She straightened. 'I wish to know exactly what my resources are,' she said briskly. At the blank look upon his face, she added, 'How much money do I have, and what is the current value of my property?'

The blank look hardly faded. 'What money are you speaking of, Highness?' he murmured in confusion.

Dorothea frowned, annoyed that the man couldn't answer so simple a question immediately. 'There is my allowance, both from my father and the prince. Since I haven't seen any of it, it must be accumulating somewhere. And then there are the revenues from the estates in Wilhelmsburg,' she went on. 'Plus the smaller properties. Those, I presume, are being held in a trust.'

Bernstorff checked a smile, seeing that the princess was speaking in all seriousness. Few women, of course, understood financial matters. Certainly the princess wasn't one of them.

'There is nothing in your name, Highness,' he explained patiently. 'All of your holdings are in your husband's name, with your son as beneficiary.'

Now it was Dorothea's turn to stare blankly. Obviously he didn't know what he was talking about, and this astonished her. Bernstorff had been with her father for many years.

'I'm afraid you don't understand,' she protested, her voice as patient as his. 'Well before I was married, the duke purchased the island known as Wilhelmsburg, plus the five estates along the Elbe. My mother showed me the deeds. They are in my name.'

Bernstorff smiled condescendingly at her words. 'I do understand, Highness,' he commented with a slow nod. 'And you are correct. The deeds were in your name.'

'Were?' The first traces of alarm warmed her cheeks.

'Yes. But your marriage contract supersedes everything.' He leaned forward slightly. 'When you married, everything you owned, including future revenues, was turned over to the prince.'

White-faced, Dorothea stared at him. The room seemed to sway precariously and she clung to the arms of the chair for support. But it is all a joke, she thought, frantic. A horrible, horrible joke!

Noting her sudden pallor, Bernstorff grew concerned. 'Are you all right?' he asked in a sharp voice.

She swallowed. 'Are you saying that I am … penniless?'

The minister threw back his head and laughed, delighted with the terminology. 'I'd hardly say that, your Highness,' he replied, feeling indulgent. He leaned back in his chair. 'After all, what belongs to your husband is, in a sense, yours as well. There is plenty of money. Plenty.'

Dorothea wet her lips and clenched her hands. 'I am not living with my husband,' she pointed out slowly, though she knew that he was aware of that fact.

'Oh, I realize that you are, right now, separated,' he replied carefully. 'But rest assured, your husband is still responsible for your support.' He nodded for emphasis.

Dorothea still didn't believe him. Obviously he had made a mistake, was misinformed. Her jaw tightened. 'I wish to see my marriage contract,' she stated firmly, ignoring his expression.

Bernstorff was frowning, deeply. But then, he was thinking, what could one expect from the daughter of Eleanor d'Olbreuse? The duke indeed had a cross to bear. As for the luckless Prince George, that man had Bernstorff's entire sympathy. Dorothea was still staring at him in a determined manner. Clearing his throat, he bent over and opened the bottom drawer of his desk, removing a metal box. After producing a key from a ring that held several, he unlocked the box and rummaged a moment among the papers inside it. At last he selected a document and then carefully placed it before her.

'As you can see, Highness, your signature is there, along with the others. It's perfectly legal and will stand up in any court.'

With hands that trembled, Dorothea picked it up. With only a brief glance at the minister, she turned her full attention to the words.

They were quiet while she read, now, the document that she had signed more than ten years ago.

Finally she put it back on the desk, feeling empty and enraged. Why had her mother and father allowed this to happen? How could they have allowed her to sign away everything? Everything! She was indeed penniless. The meanest servant possessed more than she did.

'I was only sixteen when I signed that,' she protested in an angry voice.

He shrugged, unmoved by her distress. 'But perfectly capable of reading, Highness,' he pointed out logically. 'Your signature indicates your approval. If anyone physically forced you to sign it, I am not aware of it.'

Slowly, carefully, Dorothea took a deep breath, ignoring the thunderous pounding in her ears. 'What of Celle?' she managed to ask.

The frown returned. 'Under the contract, Celle and Hanover will be united by the union of the prince and yourself when your father dies.'

Dorothea fixed him with a penetrating look. 'What if that union is broken?'

'Highness?'

'What if I get a divorce?'

He raised a shocked brow. Bourgeois. Just as her mother, he thought disdainfully. She would wreck an empire just to satisfy a whim. 'Celle, too, will go to the prince,' he advised stiffly, not at all pleased with this conversation.

Dorothea leaned forward slightly. 'But not until my father's death, is that not so?'

Startled by her astuteness, Bernstorff momentarily faltered. That was the one weak link. Legally, Celle still belonged to the Duke of Celle. If, during his lifetime, he was persuaded to change his will ... 'That is correct,' he admitted slowly, reluctantly. 'Celle belongs to your father while he lives. But,' he stressed, 'according to that contract, it reverts to Prince George upon the death of Duke Wilhelm.'

Dorothea took a moment to digest that. Then she got to her feet, murmured her thanks for his assistance, and, unsteadily, walked from the room.

Penniless! They had tricked her, they had all tricked her. The thoughts jumbled about in her brain: divorce, George, Celle, Philip. Philip. Philip!

In her room Dorothea put her hands to her ears in an effort to stem the horrendous pounding and throbbing that seemed to be captured within her head. With a small cry of despair, she collapsed, would have fallen to the floor but for Lenore, who quickly reached for her.

'It has been five months.' Wilhelm made no attempt to control his annoyance. 'Time and more for her to come to her senses. My patience is at an end.' He threw his napkin on his plate, where it sank into a puddle of gravy. He glared at his wife, seated across the table.

Eleanor gave him a pleading glance, which he ignored. But damn it, he thought, it had gone on long enough. Over the past months they had both tried to convince Dorothea to return to her husband. At first their words were reasonable, then cajoling, and at last, threatening.

Nothing had worked. Dorothea refused even to leave her room. True, she had been ill when she had arrived, Wilhelm conceded. Even the physicians prescribed rest and quiet. Well, she wasn't sick now. And she had had quite enough rest and tranquility. He glanced down at the letter that rested beside his wineglass. It was from Ernst, suggesting that his son's wife had been away from home long enough. Wilhelm heartily agreed.

'Just a few more weeks,' Eleanor began, almost timidly. She, too, was upset with Dorothea's behavior. But she was more worried than angry.

'There will be no more weeks, or even days,' Wilhelm thundered. 'She has been pampered long enough. Too much. She returns to her husband in the morning if I personally have to carry her out to the carriage.'

'I'll go back with her ...'

'No. Ernst advises that he and the electress will meet Dorothea at Herrenhausen. She need travel alone only half the distance.'

'Prince George?'

'He'll be there as well,' Wilhelm advised, nodding. He got to his feet and stood before her, hands clasped behind him. 'Do you wish to tell her, or shall I?'

'I'll do it,' Eleanor said quickly, getting up.

When she entered her daughter's room a short time later, Dorothea barely glanced at her. She was fully dressed but sprawled across the bed as if she had been napping.

Seeing the duchess, Lenore got up, smiled briefly, then left the room. It was almost time for the post to arrive. She prayed that today there would be a letter from Philip. Over these past months the only time the princess could be roused from lethargy was when she received a letter.

Eleanor faced her daughter. 'Dorothea,' she said quietly, her heart aching. 'It's time for you to return home.'

'This is my home,' Dorothea pointed out in a dull voice. She still hadn't moved and gave no indication of doing so.

'No, dear,' Eleanor responded gently. 'Your home is with your husband and your children.'

Turning her head slightly, Dorothea cast her mother an annoyed look. But she said nothing.

'You can no longer stay here,' Eleanor went on, averting her eyes. She clasped her trembling hands together in a gesture of despair. 'Your father insists that you return to Hanover in the morning.'

Incredulous, Dorothea finally sat up. 'Are you throwing me out?' she demanded, quite shocked by the words she had just heard.

Eleanor sighed helplessly. 'Were it up to me, you could stay here indefinitely. But your father is quite adamant. You must return in the morning. I'll send the servants up later today to assist you with your packing.' Watching her daughter's lovely face, Eleanor felt torn by indecision. Wilhelm was so certain that it was right to send her back to her husband. But was it?

'I don't want to go,' Dorothea said evenly. She fought the feeling of desperation that engulfed her. Somehow she hadn't counted on this, hadn't thought that her family would refuse to shelter her.

'You must.' Eleanor made her voice stern. 'You cannot stay here. Where else would you go?'

'With no money, not very far,' Dorothea agreed in bitter tones. She swung her legs over the side of the bed and glared at her mother through sudden tears. 'Why did you do it?'

'Do what?' Eleanor asked in genuine confusion.

'Why did you give away everything I possess? Why did you leave me penniless?'

Eleanor wrung her hands. 'The agreement was drawn up by your father and your uncle,' she tried to explain. 'It was thought to benefit all concerned. How could we have foreseen that you would be so unhappy?' Wearily she sat down on the edge of the bed.

'Benefit all concerned!' Dorothea repeated despairingly. 'It certainly doesn't benefit me. I have nothing!'

Eleanor bit her lip as she watched her daughter. 'I'll sell my jewels,' she offered suddenly. 'You can have that money.'

Dorothea made a face. 'Can you sell them without Father's knowledge and consent?' She laughed harshly at the look of distress she saw. Then she grew quiet. *She* had jewels. Not many – George seldom gave her gifts of that nature. But they ought to produce some money.

'I promise I will try,' Eleanor assured her. She blinked against the hot tears that shone in her eyes. 'And whatever money I get for them will be yours.'

Viewing her mother's saddened face, Dorothea was overcome with remorse. She reached out and they embraced tightly. 'I'm sorry,' she whispered. 'I know that none of this is your fault.'

After a while Eleanor drew away. 'The elector and electress are waiting for you at Herrenhausen,' she said finally, wiping at her damp cheeks with her fingertips. 'You're to meet them there. They will escort you back to Leine.'

Dorothea turned away then. Leaning forward, Eleanor patted her slim hand. 'Please try,' she urged, imploring. 'At times a woman must try very hard and very cleverly to make a marriage work.' She gave a short laugh. 'Men are, after all, not much good at it.'

Dorothea had no intention of trying, but she smiled warmly as she replied. 'I will, Mama.'

With a deep sigh, Eleanor got to her feet. 'I'll send the servants to you shortly.' She regarded Dorothea a moment longer, then left, almost colliding with the returning Lenore, who apologized profusely for her clumsiness.

When the door closed Lenore drew a letter from her pocket. With a broad smile, she handed it to Dorothea. 'It just came,' she said breathlessly.

Dorothea reached for the envelope and quickly broke the seal, then read with avid eyes. After a while she turned to Lenore with barely concealed excitement. 'Do you remember when I told you of Philip's friend, Prince Augustus?'

Lenore wrinkled her brow. 'The one who is built like a bear and drinks like a fish?'

Dorothea laughed. 'Yes.' She nodded. 'That one. Well, his brother has died. Augustus is now Elector of Saxony.'

'Marvelous,' said the doubtful Lenore, who could see no cause for joy.

'Augustus, it seems,' Dorothea continued, consulting the letter, 'owes Philip a great deal of money. Better than thirty thousand crowns. Now that Augustus is elector, Philip has gone to see him.'

'Did he get the money?' Lenore inquired.

'Not yet. But Augustus has promised to pay. In the meantime, he has offered Philip a commission as a general.' She looked up at Lenore and smiled. 'He writes that he has accepted and that the pay is far in excess of what he is now earning.'

'Does that mean he'll be moving to Dresden?'

Nodding, Dorothea replied, 'But first he's returning to Hanover to resign his commission there and to take care of some unfinished business.' She laughed happily. 'We, too, have some unfinished business, Lenore. We're returning to Hanover in the morning. It appears that my father will no longer keep me under his roof.' She tilted her head and regarded Lenore with a half smile. 'How would you like to live in Dresden?' she asked softly.

Lenore's answer was a deep sigh of resignation.

The following morning, to the delighted surprise of both the Duke and Duchess of Celle, Dorothea calmly entered the waiting carriage, cordially bidding her parents good-bye and thanking them for their hospitality.

During the ten-mile drive to Herrenhausen, Dorothea dicussed her plans for escape with Lenore. There was, she explained, little reason to pursue a course of divorce, or even continue with this formal separation which, in any event, had become a mockery. It would simply not come about. She realized that now. Running away was the only solution; they would elope.

Herrenhausen was in sight. Dorothea, viewing the splendid estate, smiled wickedly. She could picture the elector and Sofia watching for her arrival; perhaps even George, although she doubted that. As the carriage slowed, she called out to the driver: 'Keep going! We are not stopping here.'

'Ma chère,' Lenore protested uneasily. But Dorothea paid no mind.

'Continue on to Hanover,' Dorothea instructed with a wave of her gloved hand. The driver, with no alternative, obeyed the orders of his royal passenger.

The draperies had been drawn back to reveal the driveway that led to the large manor house. As Dorothea had suspected, both Ernst and Sofia had noted the approach of the carriage. They saw it slow; then, in some confusion, they watched as it again picked up speed, continuing on down the road, trailing little puffs of ecru dust in its wake.

It took a moment for them both to realize what had happened. They exchanged glances filled with dismay.

'How dare she!' Ernst sputtered at this latest disobedience. In his anger, he was speechless and could only glare at his wife.

By his side, Sofia looked appalled and confused. Apparently their daughter-in-law was returning home in no meeker state of mind than when she had left.

Monplaisir

May 1694

Seated at her writing table, Elizabeth Platen read the report sent to her from Dresden. Over the years, during her many travels, she had found it most expedient to enlist the services of at least one person in each of the various courts throughout the empire. These people were not difficult to find; there were many who were greedy and self-serving. And for any information that might be of interest to her, Elizabeth paid handsomely.

Such a report she now held in her hand. It was not, however, the usual political information normally sent to her. This was of a personal nature. Too personal, actually. Her face was white with anger as she read it again.

It seemed that Philip would shortly be in the employ of Augustus of Saxony. The two, she already knew, were old friends. In fact, it was rumored that Aurora was more than a friend to Augustus. But then that one changed mistresses almost as often as he changed clothes, and far more often than he changed horses.

Philip must have been drunk indeed, she thought, to have said such things. Though she had never seen him drunk, it seemed the only plausible explanation. In the presence of Augustus and a goodly portion of the court of Saxony, Philip had spoken jeeringly of Prince George and his 'ugly mistress.' A man would have to be a fool, he had said, to prefer that harridan to the beautiful princess who was his lawful wife.

Beautiful princess indeed, Elizabeth thought savagely.

Then Philip had gone on to say that he was most fortunate to enjoy the trust of the princess.

'And you enjoy more than that, my friend,' she muttered viciously as she read.

But it was the references to herself that made Elizabeth's eyes glitter with rage. She was, he had told the assemblage, old, and painted her face heavily to disguise it. That was bad enough, but there were innuendos as to her various lovers. He'd even had the gall to tell everyone that she had tried to convince him to marry Charlotte!

In an angry motion, Elizabeth threw the report aside. It landed face up on her writing table. There was no doubt, no doubt at all, that Ernst would receive a similar report.

Elizabeth stared down at the scrawled words for a long moment. The references to her many lovers leapt out at her. It would be best, she decided, if she reached Ernst first. It shouldn't be too difficult to convince him that this was Philip's revenge for his sister's ignoble dismissal from Hanover.

Calm now, Elizabeth got up, retrieved the letter, and put it in a drawer. Then she picked up another piece of parchment and studied it thoughtfully. It was one of Dorothea's letters to Philip. The only one that she had been able to intercept. Unfortunately, it didn't reveal the physical side of their affair, but it was quite explicit with regard to their intention of running away together.

Her red lips curved in a smile as she carefully returned the letter to its hiding place. The 'beautiful princess' was due to return to Hanover shortly. Most likely she would spend a few days at Herrenhausen first. Philip was also scheduled to return, to resign his commission and, probably, sell his heavily mortgaged house.

They would meet, of that Elizabeth had no doubt. Nor did she need to guess how. She was quite familiar with the garden gate.

Oh, yes. They would meet. And when they did, Elizabeth would have her own revenge.

You will pay, my dear Philip, Elizabeth thought as she gently closed the drawer and locked it. You will pay dearly for your unkind words.

Hanover

June 1694

'Welcome back, Count Königsmark.' Conrad Hildebrandt beamed at his employer. 'I received your letter saying that you were returning today. It's been many months.'

'Too many,' Philip agreed, entering his house. He laughed and gave his secretary a playful punch in his ample stomach. 'I see you've been keeping close watch on the larder,' he observed.

Hildebrandt looked abashed. 'Milord,' he murmured uncomfortably, but Philip only laughed harder.

'It's all right, Conrad. Although I daresay that one day you'll eat me out of house and home.' Then he grew serious. 'Have you had any luck with the house?'

Hildebrandt brightened, grateful that the conversation was again on his level. 'Indeed I have, milord. I've gotten a good price for it. There'll be money left over after the mortgage is satisfied.'

'Excellent!'

'Your letter mentioned your new commission. May I offer my congratulations?'

'Thank you, Conrad. It was indeed a stroke of good fortune. We must clear all paperwork within the coming week. I must report back in Dresden by the fifth of July.'

'I'll see to everything, milord.' Hildebrandt hesitated, wondering about his own part in the coming changes. 'Will I be accompanying you?' he asked tentatively.

Philip clapped his secretary on the back. 'I couldn't do without you,' he said, grinning at the man's flush of pleasure. 'Not only will you accompany me, but I plan to raise your wages.'

'Thank you, milord!'

'Fine, fine. I'll leave all the details to you. I'm sure you know how better to handle them, anyway.' He peered at Hildebrandt intently. 'Is the court in Hanover?'

'Yes, milord. The princess returned from Celle more than a week ago. The rest arrived yesterday.'

'The princess returned alone?' That was a surprise. Philip had thought her still in Celle. He was silent a moment as Hildebrandt confirmed this. Then he said, 'Do you have a lackey you can trust?'

'Why, yes.' Hildebrandt nodded, somewhat startled by the unusual question.

'I mean, trust implicitly,' Philip stressed as he walked into the study.

'Yes, indeed. I know of such a one,' Hildebrandt affirmed, following close on Philip's heels.

'Good.' Philip quickly penned a note and sealed it. 'I want you to see that this is delivered to Mademoiselle Knesebeck.'

'The princess's lady?'

'Yes, that's the one.'

'I understand, milord. You can trust me.' Hildebrandt's voice had fallen to a mere murmur. Although Philip had never discussed Dorothea with him, the secretary was well aware of the dangerous involvement.

Philip nodded, satisfied. 'Now, what I need is a hot bath to wash off the grime of the road.' He left the study and took the stairs two at a time, shouting for the servants to bring hot water.

Later, as he dressed, Philip looked outside, his eyes easily locating Dorothea's window. It was barely dusk but a lamp shone softly, and he smiled at the sight of it. Despite all their planning, yet another year had drifted by. But only a few more days, my darling, he vowed. Only a few more days and we will never again be separated.

The thought filled him with so much joy that he could barely contain his excitement. Even the ever-present problem of money faded into the background. And now that Augustus was elector, their position at court was assured. Philip blessed the day that he had befriended the bluff, hearty prince. Whatever his faults, Augustus was proving to be a stout friend.

It was very late. The moon had long since risen and was already on the wane when Philip left his house to make his way across the garden. He was familiar with every tree, every bush, and his progress, while cautious, was made with ease.

He put his hand on the gate and it swung in without resistance. Lenore was waiting. Without words, she beckoned him inside.

Lifting her skirt slightly, Lenore ascended the narrow stone steps, Philip close behind her. There was no light. Both of them ran a hand along the stone wall that, despite the mildness of the summer evening, was cool and damp. At the top of the stairs Lenore opened the door a crack and peered into the corridor. It was empty and silent, so she proceeded.

A moment later they were safely inside Dorothea's apartment.

Outside, from where she had been concealed in the deep shadows of the castle walls, Elizabeth now stepped toward the gate. She turned to the servant beside her. 'Nail it,' she instructed briefly. 'Make certain that it's fastened tight.'

The man nodded and set about his task, but Elizabeth didn't wait. Instead, she glanced up at Dorothea's window, a cold smile on her face. Although the draperies were drawn, she could imagine the tender scene that was now being played out. Then she quickly walked to the front entrance and entered the hall. After cornering a servant, she sent him to awaken the elector. 'I'll wait in his study,' she informed the man curtly.

The servant, an old man, whitened. 'Milady ...' he protested, but fell silent at the look on her face. If it were anyone else – anyone – he would have refused to awaken the elector. But Countess Platen ... one did not cross her.

Confident of being obeyed, Elizabeth went into the study to wait. There was time, she mused. Philip would no doubt be a while.

Almost thirty minutes went by before Ernst appeared, a

dressing robe wrapped about his spare body, his expression disgruntled and annoyed. It was, however, only a mild annoyance, for he knew perfectly well that Elizabeth would not have had him awakened without good cause. Obviously it was something that couldn't wait until morning. In spite of himself, he was intrigued.

'It's past three, Elizabeth,' he grumbled.

'I'm well aware of the time, my dear,' she responded coolly. 'You know I wouldn't have inconvenienced you for a trivial matter.'

He grunted and sat down in a deep-cushioned chair. 'Well, I'm up now. What is it?'

Calmly she handed him Dorothea's letter to Philip. She made no comment, for none was necessary. The incriminating words made it all too plain.

The duke read it, his face growing pale and flushed by turns. Königsmark! He couldn't believe it. Of course there had been rumors, but there were always rumors. He gripped the letter tightly and read it again, skimming over the ridiculous endearments and protestations of undying love. They were obviously making plans to elope. To run away. He looked up at Elizabeth, his mouth slack.

'How long has this been going on?' he managed to ask.

She shrugged. 'Three years, perhaps longer. You can understand why I was so upset over those vicious lies he has been spreading about all of us. The man will stop at nothing!'

Ernst scowled. 'A greater scoundrel never lived,' he agreed grimly. 'But he's not going to get away with *this,*' he went on, tapping the letter. 'Not if I have to lock her in her room. And when he shows his face here …'

'He *is* here,' she interrupted curtly. 'Now.'

The duke's expression went blank.

'My dear Ernst, you don't think I had you awakened just to show you that.' She pointed at the letter he still held.

'Where?' he asked inanely. His voice cracked on the single word.

'He is at this moment in the room of the princess. I've seen him enter with my own eyes.'

The elector blanched. 'My God, you don't mean they're

– they're ...' He leapt out of his chair, hands balled into fists, the letter crumpling beneath the pressure.

'Wait!' she cautioned him as he headed for the door. 'Think of the scandal should you confront him in your daughter-in-law's bedroom. A thing like this couldn't be kept quiet. We must think of Prince George and of Celle.'

Ernst ran a trembling hand through his thinning hair. 'I'm damned if I'll ignore such goings-on under my own roof!' Although his statement was strong enough, his resolve wavered with the thought of Celle.

'Nor should you,' Elizabeth soothed. 'Leave it to me. I assure you he will be placed under guard very soon, without anyone the wiser.' She walked over to him, kissed him fondly on the cheek, and placed her hand on his arm, guiding him gently back to the chair again. 'You wait, my love. When I return, it will all be taken care of, I promise you.'

He sat, but he was still agitated. 'See to it,' he mumbled, waving a hand. 'See to it.'

My God, Ernst thought as Elizabeth left the room. What if they have already gone? What if Dorothea had left – and one day pressed her claim for Celle? He put his head in his hands. The thought was too awful to contemplate. They could never remain an electorate then. Hanover would return to its status of an insignificant town.

In the hall, Elizabeth spied the same servant she had spoken to earlier. She beckoned to him. 'Summon three guards,' she instructed briskly. 'Bring them here to me. And then,' she added as an afterthought, 'you may retire. The elector will remain in his study. If you are needed, I'll summon you.' The fewer people around, she thought, the better.

This time the servant bowed smartly and hastened to do her bidding.

'I must leave,' Philip said, holding Dorothea close. 'It's almost four o'clock.' She clung to him, reluctant to release him. 'It's only for a little while,' he murmured, comforting her. 'I'll return for you tomorrow night. Be ready.'

'I'll be waiting,' Dorothea promised, kissing him hungrily. 'Never will a day seem as long as tomorrow will be.'

Gently he disengaged himself from her arms. 'Get some rest. And remember,' he admonished sternly. 'Pack only what you need.' He grinned. 'I cannot keep coming back for extra trunks and grips.' With a light kiss on the tip of her nose, Philip moved beside Lenore, who glanced cautiously into the corridor.

'All clear,' Lenore whispered, smiling at him.

Philip walked quickly, silently, along the corridor. A moment later he was stepping down the stone stairs. When he reached the gate he pushed on it, annoyed to find that it didn't immediately respond to his touch. He checked the bolt, but it was opened. He pushed again, with the same result. Then he put his shoulder to it.

The gate wouldn't budge. He tried a few more times, thinking it was stuck, but finally gave up. The sky was showing signs of lightening. Soon the whole household would be awake.

Hurrying now, Philip retraced his steps. In the corridor again, he looked about him with a sense of urgency. He didn't dare try to leave by the front door. He pursed his lips as he looked down the long dark hallway. If he remembered rightly, there was another set of stairs at the other end. It led into the huge banquet hall to the rear of the castle. There were several French doors that led out onto the back balcony; even if locked, he could easily force one open.

His mind made up, Philip moved quickly. Only moments later he was in the banquet hall.

His eyes were atuned to the darkness, but his attention was riveted on the doors. He was taken by surprise when the three men jumped out of the shadows and tried to gain a hold on him.

But Philip hadn't spent all his life as a soldier without learning a thing or two. He easily rebuffed one of them as his fist shot out and hit the stranger on the jaw. With the small respite, he was able to draw his sword. The second man was the recipient as Philip plunged the blade into unresisting flesh.

And then, suddenly, his head felt as if it had exploded. He put his hands up, and a second later felt the hot cut of steel as it pierced his own flesh.

The day, as Dorothea had foreseen, was interminable. She was so excited that she sent her regrets for meals, claiming a headache. With the assistance of Lenore, she spent the day packing, first selecting, then discarding particular items. With great care, Lenore was sewing what jewels were available into the lining of one of her gowns. When she was through, she packed her own belongings into a small valise.

Dorothea held up her luxurious fur cloak. 'I cannot leave this behind,' she lamented. 'But there's no room left.'

'Then wear it,' said the ever practical Lenore.

'In July?' Dorothea laughed. But yes, she would have to, she decided. She couldn't bear to leave it there.

After carefully closing the door to the bedchamber, which was in complete disarray, Lenore and Dorothea calmly ate their evening meal in the sitting room. When the servants had cleared away the empty dishes, they again returned to the bedchamber to wait.

With maddening slowness the hands of the clock passed eleven, then twelve. Philip was to come for them at three in the morning. Lenore urged sleep. 'The time will pass faster. I'll keep watch.'

Dorothea shook her head firmly. 'I can't sleep. Not now, not on this of all nights.'

So they waited.

The hands of the clock finally touched three, then went past it silently, as if the number were of no great importance.

At first, neither of the women was unduly concerned. Philip was cautious. If he had seen anyone, a servant, a burgher getting an early start to Celle, anyone, he would wait until the way was clear.

At three-thirty, Dorothea went to the window and looked across the gardens to Philip's house. From this angle the forecourt was obscured. But even if it weren't, it was too dark to see if a carriage waited. Restless, she returned to her chair.

'Relax, *ma chère*,' Lenore said gently. 'It's a big step. No doubt there are many last-minute details he must see to.'

'But why tonight?' Dorothea fretted, refusing to be

consoled. 'He's almost never late. Why should he be late tonight of all nights?'

Lenore shrugged. Who was she to fathom the affairs of men? She regarded Dorothea fondly. Someday, Lenore hoped, she would find a love as intense as had Dorothea. So far, no man had caught her fancy for more than a few brief nights. But perhaps that was just as well, she reflected stoically. There might be little ecstasy in her life, but neither was there any turmoil. Except of course that which was provided by her young mistress, who seemed to have an inexhaustible supply of it.

By four-thirty, Dorothea was frantic. It was only with the greatest effort that Lenore was able to restrain her from running into the night in search of Philip.

'Something has gone wrong,' she speculated, keeping her voice calm. 'We can only do harm if we act rashly.'

Almost ill with fear and disappointment, Dorothea threw herself across the bed.

She didn't think she had slept, but when next she opened her eyes sunlight was streaming in through the window. Quickly she glanced at Lenore. Still sitting in the chair, the woman smiled at her sadly. She didn't speak, for there was little need to inform Dorothea that Philip hadn't come for them.

Time and again Conrad Hildebrandt parted the draperies and peered outside. Where the devil was he? Today was the first of July. He had checked his calendar more than once. There was no mistake. Today was the day they had to leave for Dresden. Actually, he had been given to understand that they would get an early start, three-thirty, or four at the latest. But here it was, almost noon, and no sign of Count Königsmark.

Noon was the deadline. If they left later, they wouldn't arrive in Dresden at the appointed time. Hildebrandt knew where the count had gone, at least he thought he did; but then, perhaps he was wrong.

In fact, the only thing he was certain of was that Königsmark was not there. And he had said that he would be.

Hildebrandt sat down and waited. While he waited he

ate, because it passed the time and because it soothed his frazzled nerves. As he munched on leftover sauerbraten, washed down with strong beer, he kept his eye on the clock.

By three-thirty in the afternoon his concern had deepened to worry. Even cherry strudel couldn't calm his mounting apprehension.

In his carriage, Hildebrandt rode to the outskirts of Hanover, diligently picking his teeth on the short journey. He really didn't know what to do. The house was sold, the papers were in order, his bags were packed, Königsmark's things were ready, all as instructed.

With his tongue, Hildebrandt pushed against a tooth that had of late been bothering him, and at the same time hoped that Königsmark didn't turn up while he was gone. That would be a fine mess, he thought, probing within the depths of his mouth.

He belched discontentedly as they approached the camp, wrinkling his nose at the unaccustomed odors of leather, horse dung, and male sweat. Quickly he produced a white linen handkerchief and held it to his nose.

'Marshal Podewils,' Hildebrandt said cordially as he entered the commander's quarters a short time later. 'I hope I'm not intruding.'

Podewils offered a gracious smile, hiding his surprise at the sight of Königsmark's secretary. 'Of course not, Hildebrandt. Come in.'

'I won't take but a minute.'

Podewils nodded, amused by the sight of the short fat man. 'Take two, if you like. What can I do for you?'

'I was wondering if you'd seen Count Königsmark.'

Podewils's face clouded. 'He's not here,' he said. 'In fact, I thought he was in town. The last word I had from him was that he was going there to resign his commission. I understand that he's had a more lucrative offer from Saxony.' Seeing Hildebrandt's obvious disappointment, he asked, 'What's wrong?'

Hildebrandt shrugged, annoyed by the wasted trip. He'd been so certain that Königsmark was there. There was no other place for him to be. 'You are correct, Commander,' he said at last. 'In fact, we were to leave for

Dresden today. But Count Königsmark has ... disappeared.'

Leaning back, Podewils laughed heartily at the news. 'Disappeared? My dear man, Königsmark disappears only when he wants to.' He got up and put an arm about Hildebrandt, escorting him to the door. 'I shouldn't worry, if I were you,' he said, seeing the man's genuine distress. 'He'll turn up. And I'll wager he has a fine excuse for his tardiness. He always does.'

Still laughing, Podewils returned to his desk. Hildebrandt again entered the carriage. Somehow, the commander's hearty words didn't soothe him.

By late afternoon he was back in the house, waiting. Just before dinner, the front door burst open and Hildebrandt watched stupidly as the house filled with guards.

'What? What?' he said ineffectually, astounded by the intrusion.

A captain of the guards stepped forward and bowed perfunctorily. 'I regret to inform you, monsieur, that this house is under official seal.'

'You can't,' Hildebrandt began to protest. He fell silent as the captain thrust a paper at him.

'This says I can,' the man said simply.

Dumbfounded, Hildebrandt read the search warrant. It was legal, all right. And it was stamped with the elector's own seal. But what could they possibly want? he wondered as he watched the guards rummaging through the rooms. Wearily he sat down on a chair in the hall. There wasn't anything he could do, he decided unhappily. But the events told him one thing. Königsmark hadn't come home for the simple reason that he had been arrested.

Hildebrandt sat there chewing his lip, while the guards went about their business. At last his brow cleared. He would write immediately to the count's sister. Aurora was, he hoped, still in Dresden. If rumors were correct, she was a close friend of Augustus. Very close, indeed. Surely the Elector of Saxony would have some say in the matter of the arrest of one of his generals.

Some days later, Lenore, who had been gone all morning, returned to Dorothea. Seeing the questioning look, Lenore shook her head slightly. 'No one seems to know where he is,' she said slowly. 'I've even spoken to Hildebrandt. He's as mystified as the rest of us.'

'But isn't he doing something about it?' Dorothea protested, viewing her lady in distress.

'Indeed,' Lenore affirmed. 'He has managed to get word to Augustus that Philip is missing.'

Dorothea sighed and felt less alone. 'Surely the elector will be able to do something,' she murmured, still upset.

Lenore hesitated, wondering whether she could relate the rest of her information. But it was best, she decided, that Dorothea know everything. 'Philip's house has been searched,' she reported in a quiet voice. 'It's now under official seal.'

'Oh, my God.' Dorothea collapsed in a chair. It took a moment before she could find her voice again. 'Then he's in prison,' she cried out. 'They have found us out and have buried him in a dungeon!'

Lenore did not correct her mistress, but privately she thought Königsmark too important a person to imprison. The alternative, however, was one that not even she wanted to face. *'Ma chère,'* she said softly. 'They must've found your letters. It will only make matters worse if they find his here. You must destroy them.'

Dorothea drew in her breath sharply. 'No! I will never do that.' Her brow creased as she glanced about the room. 'We'll hide them.'

'There is no place they can be hidden,' Lenore protested strongly. She sighed, noting Dorothea's face. 'Wrap them together. I'll try to get them to Hildebrandt. He can send them to Aurora Königsmark for safekeeping.' When Dorothea still made no response, she added, 'I'm certain she'll return them to you whenever you want. Remember, if they fall into the wrong hands, you'll never see them again.'

Still Dorothea hesitated, unwilling to part with Philip's letters. But at last she saw the logic in the suggestion. Unhappily, she began to gather the precious mementos.

In the duke's study, where they had been closeted for days now, Ernst and George sat at the desk, the top of which was covered with a pile of paper. There were almost two hundred letters. In growing amazement they read them mostly in silence.

George positively blanched as he read his wife's candid opinion of him. Occasionally they came across one that described Wilhelm in unflattering terms: rigid, unfair, even aged. These Ernst carefully laid aside.

George was numb. He didn't love Dorothea, had never loved her, but his wife's actions appalled him. Blatantly taking a lover, then deciding to run away with him. Damn, if she'd taken a lover and had done it discreetly, he would have been generous enough to look away. But she had betrayed him in the worst manner. For that, he would never forgive her.

With a grunt, he threw a letter aside and stared dolefully at his father. 'I hope you're not going to suggest that I continue this marriage.' He rubbed his weary eyes. 'I can't accept this. Regardless of the consequences, I just can't accept it.' He got up and began to pace the room, stiff with the long hours of sitting there, reading those damnable letters. Pausing, he glanced at his father, annoyed that Ernst had even hesitated in his response. George's mouth tightened and he scowled. This time my father had better agree, he thought grimly. This time I will not return to that woman.

Ernst issued a deep sigh, momentarily at a loss for words. There was no doubt in his mind, after reading all of this, that Dorothea had actually slept with the man. Incredible, Ernst reflected. How could she have managed this liaison for more than three years without anyone knowing about it? Brazen! He'd known that his daughter-in-law had an unruly temper, but this! This *was* too much to ask of George. The prince had been patient long enough.

And yet. Just that morning Elizabeth had brought him news of the latest rumor making the rounds. 'Little Philip' they were calling George's son. Little Philip indeed, Ernst thought indignantly. The boy was George's son. Of that, at least, there was no doubt; the letters before him were proof of that. At all cost the rumors had to be stilled, for the sake of his grandson, his son, and, of course, Celle.

'I agree to the divorce,' Ernst said at last in a tired and somber voice. He ignored George's grateful look. 'But – and hear me well – there must be no hint of adultery.'

'What?' George was astounded. His eyes widened, his mouth gaped.

Ernst raised a hand, glaring at his son. 'Think for a moment,' he hissed, angry with George's obtuseness. 'There is more here to consider than your wounded pride. Think of your son. Do you want it bandied about that he is Königsmark's spawn?'

George looked pained. He walked back to the desk and sat down again. 'There's no question of that,' he protested heatedly. 'The proof is here.' He touched the pile of letters. 'They didn't even meet until after George Augustus was born.'

'For you and for me, it is there,' Ernst noted acidly. 'But at the slightest hint of adultery, your children will come under a cloud of suspicion that will never dissipate!' Thank God, he was thinking, that the letters were all dated. Even Sophie-Dorothea had been born before they had met each other.

George was regarding his father sardonically. 'So, we announce to the world that my wife is a paragon of virtue?' His lip curled.

Ernst stared steadily, nostrils flared. 'I'm afraid, my son, that that is exactly what we must do.'

'But I will not longer live with her,' George stated emphatically. 'I insist on that.'

'You no longer need live with her,' Ernst agreed calmly. 'As for the terms of the divorce, if I know my daughter-in-law – ' he fixed George with a baleful glance – 'and I think I know her better than you, she will play right into our hands.'

Hanover

August 1694

Franz Platen bowed courteously to the princess as he entered her sitting room. He was dressed in a black velvet doublet, the austerity of which was relieved by a white ruffled shirt sporting tiny pearl buttons. The austerity of his expression, however, was marked, unrelieved by even a hint of a smile.

'If I may, Highness, I would like to speak with you privately.' Platen cast a pointed look in the direction of Lenore Knesebeck. Dorothea nodded and Lenore withdrew with as much calmness as she could muster.

When they were alone, Platen again regarded Dorothea. She looked pale and had lost weight since he had last seen her. The soft gray morning gown she was wearing hung loose about the waist and hips. 'What I have to discuss with you,' he said, keeping his voice civil, 'is of a somewhat delicate nature. It would facilitate matters if I were permitted to speak frankly.'

Dorothea eyed him warily. Her nerves felt stretched to the breaking point. She clasped her hands tightly to keep them from trembling. Although she had no liking for the minister, she was glad to see him. Perhaps he would tell her where Philip was. She knew nothing. In these past two weeks only Sofia had visited her, offering the curt suggestion that she remain in her apartments until further notice. Not trusting her voice, Dorothea now merely nodded in affirmation.

'Prince George is most anxious for a reconciliation,' the minister stated blandly. 'However, if you agree, it must be a *complete* reconciliation. In other words, Highness, he must be allowed to return to your bed.' Platen almost smiled at the shocked look on the face of the princess.

In complete amazement, Dorothea stared at him. She had never expected this. 'No.' She spoke the word emphatically, then was momentarily puzzled by Platen's satisfied smile.

'Am I to understand then that you still desire a divorce?' he inquired with a lift of his black brows.

The feeling of relief was overwhelming. Dorothea was filled with exultation. At last they were prepared to give her what she so desperately wanted. 'I do. And the sooner the better.' If Philip were indeed imprisoned, as she strongly suspected, then if she were divorced there would be no point in keeping him locked up.

Again there was that look of satisfaction. Platen had long suspected that the princess was so anxious for her freedom she would be most amenable to any terms.

'Then the prince – with the elector's sanction, of course – is prepared to dissolve the marriage between you.' Platen cleared his throat. 'There are only two conditions under which the court and the church will agree to grant a divorce,' he explained. 'One is adultery by the wife in question; the other is willful desertion by either party.' He smiled thinly. 'Naturally the first is out of the question. As for the second, obviously the prince cannot have been said to leave his own home. Therefore ...' He spread his hands.

'Therefore the responsibility of desertion must be mine,' Dorothea finished for him with a sarcastic smile. Yet she could see the point of it. She could never admit to adultery; that would separate her from her children forever. 'I will go to Celle,' she said at last.

'Ah, no,' Platen interjected, sounding regretful. 'That would not be a good idea, Highness. You see, the court would have no way of knowing that your move was permanent if you went to your parents' house. You have done that before. No.' He shook his head. 'It would be better if you went elsewhere.'

'But where else can I go?' said a mystified Dorothea.

'You are familiar with the Castle of Ahlden, are you not?' he queried pleasantly. 'It's only a few miles from Celle and belongs to your father.' He smiled again. 'And you have always wanted your own residence.'

She brightened. 'Yes. It's perfect,' she exclaimed. 'If my father agrees, I shall be glad to go there.'

'Excellent.' Platen beamed, pleased with how smoothly all this was going. He fumbled in his pocket and brought forth several documents. 'Now I will need your signature, Highness. The courts are quite fussy about these things.' He walked toward the writing table. Dorothea followed, seating herself in a straight-backed chair with a hand-embroidered cushion. She was at pains to keep the excited anticipation she was feeling from showing on her face. Freedom was actually within her grasp! Her hand trembled as she reached for the quill.

'This one – ' Platen tapped a page – 'states that you refuse – now, and in the future – to cohabit with your lawful husband. And this one – ' he pointed to another sheet – 'states that it is your intent to leave your husband's house and take up permanent residence at Ahlden.' He watched as the princess unhesitatingly affixed her signature to both forms. Then he laid the final document before her.

Dorothea glanced at it, her brow creasing in a frown. 'This says I agree never to remarry!' She looked up at him in some perplexity.

Platen nodded but made no immediate comment.

Dorothea moistened her lips. 'I don't think I shall sign this one,' she murmured, and made as if to hand it back to him.

The minister made no move to take it. 'I believe that it would be in your own best interest to reconsider, Highness,' he remarked in a quiet voice.

'I hardly think that it's in my best interest,' Dorothea retorted with a flash of defiance. 'Nor do I think the court will find it necessary.'

Franz Platen pursed his lips and regarded her with cool eyes. 'If you do not agree, then I doubt that this will even reach the court,' he murmured, watching her closely.

Her brows drew together in consternation. 'Are you saying that the elector will refuse to sanction the divorce unless I sign this?'

His smile was enigmatic. 'I cannot speak for the elector,

Highness,' he answered. 'But I would venture to say that your assumption is most probably correct.' His thin face held a bland expression as he regarded her. 'On the other hand, he might decide to go ahead with it – using a charge other than willful desertion.'

Dorothea's mouth tightened, but her mind was working furiously. One thing at a time, she told herself. What she held in her hand was merely a piece of paper. There was no way in the world they could prevent her from marrying again if she chose to do so. Oh, she would not be able to marry here, in Hanover. But there were other places, other countries, that would offer no barrier. And once she *was* married, there would be nothing they could do about it. She reached for the quill.

Platen nodded, approving, then gathered the documents together in a neat pile. 'Now it's only a matter of review by the court.'

'How long will it take?'

'Only a few weeks. Although I suggest that you leave for Ahlden immediately.' He paused at the door. 'One more thing. Mademoiselle Knesebeck will not be accompanying you.' He raised a hand before Dorothea could protest. 'Trust me. It's only until all this is settled. Surely you agree that the woman deserves a brief holiday. Naturally you will not be unattended. The electress has chosen two ladies who will go with you.'

Dorothea had indeed been ready to protest. But perhaps the minister was right: Lenore did deserve a holiday. 'Count Platen,' she said, as he turned to go. 'I've heard some disquieting news about Count Königsmark. I ... was wondering if you could tell me where he is.'

Platen raised his brows in apparent surprise. 'I've no idea as to the whereabouts of Count Königsmark,' he replied smoothly. 'Quite possibly he may be on his way to Dresden.'

'I've heard that his house is under seal,' she persisted, watching him, imploring.

A shadow of annoyance crossed his gaunt features. He had been right, Platen thought, to have suggested the removal of Mademoiselle Knesebeck. 'That is true,' he admitted at last. 'There were some papers that were in his possession that the elector thought harmful to the welfare of Hanover.' He regarded her with a pointed look, gratified to see the sudden pallor. 'Naturally we would not want them to fall into the wrong hands.' He smiled then. 'If you're concerned about the official seal, perhaps it may set your mind at ease to know that it has been removed. The house is, in fact, sold. I believe the new occupants will be arriving within a week or two.'

When the minister left, Dorothea sank weakly into a chair. They had her letters, of that she had little doubt. Then she relaxed a bit. If they were planning to use them against her, they would have already done so. Perhaps, she thought suddenly, Philip was not in prison at all. Perhaps he went into hiding when he saw that his house was under the official seal. The thought made her feel better. Once Philip learned that she was in Ahlden, and free, he would contact her. She would go to him, wherever he was. Even if she had to make the trip alone, somehow she would manage.

Platen immediately reported to the elector, who was carrying on a discussion with Prince George. Platen related what had happened, including the princess's inquiry about Königsmark.

Ernst grunted. 'You were right about that woman,' he said, referring to Lenore. 'I questioned her myself with regard to her participation in this matter. But she was adamant. According to her, the princess is entirely innocent of any misconduct.' He gave a harsh laugh. 'Mademoiselle Knesebeck will not trouble us again.' He picked up the document Platen had put before him, nodding in approval as he saw the signature.

'I don't see what good all this is going to do,' George complained with a brief glance at the papers. 'Once she has her divorce, she can do anything she wants. Who is to stop her from marrying again? Then what?'

'She has agreed to never remarry,' Platen pointed out, picking up the document in question. 'It is here, in writing.'

'There's nothing to stop her from leaving the country,' George declared, unconvinced. 'She could marry in France, in Poland, in England! How are we to make certain she never leaves Hanover?'

Ernst merely smiled at her son. 'You may leave the details to us,' he noted calmly. He regarded George's disgruntled face with speculative eyes. 'It might be wise for you to go to Brandenburg until this is over. There's no need for you to be here. Franz will give you the necessary papers to sign before you leave.' He stood up and motioned to the footman standing just outside the room, giving orders for his carriage to be readied. 'I think it's time I paid my brother a visit,' Ernst announced. He picked up the letters that he had so carefully separated from the rest. He had an idea that Wilhelm would be most interested in them.

Upstairs in her bedchamber, Dorothea was still sitting in a chair when two women entered. She recognized them both. One was Gertrud von Holst, a tall, nondescript woman with a face frozen in perpetual rebuke. The other was Klara Richthoften, plump and humorless, her black hair drawn into a knot at the back of her head. Both were women would could be described as impoverished nobility, both were widows, and both were in their late thirties. Already Dorothea missed Lenore.

'Where is Mademoiselle Knesebeck?' she demanded as the women briskly set about packing. 'Am I not to be allowed to say good-bye?'

Gertrud fixed her with a stony stare. 'I believe Mademoiselle Knesebeck has been instructed by the elector to take her leave immediately.'

'Where did she go?' Dorothea hoped Lenore hadn't gone all the way to Hamburg to see her sister. If that was the case, she could be gone for months.

'That, Princess, is something I do not know,' Gertrud responded truthfully as she resumed packing.

Dorothea's mouth tightened. 'I will not leave until I see my children,' she stated emphatically. 'For the past two weeks they have not been brought to me for their daily visit.'

Fine time to think of them, Gertrud thought with contempt, but she bowed her head in a respectful manner. 'I'll get them now, if you like.' Turning, she walked toward the door. Dorothea thought she looked like a vessel under full sail.

A few minutes later the woman returned holding George Augustus with one hand and Sophie-Dorothea with the other. The boy's face lit up when he saw his mother and he rushed into her open arms.

'I haven't seen you in days,' he cried petulantly. 'They said you were ill. Are you?' He looked at her with wide blue eyes.

'I was.' Dorothea smoothed the soft black hair. 'But I'm well now.' She reached out and clasped the boy to her, then reached for her daughter. 'I want you both to listen carefully,' she said, looking from one to the other. 'I must go away for a while. And I would like to know that you both will be good while I'm gone.'

'Where are you going?' piped Sophie-Dorothea.

'Only to Ahlden, which is not so very far away.'

'When will you be coming home?' George Augustus inquired, toying with the rope of pearls about his mother's neck.

Dorothea wet her lips. 'It may be that I will live in Ahlden. However, I'll visit you both often, I promise.' She again hugged them, then stood up. 'Madame von Holst will take you back now. And remember, I want to hear only good things about you.' She watched the children with a wistful smile as they scampered away. Then she sobered. She must speak to Platen about the children. Perhaps they would allow them to come to Ahlden for visits, or she could meet them at Celle.

Platen, however, was unavailable, it seemed. George had already left Hanover. Ernst had gone hunting. Sofia assured Dorothea that she would speak to the elector as soon as he returned, assuring the princess that she would send word to Ahlden as soon as the matter was resolved.

With very little regret, Dorothea took her leave from the Court of Hanover and made her way to her new home … the Castle of Ahlden.

Celle

August 1696

Eleanor stood by the window in the drawing room, her back to Wilhelm, and pressed her fingertips to her throbbing temples. She felt as if she could no longer bear the pressure; yet it was there, relentless, persistent, demanding her attention even when she didn't want to give it.

'My God,' she said in a low voice, without turning. 'How could you have let such a thing happen?'

There was no answer. She turned then. Noting Wilhelm's cold expression as he viewed her, Eleanor felt a pang of sadness. He had been looking at her like that often lately.

Perhaps, Eleanor thought, tired, Dorothea had ended more than one marriage. She, too, felt differently. Toward Wilhelm. She knew she shouldn't have brought up the subject again. But she couldn't help herself.

'She has disgraced our house,' Wilhelm replied at last in a low, angry voice. He was, as she had suspected, irritated with her for speaking of Dorothea. Even now, after two years, the sight of those letters burned in his mind like some sort of eternal flame that refused to be dampened.

'But she is your daughter,' Eleanor pleaded. 'Your only child.'

'I have no child, madame. Nor do I wish to hear her name spoken in this house again.'

'I will not agree to that,' Eleanor said quickly, defiantly. 'At least allow me to visit her.'

Wilhelm's expression merely grew more frigid. 'No!'

'You cannot keep her locked up forever,' she protested,

on the verge of tears. 'The divorce has been granted. And you and your brother forced her to agree that she would never remarry,' she added bitterly. Eleanor thought of how hard she had fought to have that document destroyed. The trouble was, they wouldn't allow her to see Dorothea; now, or when the divorce proceedings were in progress. Dorothea had wanted so desperately to be free that she had signed anything that they had put before her.

A slight, unpleasant smile drifted across Wilhelm's face. 'Forced?' he noted, jeering. 'The little fool agreed to everything of her own free will. So anxious was she to rid herself of her lawful husband that she even appeared before the court and told them she was acting of her own free will.'

Eleanor found this logic maddening. 'She didn't agree to spend the rest of her life at Ahlden,' she said in a rising voice laced with hysteria. 'She didn't agree to forfeit the right to see her own children!'

Wilhelm straightened his shoulders. 'The elector and I did what we thought best.'

'For whom?' she challenged, at this moment hating him. 'Certainly not for Dorothea. You let your brother wrap you around his little finger. A word from him and you allowed your daughter to be imprisoned like a criminal!' Eleanor knew she was screaming but couldn't help herself. They'd been having this same argument, with slight variations, for the past two years. She had exhausted every plea she could think of and had invented a few new ones, all to no avail.

Wilhelm's expression didn't change. As far as he was concerned, Dorothea had besmirched the name of his family. He did not for one moment decry Ernst's harshness. That man had worked so tirelessly to upgrade Hanover to an electorate. He didn't deserve the bitter blow of having an adulterous daughter-in-law.

'You are hysterical, madame,' Wilhelm observed coolly as he walked toward the door. 'You may not agree never to mention her name again. But then, I don't have to listen, do I?' With that, he left the room.

Eleanor collapsed in a chair, her despair too deep for the luxury of tears.

God, how she had pleaded, Eleanor recalled, staring dully about her. But, as always, Ernst had gotten his way. It wasn't enough that all of Dorothea's property, including Celle, remained in George's hands. No, it hadn't been nearly enough.

If only they had allowed me to see her, Eleanor thought, probably for the hundredth time. But that was one of the first things Ernst had insisted on when he spoke to Wilhelm. Eleanor remembered that night so clearly, never realizing then that it would change her whole life. She had been surprised to see Ernst; his visit had been unannounced. For hours he had been closeted with Wilhelm, hours in which they had plotted the course of her own daughter's life. There had been letters, although Eleanor herself had not seen one of them, the contents of which Wilhelm refused to speak of. But Ernst's condition that Eleanor not see her daughter was only the first thing he had insisted on.

The second had been the stipulation that Dorothea never remarry. That shocked even the court, which had demanded that the princess present herself and, in her own voice, agree. Inexplicably, Dorothea had done so.

But Dorothea hadn't known about the rest, Eleanor reflected grimly. Dorothea hadn't known that instead of freedom, the price of her divorce would be confinement in Ahlden – for the rest of her life. And the children, that was another thing she hadn't known about.

Eleanor's eyes narrowed. They wouldn't allow *her* to visit her child, either. But she wouldn't give up, Eleanor vowed, clenching her hands in her lap. If it took the rest of her life, she would see Dorothea free. She would even welcome Königsmark, if he could help. But he, like the rest of them, seemed to have deserted Dorothea.

Idly, Eleanor wondered what had happened to Philip. Although she was only one of many. Aurora Königsmark has caused such a fuss that repercussions were still going on, even now, two years later. Augustus, prompted by his beautiful mistress, had sent a special envoy to Hanover. Even King William expressed a strong curiosity. But Ernst, ever shrewd, requested that the emperor intervene. He was, the elector let it be known, displeased with all this interference in his internal affairs. Thereafter, the shouts had subsided to whispers.

Ernst knew where Philip was, Eleanor was certain of it. And even Wilhelm probably knew what had happened to Königsmark, although he would not speak, even to her. That meant one of two things: Königsmark was either imprisoned or he was dead. Probably the latter. Under those circumstances he could be of no further use to Dorothea; for that fact only, Eleanor mourned him. If it hadn't been for him in the first place, all of this would not have happened.

At this thought Eleanor wrapped her arms around her stomach and rocked back and forth in anguish. What have you done, my darling child? she thought in utter despair. You've given up everything, more than you will ever imagine. All in the name of love. Love for a man who is now probably dead. And when you agreed to take Ahlden as your 'permanent' residence, you had no idea of just how permanent it would be.

Eleanor ceased rocking. My God, they even refused to let Dorothea out into the courtyard. Her daughter hadn't even been out in fresh air for two years!

A sob escaped from Eleanor's throat, already ragged and sore from countless such eruptions in the past months. Dorothea would die! No one could live without fresh air and sunshine. She would die!

Eleanor gripped her hands so tightly that her nails sunk into the palms of her hands. But not while *she* could help it, Eleanor vowed fiercely. Not while she had an ounce of blood left with which to fight.

For a long time Eleanor sat there. The afternoon sun ambled across the sky and finally sunk from view.

Eleanor realized she couldn't effect Dorothea's release. Not yet. But there might be a way at least to allow her to be able to go outside. The more Eleanor thought about it, the more she was certain that it would work.

Determined now, Eleanor got to her feet and tugged on the silken bellcord. When, a short time later, a servant entered, she sent for Bernstorff.

She was still lost in thought when the minister appeared, a questioning look on his face. The expression, however, merely concealed a mild apprehension. He hoped there wouldn't be another outbreak of the furious hysterics that had gripped the duchess in these past months. He was pleasantly relieved, therefore, when her voice came to him calmly, almost disinterestedly.

'Some time ago,' Eleanor said, her brow furrowed in apparent contemplation, 'there was a woman in Hanover for carnival. She was quite adept at telling fortunes. Do you recall her name?'

Bernstorff's expression relaxed and he laughed quietly. 'The gypsy? I believe she called herself Tamara, or some such heathenish name.' The laughter stopped, but he still smiled. She had been an old woman, wrinkled beyond belief, but she had caused quite a sensation. Of course he himself didn't believe in that foolishness with the cards, but some took it quite seriously. Prince George was especially vulnerable. He had hung on her words as if she were speaking gospel.

Eleanor smiled faintly, the expression never reaching her blue eyes. 'Yes, I do believe you are right,' she mused. 'Have you any idea where she is now?'

Bernstorff frowned in perplexity. 'The last I heard, she was in Brandenburg,' he offered. 'But I'm not certain that she is still there.'

'I would like you to find out,' Eleanor instructed in the same casual tone. 'When you locate her, have her invited to Celle.'

'Madame?' He bent forward, his eyes opening wide in acute surprise.

Eleanor shrugged, still smiling. 'These past months have been so trying. I'm certain we can all do with a bit of diversion. Don't you agree?' She regarded him in open candor.

'Of course, milady,' he responded quickly. His smile broadened. And about time it was, too, he thought as he left to do her bidding.

Despite Bernstorff's conscientious efforts, fall was well under way before the gypsy woman could be found and brought to Celle. Eleanor put the long weeks to good use.

The Castle of Celle was cleaned, polished, and

decorated in the most lavish manner. Invitations were sent to the court of Hanover and as far away as Brandenburg. These were readily accepted when it was learned that one of the entertainments was to be Tamara, the gypsy fortune-teller.

Even Duke Ernst and Prince George accepted readily, with some relief, seeing that the Duchess of Celle had apparently reconciled herself to all that had happened.

As for Wilhelm, he joined in enthusiastically with the plans for the great festivities, happy to see that Eleanor had at last emerged from the melancholia that had gripped her all these months.

October was almost gone when the merrymaking, scheduled to last all week, began.

Eleanor greeted her guests in a calm and gracious manner. She was looking particularly radiant in a satin gown, apricot in color, and was bejeweled and exquisitely coiffed. She smiled brilliantly at Ernst, was courteous to George. Even Melusine von Schulenburg was greeted in a cordial and friendly manner.

George, who had been prepared for a most awkward time, relaxed, began to enjoy himself. It was, however, quite late in the evening before he approached the screened-off area where the gypsy woman sat at a small table, reading the cards for any who cared to indulge in this bit of whimsy.

No one knew the gypsy woman's age, but it was suspected to be in the upward reaches of seventy. She wore her wrinkles proudly, defiantly. From the many creases that comprised her weathered face, black eyes shone brightly, intelligently, and appeared those of a much younger woman. Her flowing gown was of flowered silk. A red kerchief all but hid her thick black hair.

Somewhat unsteady on his feet from copious draughts of wine, George sat down before her. Immediately she handed him the stack of cards, instructing him to select one. With the movement, her many gold bracelets jangled musically. Reaching out, George chose a card – the knight of coins – and this she placed on the porcelain-topped table between them.

'It is you,' she said briefly. Then she further instructed that George shuffle the remaining cards and cut them three times. When this was done, she removed the top seven cards. Beginning at her right, she positioned them in a half circle beneath the indicator card.

George watched as the old woman ran her fingertips over the first three: the ace of coins, the eight of cups, and the king of cups. Then she regarded him.

'Your crown will rest heavily on your head,' she intoned with a brief glance at him.

'I wear no crown,' George murmured, staring at the card.

'You will,' the old woman replied, unruffled. Then, tapping the third card, she continued. 'But there is one who will greatly ease your burden and, in all but name, will rule in your stead.'

George frowned but made no comment as she ran her hand over the next three cards: the queen of swords, which had fallen in a reverse position; the tower, with its crumbling façade in flames; and the nine of swords.

That last one chilled George as he viewed the picture of a man who, in an attitude of utter misery, was sitting up in bed, weeping. Behind the man were bars; and these cast ominous shadows.

The gypsy viewed the cards a moment without speaking, then looked at George again, her expression grave. She pointed to the reverse queen of swords. 'The health of your wife is linked to your own. Your fates are bound together.'

'I have no wife,' he managed to say in a choked voice. His palms felt moist. Absently, heedless of his satin breeches, he rubbed his hands along the top part of his thighs.

'But you do,' she repeated, bringing his attention to the reversed position of the card. 'Be she widowed or divorced, she is one and the same.' She turned her attention to the next cards: the tower and the nine of swords. She tapped this last for emphasis. 'Unless accident befalls her, she will live for many years.'

'What is that to me?' George demanded in a shaken voice. I should not, he thought, have had that last glass of wine. It was resting in a most unstable manner on his stomach.

'You will survive her by no more than twelve months, nor less than six months.' She tilted her head slightly, hearing his sharp, indrawn breath.

'How can you be certain of that?' His voice sounded strange, even to his own ears.

'I am not,' she replied in her curious, flat voice. 'The cards are certain. I can tell you only what they tell me.'

With a hand that trembled visibly, George pointed to the nine of swords. 'Is that a card of death?' he asked through numbed lips.

She merely raised her eyes to meet his gaze. 'It is the final card for us all,' she noted calmly. 'Only the time is of any importance.' She touched the seventh card: the chariot. 'The outcome depends on you,' she advised. 'You may choose your own direction.'

'I don't understand,' he said, blinking.

She shrugged her bony shoulders and tightened the fringed shawl she wore. 'I can tell you only what I see,' she repeated, without concern. 'You will survive your wife by no more than one year. If she falls ill, beware.'

The gypsy watched in dry amusement as the prince stumbled to his feet. She resisted the urge to touch the fat purse of coins that lay comfortably in her pocket. The Duchess of Celle had been most generous.

Then Tamara looked at the cards again and frowned slightly. Strangely, they had fallen as if the hand of Fate had placed them there. Although paid in coin, Tamara had not had to contrive at all.

The thought was comforting.

Schafels

April 1697

Lenore got to her feet from where she had been sitting on the cold floor and viewed her handiwork with satisfaction.

The stone wall was covered with scratched-in words. From the ceiling to the floor, almost every inch was covered. Tedious; but then, she'd had nothing else to occupy her time in these past three years. She looked at her hands. Both were blackened, the right hand terribly calloused. She rubbed them on her woolen skirt, her eyes returning to the wall. Each word, each letter, had been laboriously scratched in with a small rock, worn down to an almost knife-like sharpness. A candle placed in close proximity to a stone eventually produced a black, charcoal-like substance. This she carefully scraped off with a spoon. Moistened with a bit of water, it produced an effective inking-in of the words when she rubbed it into the crevices.

It was her story that she had placed on the wall, how she had been imprisoned for no reason, how she had been shut away without trial.

For three years now Lenore had not left this room in the tower of Schafels, where she had been summarily sent after the elector had questioned her. Presumably angered by her steadfast defense of Dorothea, he had ordered her taken away that very day.

At least she wasn't in a dungeon, there was that to be said. Her cell was in the upper tower. It had a fairly comfortable bed, a table, two chairs, and even two windows. The windows were not barred; they didn't need to be. First, they were too narrow for anyone but a small child to get through, and second, it was close to a hundred-foot drop to the ground.

A noise made her turn around. Lenore watched as the heavy iron door swung inward. Karl Muntz, the only other human being she had seen for these past three years, entered with her evening meal. He was in his late fifties, stoop-shouldered and arthritic.

With an audible sigh, Karl set the tray on the table, then sat down, a practice he had begun some six months after her arrival.

'Them stairs gets to my legs,' he complained, rubbing them for emphasis.

'It's just your age,' Lenore murmured as she sat down. But she smiled. He wasn't a bad sort, actually. In fact, if it hadn't been for him, she would never have been able to get word to her sister in Hamburg as to where she was. And if it weren't for him, she wouldn't receive any letters at all. She had bribed him at first, but as the months went by he declined to take any more money from her. Which was fortunate, because the only funds Lenore had were those that her sister was able to send.

'What are you talking about?' Karl grumbed. 'I'm fifty-eight; that's not so old.' Bushy brows drew down over watery blue eyes.

Lenore was viewing her plate, wrinkling her nose as she did so. 'Sausages and cabbage again?' She looked up. 'Don't they know how to make anything else?'

Karl grinned, revealing two missing teeth. 'Would her ladyship like venison?' he inquired sweetly. 'Perhaps a little wine?'

'I wouldn't mind,' she replied tartly, beginning to eat.

'If you would be nice to me,' he suggested with an exaggerated leer, 'I might be able to arrange it.'

Lenore laughed in genuine merriment. The exchange was not a new one. 'Are you going to join me, or have you already eaten?'

He shrugged his stooped shoulders. 'I been feeling poorly of late,' he said, declining. Then he viewed the wall. 'God almighty!' he exclaimed, irritated. 'You'll have the whole damn room scratched up soon.'

She raised her brows. 'I would hardly call this a room.'

Swallowing, she pushed her plate aside. 'Besides, it's not likely to be rented out in the near future, is it?'

'Guess not,' he agreed, grinning again. Then he fumbled in his shirt pocket. 'Almost forgot. You got a letter from your sister.' He handed it to her and Lenore laid it aside. It was nice to have something to look forward to. She would let it stay there for a while, contemplating her pleasure.

'Thank you,' she murmured softly, then smiled at him. She wanted to say more, to tell him how much she appreciated his kindness, but she also knew that it would embarrass him if she did so. 'Can you bring me another candle tomorrow morning?'

Karl stood up. Frowning, he picked up the tray. 'God almighty, woman,' he grumbled. 'You use more candles than all our other guests combined.'

She laughed again. But watching him leave, Lenore knew that he would bring the requested candle with her morning meal.

The door thundered closed. A moment later Lenore heard the metallic sound as the lock was turned. The sound had ceased to bother her. In the beginning it had had the ring of death about it, had left her cold and shivering. But now the sound was a mere background noise, revealing no more than what it was: the locking of a door.

Again she viewed the wall with satisfaction. Maybe someday someone would read it and know what had happened to her. It was a small revenge, but the only one she had.

Her lips curved softly. Perhaps there was one other. She had refused, against all threats, to betray Dorothea. With the thought of her mistress, the smile faded. From what her sister wrote, Dorothea's lot had been no better than her own. Worse, for she must know by now that Philip was most probably dead. Oh, they were still speaking of the count's 'disappearance,' but there was little doubt in her own mind as to what had happened. She knew for a certainty that Philip's love for Dorothea would never have permitted him to stay away from her. Only death could have accomplished that.

Her heart ached for Dorothea. Her sister had written

that soon after entering Ahlden, the princess – now called duchess – had fallen grievously ill. And no wonder, being shut up as she was. For a time, there wasn't even a physician to attend her. But then the elector, or Prince George, must have had a change of heart because they suddenly sent medical aid. Not only that, but just as suddenly, Dorothea was allowed at least to walk about the courtyard and avail herself of fresh air and exercise. Perhaps, Lenore mused, the Duchess of Celle had been able to exert some influence, since this all came about after the elector and Prince George had paid a visit to Celle.

Lenore glanced at the letter on the table and picked it up. After a moment, she broke the seal and began to read.

Over the years she and her sister had developed a code of sorts, just in case their letters fell into the wrong hands. Because of this, the letter had to be read several times before she sifted the real meaning from the innocuous, chatty words.

Then she gave a short laugh and put the parchment with the others. Her sister still insisted that somehow, some way, she would get Lenore out of there. The woman had exhausted normal channels, because who, after all, could question the elector? Everything was on his side. If he gave an order for imprisonment, or even death, it was carried out immediately.

Lenore walked over to one of the windows and peered outside. It was almost dark. Only on the rim of the horizon was there a faint pinkish hue. Her view, because of the height, was vast. Lenore watched for some time as the color faded to a luminous purple, then, finally, black. There was no moon tonight and so she resignedly turned away. There was nothing more to see in the darkness.

There was also nothing more to do but retire. Lenore had begun to walk toward the bed when a strange noise made her halt in the middle of the room.

She waited. There it was again. Mystified, Lenore tilted her head in an effort to pinpoint the direction from whence it came.

Then, hearing it yet again, she looked up and stared at the ceiling. She blinked, thinking her eyes were playing tricks on her. She picked up the single candle and held it high. One of the stone blocks moved! She was certain of it. The sound came again and with it a small sifting of mortar drifted down to the floor.

Lenore watched, too fascinated for fear, as the stone was carefully removed, seeming to defy gravity as it was lifted out of its resting place. The second block was more easily removed. At last a man's face peered down, a finger to his lips, cautioning her to be silent.

A hand flew to her mouth as Lenore recognized her cousin Edward. There was no doubt, even though she hadn't seen him for almost ten years. She stared, wide-eyed, as he removed yet another block, then quickly lowered a rope. From his motions Lenore discerned that he wanted her to tie it around her body. Carefully she set the candle back on the table.

With quiet, sure movements, she did as he had silently instructed. Moments later Lenore felt herself being lifted off her feet. As the ceiling was not that high, when Lenore's feet were only a foot or so off the floor Edward was able to grasp her hands and pull her up. The crawl space between the ceiling of her cell and the tiled roof was not high enough to stand up in. Bending over, Lenore followed as her cousin guided her a few feet to where he had removed the tiles in the roof. A while later they were outside on a narrow stone ledge.

'How on earth?' she whispered, quite overcome with surprise.

Edward smiled broadly, his teeth very white in contrast to his black beard and hair. 'We've been planning it for weeks,' he replied in an answering whisper. 'I've been hired to replace the broken tiles on the roof. I've worked slow, waiting for tonight, because there's no moon.' Then he grew serious. Pointing down, he said, 'It's almost a hundred feet. Will you be frightened?'

Lenore shook her head in a determined manner. 'Not on your life,' she said. 'Get me out of here.'

He nodded, pleased with her spunk. The rope was tied securely to her waist, but Edward undid it and retied it again to his own satisfaction. The other end he wound about a turret. Then he carefully assisted her as she went over the side. 'There's a small ledge about midway,' he said to her in hushed tones. 'If you feel the need to rest, raise your hand.'

'There will be no need,' Lenore replied grimly. 'I've rested for three years.'

Bracing himself, Edward kept the rope taut, releasing it a bit at a time as he lowered Lenore to the ground.

Down and down she went. The rope burned her hands and bit her rib cage but she clenched her teeth, refusing to cry out. At last her feet touched solid earth. Quickly Lenore undid the rope, then raised both arms in a signal that she was none the worse for wear.

Edward brought the rope back up and in only moments was down beside her. Again he cautioned her, by placing a finger against his lips. Taking her by the hand, he began to run for the cover of the trees. There, two horses were tethered.

Gathering her skirts, Lenore mounted with her cousin's assistance. Although she hadn't been on a horse since she had been a young girl, she wasn't frightened. A short time later they were on the road.

Several miles outside of Schafels they dismounted and entered a waiting carriage. Then, with only the night as witness, they sped on to Hamburg.

Ahlden

January 1698

The first year had been the worst, Dorothea supposed, simply because she did not, could not, believe that they would have done this monstrous thing to her. 'They' were her father, her uncle, and her husband. They had again tricked her, just as they had when she had first married. They had agreed – agreed, mind you – to imprison her. To imprison the embarrassment that she had become.

She had gone a bit mad for a while, she realized that now. Nor had the matter been helped by Gertrud and Klara following her about, spying on her every waking movement. They even stood, one or the other of them, outside her water closet. It was unbearable, it was humiliating to have so little privacy. Her demands and instructions, so long as they remained in the realm of trivia, were carried out in an almost normal manner. She could command what she wished to eat, what she decided to wear, when she wished to retire.

But she could not command that the door to her prison be opened.

At first, disbelieving, she had tried to open the door herself. It was locked, and remained locked – for two years. But surely, she had cried out, she should be allowed to walk in the courtyard, in the air?

No, she was informed. It was not allowed. 'Who dares allow where I am concerned?' Dorothea had demanded. There had been no answer to that. But she had known. It was *they*.

Dorothea knew that her mother hadn't been a part of it, though even of that she had at times been uncertain. She hadn't seen Eleanor in four years. She had written: to Eleanor, to Wilhelm, to Ernst, even to George.

Her letters, if delivered, went unanswered.

The frustration, the terror, at first, had been unbearable. Dorothea felt she couldn't possibly spend the rest of her life confined within these seven rooms. Not even if she were properly attended, as she was. Within this small, confining area, Dorothea was treated according to rank ... until it came to the matter of opening the door.

But Platen had said nothing of this, her mind had raged in futile despair. He had never, never indicated that imprisonment, not freedom, would be the end result of the court's decision to grant her a divorce. Not that the court had decided that; *they* had decided that.

Yet, what recourse? Who could countermand the three most important men in Hanover-Celle? Who could even question the elector?

In desperation, Dorothea had written to Count Platen, begging him to send Lenore to her. That letter, too, had gone unanswered. Perhaps Lenore had been sent away. Dorothea didn't know.

And Philip. That had been the most tormenting thought of all. That he was dead was something Dorothea had had to accept before her wits returned to her. There was no other explanation. If he was alive, he would have contrived to contact her, one way or the other. Deep within her heart, she knew that.

Philip was dead. The knowledge had driven her to such despair that she had fallen ill and almost died.

No one, at first, seemed to care. Then, suddenly, doctors appeared, as if from nowhere. Soon after that she had been allowed to go outside, under guard, to 'take the air.'

In those first weeks the chaplain had visited her daily. A pale, dry man, he had tried to extend God's blessing upon her. But God had deserted her, leaving torment and anguish in His wake.

For a while Dorothea had suffered hallucinations, seeing Philip's dear face and form, which always remained just out of reach. Terrified of losing even this nebulous presence, she had rushed from room to room, crying out his name and clutching at apparitions, only to find her hands empty, her heart barren. In that state she had felt vulnerable, exposed, as she had never before.

It had been devastating. It still was, when she thought of it.

Slowly, from somewhere deep inside her, a reservoir of strength made itself known, born of anger and determination. This, Dorothea told herself sternly, was just what *they* wanted. How pleased they would be to see her so totally destroyed. Dorothea now had only one weapon: that of survival. That alone would defeat them.

At times she slept for days on end, opening her eyes and dully surveying the now-familiar room, finding nothing of any interest to her bruised mind. Then Dorothea would close her eyes again and find refuge in oblivion.

Oblivion. It even had color. Strange, that. It was not one color, nor was it ever the same. It was a blending of mists, some pastel, some vivid, all meaningless. There was no beauty, nor was there terror; just oblivion. She wouldn't rise from her bed on those days, wouldn't dress, bathe, eat, or speak. Those things belonged to another time. Those things had a purpose. Now she had no purpose. Once she 'awoke' to find herself seated at the dressing table, a strange woman pinning up her hair. It was not Lenore. Lenore always had a gentle touch. Dorothea had peered into the mirror and seen herself. The reflection that had stared back was only a hideous resemblance of what she remembered. And the terror again descended, as if in extremity her own body was betraying her.

Dorothea wondered wryly who had been more surprised, George, the physician, or herself, when she had emerged from the nightmare, thinner, weaker, but whole in mind and body.

And now, today, after almost five years of seeing the same faces, hearing the same voices, there had occurred another breakthrough. Two, actually. She was being allowed henceforth to ride in the carriage, weather permitting, through the six miles that comprised Ahlden. It would be the first time in five years that she would be allowed 'outside.'

And, best of all, there had been a letter for her. It was from Eleanor, who had advised her that from now on she would be able to visit Ahlden once a week.

Dorothea had spent the day dressing with much care. Then, accompanied by the ever-present Gertrud and Klara, she entered the waiting carriage.

It was a large and splendid vehicle that could be ridden with the top up or down, and it required four horses to move it. The day was cold but clear and sunny. Dorothea ordered the top down, then held her breath, waiting for her order to be denied or, worse, ignored.

But it was carried out promptly enough. With a trembling feeling of excitement that she couldn't repress, Dorothea heard the hollow clatter of hooves as the horses crossed the wooden drawbridge.

Across from her, even Gertrud and Klara wore expressions of anticipation. It suddenly struck Dorothea that the two women had been as much prisoners as she had been.

The horses ambled at no more than a walk as the liveried driver led them leisurely along the single cobbled street that graced the village.

No more than two hundred people lived in Ahlden. But the village was surrounded by many farms and these people also came to town, to shop, to go to church, or just to visit.

There was a small inn with a red gabled roof and a smart rectangular sign that swung lazily in the gentle breeze. A few hundred feet from the inn was a smithy shop. A heavy-set man, probably the owner, paused in his labors to watch the royal carriage go by.

Other villagers, too, paused in whatever they were doing to peer with curious, but not unfriendly, faces. A few smiled tentatively. To these Dorothea immediately smiled in return, nodding pleasantly.

All too soon the carriage turned around. At the same leisurely pace, it returned to the castle. When it cleared the drawbridge, the heavy apparatus again swung up and was bolted.

But even that couldn't dampen Dorothea's spirits. Hurriedly she changed her clothes and gave orders for a special tea to be prepared. Then she sat by the window so as to be certain she would see Eleanor the moment she came into view.

A tap on the door made her turn, annoyed by the interruption. 'Come in,' she said sharply. When it opened, she was startled to see de la Fortiere, Governor of Ahlden. She frowned at the tall and stocky man, who wore a white wig over his thinning gray hair. 'Monsieur?'

'Forgive the interruption, milady,' he said in quiet tones. 'I know that you are expecting the Duchess of Celle today – '

Dorothea's face lit up. 'Has she arrived?'

The governor shook his head. 'No,' he said regretfully. 'I'm afraid that she will not be coming, at least not today. You see, last night the elector died.'

Ernst dead? Although her shock was great, Dorothea couldn't admit to any sorrow. In a daze she heard the governor mumble condolences. Then he informed her that he would be going to Hanover for the funeral. There was, of course, no mention of her going. With a bow and a mumbled 'Duchess' he withdrew.

Even now, after all this time, Dorothea always gave a small start when she was addressed as duchess. That's who she was now: the Duchess of Ahlden. *They* had even tried to deprive her of her identity.

But afterwards Dorothea couldn't suppress a feeling of growing excitement. With Ernst dead, George was now elector. Surely he wouldn't continue with this farce. With trembling hands, Dorothea sat down at her writing table and penned a letter to George, conveying her condolences, begging him to relax her restrictions and allow her to see their children again.

The letter went unanswered.

Hanover

February 1698

But it didn't go unread. The letter was delivered the day of the funeral. After the lengthy services, George read it with cold eyes. He put it on the desk, then glanced about his father's study. It was his study now. Leine was his. All of Hanover was his. In the not too distant future, all of Celle would be his too.

He sighed in deep satisfaction. Although he grieved for his father as a man, he couldn't bring himself to be too unhappy. There was no one now who could tell him what to do. Before long, Melusine would be moved back into the castle, where she could take her rightful place by his side.

His eyes returned to the letter again. In fact, there was only one thing over which he had no direct control. And that was Celle. It still belonged to Wilhelm – to do with as he wished. Even now it was within Wilhelm's power to leave that domain to his daughter.

He found the thought greatly aggravating. The Duke and Duchess of Celle were here now, having come for the funeral. Eleanor had tried repeatedly to speak with him but George refused to see his aunt in private. However, he thought now, it might be worth his while to speak to his uncle before he returned to Celle.

When Wilhelm, having been summoned by a servant, entered the room a short while later, George was struck by how old he looked. He was almost seventy; little remained of the dashing gallant that he had once been. It seemed as if he had taken the death of his beloved brother hard. Wilhelm's eyes were red-rimmed with unshed tears and his skin had an unhealthy pallor.

Wilhelm glanced at the new elector with sorrowful eyes as he sat down. 'What will we do without him?' he mourned sadly. He fumbled for his handkerchief, dabbing at his nose.

George regarded his uncle with contemptuous eyes. 'We will do our best, Uncle Wilhelm,' he said softly. 'And I hope that, just as my father always did, you will permit me to seek your advice and counsel when necessary.'

'You have it, my dear boy,' Wilhelm replied in a choked voice. 'How fortunate Ernst was to have a son like you. One who will carry on for him.'

George nodded solemnly at the observation. 'I hope to do that,' he agreed. 'And I look forward to your aiding me as much as you did him.' He wet his full lips, not meeting Wilhelm's eye. 'To safeguard what my father has spent so many years in building, I must ask again for your assurance that your daughter will reside permanently in Ahlden.' When he saw Wilhelm hesitate, George went on quickly. 'I know that you will never go back on your word to your brother. Yet I feel I must ask for your reaffirmation. Because,' he added in a quiet voice, 'it was the last thing my father requested I do.'

'Of course. I would never break my word,' Wilhelm insisted steadfastly. 'I understand what a disaster it would be if Dorothea remarried.' He averted his face, staring dully at the carpet. After all these years, he still felt a burning shame.

'Exactly,' George agreed, relaxing. He would not, he decided, mention Dorothea's request to see her children. That was out of the question anyway. Certainly he wouldn't want his young daughter anywhere near a woman like that. 'Later this year, King William is to visit us,' he went on in a more normal tone.

Wilhelm brightened for the first time in days. 'That is good news. I haven't seen his Majesty for several years.'

George nodded, impatient with the interruption. 'My mother intends to present her claim, as granddaugther of James I, to the succession of the English throne.' His face went wry. 'I cannot imagine why she is so insistent, but she is quite adamant about it.'

'Well, so she should be. Her claim is legitimate,' Wilhelm noted. 'It remains only for her to be formally recognized. I'm certain that the king will agree. After all, the only other choice he has is a Catholic. Neither the king nor the queen would turn the crown over to a papist.'

'I guess you're right.' George sighed. He could imagine nothing he wanted less than the English crown. 'However, there is something that interests me more. The king's nephew and heir, William of Gloucester, is only ten, but it's not too soon to mention Sophie-Dorothea as his betrothed. Now the king will, of course, stop by Celle first, as it is on his way. It would help matters greatly if you and the duchess would broach this subject to his Majesty. In that way, he will have some time to consider it before I speak to him.'

Wilhelm smiled, feeling needed again. 'I will indeed, my boy.' He got to his feet and made a small bow. 'Hanover is fortunate in having you as elector, your Highness,' he said formally.

After Wilhelm left the room, George picked up Dorothea's letter again. Giving it no more than a cursory glance, he crumpled it and threw it into the wastebasket.

Monplaisir

April 1700

Elizabeth Platen was in her bed, her flesh simply a container for the agony that spread throughout it. She was feverish, she had been so for days. All the physician's ministrations had failed to halt the insidious horror that had taken over her once-beautiful body.

But she needed no physician to tell her that she was dying. That she knew, felt, saw. It was that last that was so painful. More than anything else, her physical deterioration in these last months had been, for her, a living hell.

She looked at her woman servant. There were two that tended her, one during the day, one during the night. Save for the physician, Elizabeth would allow no other to enter her room. Not even Franz. One look at the revulsion in his eyes that last time she had seen him had caused her to banish him from her bedchamber.

Suddenly infuriated by the woman's compassionate expression, Elizabeth screamed, 'Get out! Get out of here.'

Hesitantly the woman made for the door. With a brief look at the countess's angry face, she departed.

After falling back on the pillow, Elizabeth remained still for a moment. Then, with great effort, she hauled her body out of the bed and staggered to the mirror.

There it was. That face, once so beautiful, stared back at her, a nightmare of erupting, ulcerous sores. She peered with narrow, squinting eyes, for her vision was fading, it seemed daily. Soon she would be blind. The physician had offered no hope there.

Enraged by the monstrosity she was seeing, Elizabeth reached for a heavy vase and flung it at the mirror, shattering the glass, just as her beauty had been shattered by the awful disease that had invaded her body.

The noise brought the servant back. This time Elizabeth did not object as she was led back to her bed.

What is the use? she thought wearily, easing herself down again. Was this God's punishment? Was this His vengeance? Was it Philip's?

Turning her head, she regarded the servant. A kindly woman in her late fifties, she didn't even cringe when she sponged the wreck that had been the beautiful Elizabeth Platen.

'A priest,' Elizabeth whispered hoarsely. 'Fetch a priest.' She closed her eyes and waited. She had all but abjured her faith here in Protestant Hanover, but in her extremity it returned as forcefully as it had ever in her life.

She would have to tell the priest, confess her crime, if she were not to spend eternity with her soul rotting as her body was now rotting. Only a final confession could save her from the clutches of Satan himself.

She hadn't meant it, then or now. God knew she had loved the man; too much, perhaps. If she hadn't loved him so, her need for revenge might not have been so great. Thrashing about, Elizabeth felt as if she were plagued by demons, demons who assaulted her mind and her body. 'But I didn't want him dead!' she cried out to the empty room. 'That was not my wish.'

She fell back on the pillow, her mind fastened on that night, and with a vision that was all too clear again she saw the death of Philip Königsmark.

He had come out of the shadows, as she knew he would, seeking an exit. She, and the three guards, had been waiting.

And how he had fought. Even now, all these years later, Elizabeth could see him: his step light, his manner determined. But of course it hadn't been enough, not against three men – and herself. It had been Elizabeth who had struck him the blow on the head, intending to stun him. If she hadn't struck him when she did, he might have been able to deflect the sword-thrust that killed him. When that blade pierced his chest, Elizabeth felt as if she herself had been stricken.

She stood there, staring down at his crumpled form. 'Bring a torch,' she had said quietly, denying the ache in her own breast.

In the flickering light she had examined Philip closely. Then she viewed the guard. 'You fool. He's dead. You were supposed to arrest him, not kill him!'

The guard looked abashed yet defiant. 'You saw how he fought, milady,' he argued in grim tones. 'He overcame two of us. Had he gotten by me, he would have escaped. And you said under no circumstances – '

'I know what I said! Be quiet while I think.' She stood there a moment. In the meantime, the first guard sat up, rubbing his bruised jaw. Elizabeth flashed him a look of utter contempt. The other guard was laying where he had fallen, unconscious.

But even then, with Philip dead at her feet, Elizabeth had not yet felt the full loss. Her mind worked swiftly. Ernst, she knew, would be furious. He had agreed to have Philip put under guard; he had not agreed to have him killed.

And now what? No one must know that the elector was involved in a murder.

At last she had turned to the guard, who had been standing there, awaiting further orders.

'Get blankets and the largest sack you can find,' she instructed. 'Put him in it, then dump it into the river. Make certain that it's weighted properly,' she stressed. 'If it rises, you will join him.'

After all this time, Elizabeth still wondered at her voice, so controlled, so authoritative, while inside her heart had been breaking irretrievably. 'And clean up this mess,' she went on. 'If I see one spot of blood by daylight, I'll clean it with your hide!'

She had left them to their chores, returning quickly to Ernst. There were, she estimated, between thirty and forty-five minutes before the household, or at least the kitchen staff, would be awake and functioning. Perhaps another hour before the rest would be up and about. It was time enough.

Ernst was sitting where she had left him. In a few terse words Elizabeth related the mishap.

'Good Christ!' he swore, really annoyed with her. He was unused to Elizabeth bungling anything.

'I've told you what happened,' she protested, almost irritated. She, too, had wanted Philip alive; but for different reasons. Now he would never know that she had had her revenge. 'He fought like a madman,' she tried to explain.

'Or a soldier,' Ernst replied in icy tones. 'Did anyone else see what happened?'

'No.'

'What have you done with the ... body?' he asked. As she opened her mouth to reply, Ernst raised his hand. 'No, no. Don't tell me. I don't want to know about it. I want no part of murder.'

Elizabeth cast him a disdainful look but made no comment.

'Damn it, Elizabeth,' he went on as the full meaning of what had happened sunk in. 'This is not just any man. How will we explain it if he suddenly disappears? He's well known throughout every court in Europe.'

'Why must we explain it?' she had asked reasonably. 'No one knows that he's been here; certainly he should not have been here,' she added dryly.

'How can you say that?' Ernst demanded. 'The guards are no problem, I'll admit? But what about Dorothea?'

She had laughed softly. 'You don't expect her to admit that she let a man into her rooms at night, do you?'

Ernst was silent a moment. 'And what of her?' he asked then. 'We cannot ignore this whole business. What if Dorothea still decides to run away?'

'One has nothing to do with the other,' Elizabeth replied, her mind working at its usual speed. Dorothea was the cause of everything, the crux of the matter. 'We have the letters proving that she was involved with Königsmark and planning to elope with him. The letter does not implicate her in adultery. And I seriously doubt that she will admit to such a thing. Now, I suggest ...'

And so she had. And, as usual, Ernst had listened.

In some ways, Elizabeth mused, Dorothea was better off than she. Because she, Elizabeth, *knew* that Philip was dead. For a long time Dorothea had not known; even now, she was probably uncertain.

And no doubt the princess would never have agreed to all those restrictions in order to secure her divorce if she had known that it was all futile. Divorce or no, she could never have Philip.

That, at least, she had accomplished, Elizabeth thought with some satisfaction.

She was still deep in contemplation when the priest arrived. As he came closer Elizabeth looked up at him, almost pleading.

'Forgive me, Father,' she whispered in anguish. 'Forgive me, for I have sinned ...'

Ahlden

November 1702

Dorothea greeted her mother warmly and led her to a comfortable chair close by the fire. It blazed high, for the day was bitterly cold, the wind at times cavorting with a frenzied determination that took one's breath away.

'Mama,' she said gently. 'You shouldn't have come today.'

'And why not?' demanded Eleanor, sitting herself down with a sigh.

'Because it's snowing, and quite hard,' Dorothea pointed out, easing herself into a nearby chair. 'You know the dampness only aggravates your shoulder.'

In spite of her protests, Dorothea was truly glad that Eleanor had not forgone her weekly visit. It was only through her mother that Dorothea received any news of her children. Occasionally Eleanor even brought miniatures. There was other news, as well, as when Elizabeth Platen had died two years ago. That had not exactly been unhappy news.

Reaching over, Dorothea picked up a silver pot from the low table, then poured hot chocolate into a delicate china cup. She handed it to Eleanor. 'How are you feeling?' she asked as she poured a cup of the hot liquid for herself.

'I'm well,' Eleanor assured her, although in truth, her arm and shoulder were aching this day. Her arthritis always seemed to act up more in the winter months. 'Don't concern yourself about me,' she went on, replacing the cup on the table. 'Besides, I had to come today to tell you that the king has died.'

Stunned, Dorothea put her own cup down. 'Does that mean ...'

Eleanor nodded solemnly. 'It means that the electress is in direct line to the English throne. I'm sure you recall that the little Duke of Gloucester died a year and a half ago. Poor little thing,' she remarked, momentarily diverted. 'He was barely eleven. Now, Anne is queen, and with no children to succeed her, Sofia is Anne's heir.

Dorothea gave a short, mirthless laugh. 'I never would have believed it,' she murmured. And, in truth, it was nothing short of a miracle. The next Stuart in line for the throne was Anne's half-brother; but he was an ardent Catholic. Anne herself might have overlooked this deficiency. However, the Act of Settlement, enacted by Parliament in 1701 excluded Catholics from the throne, leaving Anne no choice but to agree to the Protestant Hanover branch of her family to succeed her.

Eleanor regarded her daughter with clouded eyes. 'Sofia is getting on in years, and is not in the best of health. I'll wager it won't be the electress who dons the crown, but her heir.'

'George.'

Eleanor gave a brief nod. A feeling of frustration engulfed her. If only Dorothea had not divorced George, she might very well be the Queen of England. Instead, she was the Duchess of Ahlden, a virtual prisoner. But Eleanor didn't say this. It was quite unnecessary to add to Dorothea's burden.

'How is Father?' Dorothea inquired then, her tone too light and too casual to be real.

'He is well,' Eleanor replied slowly. She picked up her cup again, sipping, then continued. 'I've tried to get him to accompany me here, but …'

'But he is still bitter,' Dorothea finished in a flat voice, turning away from her mother's saddened face.

Eleanor tilted her head. The fire gave a golden cast to her almost white hair. 'No,' she said carefully. 'I don't believe he is, any more,' Her mouth tightened in anger. 'In fact, I believe your father would have long since ended this foolishness if it hadn't been for George. Periodically, George demands reaffirmation from your father.'

'And Father always complies,' Dorothea retorted tonelessly. But the fact had long since ceased to hurt her.

She had gained a modicum of acceptance.

'Don't blame your father,' Eleanor pleaded. Her blue eyes misted and she blinked rapidly. She was determined that Dorothea never see her in tears on these weekly visits, although she invariably wept all the way home. 'It wasn't his idea that you – '

'I blame no one, Mother,' Dorothea said quickly. Leaning forward, she patted Eleanor's hand in a reassuring manner. But of course she did blame them. Nor could she find it in her heart to excuse her father, who had been led as if he were a child, first by Ernst, then by George.

'Perhaps I have done wrong,' Dorothea went on with an earnest look. Then she smiled ruefully. 'Although I doubt that my crime deserved life imprisonment.' At the sight of her mother's obvious distress, Dorothea was immediately contrite. 'Please don't look that way,' she begged. 'I cannot bear it when you are unhappy. I simply could not bear it if I caused you more pain.'

'Ah, Dorothea.' Eleanor sighed, wiping away the single errant tear that she had been unable to stem. 'Do not for a moment ever doubt that you are the only joy of my life. In spite of everything, I love you dearly.'

In spite of everything, Dorothea mused, watching her mother fumble for a handkerchief and dab it against her wet cheek. Some months ago, Dorothea had asked her chaplain if he thought she had committed a sin. Regretfully, for he was a kind man, he had replied in the affirmative. But despite that man's words, Dorothea had found a sort of tranquility in this past year, a serene peace in helping the villagers of Ahlden. God never ignores a penitent, or a doer of good works, the chaplain said, then assured her that God had forgiven her.

And so He must have, to have brought such peace to my restricted life, Dorothea thought now. God had forgiven her – but not her father, not her uncle, and, least of all, her husband.

Yet for all that had happened, Dorothea had to admit that she would change nothing. Certainly not those few brief years with Philip. Even now she dreamed of him, awakening at times with an unbearable sadness, a feeling of emptiness. And her body, too, treacherous thing that it was, still yearned for his touch, his caress, his kiss.

His letters helped immeasurably. Aurora, revealing great kindess, had returned them. Not a day passed that Dorothea didn't spend some time reading at least a few of them.

No, there were no regrets. How many people experienced love, real love, in their lives? Not many, she was willing to venture.

But her children. That was a regret that would haunt her for the rest of her life. 'If only I could see them,' she murmured, unaware that she had spoken aloud.

But Eleanor knew what she meant. 'They speak of you often,' she soothed. 'Mostly to me, I should imagine.'

'Do they hate me?' Dorothea inquired in a small voice.

'Oh, no,' Eleanor said quickly. She glanced about the room with wary eyes, but Gertrud and Klara were nowhere to be seen; still, she lowered her voice. 'George Augustus has a portrait of you in his rooms. The rest were ... burned. But he managed to save one and he keeps it hidden.' She smiled gently. 'The last time I saw him, only a few weeks ago, he told me that he thought you were beautiful.'

Now Dorothea's eyes filled with tears. She got up and knelt before her mother, placing her head in the ample lap. 'Oh, Mama. Will I ever see them again? Surely I cannot live the rest of my life without ever looking at the face of my son and my daughter.'

She sobbed for a length of time while Eleanor stroked her hair and thought: If it were me, I couldn't bear it. It really is inhuman. But God knew she, Eleanor, had tried everything. Even writing to Ulric, an act that had infuriated both Wilhelm and George when discovered. How very strange, she thought to herself, viewing her daughter's bowed head. Dorothea had gone through the fire but she has emerged a better person than any of us.

At last the sobs quieted and Eleanor sought to change the subject to one less painful to them both. 'The boy, Karl Clausin. I hear that he is returning next month.'

Dorothea raised her tearstained face and her lips curved slightly. 'Yes,' she said, getting to her feet. In control of herself again, she continued. 'I've received a letter from him. Although he is hardly a boy,' she commented, sitting down in her chair.

'He will be a fine physician, I've heard,' Eleanor went on. 'I'm certain that he will visit you when he returns from Vienna for his holiday. In a few years Ahlden will have its very own physician.' She smiled broadly. 'And all because of you.' She shook her head. 'I know that you receive a generous allowance from your father, but it seems to me that you spend it on everyone but yourself.'

'I've little need of money,' Dorothea noted with a short laugh and a wave of her ringed hand. 'I do not exactly regale Ahlden with fancy balls and banquets.'

'I suspect the people of the village love you almost as much as I do,' Eleanor murmured.

The sound of the door opening caught the attention of them both. Surprised, Dorothea saw Christopher Chappuzeau enter. Now in his early forties, Christopher, who had been with Dorothea from the time she left Celle to be married, had chosen of his own free will to follow her into exile. Dorothea's brow creased in annoyance at the sight of him, although he was one of her favorite and most trusted attendants. But her whole household knew that her visits with the Duchess of Celle were sacrosanct. She was not to be interrupted or disturbed.

However, before she could protest, Christopher, after a perfunctory bow, regarded her with a taut face, then walked toward the window.

'Milady, please …' He beckoned, inviting her to look outside. After only a slight hesitation, Dorothea complied with the unusual request.

The sitting room was in the uppermost part of the tower. Because of its height and three generous windows, it afforded a splendid view that went quite beyond the village of Ahlden.

For a moment Dorothea watched, confused by what she was seeing, and wondered why Christopher had called her attention to the lone rider who was approaching at a fair pace. As he drew closer, she saw that he was little more than a boy, perhaps eighteen. He seemed to spur his horse faster as he entered the village, peering behind him at intervals. Raising her eyes a bit, Dorothea saw the riders in pursuit. They wore the red-and-blue livery of the Hanoverian Palace Guard.

Eleanor, curious, had joined Dorothea at the window, and now gave a sudden start. She put a hand to her throat and drew a sharp breath. 'Oh, dear God,' she murmured. 'It's George Augustus!'

My son! Dorothea thought, aware that her heart had begun to pound wildly. With heavy impatience, she flung the draperies aside as far as she could, then opened the window. A cold blast of November air, mingled with snow, hit her sharply but went unnoticed as she waved frantically. 'George! George!' she screamed, her voice half a sob.

He either heard or sensed, for he reined in his horse suddenly and stood up in the stirrups. With one arm raised high, he waved and seemed to shout something; but his voice was carried away by the treacherous wind.

In only moments the guards reached him. Ignoring the young man's angry gestures of defiance, they took hold of the reins and turned his horse about. Then they all began to head back in the direction from whence they had come.

With eyes riveted on the receding figure, her face wet with tears she didn't even know she had shed, Dorothea watched as her son was led away. Time and again George Augustus turned and waved, but her own arms felt leaden and unresponsive. She could only stand there. Peace and serenity fled her mind. Dimly Dorothea heard her mother's frantic cry just before she slipped to the floor and blessed oblivion.

Hanover

November 1702

'You little fool!' George muttered heatedly as he viewed the defiant face of his son. His anger had been so great in these past hours that he had been quite speechless with the force of it. This morning they had started out on what was to have been a pleasurable day's hunting. Toward midmorning, George Augustus had managed to elude his numerous attendants. Moments later he was heading in the direction of Ahlden.

George knew immediately what had happened for the simple reason that the boy had tried the same thing only a few weeks ago. George Augustus seemed obsessed by the notion that he had to see his mother. Perhaps, George reflected, it was time that he dispelled the romantic images that filled his son's head.

'How dare you disobey me?' he went on, his voice rising to a shout. There was that about George Augustus that made him angry if he were in the boy's company for any length of time. Frankly, he disliked the crown prince intensely. Physically George Augustus resembled his father in a most extraordinary way, but there the resemblance ended. In all other ways, he was Dorothea's son, embodied with all her defiance and stubbornness.

'Answer me!' he shouted when George Augustus made no response. The drawing room resounded with the echo of his command.

George Augustus stood stiffly, his mouth clenched so tightly that the muscles in his jaw worked restlessly. He was still dressed in his riding breeches and leather boots, the guards having delivered him to his father immediately on their return to Leine. 'You have no right to keep her shut up, to keep me from seeing her,' he said in a voice not much lower than his father's. 'I've not seen my mother for more than eight years. You cannot keep me from her forever.'

The elector's face turned a dull red. With little warning, his hand flashed out and he struck his son full in the face.

The boy's head moved with the blow, but he neither flinched nor touched his now-flaming cheek. Instead, he glared at his father with eyes full of hate. How many times he had wished him dead; they were too numerous to count. If his father were dead, then he, George Augustus, would be elector – and his mother would be free. He lived for that day.

With very little effort, George Augustus was able to conjure up that day when he had seen his mother for the last time. Of course he hadn't known then that it would be the last time. Still, the image of her was vivid. He had her portrait hidden in his room, beneath his bed. He viewed it often. Only those closest to him knew that he had it. His sister knew. Sophie-Dorothea occasionally came to look at it, but it sent her into paroxysms of tears when she did so. George Augustus had no doubt that if his father were to learn of the portrait, he would have it burned, just as he had done with the others. There was nothing in Leine, nor in any other residence, that even hinted at his mother's existence. Her name was not to be spoken even in prayer.

So his father had decreed.

'I forbid you,' George was saying, banging his fist on a table for emphasis, causing a Dresden figurine to sway alarmingly, 'I forbid you ever to do such a thing again. You are forbidden to go to Ahlden. You are forbidden to write to her, to communicate in any way with her!' He ceased his tirade only because he was out of breath, but his eyes never left the face of his son.

'Why do you hate her so?' George Augustus asked him, truly confounded by his father's attitude. 'Other men have divorced their wives without shutting them up in a prison.'

'Ahlden is not a prison,' the Elector contradicted coldly. 'She agreed to live there permanently.'

'She didn't agree to live like that,' George Augustus protested, his flushed cheeks revealing his indignation. Did his father think him witless? he wondered. He knew of his grandmother's efforts to free her daughter. That was not a secret one could keep.

'Your mother is not fit to live among the rest of us. Even her own father agrees.'

George Augustus made a face. Wilhelm! That old man. He hated Wilhelm almost as much as he hated his father.

'A woman who cuckolds her husband deserves nothing less,' George went on. 'You revere a woman who would have been better born in the streets!'

Crimson spread quickly from George Augustus's neck to his temples. Instinctively his hand went to his waist before he realized that he was weaponless. 'Sir!'

Seeing the gesture, the elector's eyes narrowed, his mouth twisted in rage. 'You would raise your hand to your father and sovereign?' he asked slowly, his voice thick. 'Get out. Get out before I give the order to have the flesh stripped from your back. And hear me,' he called out as his son walked toward the door. 'Another attempt like the one you made today will result not only in your own confinement, but I will tighten the restrictions at Ahlden to the extent that your mother will never even leave her room! Do you hear me, George Augustus? Do you understand?'

Almost choking with anger and frustration, George Augustus nodded.

Celle

June 1705

Wilhelm, at eighty, was neither frail nor sickly. In fact, he didn't feel his momentous age at all. Yet there was no denying his years. It was presented to him in small, irritating ways. His vision was less than sharp and while the spectacles helped when he read or wrote, they were particularly ineffective when he indulged in his favorite pastime of hunting. He tired easily; that, too, was a nuisance.

For weeks now he had known that it was time and more that he put his affairs in order. Now, on this warm June morning, he had done so. With a satisfied look at the papers that littered his desk, Wilhelm sent for Eleanor.

While he waited he reflected that there was one more piece of unfinished business. But there was time enough for that. For years now, once a week, Eleanor had tried to get him to accompany her to Ahlden, at first pleading, then, as the years went by, in an almost casual, offhand manner.

But he couldn't bring himself to oblige the simple request. It would have been in some sense an admission that he might have been wrong. However, time blunts and blurs memories and feelings both, and certainly enough of it had passed. More than ten years of it.

Wilhelm shook his head in a vague manner. The years had passed so swiftly for him. He wondered if they had done so for his little girl. How odd, he thought. In these past weeks he had taken to thinking of Dorothea as a little girl. But of course she wasn't. She was … almost forty? He blinked in amazement. Indeed, she was almost forty, middle-aged, certainly not a little girl.

He was still lost in his thoughts when Eleanor entered the room. Viewing her, Wilhelm smiled fondly. There had been a time when he had thought he had lost his love for her too. But that hadn't happened. Perhaps more than the other thing, Wilhelm had resented Dorothea for causing such a rift between him and Eleanor.

'You've been working all morning, Wilhelm,' Eleanor admonished in a gentle voice. Her flowered silk gown made a soft rustling sound as she sat down in a chair that faced the desk.

'I have worked,' he agreed pleasantly. 'But mostly I've just been sitting here, thinking.'

She smiled. 'About what?'

'About you ... and your future, should anything happen to me.'

Alarm coursed through her. 'Are you feeling ill? Shall I summon the physician?'

'No, no.' He laughed at her concern. 'Stop fidgeting and listen to me. As you know, when I die you can no longer live here, at Celle.' Ignoring her pained look, he continued in a firm voice. 'The residence in Luneburg is completed. When the time comes, you may of course take any furnishings from here that you wish.'

Eleanor moved restlessly in the chair, straightening the folds in her skirt, averting her eyes from her husband. Luneburg. She'd known of it, of course; it had been under construction for some time now. But it was more than forty miles from Ahlden!

'Wienhausen is also deeded to you,' Wilhelm went on, then fell silent for a time. Eleanor didn't speak. She sat there, waiting, knowing that he would soon have to mention his daughter. For ten years he had not spoken of her. Dorothea's name was not spoken in this house unless she herself brought it up.

At last Wilhelm cleared his throat and proceeded in a normal tone. 'I have added a codicil to my testament,' he said, not looking at his wife. 'It will insure that everything will revert to Dorothea when we are both gone. In addition, on my death, there will be deposited, both in The Hague and Amsterdam, sufficient funds for her to live handsomely for the rest of her life.' He paused a moment, then added, 'Celle, of course, will belong to the elector.'

Eleanor took a deep breath. 'What good is the money to her?' she said with some bitterness. 'And all the residences that she will not be able to set foot in.' She passed a hand across her temple. 'My God, Wilhelm, this has gone on long enough. Please, please allow her to at least come to Luneburg with me when the time comes.'

Wilhelm seemed to consider this. Eleanor held her breath, but then her husband shook his head, almost sadly. 'I cannot do that,' he murmured. 'You know the reasons why.'

The anger should have been there but Eleanor felt only a profound weariness, so deep it touched her very soul. She got to her feet without speaking and walked toward the door. No matter, she thought with resignation. Whether twenty miles or forty miles, she would go. As long as she was able to get out of her bed in the morning, she would go.

She had already opened the door when Wilhelm's voice again reached her. 'Eleanor,' he said tentatively, in almost a whisper. 'I think, ... I think I would like to join you tomorrow on your trip to Ahlden.'

She turned, her eyes blinded by tears. 'I would like that, Wilhelm,' she replied softly. 'I would like that very much.'

Eleanor spent the rest of the day in high anticipation. Once he saw, actually saw, Dorothea, he could not possibly refuse to free her. She knew it!

Never had a day in her life seemed so long as this one. The hours, the minutes, even the seconds, seemed to drag in a maddening way. Eleanor couldn't wait for the evening meal to end. And when she at last laid her head down on her pillow, sleep would not come.

She was still awake at two-thirty in the morning when her maid opened the bedroom door and peered in at her. The woman was holding a candle and her hand trembled so that the light flickered and wavered. But even the warm amber glow couldn't disguise the ashen look on her face.

'Oh, milady, come. Please come. It's the duke.'

In a moment Eleanor was out of bed. Not bothering to don a robe, she rushed into the adjoining room.

'Wilhelm ...' she breathed. She ran to the bed then knelt on the floor and took hold of his hand. The physician, she knew, had been summoned. She also knew that he wouldn't be in time. Wilhelm's face was white and had a wax look about it as he struggled for breath. From the way he clutched his chest, she knew that he was experiencing great pain.

It was some moments before he could speak. When he did, she could barely make out his words.

'I'm sorry,' he rasped, clinging to her hand. 'Tell her – '

'Hush, my darling,' Eleanor said, trying to quell the panic that forced its way into her throat.

'I love you.'

'Wilhelm!' Eleanor's anguished cry released her sobs, and her mind couldn't help but rage at this final injustice to Dorothea.

Ahlden

May 1714

Dorothea smiled as she read her daughter's latest letter. It was lengthy, as they all were, and described in great detail the latest accomplishments of her seven-year-old son. She had sent miniatures of both herself and the child. Dorothea stared at them for long moments. Her daughter, the Queen of Prussia! That took some getting used to. Sophie-Dorothea had married Prince Frederick William of Brandenburg. The elector, Frederick's father, had become the first King of Prussia, and with his death the year before, the prince had become a king – and Sophie-Dorothea, queen.

The marriage, it seemed, was not an especially happy one. But it appeared that Sophie-Dorothea's indomitable spirit held her in good stead. A year after she had married, she had sent for Lenore Knesebeck, who was now her lady. Lenore, too, wrote, and it was mostly from her letters that Dorothea surmised that her daughter's marriage left a bit to be desired.

But if Sophie-Dorothea was unhappy, it wasn't reflected in her letters, all of which were bright and chatty.

George Augustus, married to Caroline of Ansbach, also had a son. But George Augustus never wrote. This, at first, had greatly saddened Dorothea, until Eleanor had explained that the young man had been forbidden to do so. Of course, she had no doubt but that George had tried to exert pressure on Sophie-Dorothea too. But one could not command a queen so easily.

So many things had happened over the past ten years, Dorothea thought to herself on this bright May morning.

Her mother now lived in Luneburg. Although in her seventy-eighth year, Eleanor faithfully made the trip to see her daughter once each week. It was she who had, only yesterday, brought Sophie-Dorothea's letter. The letters were sent to Luneburg first.

Dorothea often wondered whether George knew that his daughter wrote to her so often. Probably he did because, although Klara had died after a brief illness some years before, Gertrud was still with her. Thankfully that woman's original stiff and unforgiving demeanor had long since softened. It had been especially noticeable after the fire, two years ago. It had begun in the stables. Thence it had spread alarmingly throughout the castle and, on wind-carried embers, to the village itself.

Without the governor's permission, however, the drawbridge could not be lowered. Consequently, they had all almost perished. It was her faithful Christopher Chappuzeau who, at great risk to himself, had jumped into the moat, swum to the other side, and gotton to de la Fortier in his home. Shortly afterward, the conflagration spread to the village itself, causing great devastation.

Dorothea glanced outside and smiled. Now, after two years, there was little evidence of the damage caused by the fire. Dorothea had put her money to good use, restoring houses and shops, even the castle itself. Ahlden now had a grand church and the most expensive organ money could buy.

With a sigh, Dorothea got to her feet. She placed the miniature beside the others on the mantel.

'Milady?' Gertrud dipped in a curtsy. 'The seamstress is here. Would you like to have your fitting now, or would you prefer to wait until after the midday meal?' Briefly her gaze flickered over the new pictures. But as far as she was concerned, she had seen nothing. Over the years Gertrud had been forced to concede a great respect for the Duchess of Ahlden, grudgingly at first, but now freely given.

Nor was she the only one who felt that way, Gertrud reflected, while waiting for an answer. They all did. Down to the meanest stableboy in Ahlden, everyone felt protective toward the Duchess. Dorothea seemed to have an endless reservoir of patience, rarely lost her temper, and, if she insisted on her household being run with the strictest protocol, why, that was only her right.

'Let us do it now,' Dorothea said at last, walking into her bedchamber. She smiled pleasantly at the seamstress, a ruddy-faced woman in her late forties whose skill with a needle was nothing short of miraculous.

Dorothea allowed Gertrud to assist with the removal of her gown, then stood quietly as Madame Launays carefully fitted the pale-yellow brocade about her waist.

Dorothea glanced at her reflection in the mirror, her smile a bit rueful. The once-thin body was now on the plump side, although she was by no means fat. Her dark hair was still thick and lustrous, even if flecked with silver at the temples. But her eyes were still fine, her face unlined at forty-nine. And the dimples could still appear when summoned. She wondered if Philip would recognize her now. She turned her mind away from that; the thought of him always touched her with sadness.

Regarding Gertrud, Dorothea spoke briskly. 'Do you have the menu for tomorrow's meals?'

'Yes, milady. I'll get it.' Gertrud left the room, returning a few minutes later. Holding the paper before her, she dutifully read: 'For lunch, a *bisque de homard* and *mousse de sole*.' She looked up. 'I have not chosen a dessert, milady.'

Dorothea raised her arm slightly to allow Madame Launays to pin a seam. 'Fresh fruit and some cheese,' she instructed. 'White wine.'

Gertrud nodded and continued. 'For the evening meal, a clear consomme, *saumon poché mousselin, salmis de faisan, selle de veau …*'

'Fine,' Dorothea noted, lowering her arm again. 'Tell cook to use whatever fresh vegetables are available. But I don't want them overcooked,' she cautioned. 'And a *crême patisserie* for dessert.' At least, she thought, there was one consolation in her life. She could eat what she pleased. She no longer had to face the endless round of sausages, venison, and cabbage that used to appear on Sofia's table with such tedious regularity.

Dorothea coudn't repress a frown as she thought of her former mother-in-law. Sofia had died less than two months ago. She had collapsed while on her daily strenuous walk and was dead before they could even get her to her room.

'I'm finished, milady,' said Madame Launays, straightening.

Exercising great care, both the seamstress and Gertrud removed the pinned garment and helped Dorothea to dress again. Then Dorothea sat at her dressing table, while Gertrud began to brush her hair. The woman had become almost as expert in this task as Lenore had been. Certainly her touch had become more gentle.

'Gertrud,' Dorothea said slowly, impulsively.

Brown eyes viewed her in the mirror. 'Milady?'

'Have you ever regretted joining my court?' Dorothea studied the image in the looking glass, suddenly interested in this woman's answer. This enigmatic woman who had for so long been by her side; who, for so many years, Dorothea had not been able to call friend.

Gertrud hesitated. Ordinarily, she would have replied automatically in the negative. But for some reason something in Dorothea's tone precluded artificiality. 'I ... have no regrets,' she responded quietly, still wielding the brush.

'How so?' inquired Dorothea, with the same interested expression. 'You and I have lived a somewhat restricted life these past years.'

'So we have,' replied Gertrud. She paused, viewing Dorothea squarely. 'I'll admit that in the beginning I did not look on this assignment favorably.' She spoke carefully, searching Dorothea's face, lest she be mistaken. But no, the Duchess of Ahlden's expression was interested, inquiring. 'But then, I had little choice,' she continued. 'My husband died, as you know. I was in no position to decline this or any other post that might have been offered me.'

Dorothea tilted her head, still staring into the mirror. 'Did you love him? Your husband?'

Gertrud nodded. 'I did.'

'Was yours an arranged marriage?'

'It was,' Gertrud affirmed. 'But it worked out well, at least for me.' Again she applied the brush. 'Eric died a young man,' she murmured. 'In the battle of Flanders.'

'I'm sorry,' Dorothea murmured.

Once more Gertrud paused, viewing Dorothea's reflection intently. 'Did ... did you love *him* much?' she asked in a low voice, almost fearful of her question. But the duchess smiled gently, a faraway look in her eyes.

'Yes,' Dorothea replied softly. 'More than any woman has a right to love a man. Or perhaps,' she added with a rueful laugh, 'as a woman *should* love a man.'

Finished with the coiffure, Gertrud regarded her mistress with level eyes. 'You are fortunate, then,' she observed in a quiet voice. 'I don't think that such a harsh punishment should have been your lot.'

'There is nothing anyone can do to dim those years,' Dorothea remarked slowly. 'They've tried, but they have not succeeded.'

'Milady ...' Gertrud murmured. As Dorothea raised her brows in question, she continued. 'It is a pleasure to serve you. I've not regretted a moment of it.'

Smiling now, Dorothea reached up and patted her lady's hand. 'Thank you,' she whispered. 'You've been a comfort to me on more than one occasion. Forgive me for not mentioning it before this.'

Later that day, back in her sitting room once more, Dorothea opened a leather-bound ledger, intending to review the household accounts.

Outside the sky hosted thick gray clouds that presaged rain. A faint rumble of thunder disturbed the otherwise placid May afternoon. She stared, unseeing, at the row of neat figures, and thought of Gertrud. And having done so, smiled. How fortunate that they had at last plumbed each other's minds and discovered friendship. How she had missed Lenore all these years.

Dorothea shook her head slowly. Then, with a small sigh, she made a diligent effort to concentrate on the work before her.

She had already dipped the quill into the ink pot when Christopher entered the room.

'What is it?' she inquired, looking up at her faithful servant.

'Milady, word has just reached us that Queen Anne of England has died.' The words tumbled forth in breathless fashion.

For the moment Dorothea just stared at him with a blank expression.

'The elector, milady,' Christopher went on, seeing that she did not understand. 'He is now King George I of England. Dignatories have already arrived to escort him to England.'

At first, Dorothea seemed not to have heard. Then, suddenly, she began to laugh uncontrollably.

Christopher shifted uneasily from foot to foot. The sound was shrill, and sounded more like a sob than a laugh.

Hanover

December 1722

There had been many splendid carnival seasons in Hanover, and no doubt there would be many more. But this one would remain in people's memories for years to come. For months before the actual event, they spoke of it and little else.

For one thing, the King of England, together with Prince George Augustus and his wife Caroline, had come back to visit. His Majesty brought few of his English entourage with him, mainly because he still couldn't speak their language, and swore heartily that he would never learn. Only a few of them, notably his Prime Minister, Walpole, could converse with him on any but the most basic level. There were those who whispered that Walpole, a brilliant and ambitious statesman, actually ran the country, was in fact more of a ruler than George I. Accompanying the king, and resplendent in glittering jewels, was the Duchess of Kendal, whom many Hanoverians remembered as Melusine von Schulenburg.

Nor was King George the only member of royalty to decorate the scene. Both the King and Queen of Prussia were in attendance with full retinue.

Conscious of this, Duke Maximilian had urged that Hanover present its most glorious face to the royal visitors. And they had complied admirably. Houses were painted whether they needed it or not, streets were swept free of snow and kept clear so that carriage traffic could flow smoothly. Lanterns were strung up and down the streets and even between gabled houses, giving the town a fairytale look about it. Bells adorned trappings, filling the air with a constant musical jingle.

Even the weather cooperated. It was cold, but crisp and clear, and the air smelled of pine and chestnuts and freshly baked pastries and tortes.

Dressed in their brilliant traditional costumes, the people laughed and sang, raising their steins high to greet new visitors. When the king finally arrived, his eyes filled with tears at the remembered sights and scents of what he still considered to be home.

Even the Duchess of Celle, frail at eighty-four, and with a hesitant step, smiled at everyone, nodding her head in time to the lilting music.

Dancing and eating, masques, concerts, plays, drinking, went on from dusk until the following dawn, with no break at all. During the day, for those who wished to indulge, there were hunts, sleigh rides, and skating.

Through it all, Eleanor watched and waited. She could not approach the king until the proper occasion presented itself. But she meant to be ready when it did. As always, there was only one thing on her mind.

With her granddaughter, however, there was little problem. At the first opportune moment the young queen sent for the Duchess of Celle.

It was a beautiful sunny day, the air clear and, for the moment, quiet, in deference to those who were still asleep after the night's strenuous activities.

When Eleanor entered she made as if to curtsy, but the young queen rushed forward and embraced her elderly grandmother.

'Never in private,' she whispered, hugging Eleanor closely. 'Come, sit with me while I have my breakfast. Have you eaten?'

'Oh, yes.' Eleanor smiled as she sat down. 'You may imagine that I did not stay up until dawn.'

'Then have some chocolate with me.' Unobtrusively, Sophie-Dorothea raised her hand and another place was set at the small table. She smiled brightly while the servants saw to the repast, then she dismissed them. 'I wanted to speak with you alone,' she said as she ate, then grinned impishly. 'It's not easy during carnival.'

Eleanor's heart constricted at the sight of the face before

her, the smile that was so like Dorothea's. She clenched her hands tightly. If there was another person she loved with all her heart besides her daughter, it was this young and vibrant woman seated across the table from her. She had the same dark hair as her mother but her eyes were a vivid shade of blue.

'Tell me how she is,' Sophie-Dorothea said without preamble.

'She is well,' Eleanor replied slowly, sipping from the porcelain cup. 'I thank God daily for her good health. Your mother occupies her days constructively. The people of Ahlden consider her a saint.'

'I have heard of how much she has done for them.' Sophie-Dorothea put down the hot roll that she had been eating, her appetite suddenly gone. 'I've spoken to my father,' she said quietly, looking away from her grandmother's intent eyes. 'I requested permission to visit Ahlden, but he declined.' Her face was both sad and angry as she related this. 'Even I cannot contradict the King of England. Certainly not here, in Hanover. But it's so unfair,' she cried out. 'I haven't seen my mother for over twenty-five years.'

'I know, I know,' soothed Eleanor. Leaning forward, she patted the slim hand. 'But you know each other through your letters. Your mother reads them avidly. You must never stop writing. And, my dear, don't think of her as bitter or unhappy.' Eleanor gave a short laugh. 'Sometimes I think that Dorothea has fared best of all of us.'

'How can you say that?' Sophie-Dorothea demanded, eyes bright. 'Shut up there, year after year.'

'But she has found peace. Have you?' Eleanor looked at her granddaughter directly. Under that searching glance, the young woman turned away.

'No,' she murmured, suddenly pensive. 'My life is anything but peaceful.' She thought of her husband, the arguments, his rigid and sometimes cruel treatment of their son, Fritz. But was it worth it? she wondered. Her mother's life might be peaceful, but was it joyful? Did she laugh, sing, dance? She doubted that. 'I will write to her today,' the young queen said at last. 'I'll give it to you this evening.'

Eleanor nodded, approving. 'I wish your brother would

do the same,' she commented in a sorrowful voice.

Sophie-Dorothea's smooth brow furrowed. She didn't want to further upset her grandmother, for she was looking poorly; yet her mother should know. 'George cannot write,' she said in a flat voice as she toyed with her cup. 'Father had expressly forbidden him to communicate in any manner with our mother.'

Raising a thin brow, Eleanor said, 'I know. But he must have said the same to you. Yet you write to her.'

'The king may forbid me to visit her while I am in his realm,' Sophie-Dorothea noted dryly, her expression hard. 'But he cannot forbid me anything when I am in my own. George, unfortunately, cannot defy his father and king. But that is not the reason why he doesn't write. If it were only that, I think he would defy Father in a moment.' She studied her grandmother a moment, then reached out and took hold of her hand. It felt cold, almost weightless within her own. 'Father has threatened to tighten the restrictions on her if he disobeys.' She compressed her lips, as if to stem a cry of despair. 'Tell her,' Sophie-Dorothea went on in a low voice. 'Tell her, so that she knows. My brother still has her portrait, he told me so.'

Eleanor grew still. 'I will tell her,' she murmured.

Sophie-Dorothea produced her bright smile again, then resumed eating. She chatted gaily about her son and, when the meal at last ended, kissed her grandmother with true affection. 'I'll send the letter to you,' she whispered as Eleanor took her leave.

In her own room again, Eleanor sank down on the bed, her mind numb with despair.

She had wanted, planned, to speak with the king, to beg him if need be, to allow Dorothea to come to Luneburg. Twenty-five years was long enough. Nor could he use the excuse that Dorothea might bear more children; at fifty-five there was no chance of that.

But her granddaughter's words had chilled her heart. Eleanor knew she might do more harm than good if she spoke. God knew, Dorothea had few freedoms; Eleanor couldn't bear it if she were responsible for restricting any of them.

Oh, Wilhelm, she thought, closing her eyes. What have you done? A whole life wasted, misspent. And that life is the life of your only child.

Dorothea's crime had been love, Eleanor thought, her despair a hard knot within her frail chest. The thought so overwhelmed her that she put a hand to her breast in an attempt to calm the thunderous beat of her heart.

But then, if Dorothea's crime had been love, what was mine for you, Wilhelm? she wondered, anguished. What was mine for you?

Ahlden

January 1723

The snow had begun at first to fall gently, swirling in little powdery whirlpools, cavorting playfully before settling down to the serious business of covering the ground. But now, in late afternoon, the white of the sky molded itself to the snow-covered land. The wind moved with a fearsome determination, creating icy whorls, then capriciously destroying them.

Dorothea had her chair placed close by the window. With a light robe across her lap she watched the storm with distant eyes.

Nearby, Gertrud sat in a straight-backed chair, busily stitching a monogram on a linen handkerchief. Occasionally she viewed the duchess with mournful, compassionate eyes, concerned by the pallor on Dorothea's face. But she remained silent, feeling that words would be an intrusion on her mistress's thoughts.

Dorothea herself was oblivious to her lady's concerned scrutiny. She stared at the whiteness beyond her window.

She had received the news of her mother's death with shock. Which was odd, she thought, in view of Eleanor's advanced years. Somehow she had always thought that, whatever happened to her, her mother would be there.

The news had reached her yesterday. She had immediately written to George, who was still at Leine, and requested permission to attend her mother's funeral. Her faithful Christopher had left some hours ago to deliver her letter. And now she sat, and watched, and waited for his return.

She had wept hot, agonizing tears that had produced no

relief of the anguish and loss that gripped her mind and her heart. All these years Eleanor's love and comfort had been steadfast and courageous.

Dorothea smiled sadly. Often she had heard George or Ernst refer to Sophia as a 'real lady.' But it was Eleanor d'Olbreuse who deserved that title, Dorothea mused. It wasn't placidity or manners that defined such a term; it was courage, determination, loyalty, grace.

'Milady?' Gertrud's soft murmur broke into her thoughts. Almost surprised, Dorothea turned to her lady. They had sat for more than an hour without either one of them speaking. 'Is there anything I can get for you?' Gertrud asked.

Dorothea shook her head but made no other response.

Gertrud's brows expressed a slight disapproval. 'You have eaten nothing all day,' she complained quietly. 'At least have a bit of chocolate.'

Dorothea returned her gaze to the almost opaque window. 'Perhaps a little wine,' she said finally. Immediately Gertrud got up to fetch it.

A few moments later Gertrud returned with a tray that held not only the wine, but cheese and thinly sliced rye bread. This she placed on a table close to the Duchess, hoping that she would eat, even if absentmindedly; but Dorothea didn't even appear to notice it.

With a sigh, Gertrud sat down again.

For a long time the only sound in the room was the ticking of the clock that announced the passing minutes; and a passing lifetime, Dorothea reflected, listening to the doleful sound.

She closed her eyes and thought of Philip. As always, with the thought of him, came comfort; his presence, to her, was very real, very vivid.

Not even death has separated us, she thought, a slight smile on her lips. Someday, my darling, she mused in silence. Someday we will be together again. And this time it will be for eternity. Nothing as fragile as life will ever again interfere with our love.

With a small sigh, Dorothea straightened, still staring out at the snow. Her eyes glistened with unshed tears, but now they were not tears of grief or anguish. If she and

Philip would one day be together again, why, then she would be reunited with Eleanor as well. All she had to do was wait. Dorothea knew with absolute certainty that they would wait for her.

She thought of Karl Clausin, the young man whom she had sent to medical school in Vienna. He was home now, and a fine young man he was; nor could his arrival have been more fortunate. He had saved the life of a child, an eight-year-old girl named Inger Bernhardt.

Again Dorothea smiled slightly. She must do something for the girl, she decided. The child was bright and intelligent. She would surely benefit from a formal education. Paris, perhaps. What do you think, Mama? she mentally queried, leaning her head back. Shall it be Paris or Vienna for little Inger?

There was a soft tap on the door. Immediately after, it opened to reveal Christopher Chappuzeau. So exhausted was he that he could barely stand. He wavered before her like a drunken man.

'Christopher ...' she murmured, contrite.

'Milady,' he said, dropping to one knee. He gazed at her with an expression of unutterable sadness. 'Your petition to attend the funeral of the Duchess of Celle has been denied.' He took a deep breath in which sadness and weariness commingled and became a sound of despair.

Dorothea closed her eyes tightly, then opened them again. It wasn't a surprise; not really. And yet she had had to try. 'My poor Christopher,' she said quietly. 'I know you did your best. I really did not expect the king to agree.'

'I did not see him, milady,' Christopher replied in a bitter voice. 'I was not granted an audience. It was Minister Bernstorff who heard my request and presented it to his Majesty.'

Dorothea nodded gravely. 'And we must abide by his Majesty's decision. But somehow,' she mused in a quiet voice, 'I think that the Duchess of Celle will understand.'

Christopher got to his feet again and stood there with an oddly intent expression on his face. Actually, he was immensely relieved by the princess's reaction – as he still thought of her. He had feared another outbreak of hysterical grief, much as had occurred when he had first told her of Eleanor's death.

'Milady,' he went on gently. 'My news is not all bad.' He walked toward the door and hesitated only a moment, looking at her with a smile that was almost tender. Then he flung it open. A young man and a young woman entered the room.

Slowly Dorothea got to her feet, the robe slipping silently to the floor. She blinked, but not quickly enough to stem the tears that fell unheeded on her satin gown.

She walked toward them, a step at a time, her eyes resting first on one, then the other, as if fearful that this glorious apparition would fade.

The young woman smiled sweetly and her dimples deepened charmingly, although her eyes, too, were bright with tears. With a small gloved hand, she wiped her cheek.

The young man, however, was dry-eyed, with an expression of intense scrutiny, as though he had found something for which he had been searching for a long time and couldn't quite believe that he had found it.

Again, ridiculously, Dorothea became aware of the ticking clock, though now it seemed to strike away the years, one by one. She stood, clasping her hands, fearful they would act against her will and do something foolish of their own accord.

Should she curtsy? Dorothea wondered idiotically. But her feet were rooted to the floor, supporting legs that felt wooden and unresponsive.

The young man was the first to recover. He stepped closer to her.

'Mother,' he said softly. 'You are as beautiful as your portrait.'

Dorothea pressed her lips together but could not, as yet, utter a word. Again she blinked, momentarily annoyed to have her vision blurred for even a second.

The young queen now came closer but did not speak. Instead, she just put her arms about Dorothea and pressed her cheek against hers.

With the physical contact Dorothea's arms reached out and she embraced her daughter.

It was a moment, a lifetime, then they parted. Dorothea searched her daughter's face carefully, seeing only love and acceptance. Then she turned to George Augustus, suddenly shy.

'I saw you that day,' she whispered.

The young man embraced her. 'Did you hear what I shouted?' he asked as he drew back, smiling now.

He was so like George, Dorothea thought immaterially. Yet so unlike that forbidding, taciturn presence. 'No,' she replied. 'I couldn't hear your words.'

He grinned at her. 'I said that I had remembered, and that I had been good. And that I had not forgotten you –' His voice broke.

My heart cannot support this, Dorothea thought, looking at her son. Surely it would swell and break.

At last, reality intruded. 'How did you get here?' Dorothea asked, amazed. 'Does your father know of your whereabouts?'

The young man's expression became closed, and immediately Dorothea regretted her words.

'No,' he replied quietly. 'The king does not know we are here. Nor,' he added grimly, 'will he ever know.'

Dorothea looked confused. Hastily, George Augustus explained. 'When we learned of Chappuzeau's arrival, we knew immediately why he had come.'

'I sent for him,' Sophie-Dorothea put in, smiling at her mother. 'And I told him to wait until I had spoken to my brother.'

'When she did,' George Augustus took up the story, 'I knew that Father would never agree, never grant you permission to attend Grandmother's funeral.'

Dorothea looked away and her son grasped hold of her hand. 'Do not ever feel that we think as he does,' he said earnestly. 'Father is … difficult,' he concluded with a small laugh. Dorothea, too, had to smile. George, difficult, was worth a smile.

'But if he finds out …' Dorothea was alarmed for their welfare.

'He won't,' George Augusts assured her. 'The weather is execrable. Nothing can get through.' He grinned again. 'Except, perhaps, those who are very determined to do so.

We, both of us – ' he gestured toward his sister – 'traveled with only one attendant. And we all rode horses, fearing that even a sleigh would bog down.'

His face sobered. Dorothea eagerly watched the changing expression, knowing that this might be the last time she would have the opportunity to do so.

'He doesn't know that we've come here,' George Augustus repeated. 'And he will not know when we return.'

'Milady?' Gertrud's voice caught them all unaware, so engrossed were they with each other. 'There is food.' She pointed to the table.

Glancing across the room, Dorothea marveled at the repast that had so suddenly appeared. While she had been mooning about, Gertrud had sent for food and drink. The trestle table against the wall fairly sagged under the bowls and dishes it supported.

With the sight, Dorothea laughed, deliriously, happily, realizing how very hungry she was. Linking her arms with George Augustus and Sophie-Dorothea, she led them to the table.

Was there ever a banquet more enjoyable, more satisfying? Dorothea thought not. Their words tumbled over one another, so eager were they all to speak, to reminisce, to share.

Again the clock ticked, now relentlessly, and at last it was time for them to leave.

There were no tears now, only a sense of satisfaction, of completeness. Dorothea saw her son and her daughter, now a man and a woman, no longer children. But they were fine, and caused her heart to swell with pride.

Also, they loved her. George had not been able to quell that. She kissed them fiercely, refusing to say good-bye.

She knew now that there were no good-byes. There was only the passing of time until the next meeting.

'It may be a while until I see you again,' George Augustus said to her. 'And I cannot write.' His eyes clouded as he hugged her close. 'Please understand.'

'Don't apologize,' Dorothea said quickly. 'I, more than anyone, know the limitations placed on us all.' She then turned toward Sophie-Dorothea. 'Will you continue to write to me?'

The young queen's answer was another close embrace. 'No one can stop me,' she whispered. Drawing back, she added, 'How I wish I could have brought Lenore to see you. Not a day passes that she doesn't speak of you. She wanted desperately to come with me tonight. But she's been ailing of late and I feared the trip would be too strenuous for her.'

'Ah, my Lenore.' Dorothea was almost in tears once more. 'Please tell her how much I love her and how much I miss her.'

Sophie-Dorothea gave a soft laugh. 'She knows, Mother. There is little that can dampen her spirit. And I must confess that your loss is my gain. I really don't know what I would do without her. She anticipates my needs before I'm even aware of them.'

Dorothea smiled. 'I've never given you a gift,' she said quietly. 'And that is one of my great regrets. But Lenore is now with you. And I think, perhaps, that I could have given you no greater gift.' She kissed her daughter's cool cheek and held her a moment before she released her again.

Sophie-Dorothea stood there a while longer before she moved away, staring as if to imprint her mother's face on her mind for all time. Sophie-Dorothea was dressed not so much as a queen as a woman of nobility. She wore no jewels and her hair was simply arranged. Her gown was a plain warm woolen dress, suitable for the trip she had taken, but certainly not one whose cut would define a woman of her rank. And, in truth, Sophie-Dorothea had borrowed the outfit from one of her ladies, for she had none that would have withstood the rigors that this journey had demanded.

'I want you to know,' the young queen said in a halting voice, 'that my grandmother died peacefully.' She touched Dorothea's cheeks. 'There was no pain. She died in her sleep. And I have no doubt but that her last thoughts were of you. I spoke to her the day before it happened. She was in fine spirits.'

Dorothea regarded her daughter for a long moment. For the first time she knew what Eleanor had felt all these years. 'Thank you,' she said, not trusting her voice to speak further.

They left as they had entered, standing in the doorway, looking at her. Then, with a brief smile, they were gone.

But of course they would never be gone. Not from her heart, not from her mind, not from her thoughts.

Too excited to sleep, Dorothea returned to her chair by the window.

Gertrud, too, returned, although her hands were now idle. She sniffed and took a linen handkerchief from her pocket. No doubt I look a mess, she thought, with a small shake of her head. She had done little all this while but sit in her chair, weeping with happiness. The king would never learn of tonight's visit, she was certain. There was not one person in Ahlden, including the governor himself, who would speak of what had taken place here. And of course de la Fortiere must have known, she realized. There was no other way that the drawbridge would have been let down. Everyone, even Christopher, had to receive permission to leave the castle.

'You must be proud of them both,' Gertrud remarked finally with a small sigh, momentarily regretful that she herself was childless.

'Indeed,' responded Dorothea, almost dreamily, as she continued to gaze outside. The snow had stopped now but the wind moved just as briskly, as defiantly, as before.

Leaning forward slightly, Gertrud looked at her mistress, her expression once again saddened. 'I'm sorry, milady, that the king refused to allow you to attend the funeral. I know how much it meant to you.'

Dorothea smiled at her lady. Her expression was not sad, not despondent. 'I do not presume to judge the king,' she said quietly, leaning back in her chair. 'There will come a day when he will be judged. But not by me.'

Ahlden

November 1726

Weary from his long vigil, Christopher Chappuzeau left the castle. Unlike the Duchess of Ahlden, he had always been free to come and go.

He allowed the horse its own pace as he made his way across the heavy oak wood drawbridge, which was the only means of access to the fortresslike castle. The other three sides were surrounded by a moat.

He patted the pocket of his jacket to assure himself that the letter was safe. Although how he would be able to personally deliver a letter to the King of England momentarily escaped him. It had been her last coherent act, the writing of the letter he now had in his safekeeping. He might not be able to deliver it in the immediate future, but it was rumored that George I was to visit Hanover sometime within the next year.

When he did, Christopher would be ready.

A group of burghers approached him. In respectful tones they inquired about the duchess, for it was common knowledge that she had been seriously ill for weeks now. When he told them, their faces fell into genuine sadness. A few wept openly, unashamedly.

And why shouldn't they weep? Christopher thought, riding onward. She had given their village so much. There was the splendid organ in the town's only church, a true marvel it was, with a sound both vibrant and sonorous. There were the golden candelabrums, the imported stained-glass windows. There had been medical help for an ailing child, educational aid for others.

There were those, Christopher knew, who termed her a

saint. Her husband had not been among them. His heavy hand, filled with vengeance, had pursued her for more than three decades.

But Christopher knew better. She was neither saint nor sinner. She was a woman: warm, spirited, independent. Qualities that, together with her beauty, should have delighted any man; qualities that had repulsed that strange man she had had the misfortune to marry; qualities that had proved to be her downfall.

On a rise just outside the village Christopher halted his horse. Turning in the saddle, he looked behind him at the moss-covered stone edifice with its gray towers and tall narrow windows. It had been his home for the past thirty years.

It looked peaceful in its now snow-draped setting. The burghers, simple people who took pride in church and family, were up and about their morning chores, as if it were a most ordinary day. Nowhere in that quaint and rural scene was there a sign of the tears that had been shed, of the anguish that had been endured, of the spirit that had overcome and survived with truly remarkable grace and fortitude.

Christopher's mouth tightened, then set into a grim line. He wouldn't stay for the funeral. He knew it would be brief, a mere travesty of that solemn occasion, one more humiliation heaped on one who had suffered too many for one lifetime.

And what had she done to have caused such inhuman punishment? he thought bitterly, spurring his horse forward. He, of course, knew the answer; but it galled him more than the question.

If she had known the price that would be demanded of her, would she have done it? he mused. Would she have acted in the same way? He would, of course, never know. But one thing he did know: All the lies, trickery and deceit had failed to break Dorothea's spirit or crush her love for Philip Königsmark.

Osnabrück

June 1727

The coach rode through the early mist of the June morning, the horses moving smartly over cobbled streets that glistened with early dampness.

Inside the coach bearing the imperial arms on both doors George turned to Melusine and smiled slightly. He looked every bit of his sixty-six years. His ponderous bulk strained against satin and brocade, his face was lined and jowly.

'It's good to be home again,' he said in German. 'There exists a no more barbaric land than England,' he went on grumpily, heaving a great sigh. He had on more than one occasion wished it were possible to govern the unwanted realm so suddenly thrust on him years before from Hanover. Of course it wasn't possible. So he contented himself with visiting his home at least once each year. No one seemed to mind, least of all Walpole.

Melusine patted his arm with a hand that glittered with diamond rings. 'Indeed, it's good to be home,' she confirmed. 'And despite the years, I shall never feel comfortable there.'

And that was certainly the truth, she thought, plumping the satin pillow behind her. For years now she had had to endure those ridiculous lampoons that the English so disgracefully permitted to appear in their newspapers. They depicted her as fat and ugly. She had been so enraged at one point that she had complained bitterly to Walpole. But that man had only smiled smoothly and advised her to ignore them.

As if one could ignore being pictured as an elephant,

Melusine thought, feeling fresh irritation.

The newspapers even had the gall occasionally to lampoon the king himself. Certainly that behavior would never be tolerated in their homeland. The offenders would be dealt with in a most positive manner, quickly and harshly. Of course George could neither read nor speak English, and for the most part he did ignore the insulting pictures.

But one thing he had been hard pressed to ignore: the constant inquiries as to the whereabouts of his queen.

Queen, indeed. Melusine sniffed disdainfully. There was no queen. Couldn't the fools have seen that with their own eyes? Well, to George's credit, he had not bothered to answer. He merely turned away, his scowl indicating severe displeasure. After a while, the court had ceased to inquire. Not that it had been any of their business in the first place.

She glanced over at George, but he seemed to be lost in his own thoughts, so Melusine settled back comfortably.

George was thinking about his son. They had had another one of their violent quarrels just before he had left England. As a result, he had refused to allow George Augustus to accompany him on this, his sixth visit to Hanover.

With these thoughts of his son, George frowned. His double chin rested on his neck, giving him the appearance of a brooding walrus. *Her* son, actually, he reflected dourly. He couldn't abide the young man who was his heir. As George Augustus became older, their relationship was becoming more and more strained. Until now they could hardly speak to each other in civil tones.

Well, thank God it was all over. Dorothea had at last died. The frown deepened into a scowl. That woman couldn't even die without causing him problems. She had lived for many years at Ahlden, and should have been buried there. So he had instructed. The earth, however, had refused the coffin. With each rain the spongy clay soil had washed away. The fools claimed that each time they dug deeper, they encountered water. The duchess could not be buried at Ahlden, de la Fortiere had written in respectful words. So he had given instructions for the coffin to be deposited in the dungeons below the castle.

George had been tempted to leave it there. Would have left it there. But Melusine had had a dream and had informed him that Dorothea would haunt him if her body was not properly laid to rest. That had given him pause.

Well, now she was buried at Celle. Certainly she could rest there, George thought, annoyed. She had always wanted to return home.

As for that stupid prophecy … George snorted. Bit of foolishness, that. The year was almost gone and he was in fine health.

'With luck we'll be in Hanover by nightfall,' he now said to Melusine, his thoughts returning to more pleasurable things than death and Dorothea.

Melusine nodded at this observation, then peered outside with narrowing eyes. 'There is a man by the side of the road,' she said, suddenly alarmed. 'Why are we stopping?' In her agitation, she plucked at the satin sleeve of his jacket.

'Don't be upset,' George soothed, patting her plump hand in a comforting manner. 'He is most likely a petitioner.' He peered. 'Yes, yes. See the paper he carries? It's not all that unusual,' he remarked as the coach rolled to a stop.

The man, who was only a shabbily dressed peasant, approached in a respectful manner, cap in hand. Deferentially he handed the paper to the king, who took it, nodding curtly as he did so. The man did not speak. He bowed, then backed off until he was once again standing to the side of the road. Christopher straightened then and Melusine glanced at him sharply. He didn't look like a peasant to her, despite his dress. She was vastly relieved when, a moment later, the coach resumed its progress.

George laid the folded paper on the seat beside him, not bothering to open it.

'I think it's disgraceful,' Melusine complained, only now beginning to relax. 'You ought not allow it. What right has a person like that to so impede your progress?'

George laughed indulgently. 'I didn't inaugurate the tradition, my pet,' he protested, amused by her vehemence. 'There are few enough ways for a man like that to reach us. No doubt the poor fellow has been waiting there for weeks.'

Unconvinced, Melusine turned away, an annoyed look on her face. The expression deepened the lines about her mouth and the bridge of her nose. She leaned her head back and closed her eyes, wishing that the journey was at an end.

She loved to visit Hanover but the cross-country ride was, at best, tedious. She would, she thought, try to sleep until they stopped for lunch. She hoped George would do the same. Sometimes he felt as if he had to comment on the passing scenery, would glowingly compare this opulent land with the more delicate expanse of the English countryside. Today Melusine was in no mood to listen to his comparisons.

She heard the faint rustle of paper just as she drifted off to sleep and was glad that he was occupying his thoughts with the just-received petition, thereby allowing her to doze.

The air was getting warmer, as it always did when one moved inland, and it was this that awakened Melusine about an hour later. She straightened and groaned slightly, putting a hand to her neck. She felt as if she had been in the same position for hours. Cautiously she shifted her weight, then groaned again.

'It must be time to stop,' she murmured. 'I'm famished.' When she didn't get an answer, Melusine turned to look at George.

At first she thought he was asleep. The petition was still clutched in his right hand. But then she noted his expression; the slackness of the mouth was not normal. It seemed ... lopsided. And his left hand. It was resting, palm up, on the cushioned seat between them, the fingers oddly rigid and clawlike. His chest rose and fell, but in a labored, striving manner.

Choking down a gasp of fright, Melusine screamed for the driver to stop. He did so, with a suddenness that almost made her lose her balance.

The coaches trailing behind stopped also. Hastily alighting, Melusine waved her plump arms frantically, shouting for the physician.

With great care, the footmen lifted the ponderous bulk of their monarch. As gently as possible they laid him on the grass. Melusine watched in trembling apprehension. She reached inside the coach and picked up one of the satin pillows, then placed it beneath George's head. Then she moved aside as the physician approached with hurried steps.

Somehow, during the short journey from the coach to the ground, Melusine found herself with the crumpled petition. She held it in her hand, giving it no thought, while she watched the physician's ministrations to the man who had been, to her, more husband than king.

After many minutes passed the physician got to his feet. In his stunned face Melusine saw what she already knew.

The king was dead.

Once more there was a flurry of activity. White-faced, Melusine found herself again in the coach, this time with the physician. The man was holding the body of his dead king, now wrapped in a blanket, cradled in his arms.

Neither the physician nor Melusine spoke. The physician because it would be impertinent for him to address the Duchess of Kendal without permission; Melusine because her mind was still numb. Too numb for tears.

The coach was now traveling swiftly. The wind came in, in gusts. But Melusine was grateful for the sting of it on her cheek. It gave some indication of feeling, of life within her.

It was impossible, she was thinking. He had been all right only a short time ago. He had felt fine, he had spoken to her, joked with her.

And now he was dead. Irretrievably lost to her. She had loved him all these years. Melusine couldn't conceive of what her life was to be like without George.

After a while Melusine became aware of the petition still held in her hand. Almost defensively, so as not to have to look at her horror seated directly across from her, she unfolded the paper. A glance told her that it was not a petition at all; it was a letter.

At first the words were meaningless. She read them without comprehension. Only when she reached the end and saw the signature did shock set in. It was signed, in a strong hand, *Dorothea*.

But Dorothea was dead! Had been dead for months.

Blinking, Melusine returned to the top of the page. This time she read slowly, trying to control the trembling in her hand, without much success.

Then the last sentence caught and held her. She read: 'In less than one year from the date of this letter, I shall meet you before the Throne of God.

'He will judge us both.'

'In less than one year ...' Again Melusine returned to the beginning of the letter. It was dated November 13, 1726 – seven months ago.

The blood drained from Melusine's pink cheeks and for a long time she sat perfectly still. Then she crumpled the paper and held it outside the window of the coach. She opened her hand. The wind, grasping at this new toy, lifted it high and playfully tossed it about.